The
Last to Know

ALSO PUBLISHED BY POOLBEG

All Because of You
Wishful Thinking
Never Say Never
Not What You Think
Something You Should Know

The
Last to Know

Melissa
Hill

POOLBEG

Published 2007
by Poolbeg Press Ltd
123 Grange Hill, Baldoyle
Dublin 13, Ireland
E-mail: poolbeg@poolbeg.com
www.poolbeg.com

13 5 7 9 10 8 6 4 2

A catalogue record for this book is available from the British Library.

ISBN 978-1 84223- 294-1

Typeset by Type Design in Palatino 11/16 and Monkton 12/16
Printed by Litografia Roses, Spain

www.poolbeg.com

About the Author

Melissa Hill lives with her husband Kevin and their dog Homer in Monkstown, Co. Dublin. Her previous books, *All Because of You, Wishful Thinking, Never Say Never, Not What You Think* and *Something You Should Know* have all been bestsellers and are widely translated.

For more information, visit her website at **www.melissahill.info**

ACKNOWLEDGEMENTS

Lots of love and thanks to Mam and Dad, Amanda and Sharon and all my friends, who provide me with ongoing inspiration and are always willing to participate in my "what if?" conversations. And to Pat and Sue – our chat has already given me an idea!

A special thanks to Kevin, who as well as being a brilliant husband is also a fantastic sounding board and can come up with a solution to anything. And to Homer, who always manages to make me smile.

Heartfelt thanks and appreciation to Poolbeg – Kieran, Lynda, Niamh, David, Conor and especially Paula – an unstoppable team who don't give themselves enough credit for the amazing work they do. It's an honour to work with you all.

To Gaye Shortland, your contribution to this and all my books is immense and I just can't thank you enough.

Huge thanks to Sheila Crowley, who is not only a wonderful agent but also a true friend – this one's for you. Thanks also to everyone at AP Watt for working so hard on my behalf.

To Emma Walsh, my relentless champion, PR mastermind (and ever-willing shopping companion!) – you're the best.

Thanks to the booksellers in Ireland, the UK and beyond who give my books such terrific support – I'm so very grateful.

To all my fantastic supporters back home in Tipp, especially Bridget Cummins, Gerardine Hickey, Martina Farrell, Lorraine Browne and Noreen Quinn, who have cheered me on since day one – thanks a million.

Yet again a huge thanks to everyone all over the world who buys and reads my books, and to those who send me messages through my website **www.melissahill.info**. Thanks so much, I love hearing from you and I treasure every one.

I really hope you all enjoy *The Last to Know*.

For Sheila Crowley,
My Lucky Charm

CHAPTER 1

1. The Last to Know

Anna Edwards was enjoying a glass of her favourite wine with her favourite dish and having a lovely time in her favourite Dublin restaurant, when the man sitting across from her had to go and spoil it all by proposing.

"So," Denis urged, glittering ring in hand, his gaze locked expectantly onto his girlfriend's face. "What's your answer?"

"Oh, yes!" the girl sitting beside Anna squealed loudly, before leaping out of her seat, rounding the table and launching herself into the arms of her new fiancé. "Yes, Denis, of *course* I'll marry you!"

As the happy couple kissed and hugged in full view of the other diners, Anna took a sip of her drink and attempted to afford the two of them some privacy. So much for a quiet dinner with friends. The last thing she'd expected tonight was Denis proposing to Lauren in a packed restaurant – and especially with another couple in tow. Given what he'd planned for this evening, wouldn't dinner alone with his girlfriend have been more appropriate, instead of dragging other people along? And in all fairness, it wasn't as though they were that close friends of the couple: while Lauren and Anna got on very well, they were really just workmates, not lifelong friends!

Then again, that was Lauren's boyfriend all over, wasn't it? Anna thought a little uncharitably – showy to the last. But at the same time, what did it matter how he'd done it? OK, so she and Ronan being here too was uncomfortable (for *them*), but Lauren was totally over the moon, and Anna knew that her co-worker in the primary school in which she taught had been hoping for this for a very long time.

Anna gave a surreptitious glance towards her other half, who was watching the scene with interest, a slight smile playing across his face. What was Ronan thinking about all of this? she wondered, trying to read his expression.

But she couldn't wonder for too long, as just then Lauren sat back down alongside her, her face flushed with joy and excitement and her eyes shining with happy tears.

"Oh, my goodness, isn't it just beautiful?" she gushed, proudly extending an engagement ring on which sat a diamond the size of a small helicopter. "He has such great taste – it's *exactly* what I would have chosen myself!"

"It's gorgeous," Anna replied, hugging her friend warmly, but thinking privately that if she owned a diamond that huge she'd be afraid to go outside her front door for fear that something would happen to it. Not that she *did* have to worry about that sort of thing, she thought wryly.

A bottle of champagne (evidently arranged by Denis in advance) was promptly delivered to the table and, as the waiter poured it, Ronan shook Denis's hand. "Congratulations, mate! I'd say you had to flog more than a few motors to pay for that rock," he said jokingly, referring to Denis's profession as a car salesman.

"Nah, one or two did the job," Denis replied with a self-satisfied grin, and inwardly Anna rolled her eyes.

In truth, she still wasn't at all sure what to make of her friend's boyfriend. He and Lauren had been together a while now, and while Lauren raved about his wonderful generosity, Anna felt there was something smug and showy about him – tonight's proposal being a case in point. Still, what did it matter what she thought? The guy made Lauren happy, and that was the main thing surely?

And Denis had certainly made Lauren very happy tonight. She was positively glowing in the aftermath of his proposal, and as Anna raised her champagne glass and everyone toasted their engagement, she mentally admonished herself for thinking badly of Denis and resolved to buck up and celebrate properly. For God's sake, what kind of a friend was she for criticising Lauren's choices? It was a bit ironic, considering.

Anna took a sip of her drink and enjoyed the very rare sensation of champagne bubbles melting on her tongue.

"So, I was thinking we might as well get it over and done with fairly soon – what do you think?" Denis said to Lauren, who looked momentarily confused. "The whole wedding thing, I mean. I don't believe in this long-drawn-out engagement malarkey myself. After all, once you've made up your mind to take the plunge, what's the point in waiting around?"

At this, Lauren blushed and looked sideways at Anna.

When his girlfriend didn't reply immediately, Denis went on. "Nah, better to just get it done and dusted, I say – no point in beating about the bush."

Bloody hell, Anna thought trying to hide a smile, how many clichés in one sentence could this guy come up with?

"Well, it doesn't really matter when we do it," Lauren said meekly, evidently discomfited by the subject. "But don't forget, we'll still need time to get things arranged, stuff like the church and the dress and –"

3

"Well, all that kind of thing will be your department," Denis interjected, a touch too dismissively for Anna's liking. "After all, I've done the important bit, and it's up to the women after that, isn't it?" He nudged Ronan, who smiled uncomfortably. "Anyway," he said, addressing Lauren, "let's just try and get it done by Christmas at least – next year should hopefully be a big one for the dealership, and I don't want any distractions."

When Lauren looked a little dispirited at this, Anna bristled. Another thing she disliked about Denis was the condescending way he often spoke to Lauren. Imagine suggesting that his own wedding might serve as a distraction to his money-making! Although, Anna supposed, it was this very same money that would allow Lauren to have the big wedding, big County Dublin house and lavish lifestyle that she desired and enjoyed. Well, she could keep it if it meant being stuck with an oaf like Denis, thought Anna, relieved that Ronan was nothing like that. While he earned about a quarter of Denis's salary, he (thankfully) possessed four times the other man's humility.

"Speaking of weddings, when are you two going to get on with it?" Denis asked. Instantly Anna stiffened. Given what had happened tonight it was inevitable that the conversation would eventually take this route, but she'd hoped that Denis and Lauren would be too wrapped up in themselves to care about anyone else's wedding plans.

Or lack of.

"Seriously," Denis went on, "you guys have been together for what – since school or something, Lauren said?" He looked at Ronan for confirmation.

"That's right." Ronan's expression was carefully composed.

"And ye've been engaged for how many years now?"

"Six."

"So what's the story?" Denis persisted, looking from Anna

to Ronan.

"Honey, don't be so nosy," Lauren admonished, mortified by Denis's forthrightness and suspecting that talk of dates for Anna and Ronan's eventual wedding was possibly a sore point between them. But as Anna never really talked about it, she couldn't know for sure.

"How am I being nosy? I'm just asking them a simple question," Denis replied, scowling angrily at his new fiancée before swigging back the remainder of his champagne.

Anna shifted in her seat. "We just haven't got round to it," she said quietly. "It's as simple as that, really."

"Oh, right, I see." Denis's expression quickly changed to one that Anna was now used to whenever the subject of her and Ronan's wedding date cropped up – a mixture of confusion and sympathy.

But Anna couldn't give Denis or anyone else a definite reply as to why they hadn't set a date for their wedding, simply because she didn't know the answer to this particular question herself.

"Ah well, I suppose you'll get around to it some day," Denis said, finally realising that he'd made a slight faux pas.

"I'm sure we will," Anna nodded, trying in vain to catch Ronan's eye. "Anyway, never mind us, tonight is about you two!" she added lightly, changing the subject and determined not to let her own situation overshadow Lauren's happy night. Then she picked up her champagne glass and raised it in the air. "Here's to your big day!"

"To our big day!" Lauren echoed with a beaming smile, her humongous ring sparkling brilliantly in the candlelight.

*   *   *

"That was an interesting night," Ronan said, when later that evening he and Anna had left Lauren and Denis to their engagement celebrations and returned home to the house they shared in the Dublin suburbs.

Anna picked up his jacket from where it had been discarded on the sofa. "It wasn't what I expected, that's for sure."

"Bit of a showy bastard, isn't he?" Ronan went into the kitchen and switched on the kettle. "I mean, what was all that about, inviting us out for dinner and then springing the ring on her?" His voice drifted out towards Anna in the hallway.

He seemed pretty offhand about it all, she thought as she hung up their coats. Thank goodness. She'd been worried that Denis's pointed questioning might lead to a now long-overdue discussion about their own plans.

"I think he liked the idea of an audience," she said, entering the kitchen and leaning against the countertop. "Especially when he produced that knuckleduster of a ring."

"Puts the one I got for you in the ha'penny place, doesn't it?" Ronan said, his fingers lightly brushing Anna's tiny, six-year-old cluster ring.

Despite herself, she felt a lump in her throat. "You know that kind of stuff doesn't matter to me, Ro," she said, quickly moving her hand away.

"I know, but I wish I'd been able to afford something nicer all the same. That ring seems very old-fashioned now. Still, I suppose, it is six years . . ."

His voice trailed off pointedly, and Anna realised that Denis's interrogation about their own wedding had indeed got to him. But she couldn't talk about this, she realised, not now anyway.

"Well, I love it and that's the main thing," she said, injecting a carefree note into her voice, before speedily changing the subject. "Are you making tea at this hour?" She looked at her watch. "If you are I'll leave you too it – I want to get an early start in the morning."

"Oh, are you heading out somewhere?"

"Just for a jog," she answered quickly, having come up with the excuse off the top of her head.

Ronan smiled, but she noticed the smile didn't quite reach his eyes – those same arresting blue eyes Anna had been waking up to for the last ten years but had known for the majority of her life. In fact, she didn't think she could recall a single childhood or teenage memory without Ronan in it, such was the length and depth of their relationship. What with living only two houses down the road from Anna's, Ronan had been present at every birthday party, every celebration, every major milestone in Anna's life, and she quite literally couldn't imagine life without him in it.

So, why then, Anna thought, as she kissed her childhood sweetheart goodnight and headed upstairs to their bedroom alone, why, after so many years as a couple, and six more years' engagement, were they finding it so difficult to set a date?

CHAPTER 2

2. The Last to Know

Eve Callaghan opened her front door with what she suspected was an obviously pasted-on smile. Standing in the doorway was Sara, her neighbour from a few houses down, with her nine-month-old baby son, Jack.

"Hello there," Eve said, self-consciously running a hand through her straggly blonde hair. She knew she should have washed it that morning but she hadn't really had the time. Now she looked a fright compared to the ever-glamorous Sara.

Her neighbour grimaced guiltily, evidently not at all interested in how Eve did or didn't look. "Eve, again, I'm so sorry – you know I hate putting you out like this . . ."

Sara's voice was thick with remorse and, despite herself, Eve's heart couldn't help but go out to her.

"As I said on the phone earlier, the office need me on urgent business, and I just didn't have time to *think* of anyone else let alone –"

"It's OK, Sara," Eve smiled and waved away the other woman's apologies. OK, so this wasn't the first time that Sara had

9

landed Eve with the baby at the last minute while she went off "on urgent business", but her neighbour really did look frazzled. And the woman was probably feeling guilty enough about leaving Jack without Eve trying to make her feel worse. "He's a pleasure to look after and there's no question of putting me out." She rolled her eyes good-naturedly. "As I said earlier, I'd be here anyway."

"Oh, Eve, you're a life-saver – I really owe you one." Sara's relief was palpable. "It's just . . . well it's so hard to say no to the office – particularly when they've been so good about all this so far. And you know I'm having a nightmare trying to find a decent childminder."

Don't I just? Eve thought wryly.

"Do you have his things with you?" she asked, taking the baby from Sara's arms.

"His bag and carry-cot are in the car – I'll just go and get them."

While Sara fetched the things from the car, Eve cuddled the sleeping baby close to her chest. He was a gorgeous little thing, really, so soft and sweet – but, of course, weren't all babies? Holding his tiny body in her arms like this reminded Eve of how long it was since she'd held one of her own this way – two long years since Max and, goodness, was it really seven years since Lily? How she'd love another one like this, so tiny and needy and dependent on its mother for absolutely everything! Still, with the way she and Liam were going lately, this didn't seem likely . . .

"I'm sure your husband must be ready to throttle me by now," Sara said ruefully as she dumped the baby's things in the hallway. "He must be sick to the teeth of my doing this, landing Jack in on top of you every time I get called out."

Eve's heart plummeted as it always did when someone referred to Liam as her husband but, as usual, she didn't bother to correct Sara. What was the point? Might as well just let her neighbour continue to assume they were married, given that they were as good as anyway, what with the house, two kids and a relationship heading for nine years old.

And in truth, Eve always found it embarrassing to admit that they *weren't* married, and even more embarrassing that her long-term partner and father of her children didn't seem very interested in making things official any time soon.

"Not at all, we're happy to help," she told Sara, her casual tone betraying none of her discomfort. "Anyway, Liam's away this week – well, he's heading off this evening to Sicily for a few days." She looked at her watch. "Speaking of which, he should be back from his jog soon. I'm dropping him to the airport after lunch."

"What a great job," Sara sighed dreamily. "I think it might just be my dream job."

Eve laughed. "That's what most people say when they find out what he does for a living, but it's not all fun and games either – at least not for me!"

Liam Crowley worked for a wine import company, and he spent a considerable amount of time abroad visiting vineyards and wineries in different locations all over the world.

At the moment, he was doing a lot of business in Australia where for the last few months he'd been trying to find a selection suitable for launch onto an increasingly demanding Irish market. But this latest trip was a short one by his standards, a run-of-the-mill four-day visit to a vineyard in Sicily.

His job meant that Eve could be home alone with the children for weeks on end, while Liam was off living it up in some wine-producing destination. It could be tough at times, but it was something she was now well used to. And in truth, she really wouldn't have had it any other way. Eve loved being mum to Lily and Max, and Liam's salary meant that, unlike poor Sara, who was separated, she didn't have to go out to work and miss seeing her children grow up. So she didn't get to travel to the exotic destinations he did, but her role in the family was just as important as Liam's – if not more.

Sara shook her head. "You're fantastic, you know. I don't know how you do it all on your own with the kids and everything. I can only just about manage Jack at the best of times." Sara's husband, a drunken layabout whom Eve had never liked, had run off with another woman not long after the birth of their son, which was another reason Eve was usually happy and willing to help the woman out.

Sara looked again at her watch. "I suppose I'd better get a move on – I'm due at the airport myself soon."

"And where are you off to this time?" Unlike her useless husband – whom Eve knew had never worked a day throughout their marriage – Sara worked at a Dublin-based advertising firm and, from what Eve could make out, was fairly high up in the ranks. In any case, the woman must have been very good at her job to be deemed important enough to be called to go abroad at the last minute like that!

"Oh, nowhere near as exotic as your lucky husband, I'm sorry to say," Sara replied with a grimace. "But nice enough if I get to see any of it. They need me to go to London – to try and win over an unhappy client."

Well, Eve thought, with the amount of winning-over she herself had to do day-in, day-out with Lily and Max, she sympathised with her neighbour's plight.

But working life sounded so glamorous nonetheless! She sighed, shaking her head wistfully at Sara.

"Well, look, try and enjoy it anyway – even if it *is* only work. And try not to worry too much about Jack – we'll look after him very well."

"I know you will. I'll give you a buzz to let you know what time I get back tomorrow, OK? And again, thank you *so* much for taking him at such short notice, Eve. I owe you one, I really do. We should arrange to meet up sometime – have a night out somewhere, what do you think?"

Eve smiled. "I'd love to," she replied politely, while at the same time knowing full well that such a night out was unlikely to happen. Whatever the likelihood of Sara finding a baby-sitter, it was doubtful Eve would be able to get away for a night.

Liam found the kids difficult to handle when he was on his own with them, and now that Max had hit the terrible twos . . . Still, one must live in hope, she thought, smiling at Sara as she pulled out of the driveway in a gleaming new car. Guilty working mother or not, Sara obviously enjoyed the perks of her career.

As the other woman drove away, Eve cast a mournful glance at their older and considerably less hip Volkswagen. A family car if ever there was one, she thought, feeling bland and boring all of a sudden as she went back inside.

Not long after she'd settled baby Jack in his crib and was starting to prepare dinner, Liam arrived back from his afternoon jog.

"Don't tell me you're looking after that woman's kid again!" he moaned.

"Sara needed a favour," Eve shrugged easily.

Liam shook his head. "I think she takes advantage of you, you know, dropping him in here whenever she feels like it. We're not running a crèche here."

"She's our neighbour and she was in a tight spot so I could hardly refuse. He's easy to look after, and it's not as if I wouldn't be here anyway."

Liam grunted. "Seems to me that she's always in a tight spot."

13

Just then, from where he sat on the floor, little Max let out a delighted giggle, and his parents turned in unison to find that their two-year-old – evidently unwilling to wait for his dinner – had taken a fancy to one of Eve's potted plants, and was happily shovelling damp soil and compost into his mouth. Not to mention all over the floor and onto his clothes.

"Oh, Max!" Eve swiftly grabbed a tea towel to dry her hands but to her relief Liam managed to get there first.

Having brushed most of the offending compost off his son's clothes, he tried to get him to spit out the rest.

"Thanks, hon," she said, pleased but faintly taken aback that Liam had intervened so quickly. For much of the kids' early days, and indeed for most of the rest, Liam had generally left things up to her. Still, she'd noticed a slight softening in his approach towards Max lately, in particular as their son got older. He'd been much more reticent with Lily, primarily, Eve supposed, because she was a girl, and also because she'd been an unplanned child – unplanned to unmarried parents who at the time of her conception had been together barely six months.

Eve smiled inwardly as she remembered how shocked Liam had been back then upon learning of her pregnancy. She herself had been terrified, although admittedly less about the pregnancy and more about what her parents would say and whether or not Liam would stand by her. And although her parents had indeed been disappointed, Liam had (much to her relief) steadfastly promised to support her and their baby in every way, so there was little they could do or say. Granted, at the ages of twenty and twenty-one respectively, she and Liam had been thrust into finding a house and settling down together sooner than they might have otherwise, but they were madly in love, so what did it matter?

As far as Eve was concerned, their short time together before

Lily came along didn't matter a whit – they were blissfully happy anyway, so the new house and the new baby would have been inevitable either way. Granted, it might have been nice to go the whole hog and get married, particularly when the second baby came along, but a proposal from Liam had never been forthcoming.

Eve tried not to think too hard about why this was the case; Liam didn't seem too bothered about their making their relationship official, so why should she?

Especially, she reminded herself, watching father and son together, as they'd been blissfully happy (earlier days aside – when Liam had struggled with broken sleep and their lack of cash) ever since.

"Listen, is there any chance you can take over here and clean up this bloody mess?" Liam said then, the warm paternal display Eve had been enjoying quickly disappearing. "I've got to get things ready for this trip."

Things like what? she thought, suddenly annoyed that he couldn't look after Max for a minute when he could see that she already had her hands full preparing dinner. After all, *she* was the one who picked out his clothes and packed his bag for all these trips abroad. And she needed to get the dinner ready so early in the first place because of the trip, so the very least he could do was give her a hand!

One look at Eve's expression told Liam he'd said the wrong thing. "OK, OK, I'll do it," he said, lifting Max into his highchair before grabbing a sweeping brush and tending to the mess on the floor.

"Thank you," Eve replied, faintly irritated by the fact that lately he seemed to avoid having anything to do with the kids. Yes, it might have been her role to look after Lily and Max while his was to go out and earn the bacon, but they were his kids too!

And it was seldom enough they got to see or spend time with him!

Eve reached for the chopping board. Truthfully, she was a little annoyed with Liam for taking another long trip so soon after the last one, which had been three solid weeks in Australia. Then there was this weekend's four-day trip to Sicily which, in all honesty, sounded absolutely idyllic, notwithstanding the fact that it would be all work.

But of course, Liam didn't work all day and all night either, did he? At the end of a hard day the love of her life had the luxury of sitting back and relaxing in a fabulous *trattoria* overlooking the Mediterranean, cup of espresso (or more likely glass of Sicilian wine) in hand. Not like Eve who, after a hard week of housework and kids, could usually be found on a Friday night sitting in her pyjamas with a cup of cocoa and watching *The Late Late Show*. She sighed inwardly. She'd been thinking a lot like this lately, thinking that Liam always had it good while she was the one stuck at home looking after the children. Then again, it was what she wanted to do, wasn't it? It was what she'd insisted they do.

Still, it had been ages since Eve had a holiday, Liam preferring to spend his time off at home. It was understandable, she supposed, given the amount of time he spent away, but still *she* didn't get to spend any time away. And it had been years since they had gone anywhere together, just the two of them – they hadn't been able to manage a weekend in Mayo let alone the Med!

Thinking of Sara, her hardworking neighbour, also off on another exciting and glamorous jaunt, Eve began to feel downright depressed.

Oh, get over it, she admonished herself. Sara wasn't exactly over the moon about being called away to London, was she? No, she was too upset about having to drop everything and leave Jack. In fact, Eve recalled, she seemed downright cheesed off about the whole thing – despite the destination. Evidently, these work trips weren't as exciting as they sounded, as Liam had drummed into Eve on numerous occasions.

"If I never see the inside of an airplane again, I'll be happy," he'd moaned after a multi-stop transatlantic trip to California, not long after Max was born.

So while both Sara and Liam were each this weekend visiting glamorous locations, perhaps neither of them would get a chance to see the sights, let alone enjoy them. So maybe she was getting jealous over nothing.

"Hi, Mum! What's for dinner?" Lily bounded into the kitchen but instantly forgot all about dinner when she caught sight of baby Jack – whom she adored – in his crib. In fact, Lily adored babies and children in general. Like mother like daughter, Eve thought, smiling fondly at her. Although, with her dark eyes and almost jet-black hair, it was difficult to believe that Eve had anything to do with Lily at all; she had so much of her father's colouring.

"Oh, can we bring him for a walk in his pram, Mum, can we pleeease?" she begged.

"Not now, love – I don't have time. Dad's off to the airport later which is why I'm making dinner early."

"But I could take him," her seven-year-old told her solemnly. "How about just around the block and back again?"

Eve shook her head. "Lily, I'm sorry, but you're too young to take Jack out on your own, and we have to look after him for Sara. Unless your dad wants to go for a walk with you?" But from the stricken look on Liam's face, Eve knew immediately that this idea was a non-runner.

"Maybe later," Liam said, not meaning a word of it. "Now Daddy has to go and get ready for work, and soon we'll be having dinner."

Clearly disappointed, Lily stuck out her bottom lip and marched out of the kitchen.

"I don't have time, Eve!" Liam persisted when she flashed him a look.

Yet you have plenty of time to go jogging, don't you? she wanted to say but didn't want to pick a fight. Not when Liam was leaving soon and they wouldn't see him for another few days.

Anyway, she supposed she was lucky she'd got him to help out with Max earlier. Seeing to another child in one day would undoubtedly be way too much to ask!

After dinner, Eve bundled the kids into the car and, with Liam driving, the family set off for the airport.

"I had a look on the TV earlier, and the weather in Sicily is fabulous now," she said dreamily as they drove along the coast road towards the north side of the city. "Twenty-six degrees by day and a little under that in the evenings – heaven! Wouldn't it be nice for us to take the kids somewhere warm like that sometime?"

But Liam didn't seem interested. "Maybe. Did you pack my blue shirt? Oh and that new tie I bought last week?"

"Yes, I did," she replied, disappointed that he didn't seem to take the hint that she was badly in need of a holiday, a weekend away – anything just to break the routine.

But, right on cue, Max started wailing in the back of the car, and there was no point in trying to discuss anything. Soon after, baby Jack joined in the chorus.

"Shush, now, no need for that!" Eve tried everything to quieten the two of them for the rest of the journey but in vain. And when they eventually reached the airport's departure set-down area, there was no mistaking Liam's expression of relief.

Did he feel that way every time he left them? Eve wondered, a little discomfited. Then again, faced with the choice between a relaxing hotel abroad or a car full of wailing children, who *wouldn't* feel the same?

"See you in a few days," Liam said, giving Eve a quick kiss and doing the same with Lily and Max, although, she thought grudgingly, they got a bit of a hug as well.

"Let me know when the flight's due in, so I'll know what time to pick you up," she said, smiling at him. "And have a good trip!"

"You too," Liam replied absentmindedly, before closing the car door behind him, his mind already on the journey ahead.

Eve moved into the driver's seat. "Don't miss us too much!" she called but, as she watched her partner's retreating back, realised that she was talking to herself.

CHAPTER

3. The Last to Know

Dear Sam,

I've just finished "Lucky You" and, having enjoyed it immensely, I went straight out to the shops and bought the new one, "Lucky Stars". I'm already halfway through that and loving it so much that I had to write and tell you. Your characters are so real and you seem to know instinctively what today's UK woman wants! Thanks for many hours of fantastic (and guilt-free) reading

A Big Fan

Sam Callaghan smiled softly and brushed a strand of mid-length blonde hair behind one ear as she read her latest piece of fan mail. Well, she wouldn't say she knew *instinctively* what today's women wanted, or thought they wanted, but she certainly tried her best.

But judging from the amount of fan mail she was getting from readers lately, she must be doing something right! That particular letter was one of many that had been forwarded on from Sam's publishing house and had arrived at her London apartment earlier that day.

The response to her new novel, *Lucky Stars*, seemed to be even greater than that to the first one, *Lucky You*, published a year before. For some reason, and luckily for her, Sam thought, wincing at the pun, her stories about ordinary women facing ordinary problems had struck a chord with female readers, and since her first book had been published the previous year, Sam's feet had barely touched the ground. Never in a million years did she imagine that this could happen to someone like her, an ordinary girl from Dublin who had originally come to London to find work as a journalist.

Having moved to the city many years back, Sam had initially secured work writing periodic articles for a number of UK newspapers and, when she wasn't writing for them, she continued working on her novel, which over the years had already been rejected time and time again.

While she enjoyed journalism and especially enjoyed her London lifestyle – which was a breath of fresh air after Dublin – Sam's first love was writing fiction, and despite the setbacks and rejections she'd already received, she was still wholly determined to get her book published. The problem was that what Sam was writing about – normal everyday women with normal everyday problems – seemed out of vogue, and publishers only seemed to want stories about glamorous femme-fatale types who seemed to do little else but shop and have affairs. But as Sam wasn't one of these women, nor had any experience of them, she had no choice but to stick with what she was doing and hope that the publishing trend might change.

Eventually, she got her wish.

Years after she'd first begun work as a journalist in London, one week Sam decided to write an in-depth piece for one of the newspapers about the societal pressures facing today's UK women – ordinary, everyday women. And when the piece was eventually published, she soon discovered that she'd unwittingly tapped into some kind of zeitgeist, one that resulted in a hugely appreciative public response to the article and subsequently a surge of publisher interest in her previously rejected novel.

And since that novel hit the bookshelves the previous year, Sam hadn't looked back. Her down-to-earth writing style and normal "everywoman" protagonists had proved a huge hit with readers in the UK and Ireland alike.

Sam was enjoying her career and new-found popularity in the UK but was especially thrilled to discover that her improved profile hadn't gone unnoticed at home in Ireland. Not that she'd ever had notions of being popular or famous – in fairness, all she had ever wanted was a decent job – but at the same time there was something hugely satisfying about being recognised as successful by people back home. It meant that her decision to abandon Dublin so soon after finishing her schooling had been justified, despite her sister's insistence that she could do just as well at home.

But back then, the lure of London with all its excitement and glamour had proved too much for Sam, and she was only too happy to get out of her home city and try somewhere different.

Now, as she sat in her Clapham flat and scanned through the rest of her mail, she realised that perhaps this reader was right; maybe she did have some sort of ability to sense what today's women were feeling and the pressures they were under. Britain was experiencing something of a downturn economically, and women were feeling torn between having to go out to work or staying at home to raise their kids – situations she covered at length in her novels.

She thought about her younger sister Eve, who had never been torn in this way. All Eve had ever wanted was a husband and family – and once she'd had her first child seven years ago, the idea of any kind of work outside the home was completely alien to her. She was following in their mother's footsteps in that regard, Sam supposed. Lillian too had always seemed at her happiest when knee-deep in housework or fussing over her husband and daughters. Sam smiled as she thought about her parents, who had died some years back. What would they have made of her success? In all honesty, they probably wouldn't be in the least bit surprised. Sam had always been the one with the career vision and ambition and had little time for settling down and raising a family, so in that regard she and her baby sister couldn't have been more different.

But Sam was chuffed to think that her books were of some consolation to women out there; it justified all the hard work and thought she put into writing them. And while her books hadn't exactly lit up the bestsellers list, Sam was hopeful that they might do just that some day, and in any case she was thrilled with everything she'd achieved so far.

Just then, Sam's boyfriend, Derek Greene, entered the living room with a towel wrapped around his naked body. As they were going out that evening, he'd gone directly from work to her place to get ready, rather than travel all the way out to Wimbledon where he lived.

"Still reading those?" he said, eyes widening as he caught sight of her going through the letters at her desk. "Sam, you do realise that the restaurant's booked for eight?"

"Sure," she replied absentmindedly, scanning through yet another letter.

Dear Sam,

Like Cassie in 'Lucky Stars', I hate leaving the kids with strangers while I go out to work, but the family can't survive financially if I don't.

When reading Cassie's story I almost felt like I was reading about my own life.

"Sam, it's seven thirty on a Friday night – give it a break, will you?"

She swivelled round in her chair and flashed Derek an apologetic smile. "OK, OK, I'll just finish up with these, and then I'll start getting ready, all right?"

As a branch manager for one of the city banks, work for Derek consisted of a boring five-day week, nine-to-five, no less and certainly no more, and he still hadn't quite got his head around the fact that his girlfriend's profession didn't keep normal working hours. As she and Derek had got together while Sam was still a struggling unpublished author, her success and its resultant popularity tended to get on his nerves sometimes. Tonight was evidently one of those times.

"Sam, please," he said, heading towards her bedroom, his tone impatient, "I had to beg for this table – we really don't want to be late."

Sam stood up from her desk. "You know it'll only take me a few minutes to get ready," she soothed, faintly disappointed that her reading time was being cut short. "Don't worry – we'll be there in plenty of time."

Derek grunted but said nothing.

Why all the rush? she wondered, following him into the bedroom and going straight to her wardrobe to pick out an outfit. But then again, he was always the same, wasn't he, she thought, instantly deciding on a simple, slim-fitting black halter-dress. Too used to having staff in his division jump at his every request, often he expected the same from her. She smiled indulgently at him as he frantically rubbed a towel through his hair. After almost two years together, you'd think he'd know her better.

True to her word, Sam was dressed, fully made-up and ready to leave the flat within the half hour. In fact, it was Derek who'd eventually turned out to be the cause of a delay, and Sam noticed he seemed oddly fidgety and uncomfortable as their cab drove along the London streets. Bad day at work, she supposed.

The restaurant was situated in Chelsea and, as she and Derek followed the maitre d' to their table, Sam couldn't help but be aware of a few interested glances from other diners. Being recognised was something she wasn't exactly comfortable with but at the same time was something that went hand in hand with writing for a high-profile UK newspaper like the *Mail*. Her column consisted mostly of a commentary on the various issues facing modern British women and, while she usually tried to air her views in a thought-provoking manner, the paper generally preferred her to take a more sensationalist stance. For this reason, she longed for the day when she'd be known as a bestselling author rather than a mildly sensational hack.

She'd only just finished promoting her second novel and things had been so hectic over the previous weeks that she'd hardly seen Derek, something she knew he wasn't exactly happy about. While he'd seemed as delighted as she was when she'd first been offered her publishing deal, he hadn't anticipated the novel's huge appeal, nor the demands that the success of this and subsequent books would place on Sam publicity-wise. Sam didn't mind. The flurry of interviews, photo-shoots and launch parties that accompanied promoting her books was a dream come true, and she wouldn't swap that for anything. But she had missed spending time with Derek lately, and as she would soon need to start researching her next book, things would only get busier, so really a relaxing night out was seriously in order for both of them.

About halfway through the meal, Sam realised that while she had been chattering non-stop about everything and anything,

Derek had barely uttered a word. She sat forward in her chair.

"Derek, what's the matter?" she asked softly. "You seem very preoccupied. Are things hectic at work?"

He looked straight at her, his slate-grey eyes fixed on Sam's green ones. "No, work's fine – there's something else on my mind, actually."

"Well, what is it? Tell me. Is there anything I can do or –"

"Do you love me, Sam?" he interjected then, causing her to almost drop her fork in surprise.

How had the conversation turned so serious all of a sudden? There she was, talking about something as trivial as going shopping the next day, and then he goes and asks her a question like that? She looked around, afraid that some of the neighbouring diners would overhear, although her worries in this regard had nothing to do with her being recognised. No, this time it was because once again Sam knew exactly what was coming. *Oh dear.*

"Derek, you know I do," she replied, her heart heavy and apprehensive as she waited for the words.

"So," his gaze stayed fixed on her face, "you know what I'm going to ask then, don't you?"

Unfortunately she did. He'd already asked the same question twice before and each time he'd received the same reply.

"So, will you?"

For a long moment, Sam just stared back at him, trying to think of the right way to put it. Eventually, though, she had to look away. "Derek," she began with a deep sigh, "I . . . I just don't know . . ."

"Fine," he said, quickly shoving a forkful of vegetables into his mouth, his expression difficult to read.

"It's just that –"

"I said it's OK, didn't I?" he interjected. "You still don't want to marry me. Fine. Maybe I'll try again next year – or," he added, with a defiant shrug, "maybe I bloody well won't."

"Oh, for goodness sake!" At this, Sam shook her head. "You could at least listen to what I have to say."

"Why? Is it going to be any different from what you said last time? Or the time before that?"

"Well, not really, but . . ."

Sam wasn't completely sure why she kept turning down Derek's marriage proposals. They'd been together since they were first introduced through mutual friends two years earlier and, while she was certain she loved him, she knew deep down she wasn't ready for cosy domesticity.

And, unfortunately, this was exactly what Derek wanted. He didn't just want the ring on Sam's finger: he also wanted the house in the Cotswolds, the kids, the Labradors and the budgies, etc. And even worse, she knew he'd want her to forget all about the writing career she adored and had spent years trying to build.

"I want my kids to be looked after by their own mother, not by some stranger," he'd informed her, before going on to explain that he believed the relationship problems he now had with his own mother were rooted in the fact that she'd left him and his brother in the care of a nanny when they were younger.

Sam had been taken aback but at same time wasn't too surprised at this traditional outlook. Derek was traditional in a lot of ways. And perhaps she could understand his urgency; at thirty-eight, he was seven years older than she was and the only still-single male in his social and business circles.

But to agree to Derek's proposal would do her own aspirations a serious disservice and Sam knew she wasn't prepared to do that. It was only now that her career was starting to take off after years spent in the doldrums, wondering where her next writing job would come from and striving to get her novel published.

Yet, there was no one else she'd rather be with than Derek, and she was sure that when the time was right she'd slow down and think about marriage and family life. But not just yet.

Trying to explain this to Derek was a difficult prospect.

"Derek, now isn't really a good time for me. Maybe when I've finished the new book, we can –"

"And what about the book after that? And the one after that again? Admit it, Sam, you love those stupid bloody books a hell of a lot more than you love me!"

"That's not it," she countered, taken aback at how vehemently against it all he seemed to be. Yes, she knew that all the promotional stuff she needed to do bothered him, but "stupid bloody books"? So much for being proud of her!

"That's not fair, Derek," she replied evenly. "You know full well that I love you, but I'm very lucky to be where I am, and I can't just give it all up now. It wouldn't be fair."

"Fair to who?"

"Well, to me – and my readers, I suppose," she added almost as an afterthought.

Derek snorted. "As if they don't have enough brainless fluffy books to choose from!"

"Thanks, Derek!" Sam said, folding her arms across her chest, her expression grim. "Thanks a bloody lot."

He knew damn well how much time and effort went into those "brainless fluffy" books, and just because *he* didn't read them, didn't mean they weren't as worthy as anything else on the shelves!

"I'm sorry – that was uncalled for," Derek admitted, evidently realising how much he'd hurt her feelings. "But I still don't understand why you insist on writing a book a year and then spend any free time you have promoting the previous one. Not to mention continuing to write a column for the *Mail* when you don't need to – financially anyway," he added, when Sam opened her mouth to protest.

Perhaps he was right about all the additional time she spent out and about promoting, but going out and meeting people was Sam's greatest reward for all those lonely months spent typing away at her desk. Again, she loved the fun and glamour that accompanied a new release, the book signings, media interviews and photo-shoots – the lot. But, yes, maybe Derek did have a point in that she no longer needed to keep up the column-writing. In truth, her editor's growing influence over the tone and content of the writing was starting to make her feel uncomfortable. As far as Giles was concerned, the more sensational she could make it the better – irrespective of the topic. But journalism had paid her wages over the last few years and it was difficult to take the plunge and give it all up in the hopes that her books would really take off.

"OK, so maybe I am doing too much publicity-wise, but it's all extremely important in terms of my launching a long-term writing career. Profile is everything, as you well know. Look, it won't be like this forever," she added, putting her hand over his. "It's going well now, and people seem to really enjoy the books, but perhaps that's only the novelty factor. The important thing for me now is to ensure that the momentum keeps going and that I forge a decent long-term career out of it."

But not if Derek had anything to do with it, it seemed.

"I just think it seems a bit strange," he said. "You're thirty-one years old, Sam. Surely at this stage you should be thinking seriously about settling down and starting a family instead of obsessing over this so-called 'career'. You know well I could afford to support both of us on my salary."

Sam gritted her teeth. Why didn't he get it? Why didn't he understand how much her independence meant to her? Why did he think that now, just when her career was getting places, and with years of hard work behind her, she'd give it all up to become a housewife?

Granted, her sister had done it, and yes, Eve seemed happy enough, but then again, settling down and becoming a mum had been all her younger sister ever really wanted in life, hadn't it? As a child, Eve had always been the one dressing up dolls and pushing them around in her toy pram, while Sam had sat in a corner, poring over the latest *Malory Towers* book. But she and Eve had always been very different in that respect.

Perhaps if she'd found fulfilment in life as early as Eve had, she might have gone down the domestic route, but things were only starting to happen for her now, and she wasn't going to throw it all away just to keep Derek on side. What was the point of getting married if only one partner was happy about it? Surely both parties needed to go into such an important commitment with their eyes wide open, ready for whatever challenges lay ahead?

So, as much as she loved Derek, Sam knew deep down that she couldn't say yes now just to keep him happy. She'd always regret not taking the opportunities offered to her and might very well end up resenting him.

When she tried to explain this to Derek, he sighed deeply.

"OK then, Sam," he said, sitting back in his chair, "it seems I have no choice."

"What do you mean?" She didn't like the tone in his voice.

"Look, I love you. We've been together for nearly two years, two good years, and I sincerely hope we'll be together for many years to come."

Hearing this, she relaxed slightly.

"But, Sam, I really can't wait forever. While I understand that your career is important to you, and you want to make the most of your opportunities, I just wonder whether you're properly considering the opportunity I'm offering. How do you think all this rejection makes me feel?"

"I know, and I'm sorry but –"

"Look, you said you wanted to start researching the new book soon?"

She nodded, wondering what was coming.

"I suggest we take a break from one another while you do that – take the time apart to really think about where we're going. I think that could be part of the problem, actually. You're not thinking seriously about my proposal, because you know I'll still hang around afterwards. But, Sam, maybe I won't. Maybe I'll get tired of asking and being rejected. Maybe I'll have no choice but to look elsewhere."

A stab of jealously sliced through her at the thought of Derek with someone else. "You want us to take some time apart so you can look for someone else?" she ventured, hurt by the prospect.

"No, I want us to take some time apart in order for you to ask yourself why you keep refusing me. I want you to think seriously about it, Sam. And sometime soon, I'm going to ask you to marry me once again, *but* this time will be the last."

"So you're giving me an ultimatum," she said, faintly hurt that he was putting it so bluntly but able to understand it all the same. After all, it was true – how much must her rejections have hurt him? She'd already turned him down twice; there weren't too many men who would keep coming back after that.

"I wouldn't put it quite like that," he said, his tone softening a little, "but I do need to know where I stand. I need to know if you're ever going to change your mind about settling down with me – otherwise we're both wasting our time here."

Sam nodded silently, almost afraid to speak. An ultimatum – God! She had no idea that things would come to this. Derek really was determined to make her face an important choice, wasn't he?

Her career or marriage and babies? Why couldn't she just have both? Although it had never been high on her list of priorities, she was pretty certain that one day she did want the kids and the nice house and all the rest of it but didn't think a decision would be forced on her so soon. Yet, she loved Derek with all her heart. They had a similar sense of humour, the same interests and, up until now, had made a great team. And she knew in her heart and soul that men like him didn't come around every day. She really didn't want to lose him, but she didn't want to throw away her career either. But Derek had made it painfully clear he wasn't going to wait around . . . Sam's heart sank as the magnitude of the decision she was now facing finally began to dawn on her.

"So what do you think?" Derek said eventually, the beginnings of a smile lightening the solemn mood.

In fairness to him, he seemed to understand very well the difficult position he was putting her in.

"Do you think you could live without me for the next few weeks?"

Sam looked into the kind, handsome face she knew so well and realised that this decision would likely be the most difficult of her life. "I very much doubt it," she said, smiling ruefully at him. "But for both our sakes, I think I have to try."

CHAPTER 4

Brooke Reynolds sat back in her swivel-chair and, deep in thought, looked out the window of her tenth-floor office with its wonderful views over Sydney harbour.

This was a good one, she thought, idly watching the ferryboats leave Circular Quay and sail onwards past the Opera House – the building's famous white sail-like roof glistening brightly in the afternoon sun. The opening line of the first chapter had hooked her immediately; and she had thought it clever the way the author had successfully manipulated her assumptions about what was going on. Yep, this story had definitely piqued her interest; she liked all the characters so far (especially Eve, with her self-deprecating ways and downtrodden lifestyle) and she wanted to know more about why Anna and her fiancé still hadn't set a date and what Derek's ultimatum would mean for Sam.

Most readers would.

She swung back towards her desk and picked up the remaining pages of the manuscript. *The Last to Know*. Pretty good title too.

Judging from the setting and the dialogue, the author was likely Irish, which in Brooke's opinion was another major plus. Women's fiction by

Irish writers had always proved hugely popular amongst Australian readers and beyond.

So, as the recently promoted acquisitions editor of Horizon Group, Australia's commercial women's fiction imprint, if Brooke acquired a new Irish-written gem for the imprint, well, the publishing director would be very happy indeed. Then again, Brooke was probably biased, given that she was part Irish herself, but there was definitely something in this author's voice that worked. Additionally, she liked the contemporary Dublin setting and the way the author had very quickly established place and character.

She smiled. The fact that it was Dublin-based was probably the reason it had ended up on her desk in the first place. That afternoon, she'd come back from lunch to find the manuscript sitting there with a yellow-sticky message sitting on top: "*Think this one should certainly interest YOU!*"

Probably Karen the sales director, judging by the light-hearted tone, or perhaps even Mary, one of Horizon's readers. Both had a very good eye for what might sell.

Whoever it was, they were right; it was definitely miles better than a lot of the stuff they'd been getting lately, she thought with a grimace.

Horizon were always on the lookout for the next big thing – a new talent that would appease the voracious appetite of Australian women's fiction fans, and it had been some time since they'd received a submission like this – something that merited a serious look.

Often the submissions they received from budding authors proved to be much more Mills & Boon than Maeve Binchy and, at times, Brooke couldn't help but have grave doubts about the sanity of some of these hopefuls. One recent submission was a story told from the point of view of a sock drawer, another extolled the virtues of broccoli, while a third sought to inform Brooke that this was "the story she'd been waiting for". "*Make a quick decision now, before another publisher beats you to it!*" the author urged in his introductory letter, which was dated some eighteen months before. Sorry, mate, Brooke had thought at the time, it seems I might have already missed my chance. *"This is a highly original story, the likes of which you've never seen before!"* the writer gushed, before immediately launching into a description of his "highly original story" about precocious teenagers attending wizard school.

Brooke wouldn't mind but Horizon didn't normally publish this kind of stuff, and their submission guidelines clearly stated 'Contemporary fiction *only*'. But evidently most of these authors had either ignored the guidelines or felt that their writing was so special the publishing house would do a complete turnaround and publish it anyway. It was pity really, given the amount of work and energy that had gone into the writing, that by sending it to the wrong publisher, the authors hadn't given their work even a fighting chance. But unfortunately Brooke could do nothing about that.

So, having trundled through pages and pages of below-par submissions in recent weeks, she was relieved to *finally* have something to read that suited the Horizon list, and more importantly, something that truly excited her.

Still, while the story had started well, she would need to read much more to get a sense of what the author's writing style was like, or indeed if the story was going anywhere. Anyone could write a decent first few chapters – it was the subsequent hundred thousand or so words that usually proved difficult. So Brooke wasn't going to get too excited just yet!

Picking up the manuscript, she settled back in her chair and once again began to read.

Hopefully, *The Last to Know* would live up to its early promise.

CHAPTER 5

4. The Last to Know

Having dropped Liam at the airport, Eve decided on the way home to nip into a small supermarket to pick up a few bits and pieces to help get her through yet another Friday night home alone. She darted quickly through the aisles, picking up fresh cream cakes, crisps, chocolate – lovely comfort food – but couldn't help but dither over choosing a multi-pack of Crunchie or Kit-Kats, trying to decide which chocolate bar had the lowest calorie content. Sam would know, of course – with a figure like hers, her sister would be an expert on all this calorie stuff.

But conscious of the fact that she'd left Lily to keep an eye on the younger ones outside in the car and she didn't have much time for dawdling, Eve eventually decided on both. They'd last for a couple of weeks anyway – as long as Liam didn't get at them, that is. While they both possessed a very sweet tooth, Eve usually tried to give the kids as little chocolate as possible – usually only as a special treat.

She put her chosen purchases in a basket already full of salt-, fat- and calorie-laden food and headed straight for the cash register. She was so busy day-dreaming about Liam and whether or not he'd actually be at home to eat the chocolate that she didn't realise she'd skipped the queue.

From behind her, Eve heard a sharp intake of breath, followed by an unmistakeable "tut-tut" and, finally realising that she'd made a faux pas, she turned to apologise. "Oh, I'm sorry, I didn't realise that –"

"The bloody cheek of it!" the middle-aged woman standing behind her commented to her female companion. "Just because she's some big shot in England she thinks she can swan in here and get served before everyone else!"

Here we go again, Eve thought sighing inwardly, as she tried to move back past the queue, not at all in the mood for this today.

The other woman nodded. "Indeed. And the same one on the telly the other night boasting about how down to earth she was." Then she added nastily, "I've heard the camera adds ten pounds but in her case I think it must subtract them!"

Eve stopped in her tracks and turned around to face the women, a tight smile on her face. "I'm not Samantha Callaghan, actually," she said, her quiet tone betraying little of her humiliation. "I'm her sister."

Her tormentors stared open-mouthed, their faces reddening more and more by the second as, horrified, they realised their mistake.

"I know we're very alike," Eve went on, "apart from the odd ten pounds, that is," she added acidly, and at this, the two women looked away, ashamed. "But as you can probably tell," she said, gesturing at her distinctly unglamorous outfit of jeans and green woollen sweater, "I'm no big shot."

With that, Eve turned on her heel and walked away, leaving the two women speechless in her wake.

Embarrassed and, following the comment about her weight, no

longer quite as eager to indulge herself, Eve joined the back of the checkout queue. Blast those women anyway! she thought, getting more concerned by the minute about having to leave the kids out in the car for so long. While Lily could of course be trusted to keep an eye on them, she was still only seven after all. But what could she do?

She sighed. It wasn't the first time something like that had happened – because she and Sam looked very much alike, she was always being mistaken for her, but she sorely wished it would happen when she was doing the weekly family shop and loading the trolley with healthy fresh fruit and veg, not when she was feeling sorry for herself and indulging in a Friday-night treat!

But that was the price to pay for having a well-known sister, she mused as she handed money to the cashier, who thankfully didn't seem to 'recognise' her.

She picked up her bags and trundled back to the car, her mood greatly dampened by the supermarket visit.

Perhaps that was a tip Sam could use in one of her newspaper columns, she thought as she drove towards home: if you happen to see a woman filling up her shopping trolley with calorific treats, make it your business to point out that she's nothing but an overweight greedy-guts – that might call a halt to her gallop.

It had certainly called a halt to Eve's anyway. By the time she arrived back at the house and had settled the kids in bed, she was no longer interested in gorging herself on junk food.

Instead, later that evening she opened a bottle of wine (courtesy of Liam's complimentary stock) and spent the rest of the evening flicking through the TV channels. She was lucky that they had the UK stations really; if she had to solely rely on the programming at RTÉ in the evenings she'd go crazy! Oh – the BBC was doing some kind of holiday special, she discovered, perking up a little – she'd enjoy that.

Eve took a sip of wine, sat back on the sofa and dreamily watched the almost hypnotic images of tall palm trees gently blowing in the breeze, aquamarine water lapping gently onto the shore of impossibly pristine beaches and of course the obligatory happy couple lazing together on a hammock. She closed her eyes, trying to imagine what it would be like to be in such a warm and sunny place right now. Oh, how wonderful it would be! she sighed, trying to push away the thought that her other half was somewhere *exactly* like that, while she was once again stuck at home in front of the TV.

Eventually, Eve fell asleep, dreaming of Liam and the kids playing happily on white sandy beaches, their laughter drifting along the warm summer breeze, while she stayed in the background – vacuuming.

*   *   *

She woke up at six the following morning to the sound of Max crying from upstairs. Bleary-eyed, she eased herself up off the sofa, her joints aching from her awkward sleeping position and her head groggy from the wine, before quickly making her way upstairs to Max's bedroom. She couldn't believe she had fallen asleep on the sofa like that and –

"Oh, Max!" Realising that her son had been sick during the night, Eve groaned. And, judging by the state of the sheets, the copious amount of compost he'd consumed before last night's dinner had helped greatly in this regard.

Max continued to wail, his loud cries sending vibrations through Eve's brain, the copious amount of wine she'd consumed the night before now *not* helping greatly in this regard. "It's all right, Max – Mummy's here now."

After she'd cleaned Max up and changed his bedclothes, she

made her way downstairs to the kitchen, her son fidgeting awkwardly in her arms and proclaiming loudly in her ear that he "wanna go out!"

"You can't go out, honey," Eve replied, her tone soft. "It's much too early and you'll wake the birdies up." Not to mention the neighbours, she thought wryly, who wouldn't be at all impressed with the sound of screaming children on the lawn before seven on a Saturday morning. But this didn't go down at all well with Max, who showed his displeasure by screaming all the way through breakfast. Little Jack was a saint to look after compared to her own little horror, she thought, as she prepared to feed the newest visitor to the Callaghan/Crowley household.

Then, at around ten o'clock, Lily appeared, her daughter's sullen mood suggesting that Eve should have been able to quieten Max and let her have a precious Saturday lie-in.

"Why don't you let him watch cartoons on TV or something?" she grumbled. "That would shut him up for a while."

"Did I let you do whatever you liked when you were that age, just to shut you up?" Eve replied, the four cups of coffee she'd already had that morning only now beginning to take effect.

"No, and you still don't." Lily was petulant as she opened the cupboard and took out a box of Rice Krispies, evidently determined to make her mother suffer for disturbing her beauty sleep.

Well, it seemed the entire family was in cracking form this morning, Eve thought, going upstairs with the vacuum cleaner in tow and leaving Jack gurgling in his crib. Max was now safely ensconced in his playpen and not a bit happy about it, judging by the screams emanating from the kitchen, while Lily had been sullen all throughout breakfast.

Eve didn't understand what she'd done to upset her daughter this time, although Lily was often moody these days. Goodness, the girl was only seven years of age, Eve thought worriedly, as she vacuumed around her daughter's bed. She hoped this wasn't a warning as to what she'd be like in her teenage years.

In between spot-checks on the children and keeping a close eye on the baby, she spent the rest of the morning vacuuming and dusting the bedrooms, cleaning the bathroom and then scrubbing the kitchen.

Then, just before lunch, the telephone rang.

"Hello there, stranger," said the voice on the other end.

"Well, speak of the devil," Eve cried, pleased to hear from her sister, to whom she hadn't spoken in a while.

"Oh yes – so what's Liam been saying about me this time?" Sam shot back wryly.

Though Eve and her sister were close, these days they weren't heavily involved in one another's lives – on the one hand because Sam lived in London, and on the other because she and Liam didn't really get on.

For some reason the two had never really taken to one another. Liam had always seemed distrustful of Sam and was apparently unable to cope with the girls' closeness. It was almost as if he saw her as a rival for Eve's affections. Sam, on her part, found Liam boring and staid – in contrast, Eve supposed, to her sister's own exciting life as a well-known UK newspaper columnist and, lately, a published author.

As the years went by, their apathy towards one another hadn't changed all that much – if anything it had got stronger. Although her older sister had never said anything out loud, Eve suspected that Sam disapproved of Liam's regular trips abroad, and Liam in return disapproved – or more likely was jealous of – Sam's glamorous lifestyle.

"She's nearly thirty years old and still flitting from man to man – it's disgraceful," he'd said in the days before Sam had begun seeing Derek seriously. In fairness, her sister had been going through boyfriends at an alarming rate at that stage, but she was still young and had no commitments, so why not? Anyway, London was so glamorous and fun and totally different to life here, so why *shouldn't* she enjoy herself?

At times, Eve wished that she and Liam had had more time to themselves as a couple before settling down with the mortgage and the kids, but such thoughts were fleeting and usually coincided with the kids acting up or Sam telling her all about yet another fun-filled and fabulous party she'd been to in London.

But as she got that bit older, and particularly since her career had taken off, Sam seemed to have settled down, and her social life now mostly revolved around publicity for her new books or quieter nights out with Derek, who was older and, compared to some of Sam's previous boyfriends, had a much more calming influence on her.

And although Sam's success occasionally had its drawbacks – for her at least, Eve thought, recalling yesterday's trip to the supermarket – she was very proud of her sister and happy to see her finally focused and content with life.

"So, how's everything?" Eve asked. "Enjoying the success of the new book? Everybody's talking about it over here."

"It's great and, yes, I suppose I should be enjoying it," Sam replied, "but I'm afraid Derek has put a bit of a kybosh on things for me."

"What? How?"

"He proposed."

For the briefest of seconds, Eve felt a stab of astonishing jealousy, but this was just as quickly replaced by one of heartfelt delight.

"Sam, that's wonderful news!" she cried. "Congratulations – you must be thrilled!" But her enthusiasm faltered when Sam didn't reply. "Aren't you?"

"Not exactly," her sister said, her tone flat. "And to be honest, Eve, this isn't the first time he's asked me. He asked me twice before."

Once again, Eve's heart sank. She'd been waiting for a proposal (just one!) from Liam for goodness knew how long, so to find out that Sam had been asked (or needed to be asked!) more than once seemed unimaginable . . . not to mention totally unfair. Still, as much as she envied her sister at that moment, there was no way Eve was about to show it.

"You're kidding! You mean Derek proposed to you before now, and you didn't tell me?" She couldn't comprehend how her sister could hide something as important as this.

"There was nothing to tell."

"What do you mean?" she asked indignantly. "Oh," she added, realising, "you turned him down."

"Yes."

"Oh, Sam, don't tell me you've just turned him down again?"

Sam sighed. "I had to, Eve. Things aren't as straightforward for me as they might be for – for some people."

Eve ignored the remark and instead tried to focus on the conversation, which was all about Sam and what Sam wanted – *not* about her. "But why not?" she enquired. "He's perfect for you – he's goodlooking, has plenty of money and seems to have a good head on his shoulders –"

"That's part of the problem, to be honest," Sam said. "He can be a bit too perfect at times."

Eve made a face. "You're joking, I hope."

"No – oh, look, it's hard to explain, and yes, he is terrific, but I don't know if I'm ready to settle down just yet."

"Just yet? Sam, you're thirty-one years of age! Not that it matters what age you are, but still! I mean, I settled down when I was *twenty*-one, and I've no regrets."

"None at all?"

"No – well, OK, maybe sometimes." She glanced towards Max, who at that very moment was making a brave attempt at chewing his way out of the playpen. Dear God! "Occasionally it can be tough and, in all honesty, I'd like it if Liam were around more often. But really, at the end of the day, I wouldn't swap what I have for anything."

Sam didn't seem convinced. "You wouldn't? Not being funny, Eve, and I know this kind of life suits you, but are you telling me you wouldn't swap days of endless housework and cleaning up after a man and two kids for carefree days out shopping in town or going out on nights with the girls?"

Eve sighed. It had been ages since she'd been out shopping for anything other than groceries. "Well, maybe sometimes, but . . ."

"Exactly, maybe sometimes. But you've experienced that kind of life to a certain extent so you know what you're missing – or not, as the case may be. Derek's asking me to give up my life for a totally different kind of life, something I have no idea about other than what I can gather from visiting you."

Yes, but most importantly Derek has asked you to be his wife, Eve argued silently. *There's a big difference.*

"I mean, once we get married, he expects me to go directly into the housewife and motherhood thing, which you know I've never had much of an interest in and –"

"Well, there's nothing wrong with wanting a family surely?"

Sam sighed. "Not only does he want to have a family – he also wants me to give up journalism and maybe stop writing altogether. But I love writing and I love the financial freedom journalism gives me. And no offence intended, Eve, but I think I'd go *mad* if I had to sit at home with nothing to do day-in, day-out."

Eve's eyes widened at that last comment, and all of a sudden something inside her snapped. "Nothing to do?" she cried, stung by her sister's belittlement of her. "*You* try dealing with a stroppy seven-year old and cleaning up after a skittish toddler! *You* try being constantly landed with minding the neighbour's child and cleaning a house that seems to be constantly dirty! *You* try packing Liam's suitcases for yet another trip away – a trip that you badly need too but haven't a hope of getting! Packing endless suitcases for a man who wouldn't know what a proposal was unless it had a sales sheet attached to it! Swap places with me for a while, Sam – then see how bloody easy it is!"

There was a heavy silence on the other end and, having finished her outburst, Eve's face reddened and her hands shook as she held the receiver. She didn't really know where all that had come from, but her sister's words had really unnerved her, particularly the assumption that because she didn't work she didn't *do* anything all day. And for someone who wrote about – and was supposed to *understand* – the modern woman, well, this was doubly frustrating! Not to mention that it was something Liam hinted at now and again too, the implication that Eve had loads of time on her hands to do whatever she wished, conveniently overlooking the fact that looking after their two children was a full-time job.

God knew Liam's mother managed to get in plenty of digs about this too throughout many of her unannounced visits. But Eve hadn't intended to sound so bitter about it all, and she certainly hadn't intended to speak to Sam like that. She hoped that Sam didn't think she was going off her rocker and for a long moment was almost afraid to speak again.

Sam was horrified. "Oh God, Eve, I'm so sorry," she said eventually. "I didn't mean to suggest that you . . . I suppose I really had no idea what things must be like and –"

"No, you don't," Eve replied, but there was no longer any

bitterness in her tone. She cleared her throat. "Look, you just caught me on a bad day. I didn't really mean any of that." Horrified that she'd made her life sound so pathetic, she tried to backtrack. "And it's certainly not as awful as I made it sound."

But Sam didn't seem to be listening. "Eve, when's the last time you had a break away, a real break?"

Eve wrinkled her forehead. "Like a holiday? Never, you know that."

"No, not a full holiday – say a weekend somewhere, or a day out shopping?"

"I never go into town with the kids. It's a nightmare trying to get parking, not to mention having to get round all those one-way streets and –"

"I didn't mean with the kids – I meant on your own, or to have lunch with one of your friends."

Eve tittered. "With one of my friends? Sam, most of my friends are in the same boat as I am – too busy looking after families to be gadding off on shopping trips. Not to mention that it would be impossible anyway – with Liam away so much there's no one to look after the kids."

"There's me," her sister replied softly.

"You?" Eve couldn't resist a smile. "Sam, you're my sister and I love you to bits, but in all honesty you're the last person I'd ask to look after my kids. Now, no offence," she added quickly, "it's for your own sake. As you admitted yourself earlier, you're not exactly suited to domestic life."

Sam bit her lip. "Well, maybe that's the answer, Eve. Maybe I should find out if I could be suited to it."

"Well, yes, but how –"

"Look," Sam interrupted, "I'm sorry that I treated your life so flippantly, that wasn't my intention. I can only imagine how difficult it must be trying to keep all the balls in the air. But, Eve, this conversation has given me an idea."

"Really?" Eve was pleased. "What kind of an idea?"

"Well, as you know, I usually write about working women – women struggling to balance the pressures of home and a career."

"I know that." Eve firmly believed that a woman should be first and foremost a mother and should put the welfare of her kids before any kind of career. But that was her and of course some people were different.

"Well, maybe this time I'd like to write something from the point of view of someone who doesn't have to juggle home and career but maybe has to juggle her own different set of problems just the same."

Eve's lips pursed. "I never said I had problems juggling anything. I just get overwhelmed sometimes."

"Yes, but you did say you'd love a holiday or some kind of break, didn't you?"

Recalling the TV shows she'd been watching, Eve nodded dreamily. "It would be wonderful but it's just not possible. Not the way Liam –"

"Just hear me out for a second," Sam interjected, a little more forcibly. "You need a break, regardless of whether or not Liam is around. Now, I've just told you I turned down Derek's proposal because I'm having trouble coming round to the idea of giving up the life I have for one of cosy domesticity – a life that you already live but one of which I don't really have any firsthand knowledge. And to be honest, I think I'd like to try it out, use the opportunity as part of the research for my next book. But even more importantly, it might help me make up my mind once and for all about settling down with Derek. So, why not let me come over there and look after things for a day or two and let you take it easy?"

Eve's eyes widened. "Are you serious?"

"Why not? You said Liam's going off on another trip soon?"

"Yes, he's going off to Australia again the week after next."

"Fine. That would give us the perfect opportunity, wouldn't it? With him out of the picture, it would certainly be much easier for me, anyway," she said with a smile in her voice, and Eve had no doubts she was referring to her and Liam's mutual dislike.

Even so, Liam would go apoplectic at the idea of Sam taking over the running of the house in order to carry out research, while Eve went swanning off for a 'break'!

Anyway, she thought, shaking the thought out of her head, Sam was only talking rubbish. As if she'd let her sister come in and take over for her! OK, so she was tired and cheesed-off with her lot at the moment, but not *that* cheesed-off!

"What about the kids?" she challenged, certain that this would be the fatal flaw in Sam's not-so-well-thought-out plan. While Eve had always adored children, Sam wasn't a huge fan. "You're telling me you'd be happy to come over and look after the children without anyone else around to help? Get up at all hours of the morning with Max, get Lily out to school and help her with her homework, as well as feed, clothe and play with them both?"

For a moment Sam's enthusiasm seemed to falter but, just as quickly, she snapped out of it. "Well, that's basically the reason I want to do this, isn't it?" she shot back. "To find out if I *could* be happy doing those things if I decide to settle down with Derek. And of course I'll need to know firsthand what I'm talking about if I decide to write about it in my next book, won't I?"

"But what if you decide you don't like it – or even worse, if something goes wrong?"

"Look, if something goes wrong I'll have you on the other end of the phone, won't I? But at the same time, what could possibly go wrong? It'll only be for a couple of days at the most."

Eve rolled her eyes. "And where will I be in this little fantasy of yours?"

"Well, seeing as I'm partly doing this for your benefit, you'd think you'd be a bit more grateful," said Sam acidly. "Why don't you come and stay at my place – just slob around here and relax?"

"Go all the way over to London? On my own?"

"Eve, it's hardly a million miles away! Now that I think of it, staying here is a great idea – exactly what you need. You could go shopping, take in a couple of shows, go out on the town . . . I could get the girls to take you out if you'd like . . . they'd show you a great time, and you could borrow anything you like from my wardrobe –"

"Ha! As if any of your clothes would fit me!" Eve scoffed, picturing Sam's trim and toned figure and casting a beleaguered glance towards her own sagging middle.

"Well – just stick to the darker clothes, then," Sam advised and, offended by this, Eve sniffed. "Oh, for goodness's sake," Sam said, exasperated, "you're not much heavier than me – all you need is a bit of toning! But what do you think? Sounds good, doesn't it?"

Eve bit her lip. She really wished she hadn't lost the rag earlier and made her life sound so awful. It wasn't as if things were that bad – if anything it was just her jealousy over Sam's marriage proposal that had made her feel so frustrated.

Worryingly, Sam seemed to read her thoughts. "And Eve, I never knew that marrying Liam was so important to you," she said softly. "After all this time, I thought –"

"It's not!" Eve interjected. "I don't know why I said that, actually – I think it must have just popped out when you mentioned that Derek proposed to you. I don't honestly care."

However, the truth must have been clearly evident in her tone, since Sam replied, "You don't have to wait for him to do it, you know."

"Do what?"

"Propose, of course."

"What?" Eve laughed out loud. "You think *I* should propose to Liam? Are you crazy?"

"Why not? You two have been together for years, and you've already got the kids and the house, so it's not as though he'd refuse."

He might, Eve couldn't help thinking. "No, no, no," she said, shaking her head dismissively, unwilling to think about the prospect.

It was all right for Sam, with her independence and all that London confidence, but didn't she realise that that kind of thing just didn't happen here? There was no *way* Eve could even consider proposing to Liam. No way.

"Look, this is pointless," she said to her sister. "Liam and I are perfectly happy the way we are, and a piece of paper isn't going to change anything."

Sam seemed to sense not to push it. "If you say so, but if you ever decide you would like to get married, I see no reason to wait around for him to ask you."

"But I'm not waiting around, Sam," Eve replied through gritted teeth, almost sorry that her sister had ever phoned this afternoon, what with all the silly notions she was putting in her head. "And thanks for the offer to take over from me for a few days, but I really don't think there's any need. I'm perfectly fine."

Again Sam seemed to detect Eve's annoyance. "OK, well, I suppose I'd better let you go. I have to head out soon."

"So how does Derek feel about you turning him down?" Eve asked, curious. She'd only met Sam's boyfriend a couple of times since they started going out, and while he seemed nice enough, he struck her as the kind of man who was used to getting exactly what he wanted.

Sam's voice was tight. "Well, that's the thing, Eve . . . we're actually on a bit of a break at the moment. This time, he gave me an ultimatum. He wants me to have a serious think about our future and about whether or not I'm prepared to compromise."

"Oh."

"So, I suppose that's why I'm so keen to head home for a little while, to be honest. Ultimately, it's to give you a break, of course, but it's for my own selfish reasons too. Eve, it really could work out very well for both of us," she implored once again. "You get some time away from the housework and the kids, while I get some time to think over Derek's proposal and get an understanding of what being a housewife is really like."

"Well, if you want to see what it's really like, why can't you just come over here and watch me in action now and again? Although," Eve added grinning, "that would probably turn you off the idea once and for all!"

"It's not the same," Sam insisted. "For me, being thrown in at the deep end is the only way to learn anything. Anyway, why are you so against letting me do this? The break would do you good, surely?"

All this talk about her needing a break was starting to get right up Eve's nose. In fact, this entire conversation was starting to get to her now.

"Look, Sam, thanks for the offer, but I've really no intention of swanning off and leaving the kids, just to let you carry out some experiment."

Sam sighed. "Oh for goodness sake, it's not as though you'd be banished to the Black Hole! If anything were to happen, you'd only be on the other end of the phone, and you could come back anytime you like. I'll sort out your plane tickets. But it would be fine, Eve – I know it would." When Eve said nothing, Sam kept going. "Look, it would be a chance for you to let your hair down and have some fun – something you haven't done in years. Won't you at least think about it?"

By her tone, Eve realised that this wasn't just some madcap idea on her sister's part. She was truly serious about it.

"Please?"

But again Eve shook her head. "I'm sorry, Sam, but no. You might need a change but I certainly don't. In fact," she added defiantly, determined to bring this conversation to a close once and for all, "I'm very happy with my life, and it's perfectly fine the way it is."

CHAPTER 6

5. The Last to Know

It was the following Tuesday, and Eve was really looking forward to Liam's return from Sicily, so much so that she planned to prepare a special meal to celebrate his homecoming that same evening.

In truth, she also felt a little guilty that she'd seriously considered – if only for a brief second – Sam's proposition of a few days before. As if she'd go off and abandon the kids just like that!

OK, maybe she could understand her sister's need to try out domesticity without commitment, but what did every other woman in the world do? Family life wasn't something you 'tried out' to see if it suited you like you would perhaps a new hairstyle; it was something you actually did, something in which you were an active participant. And in all honesty, did Sam really expect her to let her children be part of the research for one of her books?

Having got up a full hour earlier that morning and spent much of it tidying the house from top to bottom, after lunch Eve put Max down for his nap and discovered – to her surprise – that she had a full hour to spare and nothing to do before collecting Lily from school and then heading to the airport to collect Liam.

She paused in front of the kitchen window and stared out at the garden. The lawn was badly in need of cutting and the flowerbeds were beginning to look a little overgrown. Eve looked at the clock. Two thirty. If she got stuck in now, she could probably get it all done within the hour, which would give her just enough time to get changed and . . .

Then she paused, remembering that same conversation with Sam a couple of days before. *"Eve, you really need to make some time for yourself!"* She bit her lip. She could leave the garden for another time and just use the hour to do . . . to do *nothing*, couldn't she?

But no, she couldn't do that, the garden would just get worse, and who knew when she'd get the chance to do it again, because as soon as Liam came home, his suitcase would need to be emptied and all his clothes would have to washed and ironed and ready for the trip to Australia the following week, and then . . .

Eve stopped short and shook her head. No wonder she felt frustrated! Never mind Liam and the kids, *she* was the one to blame for all the pressure, for creating a never-ending treadmill for herself. And not only that, but for some reason she seemed determined to keep the pace relentlessly high!

Even her seven-year-old could see that she was doing too much – wasn't Lily always teasing her about never being able to leave the house without finding some stray piece of ironing or another room that just had to be vacuumed first? For God's sake, she was her own worst enemy! No, this time, she *wouldn't* try and fit yet another piece of housework into the free time she had – instead she'd treat it exactly as that: free time!

Turning away from the window (the garden would only torment her otherwise), Eve headed determinedly towards the coffee-maker Liam had bought for her last Christmas and made herself a cup of coffee – *proper* coffee – not like the instant stuff she usually drank to save time. After that, she opened a fresh packet of chocolate digestives and, lovely steaming coffee mug in hand, went into the living room and switched on the TV.

God, she thought, as she picked up her coffee mug and swung her legs beneath her on the armchair, it almost felt as though she was doing something underhand, so strange was the notion of taking a break like this in the middle of the day!

Sam was absolutely right, she admitted, as she sipped her coffee and became more engrossed in the fashion item they were showing on afternoon TV, she really should try and relax a bit from time to time. No wonder she'd been feeling so hassled and harassed lately – anyone with half a brain could see that a never-ending, non-stop cycle of housework would get you down. And anyway, with their fashion features and cookery slots, weren't these TV programmes entirely geared towards housewives like her – and evidently *watched* by women like her, otherwise they wouldn't be on TV at all. So, was she the only gobshite in the world who spent every waking hour cleaning things up when instead she should be behaving like any other normal housewife and taking the odd break? Obviously, she thought, munching through another biscuit. Well, no more. From now on, she was going to do more of this, much more, and there was no way that –

"Working hard, I see."

Eve jumped up at the sound of a voice from behind her and, turning around, saw to her horror that Liam's mother was standing in the living-room doorway.

"Noreen! You frightened the life out of me!" she declared, quickly getting to her feet, half an uneaten biscuit still in her mouth.

Noreen eyed her speculatively. "The back door was open, so when you didn't answer my knock I assumed you were outside hanging out laundry or something . . ." her gaze travelled to the TV, "but I was wrong."

Eve wanted to lie down and cry. Why, today of all days, did Noreen Crowley have to turn up and catch her lolling around in front of the TV in the middle of the afternoon? And make that *Dr* Noreen Crowley – heavily diploma'd clinical psychologist and career-woman supremo, and a woman who had never made any secret of her derision about Eve not going out to work and depending entirely on her precious only son!

Even Liam believed his mother was too wrapped up in her own career to be healthy, and while the two enjoyed a cordial relationship, Eve knew that as a lowly wine importer, Liam believed himself to have fallen far short of his mother's immense expectations. Or at least, Noreen had wasted no time in instilling this opinion.

"Your intelligence is wasted in that kind of thing," she had said dismissively when, soon after learning of Eve's pregnancy, Liam went out and got the first job he could – a junior sales position in Morrison & Co. Dublin wine importers. "You could have sailed through Medicine."

"That was Dad's choice, not mine," Liam had retorted. His father, who separated from Noreen when Liam was ten years old, worked as a consultant in the Blackrock Clinic, and given the amount of pressure his parents' individual careers had put on their marriage, Liam had no intention of following in either of their footsteps. Or indeed, following in his father's wake and choosing a woman so hell-bent on her career that it ultimately tore the family apart.

So to say that his mother was disappointed, not only in her darling son's choice of career but also in his life-partner, would be a major understatement.

And of course, the fact that the very same life-partner had

fallen pregnant within a few months of meeting him hadn't gone down well at all, which was why Eve was kicking herself just then at being caught in such a compromising position i.e. coffee in hand, biscuits in mouth and feet up in front of the telly – especially in front of this working woman's paragon.

"Would you like a coffee?" Eve offered, her cordial tone belying her dismay. "I was just having a quick one before I went to collect Lily from school and –"

"And what's the burning topic of interest today?" Noreen drawled, casting a dismissive eye towards the TV. "Juicy gossip from the soaps? Or even, more excitingly, is today Makeover Day?" Even the TV programming schedule wasn't safe from Noreen Crowley's derision. "Honestly, I can never understand why intelligent women let themselves be condescended to like that. Or does the brain become so numb from doing nothing all day that something like learning a new bread-making recipe is considered stimulating?"

"It's just harmless, easy-watching TV," Eve said, trying to ignore her sarcasm and the pointed jibe. Yet she still couldn't help but try and justify herself. "I don't normally watch this at *all* but, as I said, I had a couple of minutes to spare so –"

"Well, I suppose one of the advantages of being a housewife is having the luxury of lazing around and doing what you like."

She might as well have been talking about Eve being a prostitute so heavy was the scorn dripping off her words, the younger woman thought, bristling.

"But it certainly wouldn't suit me," Noreen continued. "Staying busy keeps the mind alert and the body fit and energetic, whereas slobbing around in a tracksuit watching a group of airheads gabbing about another fictional group of airheads would be enough to drive me insane."

Pull up a bloody chair then, you old bag! Eve wanted to say but held her tongue. Blast Sam anyway for brainwashing her into thinking she could just take a break in the middle of the day! Now Mammy Crowley had all the material she needed to back up her theory that housewives like Eve were lazy and parasitic and did nothing but lounge around in front of the telly all day! God knows she'd suggested as much to her in the past. And even worse, Noreen had always seemed to sense Eve's long-held insecurity about the fact that Liam hadn't yet asked her to be his wife, and had no reservations about making her feel inferior in this regard too.

"I know what you mean." Eve wished she had the guts to stand up to the old wagon and tell her she could do what she damn well pleased in her own house, but in truth she hadn't really a leg to stand on. After all, Noreen was only reaffirming Eve's own guilt about taking some downtime, particularly when there were a million other things she could be doing. And, speaking of which, she'd better get Max up from his nap and allow him a few minutes to wake up properly before they headed out to the school to collect Lily.

At least by doing that she could avoid sitting here and trying to make excuses in front of Noreen.

Heading for the kitchen, Eve turned and smiled sweetly at Liam's mother who, evidently having lost interest in the "condescending" TV show, was now turning her attentions towards Eve's crying-out-to-be-washed windows. They'd had some bad weather lately and Eve was just waiting for a dry day to give her the opportunity to get started and . . . God, this was unbelievable!

"Did you say you *would* have a cup of coffee then, Noreen?" she enquired, holding her breath and willing the other woman not to notice the cobwebs she'd missed when dusting the room earlier that morning.

"Certainly not," Liam's mother replied, her tone affronted. "I don't like putting artificial stimulants in my body, Eve – you know that."

Eve resisted the urge to roll her eyes. "Of course you don't – sorry, it slipped my mind. Can I get you anything else? A glass of water maybe?"

"Orange juice would be good – if you can spare the time," Noreen replied acidly.

As soon as she heard the words, Eve grimaced, remembering. *Feck, feck, feck!*

"Actually," she said, sucking in air through her teeth and again wanting to kick the shins off herself, "we don't have any left. I'd planned to go to the supermarket this afternoon, but it completely slipped my mind . . ." *That* was why she'd had this unexpected 'window' in her afternoon! She was supposed to go and do her mid-week stock-up! *Another* point scored in Noreen's favour.

"Never mind, dear," her nemesis replied. "I'm sure such weighty matters must be difficult for you to keep up with. Oh, and now that I'm looking at it, you really should consider getting someone in to do your garden. I've never seen a flowerbed so badly in need of weeding."

*   *   *

Later that evening, as she drove towards the airport, Eve tried her best to forget the annoyance and utter mortification of Noreen's visit. Her humiliation of Eve complete, Doctor Crowley had eventually toddled off back home to her pristine pile in Drumcondra just before Eve left for the school run.

Eve now tried to concentrate on her excitement about Liam's return. In a way, their stints apart were probably good for the relationship in the long run, weren't they? Absence makes the heart grow fonder and all that. Yes, she hated it whenever Liam went away and she missed him so much throughout his trips, but yet it all seemed worth it for the huge anticipation she felt immediately before his return. And surely he felt the same way too? Surely he missed her and the kids as much as they did him and was just as excited about coming home?

But when she eventually spotted Liam waiting at their earlier agreed meeting point at Dublin airport, annoyance written all over his handsome and sun-kissed face, Eve began to have second thoughts. She beeped the horn to catch his attention and waved as, bags in hand, he approached the car.

"Where the hell were you?" Liam barked, stowing his luggage in the boot before joining Eve up front in the car. "I've been waiting for you for a solid hour!"

Eve was confused. "What? But you told me the flight would be in at four –"

"I told you no such thing. Honestly, Eve, I sometimes wonder if you go around the place with your head in the clouds! The flight was in at three on the dot, and as I've been up since all hours this morning and then had to sit through a four-hour flight, the least you could have done was be here on time."

Eve couldn't believe it. She was *sure* he'd said four. Then she thought of something. "But you know I couldn't have been here for three. I had to collect Lily from school." And after that, she'd dropped Lily over to her friend Rachel's house where she was spending the afternoon.

"And how long does it take to collect her from school? Ten bloody minutes at the most! Although with the way you mollycoddle her . . ."

Eve couldn't believe it. So much for their romantic reunion!

"Excuse me, Liam Crowley, but I do *not* mollycoddle our children. Although, if I do, it's only to make up for the fact that their father is never here to do it!"

"Oh, give it a rest, Eve. I'm back in the country two minutes, and already you're off nagging me."

"Two minutes? I thought you said you landed an hour ago?" she barked back, stung at the accusation that she was nagging.

"You know what I meant!" he said, in a voice so loud that Max, who had been sitting excitedly in the backseat waiting for Daddy to notice him, began screaming at the top of his voice.

"What a lovely bloody homecoming!" Liam sighed, his face grim as Eve tried to pull back out into the busy traffic.

Not another word passed between them throughout the entire journey home.

*   *   *

Later, with a sense of bad grace at which Delia Smith would be appalled, Eve prepared to serve dinner. She'd attempted a new recipe that she thought would be perfect for the occasion, a chicken and pasta concoction that looked and sounded delicious in the recipe book, but now on the plate looked flaccid and unappealing. Of course the fact that she had to leave out the green and red peppers, which gave Lily indigestion, was probably part of it, but either way she now had no choice but to serve the meal as it was.

She and Liam still weren't speaking, but for the sake of the kids, Eve hoped they could put their differences aside at the dinner table and start behaving like adults. And she hoped that her new recipe would impress him at least enough to pass comment on her cooking.

But yet again, it seemed she'd badly misjudged her other half.

"I won't have any, thanks," Liam said sullenly when she put the plate in front of him.

"What? But surely you haven't eaten since –"

"Eve, to be honest, I'm tired of eating the same old thing all the time. Every Tuesday without fail it has to be pasta, every

Wednesday it's some kind of lamb casserole or stew, every Friday it's shepherd's pie. All courtesy of the good people at Knorr or Campbells. You know, it might be nice to have a bit of variation now and again."

Eve was stung. "This *is* a variation, Liam – I've used a completely new recipe."

"Look, I just don't feel hungry, OK?"

"I don't believe this!" she hissed under her breath, unwilling to make a scene with the children present. Although Liam seemed to be having no such problems. "Can I speak to you a minute?" she said and ushered him into the living room so they could continue this out of the kids' earshot. "Just because you're used to being served restaurant food on your little trips abroad doesn't mean you can expect the same treatment here. I'm cooking for my family, Liam, not for a Michelin star!"

He sighed. "Look, I just said I'm not hungry. It's got nothing to do with the kind of food I get abroad, although yes, I must admit that perhaps that's part of the problem. With all the eating out I do, maybe my palate has become that little bit more sophisticated and –"

"You pompous . . ." Eve couldn't bring herself to complete the rest of the sentence. "Look, just because you're a wine expert doesn't mean you have the right to criticise my cooking. And did you ever stop to think that maybe I use packet sauces and suchlike because I'm too busy to do anything else? I'm too busy cleaning this house and looking after your kids!"

They'd been together for nearly eight years and *now* he decides he doesn't like her cooking? What the hell was wrong with him?

"Look, all I'm saying is that I don't fancy what you made tonight." His tone softened slightly. "I'm also tired and my routine is a little bit messed up after this trip – it was fairly intensive and I didn't get to bed till all hours most nights."

This admission really got up Eve's nose. To think that he was out partying like a demon while she was stuck here cleaning up Max's sick and being made feel guilty for buying a few Crunchies in the local shop!

"Well, isn't it well for you?" she cried. "My God, what I wouldn't give for an *intensive* trip on a Mediterranean island? But there's no hope of my getting that, is there, Liam? No, you prefer to keep all the fun for yourself!"

"Fun? *Fun?* You seem to have conveniently forgotten that this is my *job* – it's what keeps the family going, what allows you to stay at home and put your feet up, while I go out and put food on the table!"

Coupled with his mother's jibes earlier that day, Eve was so wounded by this she was almost afraid to speak. Put her feet up? Is that what he and his stuck-up mother really thought she did all day? He, who never tired of telling her how that very same mother had never been there for him when he was growing up! And who didn't seem to appreciate that by not going out to work, Eve *was* there for Lily and Max! How could he make so little of her, put so little value on her role in the household and put so little value on her as a partner that after all this time he still wouldn't make her his wife? How dare he?

"Food that you're now above eating, apparently," Eve eventually replied in a small voice, before hurrying out of the room, tears streaming down her face.

And as she finished tending to the children, both of whom seemed just as unimpressed with her culinary efforts as their father had been, Eve decided once and for all that big changes were in order.

Half an hour later she picked up the phone.

"Sam," Eve said to her sister, her hands still shaking with anger, "I've changed my mind – they're all yours."

CHAPTER 7

Oh, so it was going to be a life-swap story, Brooke realised, setting aside the manuscript pages she'd just finished reading. Not bad, but a shame it wasn't exactly original either.

Still, she was sure the characters in *The Last to Know* were interesting enough to carry it through – Sam's career made a nice contrast to poor Eve's downtrodden domestic existence. Brooke had taken to Eve right from the outset, with her self-deprecating ways and her busy family life. Not to mention the fact that she empathised considerably with her feelings over her long-term partner's reluctance to fully commit. Unfortunately, she had a similar problem herself! She smiled wryly as she thought about Will, her boyfriend of eighteen months.

They'd met through the surfing scene and had known each other for some time before they began seeing each other seriously, and while Brooke knew she was crazy about him, with his dark, brooding looks, bright smile and toned body, she was less sure of how he felt about her. They were both avid surfers – each spending day upon day catching the waves at Coogee and Bondi and they always had a great laugh whenever they went out on the town. Brooke knew he liked her – he wouldn't be with her otherwise – but the real question was, how much?

It was hard to tell, in fact it was hard to know exactly what Will was thinking at any given time, and despite the fact that it annoyed the hell out of her, the darker, more hidden side of his personality also intrigued her.

He was abroad again at the moment, away doing some kind of export deal in Singapore. Will worked in sales and spent more time out of Australia than he did in it, which was another reason Brooke often felt a bit sidelined in their relationship.

She supposed she felt his absence that bit more than she would have normally, as her mother had died not long after they'd got together, and she'd relied a lot upon Will to help her get through the aftermath and also throughout much of Lynn's illness. It was hard, Brooke admitted, tears coming to her eyes as she recalled that hugely difficult time, but at least she'd had lots of friends and neighbours around to help her through it. Bev, her long-time neighbour and her mum's oldest friend, had been a wonderful support and she and Brooke had spent a lot of time reminiscing about happier times when Lynn was alive and well. It had helped Brooke get over her initial grief and having her close by helped stave off much of the loneliness she often felt coming home to an empty house – the house in Manly she'd shared with her mum.

She might call over to Bev's place after work later – a good old natter and moan about Will might help take her mind off his absence and stop her fretting about their relationship.

Anyway, she should get back to work. Shaking her head, she brought her thoughts swiftly back to the present, and more importantly back to the manuscript.

She was liking it more and more as she went along, and although she still wasn't sure who'd recommended the script to her (Mary was the most likely culprit to have dropped it in before she left for her holidays), she was now fairly certain they were indeed on to something. This was *exactly* the type of thing Horizon published and very much the kind of book female book-buyers liked to read. The characters were warm and engaging, their individual storylines compelling and sympathetic and, in addition, there was something about the author's style that made Brooke suspect that there was lots of drama to come. Clearly there was much to be made of the huge differences between the two sisters and their lives, but Brooke had yet to figure out how the other character Anna fitted into the story. What was her connection to Eve or indeed Sam? It was all very intriguing.

Of course, she'd have to give it to someone else in-house for a second opinion, maybe let one of the sales directors run an eye over it, but based on what she'd read so far, she felt the manuscript had considerable potential for publication. It was such a pity Mary hadn't thought to leave more info on the submission itself before going off on her hols, though. Brooke flicked back to the beginning and pulled out the manuscript's title page, hoping to try and get a rough idea of the date of submission. No, there was no date on it, unfortunately. The problem was that if the story interested her, there was a very good chance it would also interest others, and she really hoped that *The Last to Know* hadn't already been picked up by a rival publisher.

There was always the danger of this happening, as first-time authors usually sent out material at the same time to lots of different publishers in order to give their work the best possible chance. But because Mary wasn't around to ask about when the submission had first come in, and wouldn't be for another two weeks, Brooke couldn't be sure if Horizon had already missed their chance to publish it. Perhaps the sensible thing might be to contact the author and find out if the book was still available? Still, no point in doing that until she was absolutely sure it was the right book for her, was there? Contacting the author might only get her hopes up and that wouldn't be at all fair.

Brooke picked up another sheaf of pages from the manuscript and crammed them into her briefcase before heading for home. She'd get through a couple of chapters on the six o'clock ferry home to Manly and maybe some more tonight after coming back from Bev's, which would hopefully help her make her mind up about *The Last to Know* once and for all.

CHAPTER 8

6. The Last to Know

"Well, it's about time," Anna said, when Eve told her friend all about her forthcoming London getaway. "I've been on at you to do something like this for ages, but you wouldn't listen."

As Eve's house was situated near the school in which Anna taught, she'd popped in for a visit on her way home from work. As well as knowing Ronan since childhood, Anna had also grown up in the same area as her fiancé's best friend Liam, and as a result the two couples were close.

"I wasn't sure how to go about it," Eve replied as, broom in hand, she proceeded to sweep away some microscopic dirt from the kitchen floor. "After all, it wasn't as if I could just take off somewhere on my own. Who would look after the kids?"

She was always the same, Anna thought fondly, as she sat at Eve's kitchen table and watched her sweep the floor, always pottering about looking for bits and pieces of housework that needed doing. In all the years she'd been friends with Eve Callaghan, Anna had never known the girl to just sit still and relax for a few minutes – no, there was always some hugely important bit of vacuuming or washing-up to be done.

Anna didn't think it was a question of Eve being house-proud – it was just that she didn't seem at all comfortable with the notion of doing nothing. So the idea that Eve was planning on taking up her older sister's offer of a long weekend away from the housework and the kids seemed unimaginable.

"No, it was only when Sam suggested that she wanted to give domestic life a go that it came to us." Eve paused for a moment to take a sip from her coffee mug, which was on the table alongside Anna's. "And to be completely honest, I've just had it up to here with Liam and Noreen's smart comments, and the neighbours asking for favours . . ." She rolled her eyes. "Sara was in again the other day with baby Jack – this time to go off and get her hair done. Now, I don't mind doing her the odd favour but at this stage it's becoming ridiculous!"

"Well, in a way I'm glad you reached boiling point if that's what it took to make you realise that something had to be done. You've been letting people run rings around you for way too long, Eve."

"That's exactly what Sam said." Eve resumed her sweeping, while Anna continued drinking her coffee. "And seeing as she needs a change too . . ." She shrugged.

"Why?" Anna asked.

"Why what?"

"Why does Sam need a change? The way you talk about her – it sounds as though she has a great life." Anna had never actually met Eve's sister, and whatever she knew about her she'd learned from Eve and from the odd newspaper article about her books, although Anna hadn't yet read any of them. Apparently, Sam had moved to London as a teenager and, while Anna knew the two sisters were close, Eve confessed that they saw one another less frequently since the death of their parents some years before.

Despite their apparent closeness, they seemed to be chalk and cheese – Eve with her intense love of family life and Sam with her high-profile journalistic career.

"Her boyfriend proposed, but she's not sure if she's ready to settle down just yet – what with all that's going on with her career," Eve informed Anna. She smiled. "To be honest, Sam isn't exactly the marrying type."

Anna looked up. "Right. Did she turn him down?"

"No, they decided they'd take a few weeks apart to give her time to think about it."

"I see." Anna was tempted to comment that Sam needing to think about it should be answer enough for both parties, but then she realised how stupid that would sound, given her own circumstances.

"Anyway," Eve continued, "we were chatting on the phone about things last week, and I lost the rag a bit at something she said, and to cut a long story short she asked if I'd be interested in letting her look after the kids in order to let me have a break."

Hearing this, Anna instantly felt guilty that she hadn't thought of offering to do the same. But for as long as she'd known her, Eve seemed to revel in the role of mum and housewife (or, to be more precise in Eve's case, house-partner).

"It should work out well for both of us, really," Eve went on, as she brushed debris into the dustpan. "I get some time to myself and Sam gets a taster of what being a housewife and mother is really like."

"So your sister thinks that this might help make up her mind on whether or not to accept this guy's proposal?"

Eve nodded. "Well, she also wants to use the experience as research for her next novel, but that's part of it, yes. And this was his *third* proposal, believe it or not," she added with a sigh.

"Oh."

"I know." Eve looked glum.

"Speaking of proposals," Anna said, remembering all of a sudden, "you know my friend Lauren – she teaches Second Class at the school?"

"I think so – the one with the boyfriend you don't really like? What about her?"

Anna sat back in her chair. "Well, we were all out for dinner a couple of weeks back – me and Ronan and Lauren and Denis, and guess what? He proposed to her right out of the blue – and right in front of me and Ronan!" Anna shook her head. "Isn't that mad? I was mortified, to be honest – particularly when, as you said, I'm not a great fan of Denis in the first place and, really, it's not the kind of thing you share with other people." She continued to shake her head in exasperation, expecting Eve to immediately agree that, yes, it must have all been very uncomfortable indeed. But instead, Eve looked slightly crestfallen and, seeing this, Anna's heart lurched as she suddenly realised that all this talk of wedding proposals could be really getting to her friend. As Eve often joked about Liam's hesitation in popping the question, Anna had never been quite sure if deep down Eve was all that bothered about the marriage thing, yet she realised now that the other woman's apparent light-heartedness about it all may well have been masking genuine disappointment.

"She must have been thrilled," Eve said quietly, and Anna sorely wished she hadn't opened her big mouth. "There must be something in the air – something I'm certainly not catching."

Anna went to say something, but before she could, Eve continued.

"I mean, there's Derek, Sam's boyfriend asking – no *begging* – her to marry him." Eve looked at Anna in exasperation. "And here I am, eight years with Liam, mother of his two kids and wife in all but name, yet he's never even mentioned getting married at all – let alone to me! What am I doing wrong, Anna?"

Anna didn't know how to reply to that.

Liam's apparent reluctance to marry his long-time partner and mother of his children seemed a mystery to a lot of people. The only reasonable explanation seemed to be that having experienced the breakdown of his own parents' relationship, Liam just didn't want to get married, full stop.

Liam's reluctance had to be tough on Eve, Anna thought, as she loved the man with all her heart and couldn't imagine life without him. In much the same way as Anna couldn't imagine life without Ronan, but for different reasons. Strange the way things worked out sometimes, she thought wryly.

"I don't think you're doing anything wrong, Eve," she said gently. "Liam is just Liam and that's all there is to it."

"Mmm," her friend murmured, unconvinced. "Sam reckons I should just ask him myself."

Anna nearly spat out her coffee. "You – propose to Liam?"

Eve rolled her eyes. "I know. Can you imagine the mortification of doing something like that?"

"I don't think it's a good idea, Eve. Not in the long run. Even if Liam did say yes, you'd always wonder why he didn't get round to proposing himself or if he only agreed because it was what you wanted."

"I know, but sometimes I drive myself mad trying to figure out if he's ever going to do it."

"Weird, isn't it?" Anna agreed. "Men never seem to worry about what we really think, yet we spend all our time trying to figure out what's going on in *their* heads."

"Well, that might be true for some of us but certainly *not* in your case," Eve said with a grin.

Little do you know, Anna wanted to retort but didn't. "Anyway, the break away will do you good and clear your head," she said then, purposely ignoring Eve's comment and hoping to lighten the mood. "You'd never know – you might come home and decide that Liam isn't what you want after all. That would certainly pull the rug from under him!"

Eve's eyes widened. "I should hope not," she said laughing. "For the kids' sake as much as mine! Anna – I'm going away for a long weekend, not a year. OK, so things have been hard going lately, but I think all I need is a bit of time to relax and get my head together. Whereas all Sam needs is a taste of what's to come if she ever decides to give up her precious career and settle down with Derek. It's only a long weekend, after all. What could possibly change in such a short space of time?"

CHAPTER

7. The Last to Know

Later that same week, Anna bent over the toilet and retched for what must have been the fifth or sixth time that morning. Her head spun with weakness as well as apprehension as to what it all meant.

This could not be happening. Not now – not to her.

While she'd tried her best to ignore the dizzy spells she'd been having lately – initially putting them down to overwork and stress – it was now impossible to explain away the nausea and vomiting. And while she could admit that she'd been out of sorts a bit these days, she'd told herself it was simply due to her and Ronan's mutual discomfort in the aftermath of Lauren's engagement.

He'd brought up the subject of their own wedding a few times since – in his own typical, jokey way – but at the same time Anna sensed that he was starting to feel a bit concerned that she, unlike Lauren, wasn't exactly buzzing at the prospect of a 'big day out'.

"They certainly don't let the grass grow under their feet, do they?" he said when, shortly after their dinner out together, they heard that Lauren and Denis had fixed their wedding date for September of the following year. "Makes us look like tortoises in comparison."

"Lauren's that type, though," Anna had replied blithely, hoping that he wasn't going to make an issue of it. "She's probably been planning her big day for most of her life – groom or not!" She tried her best to sound light-hearted while at the same time inwardly holding her breath.

"And where did we get you from, that you're not interested in that kind of thing at all?" Ronan replied, reaching forward and kissing her lightly on the forehead. "Although, it's probably partly my fault that you turned out such a tomboy. There aren't many girls I know who preferred exploring caves and hiding in the woods with boys to dressing up Barbie!"

Remembering their childhood exploits, Anna smiled. Things were so much simpler back then, back when they had nothing to worry them other than what their next adventure would be. They used to model themselves on the characters of Enid Blyton books – *The Famous Five* and *Secret Seven* – even though a lot of the time, there were only the two of them and not a whole lot of adventures to be had or secrets to discover in the quiet family suburb in which their respective families lived.

And now, as he once again raised the subject of what Anna supposed should be their greatest adventure of all, she couldn't help but wish that she could turn back time, back to the days when she and Ronan were just friends and playmates, and they expected nothing, least of all from one another.

But all that had changed when they had grown into adulthood together and the relationship had grown along with them. And the fact that they had experienced much of their lives through one another made Anna's current feelings much more difficult to handle, and even more difficult to explain.

"Yep, it's definitely all your fault," she replied, deliberately keeping her tone light. "But you know – there's nothing stopping you going off and finding a Barbie of your own to marry."

"Never in a million years and you know it," he said, his tone unusually serious. Then he sighed and looked away, as if he'd been bringing himself to say the words for some time, "Love, I know you're not into all the fuss, but don't you think that after being engaged for so long, we should think about setting a date sometime?"

Anna tried to keep her face blank. She hadn't expected him to come right out and say it – say that he wanted to move things forward. Usually, he'd skirted around the issue, joked about it a little, and she'd got the impression he was happy to get married whenever she wanted to. But obviously, she'd been wrong and Lauren's engagement had brought everything to the fore again.

So how could she tell him that she couldn't possibly set a date for their wedding because she still wasn't sure if she really wanted to marry him? That lately she'd become so confused about her feelings that the very mention of the word 'wedding' made her squirm with discomfort?

She swallowed hard and once again did her best to appear flippant.

"I know, I know – we're a disaster, we really should try and arrange it. But, Ro, do you have any idea how much hassle is involved in organising a wedding these days? Between the hotels and the florist and the band – never mind the church – it's almost a full-time job in itself!" She rolled her eyes good-naturedly. "And God knows neither of us has the time for all that at the moment. You're busy at work, which is great, and I'm caught up in getting Sixth Class ready for their entrance exams so . . ." The remainder of her sentence trailed off. "At the moment, the timing is not so good."

"I suppose you're right." Ronan seemed convinced by the argument. "And as well as that, it would probably be you doing most of the arranging – we both know I'm not the best at that kind of thing."

She smiled. "True."

"Ah, we'll get there eventually, I suppose," he said finally, before turning back to his newspaper. "After all, we're as good as married anyway – what's another year or two?"

"Exactly," Anna replied easily, but there were tears in her eyes as she turned away and opened up a fresh packet of cornflakes.

Now, the worst of her sickness having subsided, Anna moved away from the toilet bowl and wiped her mouth with a piece of tissue. Then, standing up she turned and stared at her drawn face and ghostlike complexion in the mirror.

What on earth was she going to do?

Ronan was bound to notice something soon – in fact, he'd already passed comment on her sombre mood and, for her, rather listless behaviour. Thank goodness he'd left for work earlier and wasn't around to see this, otherwise he's surely suspect something.

Still, with the symptoms getting worse by the day, she couldn't keep things hidden from him forever. So what was she going to do?

Her head pounding from the sickness, or the stress, she wasn't quite sure, Anna left the bathroom and went into the kitchen to fetch a glass of water. The cold liquid sliding down her throat seemed to give her some temporary relief and, as she drank, Anna realised that she would have to make a decision – soon. These last few days and the crucifying sickness this morning meant that she couldn't put it to the back of her mind any longer.

Putting down the glass, Anna reached for the telephone and dialled a number.

"I'd like to make an appointment to see Dr Ryan," she said when the call was answered.

"Certainly," the receptionist replied. "When would you like to come in?"

Anna bit her lip and stared at a recent photograph of her and Ronan. He was smiling cheerfully into the camera but there was no mistaking the faraway, distracted look in her own eyes. Almost subconsciously, her hand moved to her stomach.

"As soon as possible," she replied determinedly.

*   *   *

Later that same week, she sat in front of Dr Ryan in his surgery.

"Well, Anna, your suspicions were correct," the doctor said, his tone gentle and his eyes full of concern as he regarded her from the other side of his desk.

Although what he said was no surprise – least of all to her – Anna's stomach lurched and her fingers closed hard around the handle of her bag.

"I see," she replied, trying to appear unaffected and matter-of-fact about the whole thing. "So what are my options?"

Doctor Ryan, who was scanning through her chart, looked up. "Your options?"

"Yes, my options. What next?"

"Well, I assume the first thing you'll need to do is inform your husband – no, fiancé – isn't it? And after that –"

"That's certainly not an option," she replied quickly, her tone shaky. "I'd rather he didn't know anything at – at this stage."

The doctor regarded her speculatively for a few moments. "Well, of course that's entirely your own decision, Anna. However, I would strongly advise –"

"Doctor, I don't mean to be rude but I would like to keep this to myself. I don't plan on involving anyone – Ronan, family friends – anyone – yet."

Sensing her defensiveness, the doctor leaned forward and his tone softened considerably. "That's entirely your own prerogative, dear, and I'm certainly not going to force you into anything you're not comfortable with. However, you should be aware that what happens from here on will take considerable toll on you, not only physically but also emotionally, perhaps even more so. Most people need someone with whom to share that burden."

"Not me," Anna replied defiantly. "I'm more than capable of dealing with this all by myself."

Having discussed a variety of possibilities with the doctor, Anna left the surgery and headed for home.

As she waited at a pedestrian crossing, a mother pushing a young toddler in a buggy came up alongside her. Anna tried to appear unmoved as the little girl caught her eye and grinned, the child's huge blue eyes and cute dimples making it impossible not to smile back. All too quickly, Anna straightened up and looked away, and when the pedestrian lights eventually went green she marched determinedly across the road, leaving the mother and child for dust.

Don't let yourself be sidetracked, she warned herself as she strode further down the street. *Just concentrate on the task in hand.*

But what was her next move? Her legs began to move faster and faster almost of their own accord. What really was the best thing to do? Should she go home and confess all to Ronan, ask him to 'share the burden' as the doctor put it? But how could she – how could she expect Ronan to support her through it? Especially when . . .

No, she couldn't seriously consider that – it wouldn't be fair.

Better to just keep it to herself for the moment, while she tried to decide the best course of action. But at that moment in time, Anna knew deep down that there was only one course of action she could possible take – one that would be best for everyone.

CHAPTER

8. The Last to Know

The following weekend, Liam departed for his two-week-long trip to Australia – this time much to Eve's relief. Since telling him about Sam's suggestion to look after the kids for a weekend (but neglecting to tell him exactly what had brought it on), he'd been making her feel no better than some of those women who abandoned their kids in bus-stops or in doorways.

"You're leaving our kids with a complete stranger – just so you can go gallivanting off to London?" he'd thundered.

"Sam isn't a complete stranger – she's family!" Eve replied, almost regretting her decision to tell him at all. She could have just as easily let him go off to Australia none the wiser – in fact, Sam had even suggested that she do just that!

"What he doesn't know won't hurt him," her sister had said when they were finalising the arrangements. "And if you do tell him, he's probably going to make you feel twice as guilty about leaving the kids than you already do."

"Maybe, but there's no way I could leave here without letting him know – even if it is only for three or four days," Eve insisted.

Although, in fairness, Liam would hardly know the difference. Whenever he was away, and *especially* when he was in Australia, a week or more might pass without him telephoning home or getting in contact with home. The difference in the time zones made it almost impossible, apparently, as did Liam's irregular working hours. So, while there was no way she would keep her plans a secret from him, there wasn't a whole lot to be gained from telling him either.

"Look, things have been getting on top of me here lately," Eve had explained, willing him to understand. "So when Sam suggested helping me out, it was an offer I couldn't refuse."

"Things get on top of me too, Eve, but I don't go swanning off to London for breaks when the going gets tough, do I?"

"But you're not stuck at home all day with the kids and tons of housework, and anyway, you get lots of time away –"

"Yes, but it's not as though I'm off sunning myself, Eve – it's work! And bloody hard work too compared to what you have to put up with. Give me a week with nothing to do but bring the kids to school and stuff my face with biscuits in front of the TV any day!"

The way he said it, Eve knew that he was referring to the afternoon his mother had dropped in unannounced. Trust bloody Noreen to make it sound like she did sweet FA all day! She should have known she'd go straight back to Liam telling tales . . .

Maybe Sam had been right, maybe she would have been better off saying nothing at all to Liam, but she'd never been the secretive type and she wasn't going to start now.

"See you in two weeks," Liam said, giving her yet another perfunctory kiss goodbye when she dropped him at the airport.

Eve smiled at him. "Have a good trip, love. Give me a ring when you get to Sydney so I'll know you arrived safely."

Liam shook his head. "I mightn't be able to, Eve. You know

how difficult it is with the time difference, and I'll be at meetings most days –"

"OK – well, just give us a ring when you can – let us know you're still alive at least," she said in a jokey voice, hoping to hide her disappointment at the fact that he couldn't wish her well on her own few days away in London. Did he really resent her taking the little bit of time away that much?

She bit her lip as Liam gathered his bags and waved goodbye. Maybe this was a mistake after all. Maybe she should call Sam and tell her the swap was off. But the travel tickets were already booked and Sam would be arriving on Thursday . . .

No, Eve decided as she drove away from the airport, she'd go to London on Friday and, what's more, she'd make sure she enjoyed the little break away. It wasn't all that long ago that she was brooding wistfully over holiday programmes and a nice relaxing weekend away was surely the next best thing. Liam just didn't understand how much pressure she'd been under lately, which was part of the reason they'd been arguing so much these last few weeks. And if a few days in London away from the kids and housework went some way towards relieving that pressure, then surely the entire family would benefit?

Of course they would, Eve assured herself, now fully convinced that nothing but good would come of it all.

*   *   *

Late Thursday afternoon Sam entered the Arrivals area at Dublin airport, her luggage trailing heavily behind her. Earlier, she'd come out the wrong end of a battle with an airline official at Gatwick, who, much to Sam's dismay, had insisted she check in her medium-sized carry-case yet didn't bat an eyelid at a man with a hold-all the size of a small country! Her packing had been meticulously organised, precisely so she wouldn't need to go through the dreaded wait at the carousel, so the stewardess's fussiness had really pissed her off – as had the woman's refusal to listen to Sam's pleas.

"Look, I won't have time to wait for it at the other end," she'd argued. "It's only a small case – I promise it won't get in anyone's way,"

"Madam, I'm sorry, it might seem small to you, but in fact it's much larger than what's allowable," replied the stony-faced rep.

"And this guy's golf clubs *aren't*?" Sam retorted, red-faced, but it was no use protesting any further. Her bag needed to be stowed and, as luck would have it, was the very last piece of luggage to arrive at the other side.

So it was a tired and infuriated Sam who stood in the taxi queue outside the terminal of Dublin airport on a dark and wet November evening, waiting for a lift to Eve's house. She cursed silently when she saw the length of the queue and, typically, the corresponding shortness of available cabs. Why, oh, why hadn't she taken Eve up on her offer to collect her from the airport, she asked herself as the crowd began to shuffle forward inches at a time. If she had, by now she'd be sitting in a nice warm car and would probably be halfway to Eve's home on the southside of the city, instead of freezing her backside off in yet another airport queue. But she'd refused her sister's kind offer at the time, believing that Eve had enough on her plate without having to battle through what would undoubtedly be hellish rush-hour traffic in order to meet her flight.

"Don't worry – I'll hop in a taxi and be there in no time," Sam had insisted, conveniently forgetting that her taxi would have to battle the very same traffic! So, she'd be lucky if she got there before dawn tomorrow morning, let alone in time for dinner. She groaned at her own stupidity.

But still, she was looking forward to the prospect of a few days away from the hustle and bustle of London, and was pleased for more reasons than one that Eve had finally agreed to the swap. Granted, Sam had suggested the idea mostly for her own benefit, but at the same time it felt good to be able to do something nice for her sister and give her the opportunity to take some time for herself. Since their parents' death, and because their lives were so utterly different, they had begun to drift apart in recent times, so this would be a good excuse to rekindle the close relationship they'd had while growing up and before Sam moved to London. Eve was a sweetheart but her dedication to her family and the fact that Liam was away so much meant that visits to one another had been few and far between, so it would be good to have the opportunity to share and experience a little more of one another's lives.

And no matter how much she tried to tell herself (or Eve) that she was doing this to research her next book, there was no denying that it was more of an exercise to try out family life for size. This was stupid and probably very naïve, she knew, but unlike Eve she wasn't prepared to throw herself willy-nilly into becoming a mother and wife. It wasn't something that came naturally to her and she knew deep down that she really needed to think seriously about changing her life in such a dramatic way. This wasn't just about Derek and his proposal – it was just as much about Sam and her willingness (or not) to face change.

Little by little, the queue at the taxi rank began to shorten and soon enough Sam found herself being directed to the next available cab. She opened the car door and sank gratefully onto the back seat, pulling the offending carry-case in alongside her.

"Do you want me to put that in the boot for you?" the driver asked.

"It's fine," Sam replied, waving her arm dismissively, as she rummaged in her handbag for Eve's exact address. She and Liam had moved house since the last time Sam was home for a visit, and she hadn't the foggiest where the family were living now. Typical, she should have had the address out long before the bloody cab arrived – now she was only delaying herself even further.

She continued searching inside the bag only to discover that she hadn't brought the details with her at all. Damn, what was the name of Eve's area again? Was it Seaview – or Seafield – something like that? Blast it – no, it was neither and she couldn't for the life of her remember what it was. All she knew was that Eve had told her the house was about a ten-minute walk from Dun Laoghaire Harbour . . . but what was the name of the area?

Eventually, the driver turned around to face her. "OK, then – where are we off to?" he asked amiably.

"Oh, just give me a sec, will you?" she snapped. Then, realising her tone sounded unreasonably curt, she looked up. "I'm sorry," she began, softening her tone, "I thought I had the address with me and –"

But the remainder of Sam's sentence was cut short as soon as she came face to face with the driver. And out of nowhere, she felt a sudden jolt, a shift, a . . . revelation, almost. It was as though every nerve ending in her body had jumped to attention all at once, every synapse fired in unison.

And in that split second, she felt something that was hugely unexpected, totally irrational and impossibly strange – yet at the same time more convincing and definite than anything she'd ever felt in her life.

Sam stared at the man sitting not a foot away from her and thought with utter clarity: *This is the man I'm going to spend the rest of my life with.*

It took her a couple of minutes to compose herself after that –

but somehow she managed to mumble something to him about dropping her off in the centre of Dun Laoghaire and she'd find her way from there. And clearly the driver, an attractive guy who looked to be in his late twenties/early thirties, hadn't shared in Sam's astonishing revelation. Instead, he'd whistled softly to himself as he pulled away from the rank and out into the traffic, luckily oblivious to the shellshock his latest passenger had just experienced.

How weird, Sam thought as the car crawled along the dual carriageway towards the south of the city, yet how incredibly real the feeling had been. It was as if the world had stopped turning in that instant, in that second when she'd had her first glance of him. And although he was cute, it wasn't as though he was Mr Drop-Dead-Gorgeous – no, if anything he looked more like some *Coronation Street* extra, dressed as he was in tatty-looking blue jeans and an oversized woollen jumper. So what the hell had just happened?

"So have you been anywhere nice?" he asked, and at the sound of his voice Sam almost jumped.

"I'm sorry?"

She met his eyes in the rear-view mirror. They were nice eyes – kind eyes, Sam thought, as she tried to pull her gaze away.

"I just wondered if you'd been away on holidays or anything," the driver repeated.

"Yes – I mean no," Sam said, wondering why her heart was racing like a jackhammer. What the hell was wrong with her? OK, so he was nice to look at – but he certainly didn't possess any of the charm or charisma she was usually attracted to, so why was she feeling so wrong-footed and tongue-tied? "I mean, I'm here for a holiday of sorts, but I've just come from London."

"Ah, London's great," he said, again oblivious to her discomfort. "I get over there a lot myself, and it's a brilliant place

– always something happening." He indicated and pulled into the outside lane. "So do you work over there or something, then? Judging by that accent, you're obviously not one of the natives."

Sam smiled shyly. "No, I'm Irish – same as yourself, but I've been living in London for years now."

"So do you get home much?"

"Not really. I don't have much family left here – just my sister – most of my friends have moved on." Sam wondered why she was being so open with him when normally she didn't make small talk with London cabbies and the like. But there was something *very* different about this guy – and Sam knew it. Something that was worrying and exciting all the same. But now that she'd realised that, what should she do? Should she try and chat him up, maybe make some kind of a play for him? God, no, she couldn't do that – anyway it wasn't in her to make an idiot of herself like that! But even if had been, it was obvious from the man's tone that he was simply making idle conversation with her – the same way he did every day of the week with all the passengers he carried. He certainly wasn't trying to chat *her* up! God, he could be married for all she knew!

"And work is busy so . . ." She shrugged, deciding that she'd better shut up for a while.

"Ah, the same old story," he replied easily, keeping his eyes on the road. "Sometimes I wonder whether we live to work or work to live. My girlfriend is the same, works herself into the ground sometimes – and you'd often wonder, what's it all for? But at the end of the day, I suppose we're lucky we have jobs at all." Then, looking at Sam in the rear-view mirror, the driver's brow furrowed. "Have I given you a lift before by any chance? You look really familiar."

"No, definitely not," Sam was now only half listening to him, so surprising was the pang she'd felt at the mention of a girlfriend. Then, just as quickly, she berated herself for it. This was pathetic. So she'd felt something when she'd laid eyes on him at first but the guy was attached and – and – good God, so was she! She suddenly remembered the real reason she was here – to see if she could seriously consider settling down with Derek! And right then, Sam had her second revelation of the day, and she realised with absolute certainty – having met the man in front of her – that Derek's question of two weeks before had just become a whole lot harder to answer.

CHAPTER 11

9. The Last to Know

"I cannot *believe* you didn't know where my house was!" Eve, who had been called upon to pick up Sam from outside Dun Laoghaire shopping centre, was aghast. "I'm your sister for goodness sake! How could you *not* know?"

"I know, and I'm sorry." Sam, who was sitting in the passenger seat of Eve's Volkswagen, winced apologetically. "But I haven't been to the new house since you moved – in fairness, you're lucky I didn't end up at the old one."

"Sam, we've been at that house since after Max was born – it's hardly bloody new!" Eve tut-tutted. "Anyway, I still can't understand why you didn't let me pick you up from the airport in the first place, instead of paying out crazy money for a taxi like that."

Sam squirmed at the mention of the taxi, remembering her weird, and now utterly embarrassing, reaction to the driver.

While waiting in the street for Eve to arrive she'd quickly come to her senses and now just wanted to put the entire idiotic experience out of her mind. Nevertheless, her heart began to gallop once again as she remembered with startling clarity the jolt she'd felt when coming face to face with the driver – a man whose name she didn't even know.

What the hell had happened to her back then? How could the presence of a stranger – a man whom she had never met before and most likely would never meet again – have such an effect on her? She shook her head at the silliness of it all and sighed, deciding she was in serious need of a decent night's sleep.

"Having second thoughts about this already?" Eve asked, picking up on the sigh.

"Of course not – to be honest, I'm looking forward to a change of scenery."

"It'll certainly be that," Eve agreed wryly, as they drove towards home.

"So, where are the kids?" Sam asked. According to Eve, she usually had to take them everywhere with her. 'Even into the bloody shower,' she'd told Sam once, when Max was going through one of his difficult phases. Well, there'd be none of that once she took over, that was for certain! "Is Liam looking after them? Has he not left for Australia yet?"

She hoped against hope that there wasn't some change of plan in the meantime whereby she'd be landed with Liam as well as the kids. Then her decision whether or not to settle down would most likely be made very quickly! In her opinion, Eve's other half was a selfish oaf who didn't appreciate her sister enough and whose egotistical behaviour had partly necessitated this visit in the first place.

"Anna – you know my friend who lives up the road?" said Eve and Sam nodded politely, even though she hadn't a clue who her sister was talking about. "She was over for a visit when you phoned, so she stayed on at the house to keep an eye on them while I went to pick you up."

"That was nice of her."

Eve grinned. "You have no idea – let's just say Anna and small kids don't exactly go hand in hand!"

"Not the maternal type then?"

"A bit of an understatement," Eve said fondly. "Although I reckon she'd be a fantastic mother if she ever decided to take the plunge. She's a schoolteacher so she's well used to kids but, knowing Anna, I think she'd much prefer to stick to ordering them around."

"I suppose it's not for everyone," Sam replied, wondering if motherhood would ever be a realistic option for her. Well, in a few days' time, she should have a better idea. That was partly the whole point of all this, wasn't it? That and some hands-on experience of what it was like being a housewife and mum. She'd already sketched out a couple of plotline possibilities in her head for her new book, and her editor seemed enthusiastic enough about the idea. Soon, Sam hoped, she'd be able to write with much more confidence and authority about what *full-time* domestic life was really like, instead of making blind assumptions.

"Well, yes, experiment if you like, but at the same time don't stray too far from what you're already doing," Elizabeth said, when Sam informed her of her plans for the forthcoming book. "That's what people want."

"But to answer your question, yes, Liam left for Australia last Saturday," Eve said then, before adding wryly, "so you can take that worried look off your face."

Sam grinned, but she was relieved all the same that Eve's other half was safely out of the way. "So, did he say any more about my coming to stay at the house and you going to London?"

Eve bit her lip. "Not much more, to be honest. He seemed a bit too preoccupied with his trip to worry much about what I was doing."

Typical, Sam thought to herself. Too busy worrying about himself, as usual. If Liam was any good, he would have long ago suggested Eve take some time to herself or at least show her some appreciation by taking her away for a weekend, or offering to baby-sit while she went out for a night with friends. But that would mean thinking of someone else, wouldn't it, something that for as long as she'd known him, Liam Crowley just didn't seem capable of.

"The business isn't doing so well lately," Eve added quietly. "Liam reckons the company is losing serious ground to newer competitors. They're sourcing cheaper wines from the newer countries and selling them on at a higher profit. So Morrison & Co. really need to keep pace, which is why he's working so hard on the Australia deal."

Sam, who could still easily read her sister, knew that Eve was now most likely feeling guilty that she didn't contribute financially to the household and probably doubly guilty for moaning about Liam's absences when all he was trying to do was keep the family going. She knew they didn't have a whole lot of money to spare, which was why she'd offered to arrange flight tickets for Eve's trip to London. But no, Eve had insisted on taking the cheaper ferry across to Holyhead and then the train down to London. It would be a longer and, compared to the fifty-minute plane ride, a much more arduous journey, but despite Sam's best efforts, this was the route Eve would be taking in the end.

In truth, she'd known deep down that Eve wouldn't dream of taking money from her by letting her pay for the tickets, but she hated seeing her sister scrimp and save like that. She also knew that Eve wouldn't dream of spending the household money on flights, particularly when the family relied purely on Liam's salary, and her sister didn't have any money of her own to spend on such luxuries.

In Sam's opinion, such a way of thinking could be another reason Eve and Liam had been together for so long and yet still hadn't tied the knot. Liam seemed perfectly happy with the status quo in his role of provider, while Eve, who felt somewhat beholden to him and dependent on his money, was therefore unwilling to stand up for what she really wanted.

And unfortunately for her, becoming Liam's wife and having his children was all Eve had ever really wanted. Again, Sam felt almost guilty for needing time to think over Derek's proposal of marriage – especially when Eve would give anything to be in the same position and wouldn't have to think at all, let alone twice or three times! But that was life, wasn't it, she thought as the car pulled up outside Eve's house, and sometimes things worked out terribly unfairly.

Removing her luggage from the boot of the car, she followed her sister into the warm two-storey semi-detached house that the family had moved into two years before. The fact that she hadn't yet seen the house was simply a testament to how busy her life had been in London and how long it had been since she and Eve had spent a decent amount of time together. Considering how close they'd been when growing up, it was a shame that they didn't see one another all that often these days. In fact, despite Eve's annoyance at Sam for forgetting her address, she herself had never once set foot in Sam's London flat, so really she hadn't a leg to stand on!

She was about to remind Eve of this fact when a tall, willowy and stunningly beautiful brunette appeared in the living-room doorway.

"Hi, you must be Eve's sister – great to meet you," she said, stepping into the hallway. "I'm Anna."

Sam set down her bag and went to shake the other woman's hand, deciding at once that she liked Eve's friend, partly because she seemed so warm and friendly but also because she was the first person she'd met in ages who upon first sight of Sam hadn't immediately made reference to her column or books. But of course, she was back in Ireland now, wasn't she, and people rarely made a fuss of you here like they did in the UK.

"Pleased to meet you too. I'm sure Eve told you all about my memory loss – or gave out about it, more like." She gave her sister a sideways look and followed Eve through to the warm, nicely decorated living room.

"Imagine not remembering where your own flesh and blood lives!" Eve muttered.

"I know, I know, but I got here in the end, didn't I?" Sam said, rolling her eyes and flopping gratefully onto Eve's sofa. "So where are the kids?"

Anna turned to Eve, an apologetic look on her face. "Erm, I should tell you that while you were away, Max had a bit of an accident with a potted plant," she said, grimacing contritely. "He seemed to think it was edible."

"Not again!" Eve moaned. "Where is the divil? Honest to God, that child will *definitely* grow up to be a landscape gardener or something!"

"I thought I'd better put him in his playpen," Anna said, and Sam got up and followed the two women through to the kitchen. "I cleaned the compost up, but by the time I noticed what he was up to, he'd swallowed quite a bit of it already. I'm so sorry, Eve – you leave me on my own for ten minutes and this happens . . ."

"No need to be sorry – it wasn't your fault," Eve said reassuringly as she scooped her errant (but, thanks to Anna, remarkably clean) son out of his playpen and into her arms. "The little pup did the very same thing right under my nose a while back, didn't you? Actually, I take it back, Max – you won't be a gardener, you'll be a top-ranked CIA spy, you're so good at sneaking around undetected!" Then she looked at Sam and grinned. "I hope you realise what you're letting yourself in for?"

Sam forced a smile, inwardly wondering the very same thing herself. To be honest, she'd forgotten that, what with things being so busy in London, it had been close to eighteen months since she'd last seen her nephew – only a few weeks after he was born – and of course, back then, Max had been a tiny, harmless-looking baby. Stupidly and for some reason, Sam had expected him to be the very same and certainly not this strapping (and evidently troublesome) mini-version of Liam! Yet another example of how clueless she was about this sort of thing.

"Wow, he's got so big!" she said, tickling her nephew under his chin, the toddler staring back at her with suspicious eyes.

"Yes, babies tend to do that, unfortunately," Eve laughed, cuddling Max closer to her. "They don't all stay tiny and helpless and lovely, which is why I've been on at Liam to try for another one."

"Another one – already?" Anna said, sounding faintly shocked by the idea, and Sam remembered what Eve had told her earlier in the car about her friend's own reluctance to have kids.

"Yes, but I might as well be talking to the wall at the moment!" Eve laughed. "Not to mention that we hardly get the opportunity, he's away so much these days. By the way, where's Lily? Oh, let me guess – still sulking because I wouldn't let her go to Rachel's."

Anna nodded. "I think so – she's been in her room since you left."

"Sulking?" Sam repeated. "That doesn't sound like Lily."

Eve rolled her eyes. "Sam, the last time you saw Lily she was a shy, sweet five-year-old who wouldn't say boo to a goose – trust me, times have changed!"

Sam, who'd envisioned her niece as that very same sweet kid and not a wilful seven-year-old, was yet again taken aback by how long it was since she'd actually spent quality time with her sister, yet alone her kids!

Eve was looking at her speculatively. "Are you still sure you want to do this? Because we don't have to, you know – you could always just stay here with us for the weekend, and I won't go anywhere –"

"Of course I want to do it," Sam insisted. OK, so she'd forgotten the kids would be that bit older but, remembering her sister's distress on the phone a fortnight ago, she wouldn't dream of pulling out now. Eve needed this, and to a lesser extent, so did she. "Don't worry, I'm sure we'll all be fine, everything will be fine."

Evidently sensing Eve's hesitancy (and indeed Sam's) Anna spoke up. "I'll pop over now and again to keep you company, Sam, if you'd like. And I was planning on asking you and the kids to our place over the next day or two – for Sunday dinner or maybe a takeaway some evening, if you'd like?"

"Thanks – that would be lovely." Sam was supremely grateful that she'd have someone other than Eve for support over the next few days should things get crazy.

"And speaking of dinner, Ronan will be home soon, so I'd better head back and let you two catch up," Anna said, gathering her things. "Sam, it was really nice to meet you." Then she turned to Eve and gave her a warm hug. "See you when you get back from London. Enjoy your break and be sure to take it easy, won't you?"

Eve hugged her back. "I will – see you soon, and thanks for keeping an eye on the kids for me."

"No problem – sorry about the whole compost thing." Once again, she grimaced apologetically in Max's direction.

Eve's two-year-old was now sitting quietly at his mother's feet and looking as if butter wouldn't melt in his mouth, to say nothing of compost.

"And Sam, why don't I give you a ring over the weekend – give you a chance to settle in first?"

"That would be brilliant," Sam said, meaning it. "Thank you."

"You're sure Ronan will allow this little horror in his house again?" Eve smiled affectionately at Max.

"Well, you know Ronan – any excuse! He adores kids," she added for Sam's benefit, and although she was smiling as she said it, Sam was certain she saw a slight shadow flicker across Anna's expression just then. "See you both soon. Bye Max!"

Eve walked her friend to the front door. "Thanks again and say hi to Ronan for me."

"She seems lovely," Sam said, when Anna had gone and Eve came back inside. "It was really nice of her to invite me over for dinner like that. I hope she didn't feel obliged just because I'm your sister."

Eve smiled. "No, Anna's very genuine like that. So is Ronan."

"Her husband?"

"No, her fiancé."

"Oh, right." Sam sensed a slight catch in Eve's tone as she said this and again felt guilty. There was another person close to Eve heading for happily ever after, while she herself remained dolefully unmarried. "When's the wedding?"

Eve shrugged. "Your guess is as good as mine, to be honest. They've been engaged for yonks but don't seem in any hurry at all to get married. Some people are just like that, I suppose. And as I said, Anna isn't really into the whole husband and kids thing. She's never said it out loud – I mean, we haven't discussed it at length or anything – but you know the way you can just tell with some people?"

Sam did.

"I suppose it's just not her thing," said Eve, adding archly, "bit like somebody else I know."

Sam scooped little Max up and onto her knee, her thighs aching beneath his surprising weight. But at least he hadn't cried his eyes out as soon as he'd set eyes on her, which for Sam was a very positive start. "Well, we'll soon find out exactly how much into that kind of thing I am, won't we?" she stated firmly.

CHAPTER 12

10. The Last to Know

Early the following morning, having left detailed instructions as to how the household should be run, Eve left to take the ferry across to England and then the train onwards to London. She wouldn't reach Sam's flat till late Friday afternoon, and Sam sincerely hoped she managed to find the place OK. Eve had never been in London on her own and Sam prayed her sister wouldn't find all the hustle and bustle too intimidating. The two of them had had a lovely chat and catch-up the night before and, while Eve was a little tearful leaving the kids, she did seem genuinely glad of the opportunity to take a break. Once again, Sam was pleased she'd thought of the idea in the first place.

She wasn't so pleased, however, about having to trail a continuous shadow after Max. The child could be a little demon when he put his mind to it, and not long after Eve was out the door, he'd gone on what could only have been called a rampage with a crayon he'd picked up somewhere. Sam had only turned her back for a second in order to put some laundry in the washing machine, but somehow the child had managed to cover the four walls of, not only the kitchen, but also the living room with random purple stripes!

"How does he do that?" Sam asked Lily, genuinely bewildered by the speed and apparent ease at which her nephew had wreaked such havoc. Eve was only gone a few minutes and already Sam was up to ninety! She and her niece were on their knees in the living room, each doing their best to try and undo the damage.

"This is nothing new," Lily shrugged. "He's such a pain, though. But no matter what he does, Dad still thinks he's wonderful."

Sam smiled inwardly, remembering how, as the older sister, she too used to consider Eve an almighty pain when they were younger. Although in fairness to their parents, there hadn't been any favouritism – at least not until poor Eve let them down by getting pregnant outside of marriage. But every parent wanted the best for their child and in the end things had worked out OK for Eve and Liam. Well, to a certain degree anyway, Sam thought, remembering again Liam's refusal to make things official.

"Ah, you know what men are like," she said to Lily. "They haven't a clue. Anyway, I'm sure your dad thinks you're great too. I certainly do." She looked sideways at her. "I heard you singing in your bedroom this morning. You've got a great voice."

Lily blushed. "Ah no, I was just messing around. I'm no good really."

"You are, you know. In all honesty, I was beginning to wonder if it really was Madonna in there!" she joked and Lily reddened even further. "I think you're great."

"I'd love to be famous some day," Lily said, scrubbing at the trail of purple on the skirting board.

"Well, with the way things are going, I think you will be," Sam assured her, and evidently content with this, Lily smiled and continued removing the crayon without further complaint.

They'd just started on the living-room walls when the doorbell rang. Sam stood up and went to answer it, wondering who would be calling this late on a Friday evening. She hoped it wasn't some insurance salesman or something; they were impossible to get rid of and Sam really wasn't in the mood . . .

She opened the door to find an attractive, dark-haired young woman who, with her mini-skirt and boots and heavily made-up face, looked like she was planning a hectic night out on the town, except for the fact that she holding a young baby.

"Eve," the woman began quickly, "is there any chance you could – oh!" The rest of her sentence trailed off as she realised she wasn't speaking to the person she thought she was. "I'm sorry – I'm looking for Eve."

"She's not here at the moment," Sam told her.

"She's not?" The woman looked concerned. "When will she be back? It's just that I need her to look after Jack tonight for me –"

Blast it, Sam thought. Eve must have forgotten to tell her she'd agreed to look after a baby for someone! Well, there was no way Sam was doing that; whatever about Max (who was bad enough) she hadn't a clue how to handle babies.

"I'm sorry, but she's away for the weekend, and I'm looking after things while she's away." Sam was trying her best to sound contrite. "She must have forgotten all about this, as she certainly didn't tell me anything about –"

"Oh, I didn't tell – I mean, this is all very last minute," the woman said quickly. "I just need to pop out somewhere for a couple of hours and Eve usually obliges. "

Oh she does, does she? Sam thought, instantly recognising this for what it was. This clearly wasn't the first time this woman had dumped her baby on Eve without warning and, of course, Eve being Eve would never have had the heart to refuse. Actually, now that she thought about it, she recalled Eve complaining a few weeks back about being dragged into doing "favours for the neighbours".

"So, seeing as she's not here is there any chance you could . . .?" The woman gave Sam a pleading look.

"Excuse me?" Surely she wasn't suggesting that she baby-sit anyway! This girl didn't know her from Adam; was she really considering handing over her baby to a complete stranger?

"It's just – I really thought that Eve would be here, so I didn't think to organise . . . look, I really have to go – I'm already late as it is, so if you wouldn't mind . . ." She went to hand the baby to Sam.

"I would mind very much as it happens!" Sam cried, horrified, instinctively stepping back into the hallway. "Now, I'm sorry that my sister isn't here to free you up to go off out on the town, or wherever it us you happen to be going," she added, eyeing the woman's clothes and made-up face, "but I'm afraid you'll have to find someone else you can sponge off!"

The woman's eyes widened. "You can't do this! I have plans – very important plans. I can't just not turn up!"

"Well, you should have thought of that before you decided to dump your baby on someone unannounced, shouldn't you?"

"I can't believe this – Eve is always happy to do me a turn," the woman sniffed, seemingly coming round to the fact that she wasn't going to get her way. Then she seemed to think of something. "What about Lily? She could do it."

Sam had had enough of this. She couldn't believe the cheek of the woman – expecting to offload her baby first onto Sam, a complete stranger, and then onto Lily, only a child herself!

"Lily is seven years old!" she cried. "And it seems to me that Eve does you a good turn because she doesn't have any other choice! But I do, so if you'll excuse me I have better things to be doing than wasting time discussing this with you."

"Cow!" Sam heard the other woman hiss, just before she closed the door on her.

"I can't believe that!" Sam said, shaking her head at Lily, who was standing in hallway. "Who does that woman think she is?"

"Sara always does that," Lily said, with a slight shrug of her shoulders. "Last week, we were on our way out to the shops when she dropped Jack off without asking but she didn't bring his buggy so then we couldn't go. He's a lovely baby but I think Mum would prefer to know when he's coming."

"You mean she never asks your mum first? She just drops him off like that?"

"Yep, it drives Dad crazy, but you know Mum. She loves babies so she never says no."

"Still . . ." Sam couldn't believe that Eve would allow herself to be walked over like that. As if her sister didn't have enough to be doing looking after her own kids without with the neighbours' children being dumped on her too!

She would have to have a serious word with Eve about this when she got home and ensure her younger sister learned to stand up for herself, instead of being taken for granted by everyone around her.

"Um, Auntie Sam?" Lily's voice brought her right back to the present.

"Yes, pet?"

Lily sighed and pointed to the living-room walls Sam thought they'd just finished cleaning, but which were now – incredibly – covered with streaks of red! "I think Max found another crayon somewhere."

CHAPTER

11. The Last to Know

Sam woke early the following morning, and when she opened her eyes it took her a couple of seconds to figure out where she was. Stretching languidly out on the bed, she stole a brief glance at the alarm clock and, spotting the time, immediately closed her eyes again. Seven o'clock? Forget it!

Back home in London, Sam rarely rose before eleven on a Saturday morning, and despite the list of domestic duties that (according to Eve) she needed to get through that day, there wasn't a hope of her getting out of bed now. It wasn't like her to wake up so early at all actually . . . Sam yawned, turned onto to her side and pulled the covers back over her head.

She was just about to drift back to sleep when she heard a sound, an odd clatter that she now realised was responsible for waking her up in the first place.

Bloody hell, what was that, she wondered, deciding that it was definitely coming from downstairs. Shit, she hoped it wasn't burglars or anything. But what else could it be at this hour of the morning? Surely the kids weren't awake yet and . . .

Sam shot up out of the bed. Shit – the kids! Or more importantly, Max! Had the little demon somehow succeeded in breaking out of his cot? Last night, Sam couldn't get over his determination not to go to bed, and when she tried to lift him into the cot, he reminded her of a cat trying to avoid water the way he spread-eagled himself above it, arms and legs everywhere.

It had taken her a good half hour to get him into the blasted thing, let alone to sleep! Thankfully, though, he seemed rather spent after yesterday's excitement of having a new victim to torment and from running amok with the crayon.

"You were lucky," Lily had pronounced knowledgeably when the two-year-old finally drifted off. "It usually takes Mum over an hour to get him down."

But clearly he was finished sleeping now, Sam thought, groaning as she pulled back the covers and went to check on him. She hoped to God he hadn't escaped from the cot; who knew what mischief he was getting up to now!

But no, a quick visit to Max's bedroom revealed that, for once, he wasn't the source of the racket, and Sam frowned as she tiptoed back along the landing towards Lily's room, which turned out to be empty. What the hell? Sam couldn't envision her well-behaved niece getting up and causing such a commotion at this hour, but you never knew, did you? Hadn't Eve mentioned something about her being moody and sulky? Still, what could she possibly be doing?

Putting on a dressing-gown, she crept downstairs and into the kitchen, from which the noise seemed to be coming. And when she did, Sam almost couldn't believe her eyes.

The smell of burning food instantly assaulted her nostrils, and the kitchen – well, it seemed to Sam as though a bomb had gone off under it! A milk bottle lay on its side on the ground in front of the fridge, its contents spilling out all over the floor, a selection of empty eggshells were scattered on the countertop, alongside a partly used bag of self-raising flour – much of which seemed to be have been used for decorating the work surfaces. Piled up alongside the toaster was what looked like a half sliced-pan's-worth of blackened, charred toast, and there – in the middle of all this chaos – was seven-year-old Lily, completely *blanketed* in flour and loading a tray with what looked liked a plate of freshly made pancakes.

"Lily, what the hell is going on?" Sam gasped.

Lily turned around, her face white as a ghost, and not just because it was covered in flour. "Ah, Auntie Sam," she cried, "it was supposed to be a surprise!"

"What was supposed . . ." Then it clicked. The milk, the toast, the eggs . . .

"I got up early to make you breakfast in bed. I thought it might be nice for your first day here with us, but now it's all ruined!" Her bottom lip jutted out, and she seemed so distraught that for a second Sam was worried she'd drop the tray. "I made pancakes and toast and I was just going to boil the kettle for your tea –"

"That's very nice of you, pet, thank you." Sam didn't have the heart to say anything about the God-almighty mess Lily had made while attempting this secret task. How could she? It was really sweet of her after all. "Pancakes, wow! Aren't you great to make those?"

"Well, it's my first time making them all by myself," Lily said, calming down a little. "I usually help Mum but she only makes them on Pancake Tuesday, but in the TV shows they always give them to guests for breakfast, so I thought you'd like them."

"I would – thanks," Sam gulped, wondering how much of the flour had actually made it into the pancakes given that the majority of it seemed to have ended up all over her niece's clothes.

"You'd better eat them, otherwise they'll get cold," Lily said, presenting Sam with a plate of gloopy sludge.

"Well, in that case, maybe we should give them a few more minutes on the frying pan," she replied with a nervous laugh, but her smile quickly dropped when she spied the state of the cooker. The same thick mixture was splashed all over the hob and its surrounds, and looking like it was already starting to harden and stick fast. Oh no, it would take her the entire day to clean all of this up!

"Are they nice?" Lily asked hopefully, when the 'pancakes' were ready and the two of them were seated at the table.

"Favvoulus!" Sam replied, her mouth full, unwilling to hurt her little niece's feelings, but *so* not relishing the clean-up operation she'd now have to perform. "It's the nicest breakfast I've ever had!"

* * *

That afternoon, she got a call from Anna.

"How are you doing?" Eve's friend asked, a smile in her voice. "Is your sanity still intact?"

"Just about!" Sam replied through gritted teeth, recalling the morning's exploits. It had taken her a full two hours to get the kitchen back to normal and she'd had to do every last bit of it on her own. Lily wasn't quite as interested in cleaning up the mess as she was in creating it and after breakfast had quickly disappeared next door to a friend's house. But the little girl had had the best of intentions in trying to surprise her so Sam couldn't really say anything.

"Something tells me Auntie Sam is a lot more strict than Mummy Eve tends to be," she said to Anna. "Earlier, Max had an almighty tantrum over what to eat for lunch, so instead of trying to sweet-talk him like Mummy might do, I simply put him back in his room, and let him burn off steam. Lily was mightily impressed. She told me that Eve would *never* do something like that." She wasn't about to confess to Anna that, at that stage, she'd been sick to the teeth of her nephew's antics and was only too glad to see the back of him – if only for a little while. That same morning, while Sam was immersed in cleaning up the kitchen, he'd really gone to town – evidently deciding to make the most of his aunt's distractedness. While she was sure he'd be fine left alone in his playpen, the little Houdini had somehow broken out of it and crept into the living room where he stuck a Liga biscuit in the video player. Sam still hadn't managed to get it out. Then, just before lunch, when she was cleaning the bathroom as per Eve's instructions, she discovered one of her own shoes stuck down the toilet! The child was an absolute terror – how on earth did he manage these things? On both occasions, Sam had literally only turned her back on him for a couple of seconds and – mayhem!

"Too much of a softie, I suppose," Anna mused, referring to Eve's treatment of her youngest.

"Definitely, and doesn't the little fella know it – only two years of age and he's already running rings around her! A chip off the old block if ever there was one!" As soon as the words were out of her mouth, Sam winced, wondering if she'd said too much. After all, hadn't Eve mentioned that Anna and her fiancé were very good friends of Liam's? And here she was merrily slagging him off!

But the other girl must have picked up on her uncertainty.

"Eve certainly has her hands full with the men in her life, that's for sure," she joked. "But listen, I won't keep you. I just wanted to ask if you and the kids were OK to come over for dinner tomorrow – say one thirty?"

"Are you sure you don't mind? Don't feel you have to give up your Sunday afternoon for us and –"

"Of course we don't mind. Look, as I said before, it won't be anything fancy, and we'd enjoy the company. Ronan was thrilled when I told him you'd be bringing the kids. Eve used to come over a lot when Max was younger, but since he's started walking . . ."

"I can imagine," Sam said wryly, now truly understanding why Eve rarely went anywhere with the kids. "So I don't have to warn you to bolt down the furniture in advance then, do I?"

"Already done," Anna laughed. "For once, our house is a child-friendly zone."

*   *   *

So, Sunday lunchtime, Sam and the kids walked the short distance to Anna's house, Lily insisting on pushing Max's buggy all the way.

Sam was really impressed by her niece's good manners and helpful behaviour, although she definitely could have done without the previous morning's breakfast fiasco. Still Lily's heart was in the right place and Eve had told her before the visit that Lily was slightly awed by Sam's success with the newspaper and her books, and at school got great mileage out of the fact that her aunt was 'famous'. Contrary to what Eve had said before about her sulks and moods, Sam found her still very much a sweet young thing, although her niece's good behaviour could probably be put down to the sheer novelty of having her supposedly glamorous aunt around.

Although, on that particular day Sam felt far from glamorous. Believing that she'd be spending most of the weekend indoors and more often than not doing housework, she'd brought nothing to wear but casual tops, jeans and tracksuit bottoms. And seeing as the only decent pair of shoes she'd bothered to bring had been drowned in the toilet, she was now stuck with her trusty runners. But in a way, she didn't mind. She was enjoying just slobbing about with no make-up and letting her normally blow-dried-straight blonde hair curl up and do what it pleased.

Unlike London, there was no pressure here to look her best – and, she admitted to herself reluctantly, no pressure from Derek either. Though he'd never said anything out loud, Sam knew that her boyfriend liked her to make the effort when they went out together and especially when with his friends.

But Sam wouldn't normally dream of visiting someone's house dressed so casually; she now wished she had brought something a little smarter. Dressed in a pair of runners, jeans and a black sweater (the only item in Eve's rather dated wardrobe she could bring herself to wear) she was going to look a right state – especially alongside the beautiful Anna!

But from what she'd already gathered about Eve's friend, Anna didn't seem the competitive type and was unlikely to care one way or the other how Sam looked.

Still, it was hard to break the habit of worrying how you looked in public – especially when accustomed to ultra-fashionable and competitive London.

"Are you looking forward to going to Anna's house?" she asked Lily who clad today in a denim skirt, legwarmers and trendy pink top, was also putting Sam's appearance to shame. "She seems very nice."

"She is nice," her niece replied. "Dad doesn't really like her much, though."

"He doesn't?" Sam repeated, wrinkling her brow in surprise. Hadn't Eve said something about Liam, Ronan and Anna being great friends growing up? "Why not?"

Lily shrugged. "Dunno, but he never really talks to her when

Melissa Hill

she comes over to our house. He'd much rather talk to Ronan about football and stuff."

Oh! Sam grinned at her niece's naivety and the way seven-year-olds viewed adult behaviour with such simplicity.

"So what's Ronan like?" she asked.

"He's *very* nice," Lily replied with meaning, and when she looked sideways at her aunt, Sam realised that her niece was blushing.

Wow, she thought, smiling inwardly, did Eve realise that her seven-year-old had a bit of a crush on this Ronan? Because it certainly seemed that way!

"Really?" she teased. "So is he good-looking?"

"Nooo!" Lily's blush deepened, and she shook her head. "Just nice."

"Ah, just nice. I see."

But there was no more time to delve deeper into this, as the three had now reached Anna's house, or indeed what Sam *hoped* was Anna's house. She looked again at the piece of paper on which she'd written the address.

"This is it," Lily confirmed, opening the gate and wheeling Max's buggy up the path. "Ronan must still be at work. There's no car in the driveway."

"Work – on a Sunday?" Sam repeated, surprised. "What does he do?"

"Didn't Mum tell you?" Lily asked, before reaching up and ringing Anna's doorbell. "He's a taxi driver."

*   *   *

"Hi, Lily, Hello there, Max! Sam, welcome."

Catching sight of Anna smiling in the doorway, fully made-up and looking like she'd just walked off a catwalk, Sam's heart sank.

My goodness, this woman was a stunner! Her mid-length chestnut hair tumbled sexily around her face, and she wore a green multi-coloured dress over glam high-heeled boots, which really accentuated her slim figure and had the effect of making Sam feel like the dowdiest woman on earth. Unused to feeling so utterly wrong-footed in the fashion stakes, she immediately began to apologise.

"Anna, I'm so sorry I look such a mess, but I didn't bring anything decent to wear with me and –"

"Don't be so silly." The other woman immediately waved her apologies away as Sam and the kids followed her inside. "You look great – and don't mind me, I wouldn't normally dress up like this either; it's just that we're visiting Ronan's dad later." When they reached the comfortably furnished living room, she explained further. "It's the first anniversary of Ronan's mum's death tomorrow and there's a remembrance Mass for the family this evening. Hence the threads."

Sam was horrified. "Oh my goodness, I feel so *awful* about intruding on you now. You really should have said –"

"No, no – don't feel bad – the last thing you're doing is intruding. I asked you, remember? No, we're not going over there till later this evening, and to be honest, Ronan could do with the diversion. No offence," she added quickly. "It's just that the whole thing hit him very hard last year, so having you and the kids around today will really help take his mind off things." She smiled. "So now you know my reasons for inviting you all weren't entirely unselfish!"

Sam smiled back, although she still felt awkward about intruding.

"Seriously, Sam – it's fine. If you weren't here, Ronan and I would spend the whole day just moping around and waiting to leave. Instead, you and I can have a proper chat and Ronan can mess around with the kids. It's what he does best anyway."

Again, Sam was aware of a slight alteration in Anna's carefree tone when she said this.

"So please don't be worrying," Anna went on. "As I said, we're delighted to have you. So," she deftly changed the subject, "tell me all about how you're getting on with Mad Max!" She smiled at the toddler who was still strapped into his buggy and was almost turning himself inside out to escape it.

Well, Sam thought, if the other woman was adamant they weren't intruding then she'd just have to take her word for it. She was about halfway into telling Anna the story about Max's attempts at redecorating the living room when it happened.

Again.

She hadn't heard the heard the car pull up and was sitting on the sofa with her back to the door when it opened, yet when Anna's fiancé entered the living room – without even looking at him – Sam knew. She knew because every hair on the back of her neck stood to attention, and every nerve in her body cried out with the same reaction it had a few days earlier.

It was him.

"Ronan, there you are! You're lucky – we were just about to start dinner without you!"

Sam sat in horror as Anna beckoned her fiancé forward. No, no, this was crazy; this couldn't be happening – it couldn't be –

"Ronan, this is Eve's sister, Sam. Sam, this is Ronan."

Sam turned to face the man, this normal, innocuous-looking man who was no heartbreaker, no stunningly handsome rake, yet had – as on the other night – an almost spellbinding effect on her. And as she met his eyes, the very same thought again flashed through her mind: *This is the man I'm going to spend the rest of my life with.*

And he was Anna's beloved fiancé.

"Oh, it's you!" Ronan exclaimed as he went to shake her hand, and for a second Sam wondered if the effect wasn't so one-sided after all, otherwise how would he have recognised her so readily? "I knew you had to be related to Eve somehow – you're the absolute image of her."

"Oh . . . right." Of course, Sam thought, as she limply shook his hand, her brain turning cartwheels. The other night in the cab he'd tried to tell her she reminded him of someone but, accustomed to being recognised from her by-line photo in the newspaper, Sam hadn't given it too much thought.

"And of course she's very well-known for her books and newspaper column," Anna added, but Ronan looked blank.

"Don't you know she's writes for the *Daily Mail* as well as being a published author?" Anna rolled her eyes in exasperation. "The newspapers here are always talking about her. Honestly, Ronan, you haven't a clue sometimes!"

"Yes, but you love me anyway, don't you?" he teased, putting his arm around his fiancée and lightly kissing her on the forehead.

Sam's stomach flipped. What the hell was going on here? Why was this man having such an effect on her? He was madly in love with Anna – any fool alive could see that!

"Sorry, Sam," he said then, giving her an apologetic look. "Anna is the only reader in this house. Most of the time, I don't even bother picking up a newspaper; there's so much depressing news around these days."

"Don't worry," she managed to reply, her smile thin and forced. "The stuff I write wouldn't be your kind of thing anyway."

"Right. Hi, Lily, hey, Maxy!" Evidently nowhere near as affected by Sam's presence as she was by his, Ronan quickly turned his attention to the children. "How are you doing? Lil, you've got so big since the last time I saw you. And how's that bould brother of yours behaving these days?" With a flourish, he scooped Max up off the floor and held him high above his head, the toddler giggling with delight at his antics.

Sensing that Sam was feeling uncomfortable, but not for the reason she suspected, Anna smiled at her and nodded indulgently towards Ronan as if to say 'See what I mean?'

But still shell-shocked by Ronan's reappearance and who he actually was, never mind the effect he was having on her, Sam barely managed to nod in return.

"Well, seeing as we're all here now, I'd better start serving dinner," the other woman said briskly. "Sam, will you have something to drink in the meantime? It won't be any longer than ten or fifteen minutes tops. Some wine, maybe? We wouldn't normally have it, but Liam gave Ronan a case of the stuff a while back and there's a bottle or two left in the fridge."

. "Yes, please," Sam nodded numbly, deciding she'd better do something to try calm her nerves!

"Him and his bloody poncey wine – pity he doesn't work for Guinness," Ronan muttered, evidently unimpressed by his best friend's donation. "And what's this 'ten or fifteen minutes' business? That's an awful length of time to keep a working man waiting for his grub," he joked, following Anna out into the kitchen, Max still in his arms.

"Well, why don't you make yourself useful and pour a glass of wine for our guest?" she heard Anna reply archly. "Maybe then you'll get your 'grub' a bit sooner."

"Tell you what, why don't I give you a hand with dinner?" Sam shot up out of her chair, terrified of spending any length of time alone with Ronan – despite her attraction to him. A wholly inexplicable and obviously totally futile attraction. And even with the kids around, she didn't think she would be capable of making idle conversation.

Anna wouldn't have it. "Not at all – you're a guest!" she

protested, coming back inside.

"Seriously, I'd rather do something, and anyway it looks like the kids would much rather spend time with Ronan than with me." She affected what she hoped was a sincere smile. "Please let me."

"Well, OK then."

Sam followed Anna back into the kitchen where the mouth-watering aroma of roast pork was even stronger. "So much for nothing fancy!" she scolded mildly. "This smells gorgeous. Anna, you really shouldn't have gone to so much trouble."

"It's no trouble and anyway it's a special occasion – we're delighted to have you here," Anna said, opening the bottle she'd taken from the fridge. She then picked up an empty glass from the beautifully set kitchen table and poured Sam a glass of white wine. And as Anna handed her the drink with such a gracious and heartfelt smile, Sam wondered how on earth she could even *think* about competing with this lovely woman for her devoted fiancé's affections.

CHAPTER 14

"You need *more* time? How much more time?" Brooke's heart sank. Today she'd arranged a lunch with one of Horizon's biggest-selling authors, Margo Whyte. Margo's books were hugely successful, all reaching number one in the Australian bestseller list, her broad-sweeping historical sagas satisfying her legions of fans time and time again. But her new novel, which had been scheduled for publication in three months' time, still hadn't been delivered and, from what little she could gather from Margo, was still nowhere near completion. It was a difficult situation, and one in which Brooke needed to tread very carefully.

She'd invited the author and her agent to lunch today in order to try and get some idea of when the book might be finished. Horizon's sales director, Karen, was also joining them, and Brooke had chosen a suitably upmarket restaurant, Quay, at the Overseas Passenger Terminal which overlooked the spectacular vista of the Harbour Bridge to the right and the Opera House to the left.

"Well, I think another six months should do it," Margo's agent, Peter, informed them, while Horizon's star author sat idly studying the menu as if none of this concerned her.

"Six months?" Brooke gasped, unable to conceal her dismay.

In the early days of her career, Margo had delivered one book a year without fail (in addition to holding down a day job). Now, despite writing full-time, she preferred to deliver one book every two years, which was perfectly fine with Horizon as long as the book did indeed arrive every two years. But it looked as though this one was going to take almost three!

"Margo's gift is very fragile, you know," the agent warned and Margo smiled gratefully at him.

So is our publishing schedule, Brooke thought, meeting Karen's worried gaze. Why couldn't Margo have told her this months ago, instead of insisting repeatedly that all was going well and, yes, they should go ahead and include the new book in their catalogue? Now that, and all the promotions they'd planned for the book upon publication, would have to be completely scrapped!

The agent was still talking. "These things take time, you know – she's not a machine."

Brooke knew that, of course she did, but Margo and her agent were both long enough in the business to know the effect such lateness would have on them as publisher.

If she'd just come out and admitted well before now that she wouldn't be ready, that would be fine, but the problem was that she'd done just the opposite.

"Of course you'll have it in time," Margo had insisted to Brooke back when the first deadline had been missed. "I'm busy with a few other things at the moment, that's all."

Brooke had a pretty good idea what these "other things" might be. Since Margo's star had risen, her fantastic success had gone right to her head, and she'd quickly been seduced by the more glamorous side of the business. These days, the constant whirl of parties and social engagements seemed to have taken precedence over her writing, which Brooke thought such a shame, as when starting out Margo Whyte was one of the least pretentious authors she knew.

"But do you think six months will be long enough to finish it?" Karen asked impatiently and Brooke gave her a warning look.

"Perhaps, that's if I can get some peace and quiet." Margo seemed bored by the entire conversation. "So many people asking me to attend this and officially open that ..." She rolled her eyes, as if all this fame business was *so* draining. "I might travel to Europe for a while, see if I can get some headspace there."

"Look, if Horizon aren't prepared to wait for it, there are plenty of others who are," her agent cut in, with a barely disguised threat. "Margo *is* a huge star, after all."

Brooke took a deep breath and counted to ten. She and Karen needed to tread carefully here! "We all know that," she said, smiling at Margo, "which is why we and all her fans can't wait to get our hands on her next book. But we do of course realise that these things can't be rushed."

Some two hours later, an exhausted Brooke and an equally shattered Karen said goodbye to their star author and her agent, having eventually agreed a completion deadline of *eight* months.

"I liked her better when she used to wear Target," Karen quipped, as she and Brooke waited behind for a well-deserved dessert, the sales director needing to calm down a bit before heading back to the office. "Now it's all Collette Dinnigan and Diane Von Furstenberg . . . big money clothes and a big bloody ego to match."

Brooke bit her lip. "Ah, Margo's not too bad really. I think it's mostly Peter's fault, to be honest. Did you see the way he behaves around her, treating her like she's some kind of goddess or something? If I had someone telling me how *fabulous* I was all the time, I'm sure it would go to my head too."

"You mean the lovely Will doesn't fulfil that function?"

Brooke laughed. "Not his style – unfortunately!"

Karen smiled and poured herself another glass of wine. "It's such a pity, though – I think it's sad when authors get too big for their boots like that and forget all about what makes them great in the first place – their writing."

"I know, but at the end of the day Margo's a pro and I'm sure the book will be great when it does come in." Brooke grinned as the waiter arrived with a *humongous* portion of chocolate fudge cake. Sod the diet – for once she was going to treat herself!

"Hope so, it had *better* be worth all the aggro we're now going to have with the schedule." Karen shook her head. "Sometimes I wonder if we'd be better off concentrating on authors who actually *want* to be published and ... oh, speaking of which, I almost forgot to tell you – I'm *really* enjoying that new submission you gave me – you know, the Irish one?"

"*The Last to Know?*" Brooke replied, pleased. She'd passed the first hundred pages on to Karen for an opinion before deciding whether to pursue it any further in terms of publication. As head of sales, Karen usually had a considerable say in whatever manuscripts Horizon eventually chose to publish, so Brooke was eager to see what she thought before presenting it at an acquisitions meeting. Her colleague also had a tendency to be brutally honest in terms of a novel's marketability, so Brooke had been particularly interested in what she made of it.

Karen nodded. "Yes, that first chapter really hooked me and the characters are great, very well-drawn, but what I'm really liking is that lovely way with words – what is it about those Irish writers?" She twirled a strand of long auburn hair and grinned. "But of course, I'm preaching to the converted, aren't I? You've already nabbed yourself an Irish stud in the lovely Will."

Brooke grinned. "It wasn't just the accent, Karen. Will's a nice guy."

"I know he is – I've seen him on a surfboard, whew!" She shook her head admiringly.

"Anyway, back to business for a sec," Brooke said quickly. She didn't want to talk about Will just now. "What do you reckon on the manuscript? Has it got enough potential, do you think?"

"Well, I definitely think we need to read the whole lot before we make a final decision. It has some very good strong points, though. Character-wise I immediately liked Eve, but for some reason I couldn't take to that – what was the name of the character that's pregnant again?"

"Anna."

"Yeah, Anna. To be truthful, I thought her character a bit cold, but I *am* interested in finding out why she's upset about being pregnant and why she won't marry her boyfriend – there's enough intrigue there to keep readers turning the pages, which is obviously a plus. And I also want to find out if the other one, Sam, ends up making a play for her fiancé. Not sure why, but I think I'd like her to. So yes, I think there's definitely something there." She picked up her wineglass and took a sip from it.

Brooke nodded. She'd thought the very same thing about Sam and this surprised her, because usually, from an editorial point of view, she worried when characters went for married or attached men – it was often much more difficult for readers to sympathise with them. But interestingly, in this case, she'd actually found herself sympathising with Sam. "That's why I like it," she told Karen. "It's sort of crept up on me. I was reading it on the ferry home the other day and before I knew it we were already on the other side. That hasn't happened for a while."

"Has Julie seen it yet?"

Julie would be the one who would make the final decision on whether or not to publish *The Last to Know*.

"No, at first I thought she might be the one who'd given it to me but she doesn't know anything about it so it must be one of the readers. I don't think I'll suggest it to her until I've read the rest. And, of course, I wanted to pick your brains and see what you thought, seeing as you're the one who has to sell it to the trade."

Karen shrugged. "I'd have no concerns on that count anyway; I'm sure it'll sell fine. The Irish stuff usually finds an audience. And of course we haven't had an Irish author on the list since Katie McCarthy left, and she sold left, right and centre as you know – still does unfortunately." Irish-born but now Melbourne-based author Katie McCarthy had recently left Horizon to join a rival publisher, which meant that their books were now in competition with hers. "Well, I suppose the only good thing to come of that is that we don't have to travel to Melbourne as often now," she added wryly, "which is a huge relief."

As a fellow Sydneysider, Brooke knew she was supposed to share in her friend's supposed dislike of the other city, but in truth she liked Melbourne's smaller size and the city's varied architecture and relaxing bohemian vibe. While it had in the early days been the more commercially important of the two major Australian cities, Melbourne was now considered second best to sleek, super-confident and world-famous Sydney. As a result, the rivalry between residents of the two cities was so great it was said that Canberra was eventually chosen as Australia's capital simply because of its proximity halfway between the two opposing cities. She smiled inwardly, knowing Karen would not be impressed if Brooke admitted she enjoyed the occasional jaunt to the state of Victoria.

"What's this author's name, by the way?" Karen asked, polishing off her dessert. "Is it a good *Irrrish* name like Katie's?"

Brooke shook her head. "Do you know something, I don't actually know yet – it wasn't on the title page. But Mary probably has all those details on the original submission letter – at least, I *think* it was Mary who left it on my desk, but I haven't had a chance to ask her about it since she got back. I must give her a buzz after this."

"Do, because it's definitely got something," Karen said, signalling for the bill. "And can you let me have the rest of it when you're finished with it?"

"Of course, and I'll let you know the author's name too – see if it is a good Irish one!" she added with a grin.

"An ex-pat, I wonder?"

"Well, I presume so. If she was Irish, she'd have submitted there first, wouldn't she? Or to the UK."

"I know – I meant she could be a backpacker or something." Karen looked at her watch. "I suppose we'd better head back to the grindstone."

"Yep."

Having paid the bill, the two got up to leave. The day was hot and the humidity stifling, but as they walked further along the quays back in the direction of the office, the cool breeze off the water gave them some welcome relief.

"I doubt she's a backpacker, Karen," Brooke said, continuing their conversation about the author of *The Last to Know*. "The voice seems much older to me. Anyway, aren't backpackers too busy getting drunk and enjoying themselves to be writing about downtrodden housewives and wedding dates?"

Karen laughed and put on her sunglasses. "You're right – if you get anything from a backpacker, it's going to be an Alex Garland rip-off, isn't it?"

Brooke nodded in agreement and went on to tell her about all the *Harry Potter* and *Da Vinci Code* rip-offs she was still getting.

"Still? But there's rainforests of the stuff out there! When will it ever stop?"

"I know, I know. And none of them seem to realise that we don't publish this stuff. We specialise in *women's* fiction!"

"Well, if it sells as well as the real thing, we might just take a look at the odd Bryce Courtenay rip-off, all the same," said Karen, ever the sales director. "But no conspiracy theories and *definitely* no backpacker rants."

"Speaking of backpackers," Brooke sighed then, remembering, "did I tell you that Will wants us to head up to the tropics for Christmas?"

This would be the first Christmas since her mum's death and Brooke wasn't sure what she wanted to do. Will was convinced she should get away, while Bev had invited her to spend Christmas Day with her and the family. Granted, a week up in Queensland out on the reef sounded good, but at the same time, she wasn't sure if she'd prefer to just lay low in the house in Manly in which she and her mother had celebrated so many Christmases together. As Brooke's father had died in an accident shortly after she was born, she had no memories of him, but memories of her mother – to whom she had been extremely close – were still very fond albeit very painful. For some reason, she felt she owed it to Lynn to spend Christmas at home and to spend the afternoon with friends and neighbours on the beach, like they used to.

But Will was eager to do something more exciting.

"Two full weeks off work – I don't know when this will happen again so we have to make the most of it, Brooke," her boyfriend had said, shortly after returning from an intensive work-related trip to Europe. The company that sponsored Will's visa and allowed him to work here in Australia were in Brooke's opinion pushing him way too hard, and he rarely got a weekend off let alone two weeks. In fact, only the weekend before, he'd had to cancel on her for some last, minute work-related thing, which was why when Karen had mentioned him earlier, she'd quickly changed the subject. It was so bloody frustrating sometimes! Still, because he did work so hard, she supposed she couldn't really blame him for wanting to make the most of his time off. But at the same time . . .

"Lucky you – sounds great!" Karen seemed just as enthused about the idea of a trip to the tropics. "Where are you guys headed?"

Brooke gave her a sideways look. "Cairns probably."

Her workmate stopped in her tracks. "*Cairns?* You mean Tourist Hell Cairns? Why there?"

As the main gateway to the Great Barrier Reef, at that time of year the popular tourist city would undoubtedly be packed to the gills with tourists and vacationers. As a result, most Australians tended to steer clear of the place, preferring instead to base themselves in the nearby and considerably less bustling coastal town of Port Douglas.

"Will loves it up there," Brooke told her. "It's not my idea of a holiday, but whatever about the town, the diving is great."

"But why not do the Whitsundays? Me and Greg took a boat out there a few years back and it was bloody brilliant. Christmas in Cairns sounds . . . well, it doesn't sound great, Brooke."

"I know," she said glumly.

"What age is Will again?"

"Twenty-eight. I know,"she groaned, when Karen looked surprised, "you'd think he'd be into something less touristy, but then again, he *is* Irish, so to him it's no big deal. And apparently he's got a couple of mates going up there too so . . ." She shrugged and trailed off.

"Well, if there's a crowd of you going, it might be good fun, I reckon," Karen said eventually and Brooke nodded, unconvinced.

Shortly after she and Karen returned to the office, Brooke decided to seek out Mary and find out what her reader knew about the author of *The Last to Know* and to confirm if it had indeed been Mary who'd recommended it to her.

"Mary's out sick today," Sally, one of the assistants, informed her when Brooke phoned. "She had to leave early yesterday with a really bad migraine, poor thing."

Typical, Brooke thought. "OK, thanks, Sal, when she's back can you ask her to give me a shout? I need to ask her about a submission she passed on to me before."

"Oh, right – I think she mentioned something about that actually," Sally said conversationally. "You liked it?"

"Well, so far so good anyway."

"Great! I'll be sure to let her know."

"OK, thanks, Sal," Brooke replied before ringing off.

Well, ex-pat or not, it seemed she'd have to wait a little longer before finding out more about the author, but on the plus side, Karen really liked the story, which merely strengthened Brooke's own belief that there was something about *The Last to Know* that was well worth following through.

*   *   *

The author of *The Last to Know* (who was not – as Brooke and Karen believed – an Irish ex-pat but was in fact based in Dublin) was extremely pleased to wake up one morning and find an email from Australia in her inbox.

She was so pleased she immediately picked up the telephone to pass on the news to somebody else.

"She has the manuscript," the author said when the person on the other end answered the call.

"What? Are you sure?" the other woman said warily. "How do you know?"

"I've just got an email about it."

"I see. And?"

"And it's piqued her interest."

There was a sharp intake of breath on the other end of the line. "Do we know how much of it she's read?"

"Not a whole lot yet, apparently."

"So what do we do now?" the other woman asked, sounding nervous.

The author tightened her grip on the receiver. "We just wait."

CHAPTER

12. The Last to Know

Having spent the afternoon at Anna's house, Sam and the kids eventually headed for home around six thirty, Sam still reeling not only from meeting Ronan for a second time, but also from the realisation of who he actually was and, even worse, who he was engaged to.

After she put Max to bed – this time without much complaint (clearly he was learning his boundaries where Sam was concerned), she and Lily watched a little TV until her niece eventually drifted upstairs to her bedroom at about seven. As there was nothing much on TV, and not a whole lot else to do, Sam decided to relax on the couch and maybe read for a while. While she was tired and emotionally rather drained after the day's events, it was miles too early to go to bed too, and Eve was bound to have a few decent books lying around somewhere, wasn't she?

But her sister wasn't much of a bookworm, and the only reading material Sam could find in either the living room or Eve's bedroom was a dog-eared copy of Stephen King's *The Stand*, along with an edition of *Cosmo* that was so old it was informing readers that seventies-style flared trousers were the height of fashion.

She wondered if Liam might have a decent book lying around somewhere. With all the travelling he did, surely he must read the odd thriller or two to pass the time on the plane?

Still, despite her hunt for reading material, Sam was loath to start rummaging around in her sister's house. It was a huge invasion of privacy and something she really wasn't comfortable with. Feck it, *The Stand* would have to do – even if it would be her second or third time reading it.

She was just beginning to get nicely engrossed in the story when the telephone rang.

"Sam, I've had the most brilliant day touring around on the open-top bus!" Eve gushed when Sam answered. "How's everything? Are the kids in bed? I was hoping I'd make it back well before now, but there was some delay on the Northern Line, and it was just *awful* . . ."

Sam smiled as her sister continued to relay her sorry London Underground tale. Her sister had phoned every single day since reaching London and was keeping Sam updated on her action-packed weekend. Despite Sam's offer to have one of her friends take Eve under her wing while she was there, Eve was only too happy to find her own way around, sampling everything London had to offer. The evening before, she'd gone on her own to see some show in the West End and that day she had been out at the shops. Sam couldn't believe that Eve had taken to the place so readily and was thrilled that she seemed to be enjoying her little break.

"So, how's it all going?" Eve asked once again. "Do the kids miss me? Is Max behaving himself?"

"Everything's fine, Eve. Max is fine, Lily's fine, I'm fine." Sam was beginning to tire of repeating the mantra. "We went over to Anna's for dinner earlier."

"Oh, so you met Ronan – isn't he lovely?"

Sam gulped. "Yes, he certainly is."

"God, I hope the kids behaved themselves. Max didn't do anything too awful, did he?"

"Max was the picture of well-behaved innocence, Eve." *For once*, Sam added silently.

"Was he now?" her sister repeated, her tone sharp. "He sounds like a different Max to the one I know. Sam, if I didn't know better, I'd swear you were putting something in his food. You're not, are you?"

Sam smiled softly. She couldn't deny she'd thought about it. But there was no point in worrying Eve by going into detail about his exploits now. "Of course not. Honestly, Eve, he plays up a little bit now and then, but I think he knows now not to push it. Anyway, me being around is a bit of a novelty for the kids so they're bound to go much easier on me than they would with their boring old mum."

"Did Lily say that to you?" Eve sounded pained.

"Say what?"

"That I was boring."

"Oh for goodness sake, Eve – she said nothing of the sort." Sam rolled her eyes in exasperation. God, she couldn't win! "It was only a joke – I meant nothing by it."

"Really?"

"Really," she insisted through gritted teeth.

"Well, as long as you're sure."

"Of course I'm sure. Anyway, never mind about us, how are you getting on over there? Are you still enjoying it?"

"Sam, it's fabulous!" her sister exclaimed, delightedly. "I went to that Harrods place after I spoke to you yesterday, and I just couldn't get over the stuff in there. Absolute heaven! God, if only I had a credit card!"

"You don't have a credit card?" Sam frowned in disbelief.

"Of course not. Sure I'd only go mad with it if I had."

"So what do you do when you want to buy something?"

Eve burst out laughing. "What do you think I do? I just get the cash from Liam, that's what."

"Oh." Sam couldn't believe that in this day and age a woman like Eve could be so beholden to her partner for every single thing – even something simple like buying some new clothes. But then again, Eve didn't work so she didn't have money of her own to spend, did she? And she couldn't exactly see Liam urging her sister to spend anything on herself either, Sam thought wryly. That fella really needed telling a thing or two.

Or more likely, Eve did.

"Anyway, as I said, I did the bus thing today and I had a quick look in and out of some of those museums you're always talking about," Eve told Sam. "It was quite tiring though, so tonight I might stay in and get a video or something."

"That sounds nice. Speaking of which, I'm planning on taking the kids to the cinema tomorrow evening when Lily finishes school – what do you think? There's a Muppets movie showing, and I think they'd really enjoy it."

"Oh, they'd love that!"

"And we might go out for ice-cream or something afterwards."

"Are you sure you're comfortable bringing them into town on your own?" Eve said in a worried tone.

"Eve, they're kids, not wild dogs! We'll be fine."

"Well, if you're absolutely sure," Eve said, sounding the very opposite. "So what did Anna make for dinner today?" she continued conversationally. "She's a great cook, isn't she?"

"Roast pork – and, yes, it was delicious." Sam tried to put the image of Ronan sitting directly across from her at the table out of her mind. Although over dinner he and Anna chattered away to her and did their best to make her feel at ease, for Sam the whole thing had been excruciating. She hesitated slightly before asking. "Eve, what's the story with those two?"

"Who – Anna and Ronan?"

"Yes. I mean, I know you said they were engaged for a long time, yet there was no sign of them getting married?"

"Why, were they acting strangely around you or something?"

"No, no, no – I just wondered, that's all."

Eve breathed out. "Well, they've had a few ups and downs over the years – same as the rest of us, I suppose. Ronan's mother died last year after a long illness and I know it took him a very long time to get over it. And while she was sick, he was obviously very stressed because he had to deal with a lot of it on his own – he has a sister but she lives abroad, in France I think," she added. "So Anna and Ronan were both under a lot of pressure. She was just as worried and upset as Ronan was over it because his mother was a friend of her own and she'd known the woman almost as long as Ronan himself."

"Right – I see."

"But Anna and Ronan have been together since the year dot and no matter how tough things got, they got over it and they're as solid as a rock. They were childhood sweethearts, you know – real childhood sweethearts," Eve told her fondly. "They lived next-door to one another when they were kids and were best friends throughout school, went to each other's debs – that kind of thing. That's how she knew Ronan's mother so well and was probably the only person who knew what he was going through when she was sick."

"And they've been together since childhood and all the way through? They've never gone out with anyone else?" To Sam, the idea seemed unimaginable.

"As far as I know, neither of them has ever even *looked* at anyone else – let alone gone out with them," Eve replied. "I know – it's sweet, isn't it?"

"Very sweet," said Sam, heart sinking afresh. "Still, it does seem strange that they haven't set a date, doesn't it?" There had to be more to this than met the eye, she thought, trying to justify her discomfiting reaction to Ronan. Maybe Anna and Ronan were hesitating because deep down they weren't meant to be?

Eve's voice interrupted her train of thought. "Ah, I'm sure they'll get married in their own time eventually. I suppose the way they see it – there's no rush. I mean, it's not as though they need to worry about anyone stealing one away from the other or anything, is it?"

"No, I suppose not," Sam gulped, unable to explain why the feeling that *she* – not Anna – was the one supposed to end up with Ronan was stronger than ever.

CHAPTER 16

13. The Last to Know

Eve was really in her element in London. She almost felt like she was in some kind of fairytale.

Before she'd left on Friday, Sam had described her flat as "nothing to write home about" but to Eve it was absolute paradise. OK, so compared to her and Liam's family home, the two-roomed flat was quite small, but it was so cosy and so – so modern and so clean! Eve had nearly fallen over when Sam informed her that the cleaner would be coming in that Saturday morning. A cleaner – imagine? Eve couldn't comprehend what her life would be like if she had someone to clean the toilets and do the vacuuming. But of course she made sure the poor woman didn't have too much to do all the same.

"I knew it!" Sam exclaimed, when Eve informed her over the phone later in the day that she'd "tidied up a bit" before the cleaner's arrival. "You just couldn't resist, could you? Eve, the whole point of the next few days is for you to forget about housework and the daily grind. What about relaxing and taking it easy?"

But Eve was doing plenty of that too. She'd stocked up on magazines upon arrival and was slowly and steadily working her way through them. And despite herself, she was not so slowly working her way through London's amazing shops. Sam's flat was conveniently close to a tube station and, having got over her initial fear of the noise and bustle associated with the underground transport system, Eve was now able to hop, skip and jump her away around the city with ease. In fact, she thought now, as she waited in Piccadilly station to get a connecting train back to Sam's flat, you'd swear she'd been doing this all her life!

The sense of independence was startling. Eve had never done the independent city-girl thing and now she was beginning to realise just how much she had been missing. Not that she'd swap Lily for the world, but having her daughter and settling down at such an early stage meant that she'd really missed out on this kind of stuff. When was the last time she'd gone window-shopping on her own in Grafton St (never mind Grafton St, when was the last time she'd gone shopping on her *own*?) or spent an entire afternoon sitting in a cosy café reading a magazine and drinking hot chocolate?

But despite her intentions to have some peace and quiet, Eve did find sitting alone in Sam's flat a little bit too quiet, and so she tended to spend most of her time outside where there were plenty of people and lots of noise. Force of habit, she supposed, because while Sam was quite introverted, Eve had never been particularly comfortable in her own company.

Later that evening, having spent a nice Monday afternoon wandering around the city, Eve headed for the nearest tube station to catch a train that would take her back to Sam's.

But as luck would have it, there was yet *another* delay on the line and Eve, along with hundreds of other disgruntled London commuters, had no choice but to wait for the cause of the hold-up to clear. She couldn't believe that this happened so often; only yesterday she'd been bemoaning these delays to Sam over the phone!

Unfamiliar with alternative methods of transport back to Clapham, and terrified of her life of getting into a cab for fear she'd be kidnapped, Eve tried to ignore her tired feet while she waited a full forty-five minutes in the stale air and stifling heat for the train to arrive.

Then, feeling rather like a seasoned London Underground pro as she nipped from platform to platform, she eventually made her way back to Sam's and, before doing anything else, again phoned her older sister to see how she was getting on. She'd decided to phone a little earlier this time – when she'd phoned last night, Sam was, along with the kids, getting ready for bed!

An early night was a definite first for her party-mad sibling and, Eve thought with a self-satisfied grin, evidently a testament to the amount of work she must be doing back in Ireland!

But no, apparently her sister wasn't planning on going to sleep but was instead reading a book – a rare event in Eve's house, reading having never been particularly high on her own list of priorities. In fairness, most days she was lucky if she found the time to read the outside of a milk carton – never mind a couple of hundred pages! But Sam had always been the same, and when the two girls were kids her sister's nose was forever stuck in some boring book while Eve much preferred playing with her dolls. So it was no great surprise, really, that their adult lives had pretty much followed suit, Sam becoming a writer and Eve a housewife and mum.

The phone was ringing out on the other end, which Eve thought was rather puzzling. Oh well, she'd try again later, she thought, hanging up and going into the kitchen.

While Sam and the kids seemed to be getting on fine without

145

her, Eve still found that she missed them desperately and was really looking forward to coming home. Yes, the few days' break had been great, but she'd had her fun and now she was more than ready to come back and resume her housewife and motherly duties. The break had reaffirmed just how much she loved doing what she did and how much she truly loved her family. OK, so certain things got her down sometimes, but wasn't that the case for everyone? And after so long away from him, she was really looking forward to seeing Liam too, although she was definitely *not* relishing the prospect of collecting him from the airport! Recalling that the connecting flight he would have to take from Heathrow to Dublin usually came in at around one a.m., Eve resigned herself to the fact that their eventual reunion would be a tiring one.

Still, it would be wonderful to have the whole family back together again and this time she'd make sure to cook something for Liam that he'd really enjoy and would have his "sophisticated palate" jumping for joy!

But more importantly, she now had to come up with something for her own dinner this evening, although it was no fun cooking for just one person, she thought, opening Sam's fridge and finding the same boring healthy food that had been there since the day she'd arrived. In fairness to her sister, she had always had a gorgeous figure, but small wonder when Sam clearly had the eating habits of a saint! Not a scrap of chocolate, ice-cream or even a few chocolate biscuits . . . It was her own fault really; on her way home she should have nipped into Marks & Spencer's down the road and stocked up on some more goodies. She'd been very bold all weekend so far, getting fish and chips from the takeaway down the road and having the odd sandwich in town, before relaxing in front of the TV with chocolate and treats in the evenings. Maybe she'd pop down to the shop anyway, she thought, annoyed with herself for not thinking about it earlier, otherwise she'd have no choice but to make do with a dinner of natural yoghurt and celery – yuck!

But just as she was putting on her coat to go back out again, the telephone rang.

"Sam, hi – Gloria here," said the female voice at the other end. "Now, before you say anything, I know it's late, and I also know I promised I'd leave you alone PR-wise for a couple of weeks, but you won't *believe* this: the *Jack Nathan Show* want to do a live radio interview with –"

"Um, excuse me," Eve thought she'd better interject, seeing as this woman seemed to be able to speak without taking any breaths, "Sam's not actually here at the moment."

"Ha, good one, Sam – very funny. Seriously, you've got to do this – you *know* PR like this doesn't come round every day and –"

Eve's eyes widened as the other woman continued to babble as if she hadn't spoken. "Seriously, this is not Sam," she insisted a little more forcibly. "I'm her sister Eve."

Gloria breathed out theatrically. "Right, OK, I see what you're doing. Play the diva all you like. But didn't you hear me? This is the *Jack Nathan* show, Sam! Continental won't be happy – you know they'd normally kill for this kind of PR."

Eve's heart began to thump. She didn't believe her; the woman actually thought that Sam was pretending to be someone else in order to get out of appearing on some show! As if her sister would do such a thing! What kind of person did this woman think she was?

"Look, I swear to you – I'm not Sam. I'm just staying here for a couple of days while she's baby-sitting my children. In Ireland," she added helpfully.

"You're serious?"

"Yes."

"But Sam never said anything about taking off to Ireland!" The way she said it, it sounded as though Sam had illegally flown the country. "Shit! She's really landed me in it now. What am I going to say to the BBC – or worse, what will I tell Elizabeth when she hears that we had to turn down *The Nathan Show?*"

Eve was vaguely aware that Continental were Sam's publishers, so she knew this woman must have something to do with that, and hadn't her sister only recently talked about how her editor Elizabeth was fully behind the idea of her next book? But the woman sounded rightly cheesed-off and, even worse, made it sound as though Sam's employers would be cheesed-off too! Shit, she'd better ring Sam and find out what the story was. Maybe her sister could do the interview over the phone?

"Look, Ms – Gloria, is it?" Eve continued. "Why don't I just phone my sister and get her to call you back. Maybe you can work something out for when she comes back?"

The other woman sighed dramatically. "OK, wonderful – you do that but get her to phone me back as soon as possible, won't you? Here's the number . . ."

Eve's head was still spinning when she put the phone down. Who *was* that – that nutter? Well, whoever Gloria was, it was obvious she was an important colleague of Sam's anyway. Eve tapped her fingertips lightly on the countertop as again she dialled her own home number. Hopefully by now Sam would be back.

But still the line rang out, and for a brief moment Eve began feeling a bit worried until she remembered that Sam had said something the day before about taking the children to the cinema to see a movie.

She left it another three-quarters of an hour before trying again but still to no avail. Blast it anyway, she thought, hanging up for a third time; she'd promised your woman that Sam would phone her back, but who knew what time her sister would be home?

No option now but to just phone Gloria back and tell her the bad news.

"I'm very sorry," Eve told the other woman, "but I just can't reach Sam on the phone at the moment."

"Fuck!" Gloria exclaimed, causing Eve's eyes to widen in surprise. This wasn't exactly the reserved behaviour she'd expected from an English person! "In order for them to slot us for tomorrow morning, I need to give the producer the go-ahead before close of play today."

Eve wasn't entirely sure what that meant other than it must be sometime soon. "Well, there's really nothing I can –"

"Wait, wait, I'm thinking," Gloria interrupted, her tone impatient, and Eve waited politely at the other end of the line for her to finish thinking. A minute or so later, she spoke again. "You said Sam's away for a few days?"

"Yes, until Wednesday evening – when I go back home."

"So you're here tomorrow then – in London?"

"Yes, but –"

"What did you say your name was again?"

"Eve."

"Eve, did anyone ever tell you, you sound *exactly* like your sister Sam?"

"Well, yes, I suppose we do sound alike but –" She broke off, suddenly understanding what Gloria was getting at. "*No!*"

"What?" the other woman asked innocently.

"You're *not* thinking of sending me onto the show instead of Sam? I *couldn't* do that – I'm not Sam, I don't know anything about that stuff she writes and –"

"Darling, you don't *have* to know anything. The questions will be screened in advance – they always are so there'll be no surprises. You've read your sister's books, haven't you?"

Eve was too embarrassed to admit that, while of course she'd started to read both and thought they were great, she'd (shamefully) never got round to finishing them. It was just impossible to find the time! "Well, yes, of course, but –"

"You'd be perfect! Look, Continental will not be impressed if they find out that Sam isn't around for this. She's still contracted to promoting *Lucky Stars*, you know, so really she shouldn't have gone *anywhere* without telling me first."

Immediately Eve felt guilty. It was *her* fault that Sam wasn't here to promote her book after all.

"And people commit *murder* to get exposure on the *Jack Nathan Show* – it's PR Mecca!" Gloria went on. "So, if this doesn't happen, and it's all because Sam took off somewhere without telling us, it really won't look good for her long-term prospects with us." She let the words dangle in the air for a moment before continuing, "As I said, I worked tooth and nail to get this gig – and this kind of opportunity doesn't come round every day."

Eve was terrified. She knew this was important and that Sam not being here in the first place was all down to her but . . . no, she couldn't do what the woman was asking – no way!

"I really couldn't," she said to Gloria, but her tone was weak. "I wouldn't know what to say –"

"Of *course* you'll know! You'll know *exactly* what to say because I'll tell you." Gloria seemed to take her hesitation as a form of assent. "Seriously, Sam will be glad you did this, I'll be glad and most importantly the BBC will be glad. But if you don't do it . . ." Again, she let the remainder of the sentence hang in the air. "Let's just say a lot of people will be very unhappy with your sister."

Eve bit her lip. Although she was absolutely terrified, there was a part of her that deep down was a tiny bit intrigued about the prospect of going on the radio. It would be like being a celebrity, wouldn't it? A taste of what Sam's life was really like. And it couldn't be that bad, could it? Especially – like Gloria said – if she knew what questions would be asked in advance. And of course if Sam's career could suffer simply because she was good enough to give her younger sister a break from housework . . . well, she owed it to her, didn't she?

Ah feck it, she'd do it! Eve decided to throw caution to the wind. Any normal person would grab with both hands the opportunity to see inside the BBC instead of behaving like a terrified mouse. Maybe she might even enjoy it? God knows, she'd surprised even herself these last few days with the way she was swanning around London city as if she'd been doing it all her life!

"What time's the show?" she asked Gloria.

"You're a darling! It's tomorrow morning, seven a.m. But we'll need to be in studio at least a half-hour beforehand, so you can meet Jack and run through the questions. I'll send a car. Eve, you'll be terrific!" Gloria sang. "And you won't regret this – I promise you!"

CHAPTER

14. The Last to Know

Early Tuesday morning the telephone rang, rousing Sam out of a deep slumber. Still half-asleep, she pulled on Eve's dressing gown and slowly made her way downstairs to answer it. Picking up the receiver, she tried to suppress a yawn before speaking. "Hello?"

"For God's sake, Eve, where were you?" Liam's voice bellowed down the other end.

Sam bristled. It was bad enough that he'd forgotten her sister was away at the moment, but to think that if Eve *were* here he would dare to speak to her like that . . . Then her eyes widened when she glanced at her watch and realised the time. OK, so there was a big time difference in Australia, but this was ridiculous! She was sorry now that last night, before going upstairs to bed, she'd spotted that the phone's mouthpiece had 'somehow' managed to extricate itself from the receiver. Although it was no mystery really: Max had obviously been up to his tricks again! Still, if she hadn't spotted it, then Liam wouldn't have been able to interrupt her beauty sleep, would he?

"Liam, this is Sam," she informed him now, her tone curt. "Eve isn't due back until tomorrow – remember? And the reason I took so long to answer is because I was in bed. It's six a.m. here, you know!"

Bloody hell, what was he playing at, ringing up at this hour and waking up the whole house? From where she stood in the hallway, Sam looked up to see a bleary-eyed Lily following her downstairs.

"Sorry," he grunted, sounding somewhat chastened once he realised he wasn't speaking to Eve. "I wasn't too sure of the time difference. I'm back at the hotel – we've just finished a long day of meetings – I just didn't think."

"Obviously." Sam ignored his attempts at an explanation. "I can give you her number in London if you want to talk to her. She's at my place, but of course at this hour I'd imagine she's in bed."

"No – no need," Liam was brusque. "Tomorrow will be a busy day for me so I just wanted to check in and remind her that I'll be due back in Dublin at one thirty on Thursday morning. It's a long flight so tell her not to be late."

Sam was seething. Of all the arrogant, dismissive, condescending . . . how on earth did Eve put up with this?

"One thirty a.m.?" she clarified, wondering if Eve would have to drag a sleeping Max and Lily with her. Of course she would – she could hardly leave them alone in the house, could she?

"Yes – as I said, it's a long flight, so I don't want to be waiting around when I land. And as I won't get a chance to talk to her before then –"

"Might be a good idea to take a taxi then – instead of having Eve and the kids drive all the way up there in the middle of the night," Sam commented archly.

"Look, Sam – just pass on the message, will you? It's all very well for Eve to go gallivanting off to London, but some of us actually have to work for a living. Tell her one thirty, no later, and I'll try and let her know if there's any change."

"Fine." Sam fought to hold her tongue. "Now, will I put you on to Lily? I think she wants to say hi." She winked at her niece who was loitering expectantly in the background, evidently hoping to speak to her father.

"Look, I don't have time for that, OK? I'll see them when I get back."

"OK, I'll tell her that," Sam said, gritting her teeth and wishing she could smack him in the mouth. She smiled at Lily. "Your dad's in a big hurry, but he says he loves you very much, and he'll see you when he gets home."

But Sam could tell by the disappointment in the little girl's eyes that she knew better. Liam ringing up and not bothering to speak to his kids was obviously nothing new. What a gobshite!

"Don't forget to pass on the message to Eve, OK?" Liam said in conclusion

"Yes, sir!" Sam replied, her tone sharp as she said goodbye and promptly hung up on him. She couldn't believe the nerve of this man! There was no goodbye, no thanks, no nothing!

As she watched Lily quietly retreat upstairs to her bedroom, Sam shook her head. Liam Crowley was an unbelievable ignoramus who didn't deserve her sister or the lovely family he'd been blessed with. Not for the first time, she couldn't understand *what* Eve saw in Liam and she was sorry now she'd ever suggested that Eve should think about proposing to him herself should a proposal not be forthcoming. As far as she was concerned her sister was – and probably always had been – way too good for him, and she deserved a much better life than the one she currently had.

The few days here had really been an eye-opener. Eve's life was a continual merry-go-round of housework, childcare and favours for the neighbours, and while her sister seemed to like this kind of life, Sam was certain she was doing way too much.

Not only that but she seemed to get nothing other than grief in return.

Liam was clearly unsupportive and, from what she could make out, totally uninvolved in family life. OK, so as the only breadwinner in the family, he needed to concentrate on his work, but that was no excuse to treat Eve and his kids so dismissively.

Sam sighed. Why on earth Eve wanted to marry him, she'd never know. Not that it seemed to be in the offing anyway. In Sam's opinion, Liam seemed perfectly happy with the status quo and had no intention of proposing. But then again, she thought, maybe she was biased. Maybe Eve and Liam were perfectly happy together and, at the end of the day, one never really knew what went on behind closed doors. For her sister's sake, she'd always tried to give Liam the benefit of the doubt but, for the most part, and particularly because of the man's belligerent attitude, it was very difficult.

Sam yawned again and stretched, her body obviously trying to give her the hint that it was still way too early to be up and about at this hour. She stood in the hallway, in two minds as to whether she should go back to bed for another hour or so or just stay up altogether. A cup of coffee and a few slices of toast would soon set her right, and she could always get a start on giving the house its last going-over with the hoover before . . . Sam paused for second, hearing a faint crackling sound coming from somewhere.

Following the direction the sound was coming from, Sam's gazed eventually rested on the phone, upon which she discovered that she hadn't properly replaced the receiver when she'd hung up on Liam a few minutes before. She picked up the handset and brought it to her ear, realising that the call was still connected and the sound she'd originally thought was crackle was actually a voice on the line.

Surely Liam wasn't still chattering away to his heart's content, thinking she was on the other end, was he? Notwithstanding the fact that Liam rarely chattered, it had been a good five minutes since she'd hung up!

"Hello?" Sam spoke tentatively into the mouthpiece. "Liam, are you still there?"

But on the other end, there was now nothing but static and background noise. "Hello? Hello?" she repeated, louder this time, but still nothing.

Then, there was a slight shuffling sound, and the clinking of what sounded like glasses, or cutlery or something.

Sam shrugged. Evidently Liam had also hung up, not realising that the call was still connected on her end, and was now tucking into room service or something. She was about to hang up – properly this time – when all of sudden, she heard Liam speak again.

"To good wine and good company!" he said, his words followed by the distinctive clink of wineglasses. While his voice was audible, it was distant and Sam deduced that he definitely wasn't speaking into the phone, nor indeed to her.

"To *great* company and a job well done!" replied a female voice – but to Sam's ears, some of the sentence was fragmented. However, the follow-up was crystal clear. "Getting room service like this was a brainwave – I'm so hungry I can hardly speak. I just hope to God they don't ring now looking for something else."

"Well, if they do, they can cool their heels," Liam replied. "See? I've taken the phone off the hook so we won't be interrupted."

Interrupted doing what? Sam thought, her eyes widening. Liam was having a drink in his hotel room in Sydney with some woman – some woman with a husky-sounding voice, with whom he seemed very familiar, and he'd taken the phone off the hook so that they wouldn't be interrupted! At least, he thought he'd taken the phone off the hook and had obviously no idea that the last call he'd made hadn't disconnected properly. What was going on here? Sam thought, trying to picture the scene. Could Liam have a bit on the side in Australia? No, he couldn't have – of course not – the woman was probably just a business colleague; at least, Sam *hoped* she was just a business colleague. Her hands tightened around the receiver as she held it even closer to her ear. She shouldn't do this, of course she shouldn't, but at the same time . . .

"You were great today – as usual," she heard the woman say.

"I think it went well," Liam replied, and again Sam marvelled at how intelligible his words were. The phone must have been very close to where he was sitting – by the bedside probably, she thought, feeling uneasy. So why didn't he realise that he was still connected? Unable to stop herself, and at the same time hoping against hope that she wasn't going to hear anything incriminating, Sam stood in the hallway and continued to eavesdrop.

"Liam, you are way too modest – you had them eating out of the palm of your hand!" The woman laughed.

"Well, it was a bit of a challenge trying to get old Steve Rogers to tear his eyes away from your legs and concentrate on our proposal, but I think I got there in the end." He paused before adding, "Magnificent legs and all that they are."

Well, whoever she was, there was no mistaking the fact that Liam was flirting with her! Sam realised, her eyes narrowing in disapproval.

"You old charmer," the woman giggled, unmistakably delighted by the compliment. "What would the little wife say?"

"I'm not married, Trisha, as you know well," Liam replied tetchily, and at this, Sam breathed sharply inwards.

"Relax – I was only kidding," the woman called Trisha replied, and shortly after that Sam heard a glugging noise that sounded like more wine being poured.

"I know, and I'm sorry – it's just sometimes . . ." Liam sighed audibly.

"Sometimes?"

"Well, things aren't great at home at the moment," he finished.

Sam stiffened, afraid to – but at the same time almost afraid *not to* – listen. "Eve can be . . ."

But maddeningly, there was a brief burst of interference or something, and she was unable to make out the rest of the sentence.

Then Liam spoke again. "She's going to go mad when she finds out I need to be here for Christmas."

And so she bloody well should! Sam thought, horrified upon hearing this. How could he even *think* about going off again so soon and leaving Eve and the kids over the Christmas period? Poor Lily would be inconsolable and she could only imagine how Eve would feel!

"Liam, you and I both know you don't need to be here for Christmas," his companion said wryly and at this Sam's brow furrowed even deeper. What was he playing at? "The deal with the Barossa wineries can easily keep until the New Year."

Liam sighed deeply. "Maybe . . . oh, to be honest, I just don't know any more. Me and Eve . . . there's so much pressure, and we're just not getting along lately. "

"I'm sure it's never easy after such a long time together, and with kids and everything . . ."

To Liam she probably sounded concerned, but to Sam the woman's sympathy came across as cloying and fake.

"I'm sure it's a lot of pressure trying to keep a family going nowadays – especially when she doesn't contribute."

Bitch, bitch, bitch! Sam wanted to scream into the phone and let them know she could hear every damn word they were saying about her precious sister, her sister who had done nothing but love and support that man every step of the way throughout his career, who had raised his kids almost single-handedly while he swanned off all over the world, and who collected him from airports at all hours of the morning without a single complaint!

"I'd imagine you feel a bit trapped by it all," Trisha went on, and Sam decided there and then that if she ever came face to face with the little wagon, she would cheerfully wring her neck. "Saddled with a baby and a mortgage and all that, and at such a young age. You guys were twenty-two when you had your first child, weren't you? So young . . . I know *I* couldn't handle that."

"Well, that wasn't by choice, believe me," Liam said and then laughed bitterly. "We'd only started seeing one other when she got pregnant by accident –"

"By accident? Really?" the other woman interjected in a tone that suggested she thought Eve's pregnancy was anything but an accident.

Sam wanted to strangle her. Of *course* it was by accident! Why else would it have happened and how *dare* that woman even imply that Eve had set out to get pregnant on purpose! At the time, she remembered Eve being worried and upset but most of all terrified that Liam would refuse to stand by her.

Now, in retrospect, Sam thought, maybe Eve would have been better off if he *hadn't* stood by her, given that he'd clearly felt trapped by the entire scenario. Her heart twisted as she thought about how much this would hurt her poor sister – poor Eve, who adored Liam Crowley and who would give anything to become his wife. But by the sounds of things, it seemed unlikely that this was ever going to happen.

And how dare that cow – that complete *stranger* – pass judgement on Liam and Eve's personal life! Who the hell did she think she was?

Although on second thoughts, maybe Trisha wasn't just some stranger. Evidently, the two were close, seeing as they were happily drinking wine and sharing room service together in Liam's hotel room, and he didn't seem to have any problems discussing his private life with her. But exactly how close they were, Sam didn't know, nor did she care to find out. Brimming with anger and satisfied she'd already heard too much, she was just about to replace the receiver when Liam sighed deeply and said something else that caught her attention.

"It was partly my fault too. I should never have been with Eve in the first place. It was a rebound thing really . . . there was someone else . . . but then when Eve told me she was pregnant with Lily . . ."

Sam sat forward again, her heart pounding like a jackhammer. *What?*

"Oh?" Trisha trilled. "So, you had *two* women on the go then? Lucky you!"

"No, it wasn't like that."

To Sam's surprise – and despite the fact that he was thousands of miles away – she could detect genuine regret in Liam's voice and thought that for once he sounded almost human. "She – the other girl – didn't know how I felt, and I couldn't bring myself to tell her."

"Oh, unrequited love – how sweet!"

"Yes, well . . ." Liam sounded sorry he'd said anything. "Anyway, it was a long time ago . . ."

"Well, best not to worry about it," Trisha purred, and Sam could almost picture her patting his knee in a condescending manner, "especially not now – not when we're supposed to be celebrating another fantastic acquisition for Morrison & Co. So, cheer up and drink up!"

Again, there was the sound of glasses clinking.

"You're right," Liam replied, sounding much more like his usual self. "I shouldn't be boring you with my stupid problems – not when we've had such a good sales trip. But it's been a long day, and I'm feeling a bit down."

"Look, don't worry about it. How many times have I bored you senseless about me and Tony?" Trisha said, and Sam's ears pricked up once again. "If this job doesn't work out, either of us could get jobs as marriage counsellors," she added laughing. "Speaking of which, I'd better phone my darling husband too. Mind if I use your phone?"

With that, Sam deftly hung up, afraid that Trisha would realise the line was still open and that they could well have been overheard.

So Trisha *was* married then, and she and Liam were workmates and evidently very good friends. Did Eve know her, she wondered, as she caught sight of the framed photograph of a much younger Eve and Liam hanging on the wall above. Her heart tightened with sadness as she studied Eve's proud and delighted expression as she stood by his side. Liam Crowley was, and always had been, the love of Eve's life, but from what Sam had heard tonight he clearly didn't feel the same way.

Feeling sad and dejected on her sister's behalf, Sam padded barefoot into the kitchen and switched on the kettle and then the radio for some background noise. There was no question of her going back to bed now – how could she after what she'd just heard?

But right then, and for the first time since she'd known him, she was beginning to have mixed feelings about Liam. What was all that about him being interested in someone else when he first met Eve? And if that was the case, why had he gone out with her sister in the first place – never mind let the relationship get serious enough for Eve to become pregnant?

'By accident? Really?'

Reluctantly, Sam recalled the other woman's earlier comments about Eve's pregnancy. At the time, she'd thought them nasty and cruel, but now upon reflection she wondered if there might have been some truth to Trisha's words. It was certainly something that Eve would have subconsciously desired . . . In which case, how could anyone blame the man for feeling hard-done-by?

No! Recalling her sister's reactions at the time Sam couldn't imagine such a scenario. Eve wouldn't have done that; she wouldn't have put herself and their parents through all that worry and disappointment – it just wasn't in her.

God, it was bad enough that Liam had had feelings for someone else when he'd first met her sister, but if he'd never really loved Eve then the idea of settling down and having a baby with her was crazy! Yet Liam had gone ahead not only with that, but also had proceeded with having another child too. Why had he done that? Why had he chosen to make a life with Eve and the kids when he was clearly longing for someone else?

Of course, the fact that Liam hadn't yet proposed seemed to make perfect sense now. Why would he ask Eve to be his wife when he didn't really love her? When he was only with her because of the kids?

And this had to be the reason he was with her, Sam decided now; Liam must feel a huge obligation to Eve because of Lily and Max. But if he was such an upstanding and loving father, why didn't he spend more time with his daughter and baby son, or at least want to speak to them on the bloody telephone? It was all very strange.

But how sad for them both to be trapped in what was clearly a one-sided relationship, she thought, her heart breaking for her sister who worshipped the ground Liam walked on, while he obviously saw her as nothing more than a housekeeper and the mother of his kids.

Sam sighed deeply. She wished now that she had never picked up the phone, had never chosen to listen to that conversation. But she was doubly glad that it had been her and not Eve who had overheard them.

Imagine how devastating it would have been for Eve to hear him admit he was unhappy, never mind listening to him make suggestive comments about some other woman's legs!

But in all fairness, it didn't sound to Sam as though Liam and his business associate *were* having an intimate affair, although she couldn't account for what might happen when they finished their drinks. Still, something told her that Liam wasn't interested in Trisha nor she in him. They were friends and workmates who, what with all the travelling around the world they did together, had no doubt become very close.

Anyway, from what she'd heard, Trisha sounded like a woman who took no nonsense from anyone, least of all from men, so it was unlikely she'd be Liam's type anyway.

No, Liam wasn't interested in women like that. He much preferred the more docile, less assertive woman. A woman like her sister, the mother of his children and the one who loved him to distraction but had no idea that her feelings had, for the most part, been one-sided.

CHAPTER

15. The Last to Know

Early Tuesday morning, the car arrived at Sam's flat at six-thirty a.m. as promised.

Eve was now regretting her burst of confidence the evening before, and her nerves were in shreds. It was nearly fifteen years since she had been interviewed and that was for a job in Spar! What if she was crap? What she opened her mouth and no words came out? But for Sam's sake, she had to do this; she knew how much her sister's career meant to her.

But she still hadn't managed to get Sam on the phone to let her know that she'd be standing in for her, despite repeated attempts to try and contact her once everything had been decided. When Eve tried ringing the house yet again after she'd got off the phone with Gloria, the line had been repeatedly engaged, so Sam had either taken the phone off the hook immediately after her and the kids' return or else she'd spent much of the night chatting on Eve's phone to one of her London friends and running up an enormous phone bill! She hoped everything was OK with the kids but consoled herself with the fact that if anything had happened then of course Sam would have phoned to let her know, wouldn't she? So once again she was fretting over nothing.

"Just relax and enjoy it," Gloria had insisted once she'd eventually convinced Eve to go on the show. "There's nothing at stake here – they'll just be asking you the same questions Sam's been asked a million times before. You'll be great – I know you will."

Eve wished she could be as confident.

But when the car eventually dropped her outside the BBC offices – and she met Gloria, a slip of thing in her late twenties and far from the middle-aged glamour-puss Eve had anticipated – she became swayed by the thrill of it all and temporarily forgot her nerves.

"Eve, hi – how nice to meet you!" Gloria reached for Eve and air-kissed her on not one but *both* cheeks! Having only ever seen such a thing on TV and the like, Eve was taken aback and mightily impressed. "And so good of you to come at such short notice!" The way she was talking you'd swear that Eve had offered to be here, instead of being railroaded into it. "Now, let's take you in to meet Jack. You got a copy of the questions?"

"Yes, thank you." Gloria had couriered a press release and the expected questions the evening before, and Eve had spent much of the night learning the press release by heart and practising her replies.

"Great."

Eve followed the other woman into the huge building and tried to figure out how the hell she'd ended up here. She, Eve, boring old housewife, was actually inside the offices of the BBC! How amazing was this! As they passed through reception she stared at all the photos of the broadcasters she knew so well. Maybe she might catch sight of someone famous while she was here – oh God, what would she do if she bumped into Terry

Wogan in the hallway or something? She'd die!

"Now, before we go upstairs, I might do a little job on your make-up," Gloria said, eyeing Eve somewhat sympathetically. "Let you borrow my eye-shimmer and lip-gloss – you know, something more contemporary than that blue eye-shadow and pink lipstick thing you've got going on."

"OK."

As she followed Gloria to the ladies', Eve wondered why the fixation with her make-up when nobody would be able to see it. But then she realised that if she was supposed to be Sam, she'd have to look the part and, yes, her sister probably wouldn't dream of wearing cheap and cheerful cosmetics!

Make-up job complete, she and Gloria eventually took the elevator to the sixth floor where the two were led to a small reception area apparently outside the radio studio.

They were waiting only a few minutes when Jack Nathan, the supposedly famous broadcaster, popped in to say hello. Not being as up to speed with BBC radio presenters as she was with those from the TV, Eve didn't know the man from Adam and wasn't expecting much. But then, when she caught sight of Jack, she was almost afraid to speak. The man was gorgeous, charismatic and had the most amazing chocolately voice that made her legs turn to jelly.

"Sam, great to meet you finally," he said shaking Eve's hand. "We're big fans of yours in my house: there are three women at home and both my teenage daughters – as well as my wife – adore your column."

"Thanks" Eve barely managed to get the word out, she was so intimidated. "Um, we're great fans of your show too."

"Well, we should get along just fine then," he laughed, and if he found it odd that a newspaper journalist and supposedly seasoned interviewee seemed terrified at the prospect of a radio interview, he didn't show it. "See you in twenty."

"Twenty? Twenty minutes?" Eve exclaimed horrified, when Jack left the room. "I can't go in there!" On the way into the reception area, she'd caught a small glimpse of the headphones, microphones and the various studio paraphernalia, which had terrified her. She'd expected to see some equipment – like the radio studios she'd seen before on TV – but seeing it all like this, so terrifyingly real, was almost more than she could take in.

"Eve, you'll be absolutely fine," Gloria said briskly. "You won't have to do anything but sit there and just speak into the microphone whenever he asks you a question. And Jack's great, isn't he?"

"I suppose." Jack did seem very nice, and she did know exactly how to answer most of the questions so there really was nothing to worry about. But this was a world away from her small house and untidy kitchen, a universe away, and right then, Eve knew which world she preferred.

All too soon, it was time for the interview.

"Today, folks, our special guest is Sam Callaghan, *Daily Mail* columnist and, as author of recent popular novels *Lucky You* and *Lucky Stars*, a lady who seems to have her pulse on what's concerning the female half of the nation!" He smiled at Eve who sat at the other side of his desk, headphones on. "Sam, it's great to have you here."

After a slight pause, she sat forward and spoke into the microphone. "It's great to be here, Jack."

Omigod! Eve thought as a delighted thrill spread through her – she was live on the radio! She, Eve Callaghan, was live on the radio and despite her earlier butterflies she knew she sounded like she was doing it all her life.

CHAPTER

16. The Last to Know

Back in Dublin, Sam turned up the sound on the family radio, her mouth wide open. She couldn't believe this! What the hell was going on? Was that really Eve on the BBC pretending to be her? What did she think she was doing? And how on earth had she ended up . . .

Almost immediately, the thought struck her. Bloody Gloria! Sam knew that Continental's publicist had been trying to up her profile by getting her on one of the national radio stations, but the *Jack Nathan Show* . . .

Sam's mouth set in a thin line. Evidently Gloria *had* secured the interview and, realising Sam wasn't around, had somehow arm-wrestled *Eve* into standing in for her! Gloria could be pretty determined when it came to securing PR and that was putting it mildly. Granted getting a slot on this show was a pretty good coup and Sam would have jumped at the chance to do the interview if she'd been around at the time. But if Gloria had talked Eve into doing it on her behalf, why hadn't either of them told Sam about it – or at least got her permission to let Eve do it instead? Sam hadn't a bloody clue, but she supposed she'd better listen in properly and find out how her own 'interview' was going.

But in spite of her initial annoyance, she now found it rather intriguing and strange hearing the voice of her little sister being broadcast over the airwaves from the BBC studio. In fairness, Eve seemed to be doing just fine, Sam thought, surprised. In fact, she thought, smiling as the interview really began to get going, she was a bit of a natural!

Evidently, Gloria had coached her on the press pack for *Lucky Stars*, and Eve must have spent ages memorising her replies to Jack's questions and was now trotting out the standard answers about the book with considerable ease. Once they'd finished with that, Jack turned his attention to her newspaper columns, where Eve was obviously on much shakier ground but still managed to come across quite well.

"You have a rather strong opinion on Britain's dietary habits, don't you?" Jack asked then, and Sam knew he was referring to her slightly controversial column a couple of weeks back about the increasing reliance of British families on junk and fast food. Healthy eating had always been a subject close to Sam's own heart and she'd commented on how people today were so caught up in trying to save money by buying processed food that they were in danger of neglecting their own health and that of their families.

"Well, we need to take responsibility for our bodies, Jack," Eve answered confidently, having clearly been well-versed on this topic. "We need to treat them like the machines they are – irrespective of cost. Yes, it's important to save money in times like these but, at the same time, we need to consider that doing so could do serious damage to our health. After all, nobody would put petrol into a diesel car – it ruins the mechanism and eventually the engine gives out. Our bodies need premium fuel as much as any machine does, if not more so."

Amusingly, Eve had even managed to affect the mildly scolding tone Sam used when discussing such topics in her column. In fact, she had it down to an absolute T!

"That's all very well, but what about the people who don't have access to premium fuel?" Jack replied, and at this Sam frowned slightly. While he'd started off fairly easygoing, to her practised ears it sounded like there was a clear agenda on the horizon now. Shit, she hoped this wasn't turning into an ambush.

"Premium fuel?" Eve repeated.

"Yes, less well-off people who can't source or can't afford the healthy foods you suggest. Or people who don't have the time to prepare nutritious food every day of the week."

"Why wouldn't somebody have the time to do that?" Eve said, and Sam winced. *Don't fall for it,* she prayed.

"Well, for example, women who go out to work for long hours every day – the kind of ones you write about all the time in your column. By the time they've collected their kids from the minders, and battled through the traffic home, perhaps they don't have the time or the energy to prepare a home-cooked meal from scratch."

"Well," Eve began, her tone sniffy, "if those women are more interested in making money than in their own children's welfare, then perhaps they should think seriously about going out to work at all – *then* they might have the energy to look after their kids properly!"

Sam closed her eyes. *Oh shit!*

"I see." The delight in Jack's tone was almost palpable as he prepared to go right in for the kill. "So you're suggesting that working women aren't providing for their children correctly? That they're not taking proper responsibility for them?"

"Well, obviously they're not!" Eve said, evidently warming to her topic and, worse, forgetting where she was and who she was supposed to be representing. "If making money is more important than your own flesh and blood then . . ."

"Then?" Jack Nathan prompted.

"Then I fear for the health of the nation," she said finally, and Sam wanted to lie down and cry.

"So there you have it, folks," Jack said, wrapping up, his tone now smug and self-satisfied. "Columnist, author and self-professed *friend* of the working mother Sam Callaghan actually believes that they are selfish women who are neglecting their children's health, and that their actions are likely contributing to an already overworked NHS."

Sam dropped her face into her hands.

Oh fuck. Her career was doomed.

*   *   *

Eve was in bits afterwards.

"I don't know what happened!" she wailed down the phone to Sam later that same morning, after a grim-faced Gloria had arranged for her return to the Clapham flat. "I forgot where I was and what I was supposed to be saying!"

"It's OK," Sam soothed, although unfortunately it wasn't OK at all.

Once the press got wind of the interview, which of course they would, then Sam would be hauled over the coals for her supposed U-turn on working mothers and called a hypocrite. And seeing as those same working mothers made up a large proportion of the readership of not only her column, but also her books . . .

But she couldn't tell that to Eve – particularly when her little sister had thought she was doing her a favour by going on the programme in the first place.

"Look, try not to worry about it – these things happen. But if you knew about this interview yesterday, I can't understand why you didn't tell me about it, or at least tell me that you were thinking of standing in for me."

"But I couldn't get you – you were on the phone all last night!" Eve cried. "I tried phoning and phoning – I didn't want to do this in the first place, but Gloria convinced me I had to do it or you might lose your job!"

Well, if Gloria had said that, she and Sam were going to have some serious words when she got back. Talk about putting someone under pressure! Now she could understand why Eve had done this – and indeed why she hadn't been able to tell her about it beforehand – gritting her teeth, she remembered Max's exploits with the telephone.

"She was wrong to put you under pressure like that, Eve, and I'll make sure she knows that when I talk to her."

Sam didn't have long to wait. Almost as soon as she'd put down the phone to Eve, Gloria was next on the line. "OK, we've got some serious damage control to do here, Sam," the publicist said, evidently having located her through Eve. "If I were you, I'd get my ass back to London quick-smart and try and clean up some of the mess this woman's caused."

"Gloria, 'this woman' is my sister, who wouldn't have been anywhere near the studio only for the fact you pushed her into it!" It had been Gloria's insistence that had got them into all this trouble in the first place and Sam was not impressed. "That was a terrible thing to do, throwing her to the lions like that!"

"Well, obviously I didn't think he'd try something like that," Gloria said. "I was under the impression that it would be just a nice run-of-the-mill chat about the new book. I certainly didn't think that he'd try and set you up."

Sam sighed. "Well, he did, and now I have to try and sort it out," she conceded, feeling strangely bereft about returning to life in London at all, let alone to a media storm. "I'll be back as soon as I can – we'll talk then."

"Great. Well, if I were you, I wouldn't bother bringing a book for the journey – I'm sure tomorrow's newspapers will be more than enough to keep you entertained," Gloria said wryly before ringing off, evidently expecting a feeding frenzy.

Maybe she was right. While the UK newspapers – particularly the *Mail's* rivals – would get overexcited about Sam's faux pas, the Irish tabloids would also latch onto it with gusto – as they usually did when one of their own fell from grace, the tall-poppy syndrome very much alive and well in Ireland, particularly these days.

Oh, well, Sam would just have to grin and bear it. With any luck it would all blow over just as quickly as it had begun, although she knew that Continental would be very unhappy with their author's 'performance', particularly as it coincided with the recent publication of the new book. But while she would have to be the one to sort it out, she had every intention of letting her publishers know *exactly* who was to blame. Let Gloria take some of the heat too and blast her anyway for getting them into this mess in the first place!

So much for her sister's stress-free weekend away; poor Eve was hugely distraught about the experience and would be lucky to ever get over it.

"I've made a total mess of things," she'd cried down the phone to Sam earlier. "I don't know what the hell I was thinking sitting in the BBC and gabbing along to Jack Nathan like I've known him all my life. All this bright lights, big city stuff must have gone to my head!"

"Eve, it wasn't your fault – you did really well up until . . . well, up until you started lashing out at working mothers," Sam said wryly. "Where did all that come from anyway?"

"Oh, I don't know! I think it might be because the comparison is forever being thrown in my face! Noreen never stops making me feel bad for being a housewife and making snide remarks about how I don't contribute. OK, so maybe I don't contribute financially, but I do pretty much everything around the house and I'm there for my kids in the way I know she never was! Liam is always going on about how his parents rarely had time for him when he was growing up, yet at the same time he seems to resent the fact that I'm always there for ours! Sometimes I feel like I just can't win!"

Sam could understand her frustration – of course she could – but she sorely wished that Eve had chosen a different time to vent these frustrations instead of broadcasting them to a large portion of the population of the UK!

"I know that," she said. "I got a small preview of what you do over the weekend, even though it was probably only a fraction of it, but I do admire you very much. But just because Liam's mother is a snooty wagon doesn't mean that you should put all working mothers in the same category. Everyone's just trying their best, Eve. If anything, my stint over here has helped me realise that."

"I know," Eve said dolefully. "He just hit a nerve, that's all. And now I've ruined everything."

"Look, you didn't know any better and you walked into a trap. Jack was being very deliberate in his intentions to trip you up. Granted, if it had been me, I would have spotted that – anyone with media experience would – but you had no such experience so don't be too hard on yourself."

"I know, but he seemed so nice! I can't believe he'd set me *or* you up like that!"

"That's his job," Sam sighed, "and unfortunately that kind of show thrives on controversy. But look, please stop blaming yourself and don't forget you were lured there under false pretences, so the real person to blame for this is Gloria Jones."

"I know, but she was so persuasive, and when I met her she was so nice. They were *all* so nice!"

Eve couldn't be consoled and eventually Sam decided to change the subject.

"Well, look, everything's fine here and the kids are still in great form. They miss you, though."

"I miss them too," she replied plaintively. "The break was brilliant up to today, but now I just can't wait to get home. I don't know how you do it, Sam. A glamorous life is all very well but this kind of thing can wear you down."

Tell me about it, Sam said to herself and, oddly, right at that moment, she envied her sister's normal, relatively staid life. And while she certainly didn't envy her sister's choice of partner, she thought with a grimace, remembering the conversation she'd overheard earlier, for all his faults Eve really loved Liam and was looking forward to seeing him. As opposed to how Sam felt now about seeing Derek again.

"Oh, while I think of it, Liam phoned earlier," she said, reluctant to think about Derek for the moment.

"Did he?" Eve sounded thrilled and again, by contrast, Sam realised that over the last few days she hadn't felt any great desire to hear from Derek. That wasn't normal, was it? Not if he really meant as much to her as she'd thought? "It's unusual for him to phone from Australia what with the time difference and everything," Eve went on. "Is he OK? Was he asking for me?"

With the state she was in just then, Sam didn't have the heart to tell her sister that Liam had phoned not for a chat, but to demand a lift home. "He said he hoped you were enjoying yourself and he was looking forward to seeing you when he gets back on Thursday morning."

"Oh, I'd almost forgotten about that. That flight comes in really early, doesn't it?" The way she said it, Eve sounded like a downtrodden holiday rep instead of Liam's loving partner.

"Yes, he mentioned it was one thirty a.m. or something?"

"Yep – the graveyard shift for me and the kids."

"That's tough on them, Eve – maybe Liam should just get a taxi."

"Are you mad? Why would he spend good money on a taxi when I've got a perfectly good car at home?"

The way she said it made Sam suspect that these weren't Eve's words at all but a well-worn repetition of Liam's. Evidently, he made a habit of making her sister jump to his every beck and call. Sam shook her head. Yet, despite everything she'd learned about Liam recently, she strongly felt it wasn't her place to interfere.

"Look, I'd better let you go," she said eventually. "Try not to worry about this morning. I'll try and sort it all out in my next column – blame it all on PMT or something," she added jokingly.

"I don't know what I was thinking, Sam. I really don't. Who the hell did I think I was kidding pretending I could be you?"

"As I said, don't worry about it, and we'll talk again when you come home tomorrow. In the meantime, just relax and focus on putting it out of your mind for now, OK?"

"OK," Eve sniffed, before saying goodbye and hanging up the phone.

Sam tried to concentrate on how she was going to get herself out of this mess.

But as it was still only eight thirty, first she had to concentrate on making the kids' breakfast and getting Lily ready in time for school.

It was strange really, she thought, going upstairs to tend to Max, how easy it was to fill the day. She'd always assumed that, because her sister didn't work, she had buckets of time to go shopping, watch TV, read a book or do whatever she pleased, but in reality it was amazing how little free time there actually was. While she was – contrary to the impression Eve gave on the radio this morning – fully supportive of working mothers, her short stint here had also given her a new respect for stay-at-home mothers, and much to her surprise she found that she quite enjoyed the simple pleasures of cooking for the kids or getting the house cleaned from top to bottom.

It was such a massive difference to the whirlwind that was her life in London – the lunches, dinner parties and social life that went hand in hand with her job and her life with Derek. It was the kind of life that Sam had always thought she wanted but which she now realised seemed quite shallow and unimportant in the scheme of things. And it had been useful to hold a mirror up to her own life in comparison to Eve's, a life she'd always thought rather provincial and irrelevant.

But Eve's role was far from irrelevant. Her children were great: Lily was a gorgeous little thing, and while Max was (to put it mildly) a bit of a handful, there was something hugely fulfilling in taking care of them and being depended upon for their every need.

Granted, Sam had more than likely experienced the children at their easiest and, unlike Eve, didn't have to deal with their real foibles, illnesses or bad behaviour, but unusually for her she'd lately started to think seriously about what it might be like to have a child of her own.

Derek would be thrilled to think that her few days in Ireland had had such an effect on her, she thought wryly. He'd be absolutely shocked to learn that she was now seriously considering giving up her column in the *Mail* (although after Eve's performance earlier she might no longer have that choice) and had started to consider maybe writing a book every two years instead of one. After all, it wasn't all that long ago he'd been urging her to do exactly that, wasn't it?

But the truth was that she'd been a little bit at sea about things for a while. Yes, she'd enjoyed the glamorous side of her career and enjoyed the success and recognition that came in hand in hand with being a successful columnist, but at the same time she wasn't at all happy with her editor's growing influence on her writing and the tone he preferred her to take. It was the kind of sensationalist view that had got Eve in trouble only that morning and would surely do no favours for her career in the long run.

Maybe it was time to think seriously about whether or not she was prepared to continue in this vein and concentrate more on what direction she truly wanted her life to take. It was what Derek had been trying to convince her of all along, but the ironic thing was that, despite her growing concerns about her future, she was still finding it more difficult than ever to see Derek as part of that future. And, being honest, it hadn't just been a few days of housework and childminding that had caused her to start rethinking her life in this manner, had it? If she was being truly honest with herself, hadn't many of these second thoughts stemmed from something else entirely? Or more exactly, from *someone* else?

Sam now realised deep down that her apparent swift reassessment of her life and her reluctance to marry Derek had considerably less to do with her stint here at Eve's house and a lot more to do with the way she'd fallen so utterly for Ronan Fraser. How could she possibly think about marrying Derek when another man could capture her attention so easily? If she could feel so strongly about someone who might never even reciprocate? This had to tell her all she needed to know about her true feelings for Derek, didn't it?

In that case, she should be fair to Derek and let him know once and for all that, although she loved him, there was now no realistic chance of a future for the two of them. How could there be when she was feeling like this? And in all honesty, he deserved better, deserved someone who loved him completely and absolutely and whose head couldn't be turned as easily as hers had. She sighed, bewildered by it all. Who would have thought that a simple weekend could have changed so much for her? Meeting Ronan had really pulled the rug from under everything she'd thought she knew, everything she thought she wanted. And the frustrating thing was that, despite his immense influence on her, the man barely knew she existed. No, he seemed totally fixated – and rightly so – on the lovely Anna, his childhood-sweetheart fiancée. How could she compete with that? And more importantly, did she intend to? Sam wasn't sure. All she knew was that ever since she'd first laid eyes upon him, Ronan Fraser had sent her life and thoughts into utter disarray.

CHAPTER

17. The Last to Know

The following afternoon, Eve's heart leapt for joy as Dun Laoghaire harbour finally came into view. Although she'd enjoyed the trip to London at the beginning, she was now massively relieved to be back. What was she thinking, taking off like that and trying on Sam's life for size? It was crazy! And while it was OK while it lasted, she now knew for certain that she truly belonged at home with her children – and with Liam.

While in London, Eve had lots of time to think about her life and where it was going. And as a result, she had made a decision – a very big decision. Sam had put the idea in her head originally, and since she'd had a chance to think properly about it there was really no reason why not.

The ferry eventually reached land and she felt a shiver of excitement as she passed through the passenger terminal and onwards towards home.

Strangely, she felt like a changed woman. OK, so she had really made a mess of things for poor Sam and was absolutely mortified about that, but her sister was pretty convinced she could sort things out. She'd been such a fool for letting your woman Gloria force her into doing something like that in the first place, let alone allowing herself to lose the rag on national radio! God only knew what kind of trouble Sam would have to face now, but with any luck her sister would be able to work it out – despite her own best efforts, she thought grimacing. But if one good thing had come out of that mistake it was the fact that her radio outburst had really made her think deeply about her own life and her own frustrations. And Eve knew that most of these frustrations had been caused by one thing and one thing only – the lack of a ring on her finger.

All too soon, she was back at her house and, more importantly, back in the bosom of her precious family.

"Sam, I'm so sorry again that I made such a mess of things," she insisted almost as soon as she was in the door.

"Don't be silly – we'll sort it out," Sam replied, waving away her apologies. "I'm just glad you enjoyed the break – most of it anyway." She gave Eve a rueful smile. "How was the ferry trip home?"

"Fine – not too bumpy, luckily enough."

"I still don't know why you won't fly, Eve – the journey takes only a fraction of the time and –"

"I prefer the ferry, really," Eve insisted, picking up Max and cuddling him close to her. God, it felt great to be back! "But I did enjoy the break – up to a point," she added wryly, "and thanks for looking after things here. Did you miss Mummy?" she asked Max, who was busy trying to pull the buttons off her shirt.

"Of course they did," Sam supplied, flashing a meaningful look at Lily, who was helping her aunt gather her things together in preparation for her flight home later that evening

"We missed you loads, Mum," Lily piped up dutifully. "It's great to have you back."

"Well, Dad will be back soon too, and then we'll be a family again. Sam, did you hear anything more from Liam afterwards?"

"Not since the call I told you about," her sister replied stiffly, and Eve suspected that her sister still disapproved of her having to drive to the airport in the early hours of the following morning to collect Liam. While normally she too disliked getting up at that hour, this time would be different.

For the rest of the afternoon, the sisters chatted and caught up on their respective weekends, until eventually it was time for Sam to leave.

Then, at around five p.m, they heard a car-horn beep outside.

"It's your taxi, Auntie Sam," said Lily, waving out the window at the driver.

Eve's eyes widened. "You ordered a taxi? I thought I was taking you to the airport."

"Oh no – I wouldn't dream of putting you out," Sam insisted, "especially when you have to go all the way out there again later to pick up Liam. Anyway, I'd better go." She picked up her bags and hurried straight to the front door, almost as if she couldn't wait to leave.

Oh well, Eve thought, slightly taken aback at her sister's sudden haste to get away, Sam was probably just worried about having to face her publishers when she got back to London. Thanks to her, the poor thing had a lot of explaining to do!

"Bye, Auntie Sam – we'll miss you!" Lily cried in the hallway and, much to Eve's surprise, gave her aunt a warm hug. Hmm, she didn't make that much of a fuss of *her* when she was leaving!

"I'll miss you too, pet." Sam returned the hug. "You'll have to come to London and visit me soon."

Lily's eyes lit up. "I will!"

"Bye, Eve, and thanks for everything," Sam said embracing her sister in turn. "I'll see you again soon."

"You too – hopefully next time we'll get to spend some more time together!"

"Definitely." Sam picked up her bags and went out front to where her taxi was waiting.

"Oh!" Eve said, instantly recognising the car. "I didn't realise it was Ronan's taxi."

"He offered to drop me back when I was over there on Sunday," Sam said, somewhat apologetically. "He was the one who brought me from the airport the other day – although I didn't know it at the time."

"Really?" Eve laughed at the coincidence and waved across at Ronan, who was waiting patiently in the driver's seat for his passenger. "Look after her now, won't you?" she called to him, as Sam stowed her bag and joined him in the front of the car. And it was strange but as Eve went inside and closed the door behind her, she reflected that Sam looked almost embarrassed by the comment.

* * *

Early Thursday morning as planned, Eve and the kids collected Liam from the airport. Lily was tired and narky as she sat in the back beside Max, but luckily their youngest stayed asleep for most of the journey.

Upon arrival, Liam was exhausted after his mammoth flight but in reasonably good form considering the hour. Still, because the kids were trying to sleep, he and Eve decided to keep conversation to a minimum on the way home.

Then, much later that day, once Liam had had sufficient time to sleep off the jetlag, Eve – with the help of Lily and Max – decided to spring her surprise.

"Liam, honey – your tea and toast is ready!" she called upstairs to him, before coming back into the kitchen, her heart racing in anticipation. Then, eyes twinkling, she winked at Lily.

"Is he up?" her daughter asked from where she sat at the kitchen table.

"I think so," Eve whispered. "Now, say nothing when he comes downstairs, sure you won't?"

Lily giggled conspiratorially and put a hand over her mouth. "I can't wait! This is a great idea, Mum!"

For the first time since she'd made the decision and put her plan into action, Eve began to feel a tiny flutter of nerves. But there was no need – everything would be fine, wouldn't it?

A few minutes later, Liam appeared, freshly showered and over the worst of his jetlag. And when he entered the kitchen and saw the scene before him, his eyes widened in surprise.

"What the . . .? What's all this?" he said, his cheeks colouring as he caught sight of the huge banner hanging on the kitchen wall directly across from him.

Lily clapped her hands together and grinned. "What do you think, Dad?" she giggled.

Max sat in his high chair, oblivious to what was actually happening, but sensing the excitement clapped his hands together and grinned a toothless grin.

Eve stared expectantly at Liam – all of sudden wondering if she'd made a big mistake.

A very big mistake.

"What do I . . .? I don't know what to say . . ." Liam looked from Eve to the children and back again to the huge banner on the kitchen wall that read:

'Daddy, we love you – will you marry us? Love, Eve, Lily and Max'

"Say yes, Dad!" Lily urged, her little face shining with expectation. "Say yes so that we can be a real family!"

Eve coloured. "You don't have to decide now," she said

quickly, realising that she might have seriously miscalculated the entire situation. It had all seemed like such a good idea when she thought about it on the ferry back from London, back when she'd been full of confidence that he would say yes. But now –

"OK," Liam said quietly, and her head snapped up.

"Yay!" Lily cried, getting up from her chair and racing across to hug her father.

"What?" Eve asked, her voice barely a whisper. "What did you say?"

"I said yes, Eve." Liam's voice was gentle. "I will marry you – all of you."

CHAPTER

18. The Last to Know

"We don't have to do this if you don't want to."

Anna looked away from her reflection in the full-length mirror to where Ronan was sitting on the bed.

"Yes, we do – Lauren is really looking forward to it." Fastening the buttons of her shirt, she sighed. "I know Denis can be a pain, but I don't want to let her down. Anyway, it might be good fun."

Ronan made a face. "A bunch of fellas prancing around on a stage? Not my idea of fun."

Anna smiled indulgently. It was Friday night, and Lauren and Denis had arranged tickets for the four of them to see a play at the Abbey Theatre. As she and Ronan hadn't been out with the happy couple since their engagement, Anna didn't want to let her friend down. But as Lauren had never been a theatre buff, Anna suspected that the evening's choice of entertainment had been mostly instigated by Denis. It wouldn't have been Anna's first choice, and she knew it certainly wasn't Ronan's, but she supposed there was no harm in trying something different.

Unfortunately Ronan didn't share her enthusiasm.

"All right, we know the only theatres you're interested in are the ones with Coke, popcorn and Harrison Ford," she joked, bowing her head in order to fasten the gold chain that Ronan had given her last Christmas. She looked up. "But drama can be –"

Anna stopped short, as suddenly the room began to spin and white stars danced in front of her eyes. Then, quickly reaching for the edge of the dresser to try and support herself, she bent her head and prayed for the queasiness to subside.

"Hey, what's up with you?" Ronan leapt up from the bed, his voice full of concern. Putting an arm around her, he led her carefully towards the bed. "Here, sit down."

"I'm fine – I just got a bit of a weakness," Anna said, her head still swimming. "I just lifted up my head too quickly . . ."

Blast it, blast it, the last thing she needed was for Ronan to notice something and perhaps put two and two together.

"You didn't eat much at lunchtime either, did you, and that's not like you. Are you sure you're not coming down with something, hon?"

Anna's stomach flipped. "No, I'm fine, seriously."

"Maybe we should give tonight a miss after all," Ronan went on. "We can phone Lauren and tell her you're just not up to it. She'll understand."

"No, honestly, Ronan, I'm fine – it was just a rush of blood to the head." Her nausea having dissipated, Anna looked up and managed a watery smile. "Honestly."

"Well, the colour seems to be back in your cheeks, thank God," he said, lightly touching her face. "You were as white as a sheet just then."

Anna stood up and made a great show of continuing to get ready, even though her stomach was still doing cartwheels. "See, I'm fine. Now let's get going. We don't want to keep them waiting. "

"Well, as long as you're sure," Ronan acquiesced eventually. "You know how much I've been looking forward to this thing, so it really would be a shame to miss it." His eyes twinkled and, as his tone was once again light-hearted, Anna knew she'd got away with it.

This time.

They were meeting Lauren and Denis for a drink before the show started in some wine-bar that Anna had never set foot in before but knew by reputation as being trendy and highly pretentious. Evidently another of Denis's choices, she thought wryly as she and Ronan went inside.

For a supposed 'place to be seen', the bar was surprisingly empty, and they quickly realised that the other couple hadn't yet arrived.

"What'll you have?" Ronan asked, as they headed towards the bar. "One of these fancy-looking cocktails maybe?" He glanced through the menu and, eyes widening at the cost of the drinks, quickly put it back down on the bar. "Then again, maybe not."

"I think I'll just have a mineral water, thanks." Anna tried to sound offhand.

"What? Are you *sure* you're feeling all right?"

She grimaced. "Just to start off with – my stomach is still a little queasy. Don't worry," she added when he looked over-concerned, and she thought perhaps a little suspicious, "I'll be back to my usual later. Anyway, I thought you'd be pleased given the prices in this place." She punched him jokingly on the arm, hoping to keep things light-hearted and willing him to not to read too much into it. In truth, she should have just ordered her usual vodka and Coke and sipped it slowly, instead of drawing attention to herself like this.

"You're right – I should be thanking my lucky stars I have a nice, sensible, down-to-earth fiancée like you instead of one of those wine-swigging party-girl types."

Grinning, he turned back to the bar, and yet again Anna silently thanked God he'd left it alone. She'd have to be more careful though. A few more incidents like the weakness earlier, and he'd start to suspect something. And Anna didn't want that, not until she'd had a chance herself to work out what she was going to do. She just needed a little more time.

"What do you mean you don't serve Guinness?" Ronan's disbelieving tones brought Anna's attention right back to the present. "What kind of Irish pub doesn't serve Guinness?"

"Sir, this isn't an Irish pub *per se*," the barman explained, in a distinctly non-Irish accent but with a tinge that suggested he had spent a long time trying to get rid of it. "We're an American-themed wine and cocktail bar so –"

"Well, they serve Guinness in New York too and that's on the other side of the bleedin' Atlantic!" Ronan was horrified. "And even if they don't, at least they have a decent excuse, whereas this place is only a couple of yards from St James's Gate!" He turned and looked at Anna in disbelief. "Can you believe this?"

"That's terrible." She bit her lip, trying to hide her amusement. Very little tended to faze Ronan, but tell the man he couldn't have his pint of plain and you saw a *very* different side to him.

"Sir, I'm sorry but I'm sure you'll find a suitable alternative on our menu." The barman was unwilling to get into the specifics of how close the pub actually was to the Guinness brewery.

"Right, I'm sure a watery raspberry sherbet will taste just as good as the black stuff!" Ronan said sardonically, sliding away the menu and shaking his head in disgust. "All right then, make that two glasses of water. Or is that too bloody Irish for you too?"

"Our water comes from France, sir. Would you like sparkling, still or flavoured?"

At this, Ronan's mouth tightened, and Anna knew he was now

very close to exploding. She bit back another smile.

"Hey, guys – don't tell me you've started without us!" Just then, as if out of nowhere, Denis and Lauren appeared beside them at the bar. "How's it going, buddy?" Denis said, slapping Ronan hard on the back, ensuring the other man's mouth tightened even further.

"Sorry we're late, Anna – I hope you weren't waiting on us too long," said Lauren apologetically, while Denis beckoned the barman forward. "Hey, mate, hit me and my friend here with a couple of bottles of Bud, will you?" he swaggered. "And some Buck's Fizz for the girls."

"Certainly, sir." Evidently much more comfortable with Denis Masterson's class of patron, the barman dutifully went to prepare the drinks.

"Great spot, isn't it?" Turning his back to the bar, Denis puffed out his chest and scanned the room around him. "Best bar in the city, I reckon."

"Bleedin' fantastic," Ronan replied through gritted teeth.

* * *

Despite the actors' best efforts, the play was a complete and utter bore, and by the end of the first act, Anna was sorry she'd insisted on dragging Ronan along. Poor thing – it was bad enough his having to do without his precious pint, let alone sit through hours of this!

"I promise I'll make it up to you," she said, accompanying him outside at the interval for a cigarette and a breath of fresh air. Things *must* be bad, as it had been over three years since he'd had one!

"It's like pulling teeth, Anna," he said, dragging hard on his cigarette. "I mean, why can't they just get to the bloody point instead of all this moaning and groaning about nothing. I swear to God, I'll never complain about a half hour of *EastEnders* again. Compared to this depressing business, it's a comedy!"

Anna stifled a guffaw.

"Yeah, yeah," he said, "have a good laugh while you can. You'll be laughing on the other side of your face when I drag you over to White Hart Lane next time."

She quickly straightened her expression. "No way, nobody deserves that!"

Ronan, a lifelong Tottenham Hotspurs fan, was a season-ticket holder at the team's home ground, and was always trying to get her to accompany him to one of the many games he attended. But to Anna, watching football was akin to watching paint dry, and no matter how much her fiancé pleaded its merits, she just couldn't be turned.

"Look, let's just make our excuses to the other two and head home," she said. "I'll tell Lauren I'm not feeling well. She was wondering anyway why I didn't finish my drink earlier so –"

"I'm not surprised – God knows what kind of chemicals they put in those cocktails. They couldn't be good for you. And never mind that poor excuse for a drink that your man bought me . . ."

"Is it safe to say you won't be swapping good old Irish Guinness for American beer in the future, then?"

He gave her a lopsided grin and stubbed out his cigarette on the ground. "You can bet your life on it."

"Hello, Anna."

Anna glanced up quickly at the speaker, a man who had just come out of the theatre doors and was now standing right alongside them. And when she realised who that man was, her stomach sank to her toes. *Oh, no!*

"Hello, how are you?" she stammered, thinking that he was the very last person she'd expected to see. Or wanted to.

"Good, thanks – are you here for the play?" he enquired casually, and Anna's gaze bored onto his, hoping against hope that he'd read the warning in her eyes. "It's terrific, isn't it?"

"Brilliant," Ronan interjected whole-heartedly, certain the other man was trying to be funny. "I really can't wait to get back in there and find out what happens. With any luck they'll put your man out of his misery sooner rather than later."

Then both men regarded each other in silence, before Ronan glanced pointedly at Anna, apparently waiting for an introduction.

But Anna, still rooted to the ground by confusion and nerves, couldn't seem to find the words.

In the end, the other man beat her to it. "I'm Chris," he said, extending his hand towards Ronan. "How are you doing?"

"Oh, I'm sorry." Anna finally snapped out of her stupor. "This is Ronan," she said, before adding rather pointedly, "my fiancé."

"Very pleased to meet you, Ronan," Chris replied with a warm smile.

Then another more strained silence, as Ronan naturally waited for Anna to explain who the other man was and how she knew him.

"I'm a friend of a friend," Chris supplied again, glancing sideways at Anna who, having realised she'd been holding her breath, finally allowed herself to exhale.

"Yes," she said, urging herself to snap out of it. She was worrying for nothing – of *course* he wouldn't say anything. It wasn't his way – not to mention that it would be wholly inappropriate for him to do so, especially here. But of all the places to bump into him . . . Then again, this was exactly the kind of place he'd frequent, wasn't it? Somewhere artistic and upmarket – generally the last place you'd find someone like her and Ronan. Oh, blast Denis Masterson for dragging them along to the theatre tonight! And blast Ronan for coming outside for a cigarette. If they'd stayed indoors they might never have bumped into Chris, and Anna wouldn't be experiencing the panic she was now.

Chris and Ronan were chatting away and bemoaning the fact that they had to go outside for a smoke in the first place – as smoking wasn't allowed inside the theatre.

"They'll be banning it everywhere next," Ronan said. "This country's going to the dogs anyway and soon we'll have no pleasure doing anything. And as for the pubs, you should have seen the dump we were in tonight – a joke of a place, it was, wasn't it, Anna?" He then went on to recount to Chris the tale of the elusive pint of Guinness, much to the other man's interest and, Anna thought, amusement. "If that's the way things are going, we're in serious trouble," Ronan finished, with a weary shake of his head.

"Things aren't looking too good all the same," Chris said, nodding in agreement. Then he looked at his watch. "I suppose we'd better head back inside – the next act will be starting soon." His gaze rested heavily on Anna, who was doing her best not to let her eyes meet his. "Good seeing you – and Ronan, again, really nice to meet you."

"You too." Ronan stubbed out his second cigarette of the evening, as the other man went back into the building.

But, rubbish play or otherwise, the last thing Anna wanted to do now was go back in there. "Ro, I really think we should just head away," she said. "We have all our things with us, and I'll just phone Lauren in the morning – tell her I went back in to say goodbye but couldn't find her." Her voice sounded more insistent than she'd intended but Ronan, who was only too happy for an excuse to leave, didn't seem to notice.

"Suits me," he said, putting his hands in the pockets of his overcoat. "You're sure you don't want to let her know before you go?"

"I'm positive." At that stage, Anna just wanted to get away from the theatre, away from anywhere there was a risk they might bump into Chris again.

As the two of them walked side-by-side towards the nearest bus stop, Ronan looked sideways at her. "That Chris fellow seemed nice enough," he said.

Anna's body went rigid. "I suppose so," she replied, keeping her tone light.

"A friend of a friend, he said?"

She nodded. "Yes."

"Which friend?"

"What?"

"Which friend is he a friend of? Is it someone from the school, or one of the girls – I mean, would I know them?" His tone seemed as casual and carefree as ever, but Anna was almost afraid to answer.

"Oh – just someone who has something to do with the school, one of the inspectors. Not even a friend, just an acquaintance really. To be honest, I don't know him that well at all. I've only met him once or twice so, to tell you the truth, I'm surprised he even recognised me."

"Maybe he fancies you," Ronan teased, putting an arm around Anna and drawing her closer to him as they approached the bus stop. "Maybe the real reason he was being so friendly back there was because he wanted to inveigle his way into your affections."

"Don't be so silly, Ronan!" Anna's heart was galloping a mile a second. "As I already told you – I hardly know the man."

CHAPTER 22

"Are you still reading that?" Brooke looked up to see Will smiling indulgently at her from the doorway of her house. The door was open, as it always was in the cosy two-bed cottage she'd shared with her mum, and she'd been so busy trying to figure out what Anna was up to in *The Last to Know* that she hadn't heard him approach.

"Hi," she said, quickly putting the pages aside, before checking the clock on the mantelpiece. "I didn't realise the time."

"You've had your nose stuck in those pages since before I went away," he teased, reaching down to kiss her. "Must be a good one."

"It is," she said truthfully.

The story had really grabbed her now, and she was dying to find out what Anna was trying to hide and indeed how poor Eve would fare, now that she'd asked the horrible Liam to marry her. But she wasn't going to think about that now – not when one of her favourite people in the world was back from his latest work trip and eager to spend time with her.

Brooke got up and put her arms around him.

"How was Hong Kong?" she asked, just as eager to hear his reply.

Last weekend, he'd told her he was going on a week-long jaunt to Hong Kong to hammer out the details of some Chinese export deal the company were involved in. Apparently he was staying in the Intercontinental in Kowloon, but when Brooke had phoned the hotel late one evening to ask him something trivial – but necessary – the receptionist had no record of him or anyone from his company staying there.

Will smiled tiredly. "Great, apart from the fact that they fucked up our hotel booking."

Brooke breathed an inward sigh of relief.

It wasn't that she didn't trust him; she did, but when he was away so often it was difficult not to worry, especially when this particular time he hadn't been where he'd said he would. Or maybe this manuscript was getting to her more than she'd thought. With all this underhand business of Liam's, she was now starting to read things into her own relationship!

"We ended up in some dive on the island, which it made it twice as difficult to get around and ..." His sentence trailed off. "Never mind, you don't need to hear my work problems. They'll just bore you to tears. So anyway, how are you? Did you miss me?"

"Of course I did," Brooke said, drawing him closer. "I always miss you when you go away – you know that."

He tensed slightly. "Well, then, you're probably not going to like what I have to say next."

Brooke stepped backwards, her face falling. "What? Don't tell me you're cancelling on me again like you cancelled our trip at Christmas?"

OK, so she hadn't exactly been over the moon at the prospect of spending Christmas in Cairns, but at least she would be spending it with Will instead of at home on her own and feeling sad about the fact that this year her mother wasn't around.

At least, she'd *thought* she'd be spending it with Will, but as it turned out he'd changed his mind at the last minute and decided to go on a lad's holiday to Kuta with his mates. Brooke had been furious and more than a little hurt that he'd chosen to go off to Bali without her and had phoned her only once that week on Christmas Day. Granted, the neighbours had rallied round and, knowing better than anyone that it would be a tough day for her, Bev had renewed her invitation for Brooke to spend Christmas Day with her and her family. It had been good fun and later that afternoon she'd taken out her board and met up with some of her surfing friends on Manly beach. But nothing could take away from the disappointment she'd felt knowing that Will had blown her off. What was going on with them? Why, at twenty-eight years of age – a good three years older than she was – did he have to behave like such an immature rat-bag sometimes? No wonder she identified with Eve so much in that story!

"I'm sorry, Brooke," he was saying now. "There's a much longer trip coming up soon that'll clash with that work thing you wanted me to go to next week. They want me to go back to Europe – this time for another three weeks."

"But why are you the one who always has to go? Aren't there other people in the company that can handle this?" She tried not to sound too whiny and clingy, but she couldn't help it. Following a bumper sales year for the publishing company, Horizon had organised a celebratory staff party in Icebergs in Bondi – an ultra-trendy bar/restaurant situated on the cliffs with magnificent views over the beach – for the following weekend. Spouses and partners were invited, and Brooke really wanted Will to go, especially as they rarely socialised with her friends and spent most of their time with his. And going to Icebergs was a huge treat; the food was great and the place was one of the hippest spots in Sydney, unlike a lot of the more low-key places she and Will usually frequented together. For some reason, he disliked going out in the city, preferring instead to go for nights out locally in Manly. But then again, the Irish loved their local pubs, didn't they, and unlike most of her publishing colleagues Will wasn't at all into the 'hip and happening' Sydney bar scene. But while she usually tried to be easygoing where Will was concerned, being the patient accepting girlfriend up to now hadn't got her very far.

Will's handsome face was impassive. "It has to be me. I've been negotiating this deal from the very beginning, and if I don't do it, then the whole thing could fall through. I really thought you'd understand."

Brooke sighed, and she slumped back down on the couch. "Fine."

"Ah, come on, Brooke, don't be like that!"

"Well, how do you expect me to be? I never see you any more. You're always out of the country! Anyone would think you . . ." She shook her head, willing the idea out of her mind. Will cared about her; he wouldn't do anything to deceive her.

Would he?

Oh, this was crazy, Brooke thought. That story really was putting ideas in her head, what with all these secrets the characters seemed to be keeping from one another!

"I'm sorry," she said to Will then. "I don't know what's wrong with me lately. Don't mind me – of course you should go on this Europe trip."

He sat down beside her and pulled her close to him. "I'll make it up to you when I come back, I promise," he said. Then, in an attempt to cheer her up, he started to tickle her mercilessly.

Brooke screamed with laughter and wriggled away from him. Oh, she shouldn't be so hard on him, really. Look at them now, getting on like a house on fire. So what if he put a lot of effort into his professional life? She did too, didn't she? And really, wouldn't it be much worse if Will were a lazy gallah who didn't give a damn about anyone but himself?

Which he clearly wasn't, Brooke thought happily as she wrapped her arms around him and kissed him urgently on the lips.

*   *   *

"I don't think I can take this any longer!"

Thousands of miles away in Dublin, the senders of *The Last to Know* were losing patience. "It's been weeks – surely she must have finished it by now! And if she has, why hasn't she got in touch? Why hasn't she emailed? She has the address, doesn't she?"

"Relax – I'm sure we'll hear from her soon," the author said, trying to soothe her companion, although she too was concerned that Brooke Reynolds hadn't yet been in touch. While these things did take time, she now worried that they might have played this all wrong.

Was there a chance that she hadn't made things clear enough in the story – clear enough for Brooke to make the connection?

OK, so they had always known that this thing with the manuscript was a very long shot and could very well fall flat, yet it seemed the only realistic way of achieving their objective. Especially when they'd come up with a foolproof way of getting it to her. And when composing the story, she'd been hoping to get the message across without alerting the other woman to too much too soon. That had been very important.

But had she been *too* subtle in revealing things, so subtle that Brooke – no doubt used to reading much more imaginative attempts at fiction – had overlooked the hidden clues and understated pointers altogether? Although when it came to the ending, she'd really had no choice but to let subtlety go right out the window . . .

But what if Brooke hadn't bothered reading the story to the end and had become bored halfway through? That was a possibility, certainly, and it wouldn't have been the first time an editor had changed her mind about a manuscript's potential.

Yes, trying to maintain the momentum mid-way had been rather tricky, but what else could she do? She had to try and keep it all as realistic as possible, and while people often said that truth was stranger than fiction, in this case, maybe the truth had been too confusing – or even worse, too improbable, for the Australian woman. If not, they'd have little choice but to fall back on Plan B, which she for one didn't relish.

No, this wasn't worth thinking about; Brooke simply had to read to the end. Otherwise, this would have all been for nothing.

But she couldn't share these doubts with her companion, who was tense and anxious enough as it was.

"I mean, if she has read it to the end, why hasn't she said anything?" The aforementioned was now pacing the room, face drawn and features agitated. "Why doesn't she want to know more? I know *I* would."

"Look, as I said, she might not have finished it yet," the author appeased. "Chances are she's up to her eyes at work and hasn't got back to it yet."

Or horror of horrors, maybe she'd passed it onto someone else – one of Horizon's readers maybe, in which case all was lost, as the story had been written for Brooke, and Brooke alone. No one else would be able to spot the parallels or realise their significance.

She sighed, deciding that her companion was right – they really should have heard something by now. It seemed to be taking her a very long time to read through it, much longer than they'd anticipated. Maybe it was time to think about Plan B. They had been on tenterhooks long enough over this and she knew neither of them would be able to bear it much longer.

Brooke Reynolds really needed to finish this manuscript, and for the sake of the parties involved, she needed to do so soon.

CHAPTER

19. The Last to Know

Thursday morning after her return to London, Sam had gone straight to see her editor at the newspaper to what she anticipated would be a very lukewarm welcome. But no, instead of letting his minions wait outside his office cooling their heels like he normally did, when Sam arrived at his office, the *Mail* editor practically had the red carpet out!

"Sam, you sly dog," Giles said, before she could open her mouth to apologise for Eve's disastrous performance on the *Jack Nathan Show*. The day after the show was broadcast, all their rival tabloid newspapers had carried the story of Sam's 'hypocrisy' and some broadsheets had included at least a paragraph reproducing Sam's so-called broadside against the working women of Britain.

So while there had been some commotion, it wasn't exactly the knives-out situation she'd been imagining. And far from the rap on the knuckles she'd expected from the *Mail* editor, who up to now had been supportive of – but often ambivalent about – the subject matter of her column, Giles seemed thrilled about the controversy she'd created.

"All this publicity's done wonders for our circulation," he said, as Sam took a seat across from him.

"Really?" She was taken aback.

"Yes." He sat back in his chair. "Everyone's wondering who you're going to attack next."

"Giles, it's not like that – the whole thing was a big mistake – it wasn't me –"

"It certainly *wasn't* you – that stuff you usually write bores me to tears. Sorry," he added quickly, seeing the look on Sam's face, "but all that women's lib stuff – 'I'll support you and you support me'." He rolled his eyes. "Quite frankly, Sam, it bores *most* people to tears. We like to see you girls sticking it to one other for a change – how many times have I asked you to try and shake things up a bit?"

Sam's mouth opened, but she couldn't get the words out.

"So what I want to know is, what's the next one about and when can I see it?"

Well, Sam's next column, which had been largely written on the plane back to London on Wednesday evening, was a complete rebuttal of what had been said on the *Jack Nathan Show*. Sam was planning on coming out fighting and explaining how she'd been set up. But not, it seemed, if Giles had anything to do with it.

"Why not follow it up with a swipe at the PM next?" he suggested. "And after that, you could castigate all those war protestors, and maybe after that –"

"*Giles*," Sam interjected firmly, deciding that she needed to tell him now. This was the last bloody straw. In truth, she hadn't intended on saying anything today – not until she'd apologised for the show in her next column – but it seemed now that Giles wouldn't allow her do that. And listening to him now, if that was the kind of journalist he wanted her to be, well, then, it was just as well he'd given her an excuse. She'd been thinking seriously about giving up the column for a little while, but with all this talk about *attacking* people, Giles had now made the decision for her. Enough was enough.

"What?" said Giles.

"There won't be another column."

"What do you mean?" Giles frowned. "Haven't you finished it? You know when the deadline is, Sam!"

"I'm sorry – I've enjoyed writing for the paper these last few years, and thanks for giving me the opportunity to work for you, but . . ." Sam shrugged her shoulders. "I just don't want to do this any more."

"You mean you're giving up the column?" Giles didn't seem as upset as she'd thought he'd be. Despite his apparent delight about the publicity she'd generated, maybe he had been looking for an excuse to get rid of her anyway.

"I'm sure – I've been thinking about it for a while anyway, thinking of giving more time to my novels. I'm sorry – I hope I'm not leaving you in the lurch like this –"

"Christ, you certainly know how to go out with a bang, don't you? But never mind," he said, waving away her apologies, "I suspected you might jump ship at some stage – you writer-types usually do – the slightest sniff of a publishing deal and you're off! And as it happens I already know someone who could fill in – Moira North – sarky bitch, she is – she'd be perfect for that kind of thing."

Sam couldn't believe it. Far from being put out by her departure, Giles was already planning his next move and was already so preoccupied with replacing her he barely acknowledged her goodbyes. But she'd done it; she'd made the break at last, and although she strongly believed that she'd made the right decision, only time would tell.

It was now Monday morning – a full week after Eve's

appearance on the BBC – and Sam was due in for a meeting at the publishers' offices at eleven. The resultant controversy had died down somewhat now, and the newspapers had since moved on to other more weighty and scandalous issues, but still Sam wasn't sure what to expect from Continental.

Strange the way things worked out sometimes, she thought now, as she got ready for the meeting. She'd spent so long trying to make her way in journalism that she thought she'd feel more upset at the idea of giving it up.

But of course she had her novels to concentrate on now, assuming she had any sort of a career left there, either, she thought wryly. Maybe she shouldn't have been so hasty to pack in the *Mail* job all the same . . . chances were she might need it as a source of income should her books fail to sell and her readers abandon her in droves as a result of the interview. Chances were Continental had called her in today to tell her exactly that. Still, if her writing career didn't work out she could always try and get work with one of the more serious broadsheets or even a women's magazine – anything that meant she didn't have to compromise her principles in the way the *Mail* expected. Either way, she'd have to wait and see. Almost immediately after Eve's interview she'd phoned her editor from Ireland in order to explain what had happened and hoping to carry out some sort of damage control.

As expected, Elizabeth had been horrified.

"Well, we all know Gloria can be like a dog with a bone when it comes to securing publicity, but this is over the top. I heard the interview when I was getting ready to go out to work, and I must admit I was more than a little puzzled by it all, Sam. I was thinking it didn't sound like you at all. And as it turned out, I was right."

Elizabeth, who was herself a working mum, as well as being puzzled no doubt would also have been offended, Sam thought ashamedly.

"I would never attack or hit out at anyone like that," Sam told her. She sighed. "This is really going to hurt my readership, isn't it?"

"Maybe, maybe not," her editor had said diplomatically before making arrangements for Sam to call into the office as soon as possible to discuss the situation. "We'll have to wait and see."

Well, Sam thought now, as she hailed a cab that would take her to the publishers' offices, chances were she was about to find out.

"Well, it might be a cliché," Elizabeth announced some thirty minutes later, once Sam arrived in her office, "but it's certainly a true one. There really is no such thing as bad publicity." She smiled. "With all the newspaper coverage generated from that interview, it seems everyone wants to read your books now."

"What? You're joking!"

Whatever about the newspaper, for which controversy always gained readers, Sam was truly amazed by this. She'd been afraid (but at the same time fully prepared) that her writing career could well be ruined. But instead, the exact opposite had happened and, according to Elizabeth, people were going out and buying *Lucky Stars* in droves and, as a direct result of the interview, book sales had practically doubled! Sam shook her head in amazement as Continental continued outlining the effects her supposed negative comments, and the resultant publicity, had had on her profile. The sales director went on to tell Sam that they'd been getting so many orders from bookstores for *Lucky Star* that they could hardly keep up. It seemed she owed Gloria – and indeed Eve – a huge favour for (inadvertently) sending her sales into the stratosphere.

"There's a good chance it could hit the list next week," Elizabeth informed her finally, "which is fantastic, as sales had begun to drop off since publication. So, well done, you."

"The *bestseller* list?" Sam could barely form the words.

"Yes," Elizabeth beamed. "Seems Gloria did you a favour after all."

*   *   *

Hours later, Sam returned to her flat, still walking on air.

Knowing that Eve would no doubt be worrying herself to death over the effect her actions had had on Sam's career, upon her return she decided to phone her immediately to tell her the news.

But when her sister answered the phone, Sam had only barely managed to give her the good news, before Eve blurted some surprising news of her own.

"That's wonderful, Sam!" her sister enthused. Then she paused slightly. "Well, I'm not really supposed to say anything . . . but feck it, I can't hold it in any longer!" she went on, her voice practically shaking with delight. "Sam, I'm engaged!"

On the other end of the line, Sam wasn't sure she'd heard right. "You're what?"

"I'm engaged!" Eve repeated happily. "I took your advice and asked Liam to marry me – and he's agreed! Now, we weren't planning on telling anyone until we got the ring this week, but what the heck – now you know!"

Sam's heart sank. Oh God, why had she made such a stupid suggestion?

But of course at the time she hadn't yet eavesdropped on his conversation with Trisha and heard him admit he wasn't happy and – hold on, *why* had he agreed to get engaged if he wasn't happy? What was he playing at? Now she was really confused.

"Sam? Are you still there?" Eve's uncertain tones brought her right back to the present.

"Yes, yes – I'm just . . . wow, Eve, this is such a big surprise!"

Sam tried to inject the right amount of enthusiasm into her tone. This was a big deal for Eve – her sister had wanted this for most of her life – and Sam didn't want to ruin it for her. "It's fantastic news, congratulations!"

"I know, isn't it brilliant? You were right, you know, I can't understand why I didn't do it ages ago! And the kids are over the moon about the wedding, well, Lily is, Max doesn't really understand but –"

While Eve continued to chatter away a mile a minute, Sam tried to get a hold on her thoughts.

"But when did this all happen?" she asked. She'd barely been back in London a couple of days. What had prompted Eve's seemingly out-of-the-blue proposal?

"Well, again, it was all down to you," said Eve. "While I was in London and you were here I got to thinking about how stupid and pointless it was waiting around for him to ask me. I don't know, Sam – I think I realised just how important my family really was to me and how important it was that we *were* a proper family. So on the way back on the ferry I made my decision. I was going to ask him. What could he say but yes or no? And I was pretty certain he wouldn't say no – not when all three of us were proposing and –"

"All three of you?"

"Yes." Eve went on to explain how Lily had helped make the banner asking Liam to 'marry us' and Sam's heart sank to her stomach. Oh God! Little surprise then that Liam had said yes – in those circumstances how could he refuse? But no, maybe she was being over-analytic in light of what she knew or, at least, what she thought she knew. Maybe Liam had said yes because he was genuinely happy to marry Eve.

But no matter how much she tried to convince herself otherwise, Sam knew deep down that this wasn't the case, and what Eve believed was the best thing that had happened to her could very well turn out to be her worst nightmare.

"So, look, I know you're probably still busy what with everything that's happening with you, and I understand completely if you can't make it, but obviously this is a big deal for us so we're having a bit of a party to celebrate." Eve tried to sound nonchalant, but there was no mistaking the absolute delight in her tone. "Nothing major – just friends and family – and we're hoping to organise it for next weekend. What do you think?"

Well, yes, Sam was busy, but things had worked out OK for her in the end – better than OK judging from what the publishers had told her that morning. And while she'd been hoping to get the Derek situation sorted out as soon as possible and confess to him that their 'break' would be permanent, she couldn't do that until he returned from his work trip the following week.

So she was hardly going to refuse to attend Eve's party, was she? Not when her younger sister was so excited about this engagement and deserved something to celebrate.

Not only that, but Sam thought she'd better go and see if she could determine exactly how Liam felt about all this, and whether he was agreeing to marry Eve because he had no choice or because he genuinely wanted to.

"And of course Anna and Ronan will be there too – we haven't told them yet, but I know they'll be thrilled," Eve added casually, and at this Sam's heart gave a little flip. It was wrong – it was totally wrong – but once she heard that the object of her affection would be in the same room as her, Sam knew that wild horses couldn't keep her away from Eve's engagement party.

CHAPTER

20. The Last to Know

The following Saturday afternoon, Sam was barely in the door of Eve's home when her delighted sister flashed her engagement ring at her.

"So what do you think?" Eve gushed happily.

"It's gorgeous, Eve – congratulations." Sam hugged her effusively. And it was. Whatever his thoughts on the matter, Liam had clearly not stinted on stumping up for a truly impressive diamond ring.

"Lily helped me pick it out, didn't you, love?" Eve said, as she and Sam went into the kitchen where Lily and her friend Rachel were busy blowing up balloons for the party.

"Hi, Auntie Sam." Lily greeted her with a grin. "Isn't it great about Mum and Dad? I'm going to be a flower-girl, and Max is going to be a page-boy, although knowing him he'll probably totally mess up his suit and ruin everything." She wrinkled her nose. "He's already burst *half* the balloons for the party."

Sure enough, there was Max hiding under the kitchen table and gleefully stabbing any balloons that were unlucky enough to come his way.

"Ah, sure, he's only enjoying himself, Lil." Eve smiled fondly at her youngest, the euphoria of her engagement rendering her positively Zen-like when it came to Max's behaviour.

Seeing her sister so happy, Sam wanted to kick herself for even thinking that Liam's intentions might be dishonest.

And speak of the devil himself . . .

"Hello, Liam," Sam said as Liam quietly entered the kitchen. "Congratulations – it's wonderful news." She reached across to hug her brother-in-law-to-be.

"Thanks very much," said Liam, and the slightly jaded way he said it, coupled with his half-hearted hug, told Sam everything she needed to know.

Later that evening, the rest of the guests arrived, neighbours and friends of Eve's, some work colleagues of Liam's (although oddly, Sam thought, there was no sign of the famous Trisha) and of course Anna and Ronan.

Yet again, Sam couldn't help but be acutely aware of him, even though he seemed totally oblivious to her. She'd been aware of his and Anna's arrival almost as soon as the doorbell rang and before he'd set even set foot in the house! As Eve and Liam were deep in conversation with another couple who'd just arrived, Sam took it upon herself to answer the door.

"Sam, hi – good to see you again," Anna said, stepping inside and giving her a warm hug.

Ronan grinned, his huge blue eyes twinkling. "You're becoming part of the furniture around here, Sam!" he joked, reaching forward and giving her a quick and – for Sam – totally unexpected kiss on the cheek.

"I know . . . yes," she spluttered, the shock of having Ronan in such close proximity rendering her almost speechless. "Um . . . come in – everyone's inside."

Closing the front door, Sam followed the two of them in to the living room and tried to calm herself.

"Anna, Ronan, hi!" Eve, who was standing alongside Liam on the other side of the room, looked positively radiant as she waved to her friends.

Sam sorely wished the same could be said of her betrothed. By contrast, Liam looked as though he wished he were anywhere else but here in his living room welcoming guests to his engagement party.

Then Sam noticed something else.

Under normal circumstances she was pretty certain she wouldn't have spotted it at all; it was just that she was being particularly over-watchful of Liam's behaviour and his reaction to people's congratulations. But to Sam there was absolutely no mistaking the expression that passed across Liam's face when Anna entered the room or the look he gave her when she reached forward to congratulate him.

Oh my God, Sam thought. The woman that Liam had spoken to Trisha about in the hotel room in Sydney, the one whom he'd supposedly been afraid to confess his feelings to all those years before . . .

Could it be Anna?

Sam watched them both from afar for the remainder of the evening, her heart sinking to the depths of her stomach as she realised how hopeless this all was for Eve. Clearly, Liam had been railroaded into this engagement.

And she realised another thing. Anna also seemed to be going out of her way to avoid Liam, to avoid speaking to him, standing near him, having anything at all to do with him, which sent Sam's imagination into even greater overdrive.

Did Anna know that Liam had feelings for her? Had she always known?

She recalled Eve telling her how Ronan and Anna had been childhood sweethearts and that Liam and Ronan had also been friends since they met as teenagers. Was it possible that as they'd got older Liam had also fallen for Anna's charms, but because she already 'belonged' to Ronan, he couldn't do anything about it?

And did Anna know how he had felt, or perhaps how he *still* felt about her? Sam was pretty certain she did; it would certainly explain why she'd spent much of the evening avoiding him, while at the same time, Sam was sure, being aware of his every move. She remembered Lily's comment about how she thought Liam didn't like Anna because he never really spoke to her when she visited their house. At the time, she'd thought it was just Lily's childish and simplistic way of looking at things, but thinking about it now . . .

So where did all of this leave Anna and Ronan? Sam tried to tell herself that she was being overly suspicious because of her own feelings where Ronan was concerned, but in all honesty she didn't think so. Eve had already suggested that Anna had some commitment issues; why else hadn't she agreed to set a date? And why did she and Ronan seem so patently wrong together when everyone was convinced they were love's young dream?

It seemed to Sam that they were more like brother and sister; there certainly didn't seem to be any sparks between them, and while Ronan was the jokey, playful one, Anna seemed austere and rather cool in her reaction to him. In fact, as the evening went on, Sam was the one laughing at his jokes and bantering with Ronan, not the long-time love of his life.

No, to Sam something had always seemed slightly out of kilter where this couple were concerned, and now she thought she knew why.

And it gradually became clear to Sam that, despite Anna's determined attempts to stay out of Liam's way, she in turn couldn't keep her eyes off him.

*   *   *

The following morning over a late breakfast in the kitchen, Sam dissected the previous night's events with Eve, and despite herself she couldn't help but eventually steer the conversation round to Anna and Ronan.

She was dying to find out more about their history, on two counts – one, because she was certain Anna really wasn't the right person for Ronan, and two because she wanted to figure out how Liam fitted into the picture

"So, how long have they been together?" she asked Eve, who was pouring them another cup of coffee.

The party had been a late one, and Liam and the kids were still in bed. Even the usually animated Max had been knocked out after all the celebrations or more likely, Sam thought wryly, after all the party food he'd gobbled the night before.

"Anna and Ronan?" Eve replied. "Donkey's years, really. " She sat back down beside Sam at the kitchen table. "I think I told you before that they lived right next-door to one another and have been together ever since."

"And Liam knew them too, you said?"

"Yes, but he and Noreen didn't move into the area until much later – when they were teenagers, I think. Liam was going through a hard time – his parents had just separated, and his mother had uprooted him from everything he knew, his school, his friends, everything. He and Ronan hit it off immediately. They were in the same class in school, I think."

"And Anna too?"

"Anna what?"

"Did Anna hit it off with Liam too?"

"Well, I'm not really sure. I suppose she got to know him as a friend of Ronan's, really," Eve replied. "Anyway, why are you so interested in Anna and Ronan? This isn't the first time you've quizzed me about them and . . . Sam?" She sat up in her chair, her eyes narrowing suspiciously. "Sam, why are you blushing? What the hell is going on?"

Sam was caught. Obviously she didn't want Eve to think anything untoward about Anna and Liam, so now she had no choice but to tell her sister the truth. And in all honesty, she needed to tell her, to tell somebody about the strong and very odd feelings she experienced whenever Ronan was around.

"Sam?" Eve prompted, her tone sharp. "I asked you what was going on."

Sam took a deep breath before answering. "I'm not sure, to be honest. I think . . . I mean, I know this is stupid and kind of pathetic, but well . . . I think I've fallen for Ronan." She looked away quickly, unsure what to say next.

Eve's eyes nearly popped out of her head. "What? What do you mean you *think you've fallen for Ronan?* You barely know him, for goodness sake!"

"I know," Sam's voice was plaintive. "Believe me, I'm just as perplexed as you are. But there's something about him, Eve – something that I can't explain. From the very first moment I met him . . ." She went on to tell Eve about that strange flash of insight she'd had that first night in the taxi and how the feeling had repeated itself almost every time she came into contact with him.

"Sam, this is so unlike you! I mean, you're so practical and normal and . . . well, you don't believe in that kind of thing!"

"What kind of thing?"

"Well, love at first sight and all that. You laughed at me, back when I told you that Liam was the love of my life, that I could and never would want anyone else."

Sam's stomach dropped when her sister said this. Eve was right, she had poked fun at the notion, but now she understood a little better why her sister *had* been with Liam for so long. If Eve felt even half as strongly for Liam as she herself did for Ronan . . . well, then, of course her sister's choices made perfect sense. But – and here was a disturbing thought – was Sam kidding herself to think that anything could come of her infatuation with Ronan, in the way that Eve was kidding herself to think that she and Liam were now heading for happily ever after?

"I can't explain it either," she told Eve. "I wish I could. All I know is that whenever I'm around him, I feel something – something very strong. Jesus, Eve, almost as soon as I'd met him, all thoughts of marrying Derek went straight out the window!"

"But I thought . . . I thought you'd made the decision to split up with Derek based on your experience here," Eve argued. "That was the whole point, wasn't it?"

"Well, yes, it *was* based on my experience here, my experience of meeting Ronan."

Eve folded her arms across her chest. "I can't believe you're planning to finish with someone like Derek just because you like the look of Ronan!"

"It isn't anything to do with the look of him," Sam said and smiled. "You've seen him – he's not exactly Tom Cruise, is he? No, it's something more than that – something that goes way beyond looks. He seems like a lovely person and everything, but I don't think it's that either. I don't know, as I said, I can't explain it. I just know there's something about Ronan that made me react the way I did when I first met him, and I've been reacting the same way since. Even last night when he was here, I just felt – drawn towards him or something. All those funny little comments he makes, I don't know, there's just something really endearing about him."

217

"Well, yes, I did notice you two having a bit of a laugh in the corner last night, but I had no idea that you fancied him!" Eve shook her head. "To be honest, he's one of the last people I thought you'd be attracted to – never in a million years did I –" Then she gave Sam a stern look. "Had I known what you were up to, I would have put a stop to it."

"I wasn't up to anything, Eve – we were just having a chat. And despite what I'm telling you now, I wouldn't dream of making a play for him."

This was true. While last night she'd appreciated the opportunity to talk to Ronan on his own and enjoy the bit of banter, she had tried to ensure she didn't come across as flirtatious. Anyway, Ronan seemed the type that wouldn't notice if she *was* being flirtatious. As far as he was concerned, she was Eve's sister and he was simply being friendly. Sam suspected the same man would die of embarrassment should he realise the truth. And as much as she wanted her feelings to be reciprocated, she knew there was no chance of that once Anna was in the same room.

Eve seemed determined to remind her of that very fact. "Sam, he's engaged to Anna – they've been together forever and are madly in love so there's no possible way that you could ever –"

"Well, if they're so madly in love, then how come they haven't got married yet?" Sam shot back, and even though Eve was merely repeating what she'd told herself over and over again, it still got to her. "Why haven't they even set a date?"

"Well, because they haven't had the opportunity, I suppose. Anna's been busy and so has Ronan and –"

"Busy doing what? Going to work and coming home every day – same as everyone else? And they're both working, so it's not as though they're stuck for money and can't afford the wedding or anything like that. And although you say they're madly in love, haven't you noticed how Anna behaves around him?"

Eve's eyes narrowed. "What do you mean?"

"The way she seems to shrink away from his touch or rolls her eyes at his jokes!" said Sam, on a bit of a roll now that she'd begun poking holes in Ronan and Anna's so-called 'perfect' relationship. "They don't strike me as a couple in love, Eve, they strike me as a couple in trouble!"

She hadn't meant it to come across so vehemently, but she'd been through this in her own mind so many times that it was almost a relief to let it out. And no matter what Eve might believe, Sam knew she was right. There was something up with Anna and Ronan, and despite her own feelings on the subject, she hoped against hope that that something wasn't Liam.

Eve was staring at her. "Sam, you've got things all wrong. Anna and Ronan are my friends and I've known them for a very long time. You've met them what – once or twice? Now, you listen to me. I'm very sorry that you seem to have feelings for Ronan, but you cannot under any circumstances even *think* about acting on them! I know you're my sister, but Anna is a very good friend of mine and I won't have you coming between them."

"What do you think I'm going to do – try and seduce him? The man doesn't even know I exist!"

"He doesn't know you exist because he's madly in love with Anna and always has been. Sam, don't make a fool of yourself over this. There's nothing in it for you."

Sam was tempted to retort that that was a bit rich coming from Eve but she couldn't bring herself to say it. There was no point. Anyway, if she said something like that she'd need to explain the reasoning behind it – her suspicions about Liam and his feelings towards Anna.

Sam sighed. Jeez, the whole world and his mother seemed to have feelings towards Anna and, while she was attractive and seemed nice enough, she wasn't *that* bloody great!

She shook her head, realising once again that the whole thing was totally futile. Eve was right. There was nothing in this for her but trouble. God, as it was she was practically turning into some obsessive stalker-type – like something you'd see in the movies!

"Sam, you must promise me that you'll forget all about Ronan," Eve implored now. "I'm sorry that you're attracted to him, and I feel for you, really I do, but you have to forget about him. That vision or revelation or whatever it is you had about spending the rest of your life with him – well, that's just crazy. It's not going to happen. Not while Anna is around anyway."

"I know," Sam said quietly, but as she took another sip of her coffee, she couldn't help but wonder if Anna really *would* be around for good.

CHAPTER

21. The Last to Know

"So that was a bit of a turn-up for the books, wasn't it?" Ronan said to Anna the morning after the engagement party.

"What was?" she replied idly, putting a slice of bread into the toaster.

"Eve and Liam getting engaged, of course!" he said shaking his head. "I must say I never thought I'd see the day."

"Why not? They're as good as married, anyway. Why wouldn't they take the next most logical step?"

Ronan spooned sugar into his coffee. "I don't know – I just didn't think they'd ever get round to it. I didn't think Liam . . ."

"You didn't think Liam what?" she prompted, when he didn't finish the sentence.

"I didn't think Liam was into marriage and all that," he went on. "Especially after what happened with his own parents, you know – the separation and everything. I know all that really got to him."

"Ronan, he was barely a teenager at the time, and I'm sure all kids are massively affected by their parents splitting up. But that doesn't mean the same thing will happen with him and Eve. They've been together for years and have two children. They're practically married as it is. And besides," she added then, "Eve worships the ground he walks on."

"That could be part of the problem," Ronan said as his fiancée joined him at the table. "Now, nothing was said, but I get the impression that this wedding was all Eve's idea. Didn't you see Liam at the party last night? He certainly didn't look like a happy bridegroom – there was a face on him that would trip a jackass!"

"I can't say I noticed." Anna picked up the milk jug. "But speaking of happy," she teased, hoping to change the subject, "I see you and Sam were getting on like a house on fire . . ."

To her immense surprise, Ronan blushed. "Ah, Sam's sound," he said. "Very like Eve in ways, but at the same time different – more sensible, I think."

"I know what you mean," Anna agreed. She liked Sam too, but you'd want to be a fool not to notice the way Eve's sister reacted whenever Ronan was around – last night especially. In fairness, she did her best to hide it, but Anna was now pretty certain that Sam had taken a bit of a shine to her fiancé.

Which was interesting.

"I wonder if she and the boyfriend are still together?" she mused out loud. "Eve told me she was thinking over a marriage proposal from some guy she was seeing in London, that time she was over to look after the kids."

"Right." Ronan seemed uninterested in the details of Sam's personal life. "He wasn't there last night, was he?"

"Who?"

"Well, aren't we talking about Sam's fella?" Ronan said, slightly exasperated. "Jaysus, Anna, you're away with the fairies these days!" He shook his head. "And why aren't you eating that toast? Tummy giving you trouble again?"

"Not at all," Anna said, quickly taking a bite out of the slice to prove it. Her stomach *was* a bit iffy again today but she wasn't going to let Ronan know that. Although very soon he'd start noticing a lot more than just a dodgy appetite, and she didn't know how she was going to cope with that.

It had been a whirlwind of a few weeks and, despite being able to think about nothing but her condition, she still didn't know what she was going to do about it. And then – as if that wasn't enough – there was the small matter of Eve and Liam's engagement. Surprise engagement – at least it had been a huge surprise to her, and evidently to Ronan too.

But had it, as Ronan suspected, also been a surprise to Liam? Eve would never have taken the plunge and proposed to him, would she? No, Anna was certain Eve didn't have it in her. And she genuinely didn't notice that Liam was behaving anything other than happy last night. As usual, she had tried to ensure that she didn't notice Liam at all. That way it was much easier.

For all of them.

*   *   *

Eve was living the dream. She couldn't remember ever feeling so happy, ever feeling so positive and optimistic about life. She had a nice house, two lovely children, a loving partner and – this was the best bit – a wedding to plan!

She still couldn't believe that it had finally happened and that she and Liam were really going to get married. Fair play to Sam for putting the idea into her mind and for giving her the headspace to think about her life properly. If it hadn't been for her sister, she would never have gained the courage to come right out and propose to Liam herself.

And hadn't it really been a brainwave getting the kids

involved too! It was only right though, Eve thought as she cleaned and dusted in an attempt to restore the house to its former pristine state after the weekend's celebrations; the four of them had been a package for so long now that the kids had to have a part in any family decisions.

Lily had been tickled pink when Eve had confided her plans to her, the day after her return from London, and it had been Lily who had come up with the suggestion of the banner.

Eve smiled as she recalled the scene that morning. Liam had been totally taken aback by the unexpectedness of it all, and for a split second she had worried that she'd made a mistake, but no, he seemed just as happy about it all as she was. They hadn't really discussed dates for the wedding – in fact, Liam had been so busy since that they hadn't had much of a chance to discuss *anything* about the wedding at all, but sure there was plenty of time yet. Maybe after he got back from his next work trip to Australia, they could talk about it in detail. And hopefully, she thought smiling, Liam might also be in the right frame of mind for her to broach the subject of their having another baby. After the wedding would probably be an ideal time, really, and oh, wouldn't a honeymoon baby be just perfect! Eve sighed with pleasure, thinking of all the wonderful things she now had to look forward to – including a lovely holiday. Where would they go for their honeymoon?

Liam was always going on about Australia and how much he loved it over there, and, yes, it certainly sounded lovely, but Eve didn't like the idea of travelling too far afield – especially when they'd have to leave the kids behind. And it would probably be too expensive anyway, seeing as it wasn't a work trip and they would be paying for it themselves. No, she thought with a grin, a big fancy trip like that would be way out of their league; instead maybe they could go somewhere closer to home but just as nice.

In any case, she thought now, wherever she and Liam

eventually ended up going, she'd definitely need a passport, so the first thing she'd do on Monday was call into town and get an application form. No harm in getting it done well before time, as knowing her, with all the other things she had to think about for the wedding, she'd forget all about it until a week before they were due to leave or something, and then they wouldn't be going anywhere! She supposed she'd better get the kids put on it too while she was at it, just in case they ever did get round to a nice family holiday. But in the meantime . . . God, it would be so exciting to go somewhere exotic with Liam for the first time, to go to one of those places she was always admiring on the holiday programmes on TV!

Eve couldn't wait.

She smiled as she caught sight of her engagement ring. It had been a lovely suggestion of Liam's that she and Lily should go to the jeweller's and choose the ring instead of taking him along.

"You know me – I wouldn't have a clue what to pick out, and I'd only get it wrong. It's more of a woman's job," he'd said.

Lily had been thrilled, and the two of them had had a lovely girlie mother and daughter day out in town choosing rings until Eve had eventually settled on her diamond cluster. Granted, the whole thing was a little unorthodox in that he hadn't been involved in this at all, but then again hadn't Eve and Liam's life together always been that way?

She still couldn't believe that it was really happening, that she was actually an engaged woman, and even better, she was engaged to Liam!

But there was no mistaking the diamond ring on her finger, the weekend's brilliant party or indeed the cluster of engagement cards on the sideboard.

Temporarily calling a halt to her cleaning, Eve picked up the cards and began re-reading them. There was one from Sam (who had returned to London the day before), loads from the neighbours, a lovely one from one of Liam's work colleagues and of course one from Anna and Ronan.

Eve frowned as she recalled Anna's initial reaction to the news. Being as close as they were, Anna was obviously one of the first people she'd told about her engagement, and when she'd called to the house and broken the news, Eve had expected her friend to be almost as excited about it all as she was, but instead Anna seemed rather . . . well, thinking of it now, shocked would be the best word to describe it.

But at the same time, Eve couldn't worry about this too much. Anna had been a bit off form these last few weeks anyway and was probably under pressure with work or something. She seriously hoped that Anna hadn't got wind of Sam's attraction to Ronan, which would naturally put her friend's nose out of joint and perhaps explain Anna's recent rather distant behaviour towards her.

She was still reeling from her sister's admission of feelings for Ronan.

Ronan Fraser of all people! Yes, he was a lovely guy, and Liam's best friend, but really you wouldn't look at him twice! And she wouldn't mind but Derek, the man her sister was planning on dumping, was an absolute Adonis compared to Ronan.

Eve didn't know what was going on. Obviously, while she was here Sam must have been hit over the head with something to have gone and fallen for the likes of Ronan. Especially as he was clearly in love with someone else! But didn't she know well that you couldn't choose who you fell in love with?

Either way, she hoped her sister would soon come to her senses and forget all about this silliness. Although, it was probably just a phase she was going through, Eve decided. Sam could be a bit like that sometimes.

No, she thought, getting back to her cleaning, as soon as her sister settled back down to her exciting life in London, all this Ronan nonsense would be a distant memory.

* * *

The following weekend, Ronan and Liam arranged to meet in the local pub to watch a game of football.

Taking their usual spot up at the bar, in good view of the TV overhead, they chatted briefly over their respective pints while waiting for the match to kick off.

"Good party last week," Ronan said, once they'd finished their usual discussion about football, work and property prices. After that, the only other topic left was women.

"Yeah," Liam said noncommittally.

"I have to say, I never thought I'd see the day – the two of us engaged and settled." Ronan grinned and shook his head.

"I know."

"Well, in fairness, you've been pretty much settled for a long time, what with the kids and everything, but I didn't know marriage was on the cards. You never said a word."

"Well, you just never know, do you?" Liam said, with a slight edge to his tone.

The two men sat and supped their pints in silence for a few minutes before, eventually, Liam spoke again.

"What about you?" he asked Ronan. "Any sign of her walking down the aisle with you?"

Ronan smiled tightly. "We're in no rush," he replied, almost his stock response at this stage.

"Still, it's been a few years now, hasn't it?"

"It has, but we've been busy and what with Mam being sick last year and everything, it hasn't been easy to organise.

Anyway," he added cryptically, "with the way things are shaping up lately, I don't think it'll be on the cards anytime soon either."

Sensing the change in his tone, Liam looked sideways at him. "Why's that?"

Ronan was hesitant. "Well, to be honest, I'm not sure yet, and in fairness I could be barking up the wrong tree altogether, but I have a feeling that myself and Anna might soon be welcoming a new addition to the family."

Liam frowned. "I don't get you."

The other man looked at his friend and grinned. "Jaysus, you're not very bright, are you? A new addition?"

Liam still looked blank.

"Well, don't breathe a word of this to Eve, but I have a funny feeling Anna might be pregnant."

Suddenly, Liam's pint glass fell to the floor. "Fuck!" he yelled, leaping up off his stool. Then he grabbed a beer mat and began wiping down his trousers.

"It's a bit early in the night for that carry-on, isn't it?" Ronan joked, moving his stool back out of the way to allow Joe the barman clean up. "We've only had one."

"I hardly meant to spill the shaggin' pint on myself, Ronan!" Liam shot back sharply. Then he turned to the barman. "Sorry, Joe, the thing just slipped out of my hand."

"No worries." Joe duly mopped up the mess and removed the glass.

"For a fella who's only recently got engaged, you're in fierce bad form altogether," Ronan said when the broken glass had been cleaned up and they were once again on their own.

"Sorry," Liam grunted, sitting back on his stool. "Work is hectic, that's all. These days I hardly know my arse from my elbow what with all that's going on. I'm not long back from Australia, and I've another stint down there coming up soon."

"I'm not surprised you get narky what with all the travelling around the place you do," Ronan quipped, unwilling to get into the reasons for Liam's poor form. "It's a wonder you're in the same time zone as the rest of us at all. But sure, it has to be done, doesn't it?" He cast an eye up at the TV to where the opposing teams were starting to line out on the football pitch.

"It does." Liam looked in the same direction.

"But look, you won't say a word about it anyway, sure you won't?" Ronan said then.

"About what?"

"About Anna being pregnant. As I said, I'm not too sure myself as she hasn't said a word, but all the signs are there. Feeling dizzy in the mornings, tired in the evenings and not eating much at all. They're the signs, aren't they?" He gazed at Liam, who looked blank. "Well, you should know. What was Eve like when she was having your two?"

"I can't really remember," Liam replied truthfully. "I know she was sick for a while but, as for the rest of it, I couldn't tell you." He continued staring at the TV. "Anyway, why don't you just ask her about it?"

"Who – Eve?"

Liam rolled his eyes. "Anna, of course, who the hell else? Instead of all the guessing and surmising. Surely she'd tell you straight out if she was or she wasn't?"

"Maybe. I don't know why I don't do that, to be honest. She's been a bit moody lately . . . although I suppose that's another one of the signs, isn't it? But I don't want to risk her taking the head off me if I'm wrong either. She'd start accusing me of calling her fat or something. You know what women can be like."

"Yeah, but Anna's never really been like that, has she? You know – into clothes and all that shite like the rest of them are. She was never like that in the old days anyway," he added quickly.

"Yeah, our Anna was definitely never a girlie girl," Ronan grinned. "Remember the night we camped down in the Witches' Cave – I think we were only thirteen or fourteen or something – and yourself and myself were feckin' petrified heading down there in the dark?"

Liam nodded remembering. "Yep, and not a bother on Anna – even when we heard all those squirrels or bats or whatever they were scratching at the back of the cave. Anyone would think she could see in the dark, she was so cool about it all."

"Ah, they were good days all the same, weren't they, Liam? Just all of us having the *craic*, no jobs or mortgages or nothing to worry about."

"I know what you mean."

"And now here we are, both mortgaged up to the hilt, both engaged – you with two kids and me with one on the way," he winked, before adding, "at least I *think* there's one on the way."

"Yes," Liam said, his voice tight, "here we both are."

"Ready for another one?" Ronan asked then, indicating his near-empty glass.

"Just about."

"Grand. Same again, please, Joe," Ronan called to the barman. "But listen, you won't say anything to Eve about that, will you?" he asked, just as the game was about to kick off on TV. "You know – about Anna maybe being pregnant. You know what the two of them are like when they get talking and I'd hate for it to get back to Anna that I said something to you without speaking to her about it first."

"No problem," Liam said, watching the pints of Guinness settle slowly on the countertop. "I won't say a word."

CHAPTER

22. The Last to Know

Sam battled her way through the scores of Saturday-morning shoppers on Oxford Street. She'd arranged to meet an old workmate from the *Mail* for a coffee that morning, and having spent an hour or so catching up in a café on Leicester Square, she and her friend parted ways at around noon.

As it was such a lovely day weather-wise, she had intended to have a relaxing browse around the shops afterwards but thought twice about it when she realised how busy the streets had already become. Instead, she decided to pop into a relatively calm Waterstones, choose a good book and spend the afternoon out on her balcony enjoying it.

It had been well over a month since she'd returned from Eve's and, in the meantime, she'd finally ended her relationship with Derek.

They'd met for dinner the week after Eve's engagement party and while he'd seemed in good form, Sam suspected that he knew what was coming.

"Derek, this is not working out, is it?" she said, when they'd finished their main course.

"You tell me, Sam," he replied, his face impassive as he studied hers.

She looked away, unable to meet his eyes. She'd been with the man almost two years and up until a few weeks before she'd truly believed she loved him, yet as soon as she'd met Ronan . . . "I don't know, Derek," she said finally. "I've enjoyed our time together and care deeply about you but I just don't –"

"You just don't want to marry me," he finished for her.

Sam nodded, a lump in her throat. She was surprised at how difficult this was turning out in the end. Beforehand, she'd been so sure she would just walk right in there and tell him straight. But when she'd seen his face and remembered all the good times they'd shared . . . Still, there was no point in carrying on for the sake of it. Sam's heart was elsewhere and no matter how silly that might seem to Eve, or even to herself, she still couldn't change it.

"I'm sorry," she told him. "As I said, I care about you a lot, but I know now that I can't marry you."

"And it's taken you this long to realise it?" he said, clearly aggrieved. "Or have you always known that you weren't that bothered but decided to keep stringing me along for the sake of it?"

"God, no, it wasn't like that," Sam protested. And it wasn't. She'd loved Derek – still loved him – but it was nowhere near the strength of the feelings she'd discovered she had for Ronan. And that just wasn't right.

But of course she couldn't confess this out loud. "I would never string you along like that," she assured him. "As I understood it, the point of this 'break' or ultimatum or whatever was to give me some time and space to think seriously about where we're going and what compromises I was prepared to make for our future. But the truth is, Derek, that I *can't* compromise. And it isn't fair to either of us to expect me to." Much better and less hurtful to let him believe that this was something she'd decided after much thought, rather than admit that the decision had more or less been made for her through meeting Ronan.

"Well, to be frank, I did a bit of thinking too," Derek said, his body stiffening even more, "and it struck me that if you had to think so long and hard about how much I meant to you, then really I mustn't mean very much at all."

"But –"

"Just let me finish, please. Things haven't been right for a while, have they? You're obsessed with this career of yours and, while for your sake I'm pleased that things have taken a turn for the better in my absence," he was referring to her recent spike in sales, "it means that you're now even further away from wanting to start a new life with me. Am I right?"

When Sam didn't answer, preferring him to draw his own conclusions, she knew he took it as a yes.

"So you're right. There *is* no future for us so perhaps it's better we call it a day now, before we do more damage to one another."

"I'm sorry," Sam said, tears in her eyes as she realised that this truly was 'it' although she was relieved that it had been Derek who had chosen to eventually say the words.

Ever the gentleman, he'd insisted that they stay on and finish dinner and conducted himself with such decorum throughout the remainder of the meal that Sam felt like an absolute heel when they eventually said their goodbyes outside the restaurant.

"I'll keep an eye out for your name in the newspapers – no doubt you'll become even more famous as time goes on," he joked, although his eyes were sad. "And then I'll be kicking myself for not snapping you up before you made your millions."

Sam smiled. "I very much doubt that." But she was pleased

that he'd finally acknowledged her career as being worth something after all.

They hugged and parted ways, Sam realising with a start that she was yet again a free woman.

And weeks later, she still found it strange how much time she seemed to have on her hands now that she was no longer attached.

Although she missed Derek occasionally, she was glad that she'd plucked up the courage to end things once and for all. What was the point in staying with him just for the sake of it? Life was much too short to settle for second best. She shook her head as she thought again about her sister's out-of-the-blue proposal to Liam a few weeks back. She still didn't know how to feel about that or, worse, what to do about it. Should she tell Eve what she'd overheard that time on the phone? That she'd overheard Liam admit to some woman that he'd felt trapped by Eve's pregnancy and their subsequent life together?

It was all her fault in the first place for suggesting that Eve should propose. Of course, back then she hadn't realised the kind of life her sister led and how imbalanced the relationship really was. Granted, she'd never particularly liked Liam but she had always believed he loved her sister and had her best interests at heart. But she'd been wrong.

She'd have to say something to Eve . . . but how? Eve was over the moon about getting married and since then was throwing herself into the wedding plans with gusto. How could Sam shatter her illusions about the man she was going to marry, shatter her dreams of marriage and happily ever after?

Yet she couldn't just stand idly by and let her sister's life be ruined. Eve deserved better than that, and in fairness, so did Liam. That was something else she needed to consider. As she paid for her chosen purchase in the bookshop, she wondered whether she should confront Liam about it all. She didn't relish the thought of doing so; Liam was difficult to engage even in idle conversation at the best of times, so Sam couldn't imagine sitting down and having a heart-to-heart with him. Yet she had to do something. This was her sister's happiness she was talking about.

Sam walked out of the shop and headed further along the street until she reached Oxford Circus Underground station. As usual, the station was thronged with commuters, tourists and shoppers, and she was relieved to get through the ticket barriers in one piece, such was the urgency and impatience of the crowds trying to rush through. As the escalator slowly descended, she began idly scanning the rows of people on the way up, all eagerly heading for the mania that she was trying to escape. Then, all of a sudden, her breath caught in her throat. Just as the escalator was about to reach the end of its descent, she had spotted someone moving along in the crowd below and heading in the opposite direction.

Someone she knew.

Sam's stomach did a double flip and she blinked twice. Was it really him?

"Ronan! Hello!" Sam called out, stepping off the escalator just as he was about to step onto the one going up.

Hearing someone call his name, Ronan stopped short, and when he spotted Sam coming towards him, his features broke into a smile of recognition – one that sent Sam's stomach into a series of somersaults. Immediately he stood back and let the other commuters pass.

"Sam? Jaysus, it *is* you!" Ronan grinned in disbelief. "Fancy bumping into you in a place the size of this!"

"I know – I wasn't sure for a minute if it actually was you either," Sam smiled back, her heart thumping a mile a minute as she faced him. "What are you doing in London?"

"Can't you guess?" he said, proudly displaying the white football jersey he wore beneath his jacket.

"You're here for the Spurs match?"

"Yep. Wouldn't miss it for the world."

"But how on earth did you get tickets for *that*?"

From her time with Derek, Sam knew a little bit about football and was aware that the Spurs/Arsenal derby match was taking place that same afternoon in White Hart Lane, Spurs' home ground. As both teams were currently vying for a place at the top of the league table, the game would be even more of a must-see game for fans of either London club. To have secured tickets for this particular match, Ronan was obviously an extremely dedicated (and well-connected) Spurs fan. Derby games were highly competitive and normally sold-out affairs.

"I'm a season-ticket holder," he said proudly. "Have been for as long as they've been issuing them, so I rarely miss a home game."

"Wow! Bet you're looking forward to today's match then," Sam said, before adding. "Is Anna not with you?" The words were out before she could stop them, and already Sam felt guilty (and *very* stalkerish) for even asking.

Ronan laughed. "Not a chance. She hates football. No, I usually go with one of my mates, but his kid's first birthday party is on today, so he couldn't make it. Poor bastard – he was really torn, but there was no way the wife was going to let him miss it for a football game!"

"I'm sure he was. It's not often you get a derby match as big as this."

Ronan looked impressed. "Obviously you know your football."

"Well, I wouldn't say that. I know a little, that's all. But I do keep an eye on the London teams, the derby games especially."

"So who are you up for today then?"

She smiled. "Well, I have to say Spurs, don't I?"

"Good woman! I knew by you that you couldn't be a Red. So tell us, do you live around here then?"

"Oxford Circus? Are you mad? No, I'm out near Clapham."

"Right. Might as well be Timbucktoo for all I know of London."

"Well, I presume you know enough to know that you're heading in the wrong direction for White Hart Lane," she said with a smile.

"Course I do, but the match is ages away yet, so I thought I might as well kill some time around here."

"Well, good luck – the place is thronged at the moment, which is why I'm getting out of it and heading home for lunch."

"You haven't had lunch? I was just getting a bite to eat myself – do you know anywhere decent we could get something?"

The casual, almost familiar way the invitation was issued convinced Sam that she'd be doing nothing wrong in accepting. And it wasn't as though she'd asked *him* to lunch, was it?

Anyway, it was exactly that, lunch, not a bloody marriage proposal! But the fact that she wanted so much to spend time with Ronan made Sam realise that accepting his invitation would be almost impossible.

Almost.

"I certainly do," Sam said, turning and heading back in the direction from which she'd come, the man she was convinced was the love of her life walking duly by her side.

Suspecting that Ronan was a man who liked his food, Sam brought him to a small greasy-spoon café she knew off Oxford Street, where the two tucked into a decent-sized fry-up and a mug of tea.

Sam still couldn't believe that she had bumped into him like that, in the middle of a busy tube station through which hundreds, if not thousands, of people passed every hour. These things just didn't happen normally, so it had to be destiny, hadn't it?

But while Ronan had issued the invitation to lunch, by accepting it and by enjoying herself so much in the process, Sam now couldn't help but feel as though she was going behind Anna's back. She had feelings for this man, strange and weird feelings, but feelings all the same. And she shouldn't be acting on them, as she most certainly was now.

"So, you think Arsenal will manage it in the end?" Ronan was saying, seemingly delighted to have found a like-minded person to chat with, particularly on match day.

"Maybe not today, what with Spurs being at home, but certainly in the long run. I think they've got a better squad."

"Maybe, but we've got the hunger. Arsenal have had the upper hand for so long, I really think this is our chance to do the business."

"We'll see. Your strikers haven't been doing so well lately, though, have they?"

"A derby game is always different, you know that. Rival clubs from the same city trying to get the better of one another."

"I don't actually," Sam replied. "Believe it or not, I've never actually been to a live game, let alone a derby one."

"Well, why the hell didn't you say so?" said Ronan. "Sure can't you take Mick's ticket and come along with me this afternoon!"

Sam's heart thumped. She hadn't meant to lead him into asking her, or had she? But now he had, so she needed to decide. She wanted nothing better than to spend the afternoon with him, this man who held so much appeal and with whom she really felt a strong connection.

But he was engaged to somebody else, and irrespective of her own feelings, Sam had to remember that.

She shook her head. "No, I couldn't. I'd love to, but I have something else on this afternoon."

"Oh right."

She was certain his face fell.

"Pity," he said. "It's a shame to waste it."

"Couldn't you offload it to one of the touts or something?"

"Not a chance!" Ronan said, as if she'd insulted him. "I'd rather it went in the bin than let those chancers make a profit at the expense of the club."

"Well, I'm sorry," she said again, although it was killing her to refuse. "Ordinarily I'd love to, but I promised one of my friends I'd meet her later."

"Not to worry – maybe some other time," Ronan said amiably. "Still, whoever she is, she'd better be worth it for you to miss an afternoon like this one!"

Don't I know it, Sam thought, torn but certain she had made the right decision.

Despite the fact that it had almost killed her to do so.

CHAPTER

23. The Last to Know

That same morning, Eve called to Anna's house for a visit, little Max in tow.

"Seeing as you're on your own," she said, "I was thinking it might be nice for us to go shopping for wedding dresses this afternoon – what do you think?"

"I'm not sure." Anna couldn't think of anything worse than traipsing around bridal shops on a Saturday afternoon. With the way she was feeling these days, she wouldn't last ten minutes in a crowd. It was a relief that Ronan had gone off to London for the match that day; it meant she had a chance, if only temporarily, to let her guard down and stop trying to hide things from him. But now, with all this talk of shopping for wedding dresses, Anna realised that she wasn't going to get any peace.

"We could look for both of us?" her friend suggested. "You're going to have to start looking eventually too, and if nothing else you could get some ideas."

"I don't think so, Eve," Anna said, wishing she wouldn't push it. Fair enough, Eve was hugely enthusiastic about her forthcoming wedding, and yes she was pleased for her but –

"Anna, what's going on?"

She looked up sharply at the tone of the Eve's voice. "What do you mean?"

"Why are you being so weird about all of this? About getting married? I know it's your own business, and maybe I shouldn't be asking –"

"Yes, maybe you shouldn't," Anna said, her tone curter than she'd intended, and almost immediately she felt guilty.

"Anna, we're friends, aren't we?" Eve said, putting a hand on Anna's shoulder. "So why won't you tell me what's going on? You've been acting a bit strangely these last few weeks, and especially since Liam and I got engaged. Is there something up – something you're not telling me?"

Anna was about to answer but, before she did, Eve spoke again.

"Are you having second thoughts about marrying Ronan – is that it?"

Anna took a deep breath. Oh, she might as well tell her; it was going to come out sooner or later anyway.

"I'm pregnant, Eve."

The other woman's eyes widened and she looked down quickly at Anna's stomach. "What? No way! I thought you'd put on some weight recently, but I didn't think for a second that – Anna, that's fantastic news. Ronan must be over the moon!" Eve reached across to give Anna a hug but, realising that her friend seemed less than enthused, she stepped back. "Isn't it?"

Anna averted her eyes. "Kind of. I mean, of course it's good news but the thing is – well, the thing is, I'm not sure if –"

"If what?" Eve asked, her brow furrowing.

Anna wasn't sure how to put this. "I don't know – I can't really explain it. It's just lately me and Ronan . . . well, it just feels different, more like we're best friends than anything else."

Eve smiled indulgently. "Anna, Ronan adores you –"

"Eve, don't you think I know that?" she shot back quickly. "This is what makes all of this so hard!"

"But I don't understand," said Eve, looking genuinely puzzled. "Makes all of what so hard?"

"All of this – this thing with the baby." Now Anna was sorry she'd started this conversation. It was hard enough to get a hold on her own feelings herself, let alone try and explain them to someone else. "Look, he doesn't know yet but once he finds out about it, he will be over the moon, and then it'll be all out of my control, and I won't even be able to think and . . ." Exasperated her voice trailed off.

"Are you trying to say that you don't want to tell Ronan about the baby?"

"Well, I have to tell him, don't I?"

"Well, yes, unless . . ."

Anna could see Eve's mind trying furiously to work things out.

"Surely you're not thinking of . . . well, you know, of going to England or anything?" her friend asked, sounding horrified for mentioning such a thing out loud, let alone the thought of someone actually doing it.

"No," Anna said, but she knew by Eve's doubtful expression that she hadn't sounded convincing enough. "Well, OK, I'll admit that I did think about it at one stage, but no." She remembered how she felt a couple of months back after coming from the doctor's and having her worst fears confirmed. Back then she'd been so shocked and confused that she'd tried to consider all the options. But at the end of the day, and no matter how confused she might have been, there was no way in hell that she would realistically do something like that.

Eve seemed flabbergasted. "But where is all this coming from?

I've always thought you two had the most perfect relationship and . . . Anna, don't you love Ronan any more?" she finished tentatively.

Anna sighed. "I don't know, Eve – and I really wish I did." For the first time in a long time, she was speaking the truth. "To be honest, I don't know how I feel anymore. And trying to keep the pregnancy from him has been incredibly difficult. Lately I get the feeling he's beginning to suspect something but I've been trying to put him off."

"How far along are you?" Eve asked, looking again at her stomach.

"Just under six months."

"Six months? Goodness, Anna, where have you been hiding it? I mean, I remember thinking at the party that you looked a little heavier round the middle lately, but . . ." She shook her head. "At six months when carrying Max, I looked like the side of a house!"

"I know – my doctor tells me I'm very lucky." She bit her lip. "Little does he know."

The two were silent for a moment, as Eve seemed to digest all this.

"So what are you going to do?" she asked Anna eventually. "If things aren't right between you two, then you have to sort it out – especially before the baby is born."

"I know we do," Anna said, gently rubbing her rounded stomach and feeling just as confused as ever.

CHAPTER

24. The Last to Know

A couple of months after her last visit to Dublin, Sam phoned Eve to pass on a piece of news that she was pretty certain her sister would be in two minds about.

"I'm thinking of moving back home," she announced. "For good."

"Back home – you mean back home *here*?" As anticipated, Eve was not at all impressed. "It's because of Ronan, isn't it?" she said, her tone disapproving.

On the other end of the line, Sam sighed. She'd expected this, of course, but it didn't make hearing it any easier. "That's not it."

She'd been trying to convince herself that the decision she'd come to recently had more to do with her being tired of London than anything else. And in truth that *had* a lot to do with it. Since breaking up with Derek and leaving the job at the newspaper – the two things she realised that had really bound her to the city – she'd begun feeling a little at sea. Many of her friends there were also Derek's friends, so while it was only natural that there would be some awkwardness between them following the split, Sam discovered that she really didn't miss their company all that much. Similarly, it was becoming more and more difficult to keep up her friendship with her old colleagues from the *Mail*, as without Giles to complain about, or work to gossip about, it was surprisingly difficult to find common ground. Additionally, London no longer felt as safe as it used to, what with the terrorist risk now always there in the background.

But most importantly, while in Ireland she had come to the significant realisation that Eve and the kids were the only family she had left, and up to now she'd been so immersed in her London life that she'd almost forgotten that.

If anything, the swap had made her realise that she and Eve now only had each other, so maybe it was time they played a bigger part in each other's lives and she started becoming more involved in the lives of her niece and nephew.

But also, and stupid as it might have been, Sam had to admit that her powerful, almost magnetic attraction to Ronan had something to do with it.

Now that she was concentrating solely on writing her novels, there was no reason why she couldn't carry on with her writing career in Ireland. Granted, she'd need to return now and again to publicise and promote new releases, but realistically she could write her books from anywhere. And Dublin would be a welcome relief from the hustle and bustle of London – a quiet, more restful place in which to write.

She'd decided to put her Clapham apartment on the market in the hope of securing enough money to help her eventually buy something smaller back in Dublin. As the apartment was situated in a reasonably sought-after area of London, she was confident of a quick sale, but in the meantime, while waiting for the sale to go through, she planned to move back to Ireland and rent somewhere temporarily.

And despite the haste with which she'd made her decision, and the huge change in lifestyle she'd be making, Sam realised that she was truly excited about returning home to the country she'd had no choice but to leave a decade before. The thought of coming home to Dublin to work and live at what she knew would be a much slower pace was enormously appealing.

OK, so she couldn't escape the fact that she was still experiencing something of an obsession with Ronan – the feelings were just too strong to ignore – but despite Eve's concerns, she had no intention of interfering with his current relationship. From what she could make out, and judging by Anna's odd behaviour around him, Ronan's fiancée was doing a good enough job of this all by herself.

"Eve, there's a lot more to it than that," she said now, trying to reassure her sister that she wasn't planning on becoming a home-wrecker. "I just think it's time for me to come home, that's all."

"So you *do* admit that all this nonsense about Ronan *does* have something to do with it," Eve replied sternly. "Sam, he's engaged! And not only that but they have a baby on the way."

At this, Sam almost dropped the phone. "W-w-what?" she stammered, her heart twisting with shock, disappointment, despair – she wasn't sure exactly what.

Eve sighed. "Look, I'm not really supposed to tell you. Ronan doesn't even know yet but –"

"Eve, you cannot be serious!" She just couldn't take this in. Anna was pregnant – with Ronan's baby! How could there ever be a future for them now?

"I am serious," Eve's tone softened considerably. "Look, Sam, I know you've convinced yourself that Ronan and Anna were having problems, but surely you must realise now that you've been deluding yourself? Anna is almost seven months along now. Granted it was a bit of a shock to me too, as she's hidden it well –"

"Seven months! And he doesn't know?" Sam's heart began to race a mile a minute as a thought struck her. "Why hasn't she told him? What has she got to hide?"

"Sam, that's entirely her own business and –"

"No, seriously, Eve, think about it," Sam went on, her mind racing as she tried to convince herself as much as Eve that something wasn't right here. "You said she's almost seven months along. Why on earth *wouldn't* she tell him? Any normal woman would unless . . . unless she had a very good reason not to."

"You don't think . . ." The remainder of Eve's sentence trailed off as she began to understand what Sam was getting at. Then her tone changed. "Sam, that's enough. What you're suggesting now is totally out of order!"

"And what do you think I'm suggesting?"

"Well, I think you're trying to suggest that Anna might be hiding her pregnancy from Ronan because . . . well, because she might have been up to no good, or something like that."

"Yes, up to no good with someone else you mean!"

Eve was incensed. "Sam, that's a ridiculous and very, very hurtful suggestion, not to mention hugely insulting to Anna!"

"Well, if the baby *is* Ronan's, isn't it a bit hurtful of Anna not to tell him about it?"

"Sam, please stop this, you're deluding yourself! You don't know Anna. And to be perfectly honest, it's not for you or anyone else to decide what she should and shouldn't do!"

"I know that but still . . ." Sam shook her head.

There was definitely something very dodgy about all of this. She remembered the way Anna seemed so ill at ease at Eve and Liam's engagement party and how she'd seemed to do everything she could to avoid being near him. Was there a possibility that . . .?

No, Sam didn't want to even entertain that fact. Still there was no denying that there had been considerable tension between Anna and Liam that night. It was the first time Sam had seen the two of them in a room together and, even though she'd been uncommonly sensitive to Anna's behaviour back then, she was sure she wasn't just persuading herself that there was something up between Eve's best friend and the long-time love of her life.

But of course, she couldn't admit any of this to Eve now, could she? Apart from the fact that Eve wouldn't hear of anything untoward about Anna and Ronan, the mere suggestion that Liam might be involved in any of this would be enough to break her heart. And seeing as Sam had nothing to confirm her suspicions other than Liam's earlier admission of unrequited love and Anna's discomfort at being around him, she couldn't exactly confess those suspicions to anyone, could she? Sam shook her head, wondering if her obsession with Ronan was driving her insane.

"I don't know," she said to her sister then. "If Anna and Ronan are as happy as you say they are, it seems a bit odd to me that Anna wouldn't be jumping for joy not only at being pregnant, but also about marrying him. Yet, in both cases, that isn't true."

"Look, Sam, you don't know Anna and you certainly can't presume to know what she should or shouldn't be feeling!" Eve sounded mightily annoyed. "She *is* happy about the baby, but at the same time, it was unplanned and it's taking her a little time to come to terms with that. Anna isn't exactly the maternal type – I told you that – whereas Ronan adores kids."

"All the more reason for her to tell him then, isn't it?" Sam shot back. "Or doesn't she care about his happiness?" She knew she sounded childish but she couldn't help it.

"Sam, stop it – that's enough!" Eve cried. "I won't listen to any more of this nonsense! Ronan and Anna are my friends, and what happens in their relationship is nobody's business but theirs! God, you're nearly as bad as Liam!"

At this, Sam's head jerked up. "Why, what does he think about all this?"

"Oh, he's the same as you, always giving out about Anna and the way she keeps Ronan at arm's length and putting off the wedding. The one who's talking . . ."

As Sam heard a smile in her voice, she knew that Eve didn't think anything suspect about her fiancé's comments. But the remark only made Sam more convinced than ever that something was wrong about this entire situation. And more convinced than ever that Liam might be involved.

"So, look, I'd really appreciate it if you'd stop acting like a lovesick teenager trying to insinuate that there's something wrong with Anna and Ronan's relationship," Eve continued. "Act your age! And while you're at it, forget all about Ronan. There are plenty other men out there you can fall in love with. Why choose one who's already taken and perfectly happy with the woman he has? It's not right, Sam, and you should be ashamed of yourself!"

Sam bit her lip, suitably chastened. OK, maybe she *was* acting like a lovesick teenager and, yes, maybe it was unfair of her to be questioning Anna's motives in keeping her pregnancy under wraps. But in work and everyday life, Sam had always relied on instinct and the more she thought about it, and the more she learned about the Anna and Ronan situation, the more she believed her instinct that their relationship was doomed was spot on.

*   *   *

Anna couldn't hide it any longer. It had now been weeks since she'd confessed her secret to Eve, and until then it was almost as if the baby had been in hiding, waiting for its reluctant mum to admit its existence. Because almost as soon as she had told Eve her news, her bump had grown to the point where it was impossible to deny any further what was happening to her.

And as it turned out, she didn't have to.

"Hon, how long are you going to keep this up?" Ronan asked her one night in bed, just as they were about to drop off to sleep.

"Keep what up?" Anna asked, her heart racing fearfully.

"You know." He turned to face her, and at that moment it was as though his blue eyes could see right into her soul. "About the baby – our baby."

Anna's eyes filled with tears as a multitude of emotions overwhelmed her. She was relieved, sorry, glad . . . it was difficult to ascertain exactly how she felt at that point.

"When were you going to tell me? When you were in the delivery room?" he said, with a grin and, very hesitantly, he laid a hand on her now greatly rounded belly.

"I'm sorry – I don't know why I didn't – I just couldn't –"

"Sssh, it's OK," he soothed. "I think I know why you didn't say anything."

"You do?" Anna held her breath.

"Of course I do. I know that babies weren't part of the picture for you, they never have been, have they? So I can understand why it's taken some time for you to come to terms with it, never mind having to deal with my reaction too."

"Thank you," she said, relieved that he understood some, if not all, of her reasoning.

"I can see why something like this would scare the life out of you, Anna. The loss of control, the huge changes it will bring to our lives or even to our relationship. And I don't blame you for being worried. To be honest, I'm a little bit worried myself!" He laughed lightly. "Hon, I know this wasn't part of the plan – at least not for you – but please don't think that I'm unhappy or that

I don't want it. Of course I want it. It's a piece of you, isn't it? A piece of both of us."

Anna's heart twisted, and she wanted to cry with remorse. *A piece of both of us.*

And right at that moment, Anna's future finally became clear, and she knew exactly what she was going to do, what she *had* to do, not only for Ronan's sake but for the baby's sake too.

"You know that wedding date we keep putting off?" she said, running her hand tenderly along the side of his face.

"Yes?"

"Let's do it," Anna went on. "Let's set a date once and for all. Obviously it'll have to be sometime after the baby's born, but –"

"You're absolutely sure?" he interjected. "You're sure you want to do it?"

"I'm absolutely sure," Anna replied, knowing deep down that this was the right decision, if not for herself, then at least for Ronan and the baby. He was a good man and deserved better, better than someone like her, better than someone who'd wasted so many years trying to decide what she really wanted.

But right then, the decision had finally been made for her.

CHAPTER

25. The Last to Know

Sam was back in Dublin, and not once did she regret her decision. Granted, Eve was still a bit off form with her after their initial conversation about the move a month before (and her rant about Anna), and Sam had only been around to visit her sister once or twice since securing her rented apartment on the city quays.

Her Clapham flat had since been sold, and the proceeds would go some way towards the purchase of a new home in Dublin, whenever she decided to do some serious house hunting. As it was, there hadn't been a whole lot of time for that, as she had been concentrating on writing her next book, which with any luck would help keep her mind occupied and therefore stop her thinking about Ronan and Anna.

Still, she was really happy with her decision to return home, and apart from her friends and one or two of her work colleagues, there wasn't all that much about London life she missed.

But a twenty-four-hour corner shop was definitely one of those things, Sam thought now, realising that she was all out of coffee. It was one in the morning and she'd been working on the new book all that evening. As she was on a bit of a roll, she didn't want to leave the chapter she was working on unfinished, but at the same time, without a coffee fix soon, she knew she wouldn't be able to write "Baa Baa Black Sheep". So she realised she needed to go out and stock up.

The problem was that in this part of the city finding an open shop after midnight was a bit of a challenge, so she had no choice but to walk the fifteen minutes to the nearest petrol station, which she knew had a kiosk that stayed open all night. It was a pain, really, but nobody's fault but her own for not stocking up sooner.

Putting on a warm top to protect her against the outside chill, Sam took the lift downstairs and let herself out of the apartment building.

She hummed softly to herself as she strolled along the street towards the petrol station. It was a Tuesday night so there wasn't a whole lot of late-night activity, save for a few die-hard students evidently on their way home from a night in the pub. Lucky things.

God be with the days when she and her friends were able to go out drinking on a school night, not a care in the world amongst them, she thought smiling, as she passed by the lively and jubilant group standing on the path. As she did, she heard one of the guys wolf-whistle loudly in her wake.

Minutes later, she reached the petrol station and bought the requisite jar of coffee, and what the hell – a Cadbury's Creme Egg to go with it as a treat. After all the great work she'd done tonight, she deserved it. Then, having paid the friendly guy on duty at the kiosk, Sam put her change in her pocket and headed back to the apartment.

She was only a short distance down the path when she came across the students she'd passed on the way, the small group evidently dilly-dallying on their way home. Feeling slightly uncomfortable at having to pass by the group again, Sam feigned nonchalance by casually tossing the jar of coffee from one hand to the other as she approached.

"Hey, blondie!" one of the boys called out to her. "Got a smoke?"

"'Fraid not," Sam murmured in reply and, without looking up, quickened her pace as she walked past.

"Hey!" the same boy called again as Sam continued on, his tone now louder and, she thought, somewhat menacing. "Give us a smoke!"

"I don't have any cigarettes," Sam said, trying to sound assured and confident, but inside she was starting to feel slightly nervous. She was a woman out at night on her own and, although they were young and looked harmless enough, there were four of them and they'd been drinking.

"Lying bitch," said another lad and, to her horror, Sam realised that they were following her along the path. "I seen her buying smokes from the garage."

Sam's hands clenched tightly around the coffee jar as she kept walking, altogether unsure whether to keep on denying that she had cigarettes or to just stay quiet and keep moving. The street wasn't entirely deserted; there were a few cars passing by and there were other headlights in the distance, so it wasn't as though they'd try anything, was it?

But it seemed she'd seriously underestimated the boys she'd earlier dismissed as being harmless students out for the *craic*. Without warning, the lad who'd been harassing her about the cigarettes made a sudden lunge from behind and before she knew it Sam was thrown up against the nearest wall.

"Get away from me!" she cried, as the shock of what was happening struck her. What the hell had she been thinking going out alone in the middle of the city centre so late at night? And why had she dismissed these guys as harmless? They were all drunk and right at that moment one of them had her backed up against a wall while holding both of her wrists in a vice-like grip.

"Look, it's a just jar of coffee, see?" she insisted, hoping that he'd listen to reason. "If I had cigarettes I'd give them to you, believe me."

"Ah, leave yer woman alone, Kev," one of the other boys said then, much to Sam's relief. "She has no fags."

"I'll leave her alone when I'm bleedin' good and ready!" the one called Kev snarled at his friend while Sam stayed still, her body rigid with fear.

Out of the corner of her eye she saw the headlights of a car approach and hoped that its occupant would realise that she was in trouble and help her out. But evidently the driver didn't recognise anything out of the ordinary and the car moved on, leaving Sam once more alone with her attackers.

"Please," she said, "just let me go! My boyfriend knows I went to the shop and he'll come looking for me."

"Bit of a gobshite, isn't he – sending you off out on your own in the dark like that," said Kev in a tone that suggested he knew well she was lying.

"Please," Sam repeated, her mouth dry. "I don't have any cigarettes on me but I can give you money to buy some if you want. If you let me go, I can get my purse."

Again, another pair of headlights approached, and this time Sam thought the car did seem to be slowing down.

"Aw, aren't you very nice, offering to buy them for us and everything?" Kev slurred. "While you're at it why don't you –"

But the remainder of his sentence was cut off as just then a car door slammed behind them and a male voice shouted, "Hey! What the fuck is going on here?"

In that split second, in the same instant that Kev's attention was diverted and his grip on her loosened, Sam had her chance. Using every ounce of strength she had, she jerked her body forward and her leg upward and kneed him squarely in the balls.

Stunned and in a considerable amount of pain, Kev fell backwards, releasing Sam from his grip. Without thinking, she raced forward and into the arms of the car driver who had mercifully become her saviour.

Into the arms of Ronan Fraser.

*   *   *

"Jesus, Sam, I thought I was seeing things!" Ronan was saying, as he drove down the street away from the lads, a much-relieved Sam now safely ensconced in his taxi. "I knew it looked like someone was up to no good, but when I slowed down to take a look and realised it was you . . ."

Sam too had thought she was seeing things when, having given Kev good cause to worry about his future fertility prospects, she realised that the Good Samaritan who'd got her out of a very dangerous situation was none other than Ronan.

"I mean, what the hell were you doing out on the street at all hours of the morning? Jesus, with all those years living in London, I thought you of all people should know –"

"I know, I know. It was stupid." Sam was still too shocked to fully appreciate what might have happened to her.

"Still – no one could say you couldn't hold your own," Ronan said, shaking his head in admiration. "You gave that fella one hell of a kick." He smiled. "Remind me never to get on the wrong side of you!"

Despite herself, Sam raised a smile. Still shell-shocked by what had happened, and even more by what *might have* happened, she could barely bring herself to speak, never mind explain how she'd got the strength to do what she had.

"Now are you sure you don't want to report this to the guards?" Ronan asked. "I know those lads took off like the hounds of hell, and it's unlikely they'll catch them, but you'd never know."

"There's no point, Ronan," Sam said. "All I want to do now is go home."

"You should come and stay with me and Anna," Ronan said. "I'm on my way home now anyway, I'd just dropped off my last fare and –"

"Ronan, thanks a million for the offer, but I'd really rather go home to my own place if you don't mind."

"You're sure?"

"Yes."

"Well, then I'll come back with you. You don't want to be on your own after a shock like that. It'll probably take a while to sink in."

Despite the trauma she'd just experienced, Sam couldn't help but feel a tiny shiver of excitement at the thought of Ronan accompanying her back to the apartment. For God's sake, stop it! she admonished herself.

But once again, she couldn't help but think about fate, as she had that time they'd bumped into one another in London. In a city the size of London, what were the odds of the two of them meeting in a busy tube station? And again, in a city the size of Dublin, what were the odds of Ronan being the one to pass by while she was being attacked?

And why did it make Sam more convinced than ever that – despite Eve's protests – she and Ronan really were meant to be together?

* * *

"So you just *happened* to be wandering around the streets at night, and Ronan just *happened* to be passing by while you were being mugged?" Eve couldn't contain her astonishment, coupled with more than a little scepticism.

It was the day after the incident, and Sam was still feeling pretty shook up. Ronan had, as promised, dropped her home safely and then insisted on staying for a while and making her strong cups of coffee.

His unabashed concern, as well as his feeble attempts at being funny to help cheer her up and try and take her mind off things, made him even more attractive than before and merely deepened Sam's conviction that he would eventually turn out to be someone very important in her life.

When Eve had called to the apartment earlier that morning with Max, having heard about the incident through Ronan, Sam could tell her sister was finding it difficult to balance her concern for Sam's welfare against her disbelief that Ronan had been around to 'rescue' her merely by chance.

"Thank goodness he was just passing by – otherwise I don't know what those guys would have done," Sam said now.

"But it just seems so weird!" Eve unbuckled Max out of his buggy. "I mean, of all the people . . ."

"He's a taxi driver, Eve. He drives a cab all over the city at night and, luckily for me, he recognised me and realised I was in trouble. Thanks for your concern, by the way," she added dourly, becoming annoyed that her sister seemed to think she had somehow engineered the whole scenario.

"Of course I'm concerned. And relieved that you did get away. Did you call the guards?"

"No point – you know that as well as I do. Those lads took off like rockets when Ronan arrived and I managed to get away."

Eve gave her a sideways look. "I know – I heard. Fair play to you: I know I wouldn't have had the courage to do something like that." Then, having satisfied herself that Ronan being around at the time really was a coincidence, her voice softened. "You really should be more careful you know, Sam. Going out on the streets on your own like that in the middle of the night – it's crazy."

"I know, I know." Although Eve was right, Sam was tired of hearing this by now. "But, naively, I think I had it in my head that Dublin was a safe place – compared to London anyway. It was never like this years ago."

"Yes, well, I hope you've learned your lesson," her sister chided. She sat down beside Sam on the sofa, Max in her lap. "So, did Ronan stay long?"

"A couple of hours," Sam told her. "Long enough for me to get over the shock of it all, I suppose. Don't look at me like that, Eve. It was all totally innocent." She turned away from her sister's accusing gaze. "He's a lovely guy and Anna's very lucky to have him."

"Yes, she is. So you've forgotten all your nonsense then?"

Sam sighed. No point in telling Eve that after last night her feelings for Ronan were stronger than ever.

CHAPTER

26. The Last to Know

"So what about August?"

"I'm in the States in August – you know that."

"OK, what about September? The weather should still be good around then."

Liam sighed with irritation. "Eve, we have stocktaking at Morrissons in September – it's one of our busiest months. It's just not a good time."

Eve sat back in the kitchen chair and crossed her arms across her chest. "Well, when is a good time to get married, Liam?"

It had now been months since they'd got engaged and, despite his initial agreement that they should set a date for their wedding as soon as possible, this was so far proving very difficult. *Liam* was proving very difficult.

Notwithstanding the wedding date, he seemed to have little interest in anything to do with this wedding – booking the hotel, the flowers, inviting guests, and Eve's earlier elation about their engagement had soon deflated.

Granted, there weren't many men who got overexcited about

wedding arrangements in general, so she couldn't really blame him for that, but surely he had to have *some* input into setting the date?

"Well?" Eve repeated her question when Liam didn't reply. "When is a good time for you?"

"Well, does it all have to happen so soon? Why can't we wait until things calm down a bit?"

"Because your eldest is hugely excited and can't stop talking about being a flower-girl. Because your partner of nearly eight years – i.e. me – has quite frankly been waiting long enough for this! And I'm getting older and you know I'd like to have another baby and we can't do that until after the wedding."

Liam groaned. "Eve, we've talked about this. Babies mean money, and the other two are hard enough to keep as it is. And you know as well as I do that things are tough at work these days."

Eve's face fell. "But I thought things had improved at work and that the last Australian trip had been the best ever. At least, that's what you said at the time." The fact that the business seemed to have got better, and that the family were now financially back on an even keel, had given Eve the confidence to broach the subject of the third baby.

"Look, maybe some time in the future," Liam said then. "But the timing just isn't great at the moment. I still have a lot of travelling do over the next couple of months and, if we were to have another one, leaving you on your own so much wouldn't really be fair, would it?"

Well, it would certainly be nothing new anyway, Eve thought sourly.

"Well, OK, then," she conceded, trying not to betray her disappointment. "Maybe we'll talk about the baby some other time. But what about the wedding? Liam, it was embarrassing enough having to propose to you myself, let alone having to now poke and prod you into setting a date too."

"Exactly!" Liam shot back, quickly standing up from the table.

"Exactly what?"

"Exactly what you said. It was *you* who wanted this wedding in the first place, Eve, not me! And now you expect me to get involved in all this hullabaloo along with you. I can't just drop everything at the drop of a hat – work is too busy and –"

"Well, if you didn't want this wedding, why on earth did you agree to marry me?" she cried, her heart almost breaking in two. "Why did you say yes?"

"I said yes because . . ." Liam shook his head, and the remainder of his sentence trailed off. Then his tone softened and he sat back down at the table. "I said yes because I wanted to marry you, Eve. You're right – we should be a proper family. But all this wedding stuff, well, to be honest, it's giving me a headache. I've got so much going on at work at the moment – I've got another Australian trip lined up soon which needs a lot of preparation and I'm just finding it all hard to take in."

"Fair enough," Eve said, realising that, yes, perhaps Liam was finding it all a bit much. It was OK for her, she had nothing else to do but plan and look forward to the wedding, so much so that it was occupying her every thought and was the main topic of conversation these days, that and Ronan and Anna's newborn baby.

A few days earlier, Anna had given birth to a baby girl whom she and Ronan had named Ciara. Although five weeks premature, she was a gorgeous little thing and the absolute image of Anna. And despite the fact that she'd worked herself into such a state before her arrival, Anna was now totally enthralled with the baby, as was proud dad Ronan.

Eve was thrilled for them and also relieved that Anna had got over her brief period of panic or disarray, or whatever it was that had made her keep her pregnancy a secret from Ronan for so long. And, contrary to the rubbish Sam had been spouting about their relationship for the last while, from what Eve had seen at the hospital the other day, Anna and Ronan couldn't be happier. Good for them.

But of course Anna's new baby had merely brought Eve's desire to have another one of her own to the forefront, which was why she'd lately become so impatient with Liam. But whatever about a new baby, if Eve could just get her marriage plans back on a decent footing, she and Liam wouldn't be too far behind Anna and Ronan in the happiness stakes.

"I can understand that you're under pressure with work, and maybe I shouldn't be so obsessive about this wedding," she said to Liam then. "But I'm so excited about it! And as I said, I've waited a long time for this. Perhaps the reason I'm so anxious to set a date is . . . is because I just can't wait to marry you." Eve didn't think she'd ever been so frank with Liam about her feelings for him.

Before, she was always slightly afraid to be, afraid to come across as clingy or needy. But now that they were getting married, now that she knew Liam wanted to spend the rest of his life with her too, then it was stupid to hide it, wasn't it?

"I know you're excited and that the kids are excited. Believe me, I am too. But, Eve, there's a lot of stuff going on at work at the moment that really needs my attention. Can't we wait a little while longer before deciding on a date – until I get everything sorted? At least until after this next Australian trip anyway."

Eve nodded and reached for his hand. Upon reflection, she really should have been more understanding and more aware of what was going on with him. The Australia trip had been looming for some time and apparently there was quite a lot at stake, so it was understandable he'd be anxious about it.

No, let Liam go and do what he had to do for the next two weeks. After that, he'd be all hers.

"Of course we can," she said smiling. "After all, we've already waited this long, haven't we?"

"Thanks, love," he said, the relief so visible in his expression and overall demeanour that Eve felt doubly guilty for being so hard on him.

Just then, Lily entered the room, Max shuffling along behind her as she held his hand.

"Mum, when is dinner? We're really hungry."

"Hungee!" Max repeated after his sister.

Eve looked at the clock. What with all her trying to get things arranged with Liam, she'd forgotten to put on something for dinner. And as it was heading for six and her family were clearly hungry, waiting another hour or so for her to prepare something wouldn't go down well!

Sensing her thoughts, Liam stood up. "I'll head down and pick something up from the takeaway."

"You're sure?"

"Absolutely. I'm starting to feel a bit peckish myself. Anyway, it's a Friday evening and you deserve a break from cooking."

Wow, this was a turn-up for the books! "As long as you're sure," Eve said, pleased. "I'd quite fancy a takeaway myself."

"Can I come with you, Daddy?" Lily piped up.

"Me, me, me, me!" Max said, determined not to be left behind.

"No problem," Liam said.

Eve looked at him, startled. This *really* wasn't like him to be so agreeable where the kids were concerned. She'd definitely been too hard on him lately!

"OK then, see you guys later." Having given Liam their order, Eve beamed with pleasure as she watched her husband-to-be pile their kids into the car and drive off in the direction of their local takeaway. Smiling, she closed the front door and went back into the kitchen to arrange the drinks and cutlery.

As she opened the drawer, Eve glanced down at her engagement ring and felt another shiver of delight. Sometimes, life was great.

* * *

Liam had driven only a short distance down the main road when he thought of something.

Did he have his wallet with him? He frowned, trying to remember whether it was still in the pocket of his suit jacket or if he had left it at home.

He turned down the volume on the radio, immediately cutting short Michael Jackson's "Billie Jean" rendition. Lily, who had been boogying along to the music in the passenger seat alongside him, gave her father a disappointed look.

"Lily, is my jacket on the back seat?" he asked, trying in vain to spot the jacket in his rear-view mirror. "My wallet should be in there but, if it's not, we'll need to go back home and get it."

"It's OK, Daddy, I have money," she replied, patting the pink and white Barbie handbag she carried everywhere with her.

Despite himself, Liam smiled. God love her, his daughter still hadn't a clue about what things cost.

"Well, see if you can find the wallet just in case we don't have enough, OK?"

"OK, Daddy."

Lucky her, Liam thought wryly. Thanks to his daughter's unanticipated appearance seven years before, he – who was barely out of his teens at the time – had found out what things cost very quickly indeed!

It was hard to believe that he and Eve were still together after

266

all these years, really. No one – his mother, his friends and, in all honesty, least of all himself – had truly expected it to last.

"Do you love her?" Ronan had asked back when Liam first learned of Eve's pregnancy. They had only been seeing one another for a couple of months at the most, when she'd made the announcement out of the blue.

"I don't honestly know," Liam, still shell-shocked by the news, had replied. "She's a nice girl, and we have a good laugh but . . ." he shook his head, "either way, I have to stand by her, don't I?" Whatever his feelings towards Eve might have been, there was no question of him abandoning her. Only a right bastard would do that.

"Does standing by her mean marrying her?" Ronan replied. "Because, you know there are other ways of standing by someone, and if you're not sure of your feelings towards her, then the last thing you should do now is make a hasty decision. You of all people should know what an unhappy marriage can do to the people involved."

At that stage, his parents had been separated for a couple of years, but Liam recalled the misery in their household before Noreen and Peadar eventually decided to split. Ronan was right. He shouldn't do anything too hasty.

At the same time, Eve, or indeed her parents, had never put any immediate pressure on him to marry her and seemed relieved that he planned to provide for the child at all. Still, at the same time, Liam knew that Eve must have been disappointed back then, and again over the subsequent years. She'd admitted as much to him earlier in the kitchen, hadn't she? Admitted that she'd wanted to make things official between them for a very long time.

But they'd moseyed along happily enough for the last few years, and Liam had never really seen the point in rocking the boat, especially when they were as good as married anyway, and while sometimes the pressure of keeping the family going got to him, at the same time he didn't know what he'd do without them.

But it seemed that Eve had grown tired of waiting and decided to take matters into her own hands.

Her proposal had knocked him for six, that was for sure, but with the kids around, and indeed the expectant look on Eve's face, he hadn't the heart to say no. Anyway, now that he thought about it, it wasn't such a terrible idea after all. OK, so Eve might not have been the love of his life, but she was the mother of his children and he did love her all the same. And seeing as the person he'd *thought* was love of his life had evidently moved on, there was no point in waiting around any more, was there?

"Ah, Max, let go of that. You'll ruin it!" Lily cried, having reached behind to retrieve the jacket and found that her baby brother, who'd been hurriedly strapped into the back by Liam, had somehow extricated himself from the safety belt and was now sitting on his father's favourite Louis Copeland jacket and happily chewing on one sleeve.

"Bloody hell, Max!" Liam groaned as he caught sight of the scene in the rear-view mirror. Terrified that his precious (and bloody expensive!) jacket would be ruined, he kept one hand on the steering wheel and quickly reached behind to yank the jacket from beneath his baby son.

The split second he'd taken his eye off the road was the one in which a pedestrian decided to dash out in front of the car, and by the time Liam finally noticed the danger and slammed on the brakes, it was much too late.

Swerving wildly to try and avoid the pedestrian, he made the erroneous decision of steering the car onto the other side of the road – right into the path of a large truck laden down with building debris.

The inevitable collision was devastating, the screech of brakes and the sound of shattering glass and ruptured metal deafening. And while ultimately Liam's brief lapse in judgement served to burden the pedestrian with insurmountable guilt, and caused serious injury to the skip driver, its most devastating legacy was that the resultant crash managed – in one fell swoop – to wipe out entirely the three people in the world Eve loved most.

*   *   *

Sam was over the moon. She'd come up with an amazing plot twist for her new book and best of all she hadn't needed to spend ages and ages thinking about it – nope, it had come to her just like that, right in the middle of a scene. She loved it when things like that happened while writing, adored it when things were going well and the words on the page just kept on coming. It was the best part of the process, the part when all the parts just seemed to click together nicely, when everything fell magically into place.

Well, that was that, she thought, standing up from her desk and stretching her arms high above her head; she might as well pack it in for the day and give herself a break. She looked at the clock in the kitchen – almost seven o'clock! Shit, she had no idea she'd been working that long – no wonder she was feeling aches and pains!

Time for a treat, she decided. It was Friday evening and she'd had a hell of a good week writing-wise so why not reward herself with something nice? Luckily, there was a big block of raspberry ripple ice-cream in the freezer that would be lovely to dig into after dinner.

Sam went into the kitchen and switched on the radio. She liked having it on in the background when cooking – the music gave her a boost and put a spring in her step. Not that she needed it today, she grinned, thrilled with the way the new book was going.

In fact, things were going well all round.

She and Eve were getting on much better now that Sam had finally decided to put her stupid infatuation with Ronan to the back of her mind. He was a new father now and an elated one, according to Eve.

Sam shook her head. She'd been an idiot really and was glad that Eve had forgiven her for being so silly – particularly as part of the reason she moved back to Dublin in the first place was to spend more time with her sister! So it would have been ironic really if they ended up not speaking over that. No, she and Eve were grand now and Sam was doing her best to help her out with the preparations for her wedding – that is, if she ever managed to get herself a willing groom! Liam was – as always – up to his tonsils in work but, according to Eve, at least the worst of it seemed to be over and the wine business was getting back on track.

Sam went to the fridge and took out some fresh carrots and onions, only half-listening to the news broadcast, which as usual was full of bad news, more job losses, nurses on strike and . . . what was that? Three people killed in a car crash? How awful, she thought, pausing as she began to slice a carrot in order to listen to the rest of the bulletin. Apparently a male driver and two young children were the victims. Terrible, she thought shaking her head sadly. What a horrible, horrible thing to happen to someone.

A few minutes later the news finished and the music started back up again with the newest release from the latest U2 album, which quickly restored Sam's earlier high spirits.

She was still in the middle of chopping vegetables when in the background she heard the telephone ring.

"Hello?" Sam said cheerfully into the receiver, still shaking her hips in time to the song.

But only seconds later, the smile died on her face and the knife she held in her hand thudded heavily to the floor.

CHAPTER 31

Brooke put a hand to her mouth, unable to believe what she was reading. What the hell was the author *playing* at killing off three people like that? It was *way* over the top, way too melodramatic – she had clearly bitten off more than she could chew here! Which was such a disappointment as the story had been moving along very nicely up to this point . . .

Brooke had only started reading the manuscript again recently, having had to grudgingly leave it aside for the last couple of weeks. A new submission by one of her existing authors had necessitated a ton of revisions, and as they'd also launched a new book by a debut author, the preparation for this, as well as the rest, had taken up much of her time.

But since she'd picked up *The Last to Know* again a few days ago, she'd hardly been able to put it down, trying to figure out what would become of Eve, particularly when it seemed something was going on with Anna and Liam. But now . . . what would happen now? Liam and the kids couldn't really be dead, could they? The author was in danger of losing the plot completely here, unless she had something else up her sleeve and managed to rescue it further down the line . . .

Just then Brooke's internal office line rang, interrupting her musing.

"Brooke, it's Sandra Moore," Horizon's receptionist told her. "She says she needs to speak to you immediately."

Brooke sighed inwardly at the unwelcome interruption but agreed to take the call. Sandra Moore was an author whose second book they'd recently published and whose career they were trying to build. She'd delivered her third novel a couple of weeks back and, while Brooke normally got through her authors' new material over a weekend, this time she'd been so engrossed in trying to finish *The Last to Know* that she hadn't yet managed to read through much of Sandra's manuscript. She picked up the line.

"Sandra – hi," she began warmly. "I've been meaning to phone you actually. I'm loving the new book so far, but we've been so busy I haven't had a chance to –"

"That's not what I wanted to talk to you about," the other woman interjected shortly.

Brooke frowned. Sandra did not sound impressed. Oh dear. "Oh?"

"Well!" Sandra exclaimed breathlessly. "I've just been in Dymocks and I see that Casey Mills is their book of the month."

Brooke grimaced. Casey Mills was the debut author whose launch preparations had taken up much of her time in the last few weeks, and she and Sandra both had new books released this month. "That's right," she said tentatively.

"Well, how the hell am I supposed to sell anything when the bookstores are practically thrusting bloody Casey Mills' books at people?" Sandra cried. "It's not as if she needs the bloody exposure," she added bitterly.

Casey, a popular TV soap actor in Australia, was part of a new trend in publishing – the celebrity author. Although Brooke didn't necessarily believe that celebrities putting their names to fiction was good for literature, there was no denying that it was fantastic for sales. Readers went out and bought these books in their droves, the author's name and the associated widespread publicity sending sales of such books into the stratosphere.

"It's bloody pathetic," Sandra went on, her tone deflated. "The least you guys could do was give me a fighting chance! Instead, my books get stuck in the back beside the travel guides, while Casey Mills practically gets an entire bookshop to herself!" Brooke agreed with her entirely, but unfortunately she didn't have a whole lot of say in how the bookshops promoted certain authors above others. That was a matter for the sales team.

"Every time I open a newspaper the silly cow is smiling back at me and talking about how the story just popped into her head one day and how she never thought she'd get it published!" Sandra was on a bit of roll. "Give me a break! At least I went to the trouble of actually *writing* mine!"

"I know you did," Brooke soothed, "and it's a great book too –"

"Well, if it's so bloody great, why didn't *I* get book of the month in Dymocks?"

God, Brooke hated this part of being an editor. She felt sorry for authors having to compete with names who often hadn't even *read* the stories they were supposed to have 'spent hours on end' writing. And she could imagine how frustrating it must be for Sandra to see Casey Mills' face and the cover of her book splashed all over the national newspapers and glossy magazines, while her own barely got a mention in one of the local rags. And yes, it must be soul-destroying to find the same author's books being pushed to death by the bookshops, particularly at the expense of her own.

"What am I going to do, Brooke?" Sandra said, her voice small. "How the hell I am going to compete?"

"Look, we've got plenty lined up for your book too," she soothed, realising that by the time she'd reassured her distressed author, it would be some time yet before she could get back to *The Last to Know* and its unexpected plot twist.

CHAPTER

27. The Last to Know

It was just a dream. Eve was fast asleep and this was all just a dream. Any minute now, she'd wake up and hear Max giggling in his playpen and Lily in her bedroom singing Madonna songs into her hairbrush.

And Liam . . . Liam would either be barking orders into the phone at someone in the office or watching football on TV.

Yes, Eve was sure it was all a dream. How else could she explain the fuzzy, almost surreal world she'd inhabited since getting that strange visit a while ago? The one where a stranger on the doorstep had told her in a stilted voice that Liam and their two children had been killed outright in a car accident. As if someone could go a mile down the road for a takeaway and, just like that, never come back.

They'd tried their best, the other strangers at the front door told her. They'd tried to save them, tried to get them out of the car. But it had been no use as, according to them, the pile of heavy building debris that had landed on Liam's car after impact had made the task even harder.

But of course one of them was already outside the car: Max had been thrown out of his seat upon impact apparently. Eve knew well that this was definitely a lie. There was no way Liam could have forgotten to belt him up in the back seat, was there?

No, it all had to be a dream because if it were real, Eve would be feeling uncontrollable anguish right now, whereas instead she felt – she felt almost detached from the whole thing, disassociated, disconnected. And really, any normal person who'd been told such a thing, who'd been told that their entire family had been lost to them forever, who'd been told about such an immense tragedy, surely they would feel much, much more than this?

No, it would all be fine when she woke up, and the watery, muddled sensation in her head, along with the dull feeling in the pit of her stomach, would soon go away and she'd be back to normal.

Back to normal and back with her family.

*   *   *

Sam sat on the sofa with one arm around her sister, tears still streaming down her face. She still couldn't believe what had happened, couldn't believe that Liam and the kids were dead.

And if it was difficult for her to believe it, to come to terms with the fact that her sister's fiancé and children had a few hours earlier been killed in a car crash, then how on earth was Eve dealing with it?

She recalled her sister's cool, almost detached tone on the other end of the phone earlier that evening, when Eve had phoned the flat and calmly informed her what had happened. For a brief moment, she'd wondered if her sister might be having her on, but what kind of cruel sadist would joke about something like that?

But Sam knew it was no joke when footage from the crash had

been featured on the evening TV news, and she saw the family's battered and mutilated car – the twisted metal almost unrecognisable and covered in what looked like cement and broken paving slabs. With the help of eye-witnesses, most notably the pedestrian who had wandered out onto the road, the rescue services were able to deduce that Liam had been trying to get something out of the back seat before the accident occurred.

The force of the collision, combined with the falling debris from the skip truck, had most likely killed Liam and Lily instantly, and evidently poor little Max had not been belted in securely in the back seat.

Yes, it was all too real – at least, it certainly was to Sam. Poor Eve didn't seem aware of what was happening at all, and in the few hours since she'd been informed of the tragedy, she had just sat in the living room – dazed and staring into space.

Even when Sam had first arrived at the house, white with shock and almost unable to speak for crying, Eve had almost indifferently returned Sam's hug and without another word had closed the door behind them and sat down on the living-room sofa.

She'd stayed there ever since, not uttering a single word, just staring into space and no doubt lost in her own grief.

Even when other people began to arrive, Ronan and Anna, Liam's mother Noreen, their friends and Liam's work colleagues, Eve still maintained that eerily blank look. Yet Sam knew that it was only a matter of time before her sister realised the magnitude of what had happened to her and the impossibility of trying to come to terms with it. And in the meantime, Sam felt frustrated and useless, totally unable to comfort her and unsure as to whether or not it would ever be possible to do so.

CHAPTER

28. The Last to Know

Anna was inconsolable, and Ronan was worried. While he too was utterly devastated over his friend's death, he knew that such a huge amount of stress wouldn't do Anna any good after all the anxiety of baby Ciara being in the incubator. The baby was due home soon and Anna needed to be in good form to cope with the little one. He lay in bed beside her as she cried silently in the darkness, perhaps thinking that he was asleep or that he couldn't hear her.

The funeral had been heartbreaking. Ronan still couldn't get out of his head the blank, almost shuttered expression on Eve's face when two little white coffins and one larger one were laid to rest in the ground. All around her, family and friends were sobbing their hearts out while the poor woman clearly hadn't a clue what was going on, or if she did, simply couldn't summon the resources to deal with it. Ronan had found it incredibly agonising, especially having to help carry first the children's and then Liam's coffin into the church. Losing one person you loved was enough for anyone, never mind three. How could anyone get over that?

But the fact that even now – a full week after the funeral – Anna still was wildly upset bewildered him somewhat.

Granted, to lose a fiancé and two children at once was an inconceivable tragedy, and of course Anna would be worried and heartbroken for Eve, but what Ronan couldn't figure out was why she seemed almost as upset as Eve was, if not more so.

And Eve, the poor creature, was apparently still in denial. According to Sam she was still, even now, insisting that it was all a dream or some kind of cruel hoax.

Again at the funeral, she'd refused to accept commiserations and condolences from friends and neighbours and vehemently insisted that it was all a mistake, a conspiracy even, and that Liam and the children would be coming home soon.

The doctors had prescribed something for her, but Ronan reckoned there was no medicine in existence that could truly take the edge off a person's grief, nor was there ever likely to be.

Still, now as he lay in bed beside his weeping fiancée, Ronan really wished there was something, anything he could do to make the pain of it all easier for Anna to bear. It was difficult to describe really, but she'd taken it so hard it was almost as if she had lost her own children and the love of her own life, instead of still having him and their baby with her. In fairness, perhaps it was exactly this that made it all so hard for Anna. She was probably feeling guilty knowing that she still had him, the new baby and their lives together to look forward to, whereas poor Eve had nothing.

So, yes, Ronan decided, as he reached across and drew his fiancée towards him, all this was probably just a combination of shock, grief and hormones along with an unreasonable, but perhaps understandable, dollop of guilt.

* * *

Despite what Ronan thought, the root of Anna's distress wasn't just grief and shock over the accident. And it wasn't guilt that she still had Ronan and the new baby, while her friend had nothing. There was an element of this, certainly, but it wasn't the main cause of Anna's intolerable angst.

She was of course grieving heavily for Max and Lily and the way their little lives had been cut so short so soon. Additionally, she was racked with sorrow and sympathy for poor Eve, who after hearing news of the accident had shut down and retreated into herself and had stayed that way every since.

But the main reason, the ultimate reason, Anna was suffering so much in the wake of the accident was because the first thing she felt upon hearing the news of Liam's demise, the very first emotion she experienced – was pure unadulterated relief.

And Anna hated herself for it.

CHAPTER

29. The Last to Know

It was now almost a month since the accident and still Eve was behaving as though nothing at all had happened.

She hadn't shed a tear, hadn't talked at all about the crash and seemed to be living in an alternate reality where all was well and Liam and the kids were just away somewhere else and would be coming home soon. And whenever Sam or anyone else tried to talk to her about what had happened, she'd shut down completely.

This was hugely disturbing to Sam, but according to the doctors a reaction like this could be common enough in the wake of such an immense tragedy.

"It's a kind of coping mechanism," Eve's family doctor explained to Sam kindly. "I know it might seem disconcerting but she's had a massive shock, one that she's not yet equipped to handle. Just give it some time."

Sam was reluctant to play along and pretend that everything was normal, but for the time being she had no choice. It was also difficult to tell whether her almost constant presence in Eve's house since the accident was doing her sister any good, but for the moment it was the only way she felt she could help.

Then early that morning, a large package addressed to Eve and marked *Personal Belongings* arrived at the family home. Judging by the return label, it was from the crash recovery centre that had processed the family car, and as well as a sympathy card, the package contained a number of items including Max's favourite Action Man toy, a pink Barbie handbag that belonged to Lily, and Liam's ill-fated suit jacket.

Eve's reaction as she sorted through each of these items one by one was painful to observe, and for the first time in weeks, Sam thought she saw a slight crack in the wall of denial that Eve had so solidly erected since the accident. Then, almost as quickly as it had appeared, the brief sense of recognition was gone.

"I'd better hang this up," she said, picking up Liam's jacket and drawing it close to her. "Liam hates it when his suits get crumpled."

But the raw pain in her voice as she said this suggested to Sam that her sister was finally coming round to the realisation that he and the kids were really gone, that they weren't merely biding their time before coming back. And she decided that it might finally be time for her to give Eve some space.

"I fancy a cup of coffee, and we've run out of milk," she said casually. "Do you need anything at the shop while I'm there?"

Eve barely gave a faint shake of her head in return. "No, I'm fine," she said softly, her thoughts evidently a million miles away but, Sam hoped, on their way back to reality, however painful that reality might be.

*　*　*

When Sam left for the shop Eve picked up the jacket once again and held it close to her. She could still smell Liam – her Liam – on it but yet there was no sign of Liam, had been no sign of him in a very long time.

If this really was a dream, then why hadn't she woken up by now? And why hadn't they come home? Was there a chance that what Sam, Liam's mother and everyone else were talking about had really happened? That Liam and her babies were gone for good?

There was a very good chance but still Eve wouldn't allow herself to believe it. She couldn't allow herself to believe that Liam would put his own and their children's lives in danger like that. Liam was a good driver, a safe driver, and there was no way that he would have swerved out onto the other side of the road like that.

Once again laying the jacket aside, she began to go through the rest of the items in the box. There were some more toys belonging to Max, a pink sparkly hairclip that was Lily's and right at the very bottom of the box lay an empty carrier bag from a popular gift store which was based locally.

Eve picked up the bag, idly wondering why it had been in the car and what it contained. She knew it hadn't been there before. Always meticulous about keeping the car free from clutter and rubbish, she had cleaned it out only a day or two before the – nightmare happened.

Then she remembered something. Her birthday had been three weeks ago, not that she had taken much notice at the time what with everything that had happened. Had Liam that evening – using the takeaway as an excuse – gone out and bought her a present and maybe conspired with the kids to keep it a secret? Had they gone to the gift shop first, before continuing to the takeaway?

She recalled how uncharacteristically eager he'd been about getting something in for dinner and how unusually game he was to take the kids along with him.

Had buying her a present – either for her birthday or to make up for their recent disagreement about setting a date for the wedding – been part of the plan then?

Eve wasn't sure. Liam had certainly been acting differently in the run-up to . . . That Day, but in a good way. And despite his unwillingness to involve himself in the wedding plans, he had definitely been taking a lot more interest in family life. In fact, in the weeks leading up to – what had happened, Eve felt more content and secure in their relationship than she'd done in the entire eight years they'd been together. It was as if the decision to get married had finally anchored both the relationship and the family, in the same way that parenthood had anchored Anna and Ronan.

But, she discovered, disheartened, the bag was empty, so if Liam had indeed bought her a present, there was no sign of it now. Actually, no, it wasn't empty, there was still a receipt inside, she realised, reaching for the slip of paper at the bottom of the bag. Well, she'd been wrong on one count. The receipt was dated the previous day to . . . That Day, but Liam had indeed bought her a present. She read the details printed on the receipt.

Care Bear – Pink 6.99

Obviously, he had taken the teddy bear out of the bag and maybe wrapped it up and hidden it somewhere, waiting for the right moment to give it to her.

Then, tears in her eyes, Eve smiled sadly and brought the tiny slip of paper to her lips, a remnant of one of Liam's final, loving actions towards her.

She looked again at her family's belongings and, with a painful and startling clarity, finally realised that this was no dream – no nightmare from which she would soon wake up.

Liam, Lily and Max really were gone and they were never coming back.

CHAPTER

30. The Last to Know

A few days later, Anna phoned the house, wondering if Eve and Sam would like to call over for a visit. The baby had since left the hospital, although Anna and Ronan had had a recent scare involving a chest infection, which had necessitated another visit to the paediatric ward.

"Ciara's well over the worst of it now, and we'd love to see you," she said to Sam, before adding, "and I think it might do you both some good to get out of the house."

Sam agreed that this was a very good idea, as since the arrival of the personal belongings earlier that week, poor Eve had been inconsolable and it seemed had finally begun to break through her denial and begin the grieving process.

"I'll talk to Eve about it and get back to you," she told Anna. "As you can imagine she's up and down a lot these days so . . ."

"I understand. It's just . . . well, I haven't been able to do much or be there for her since . . ." Anna's voice trailed off, and Sam knew that understandably the other woman must be feeling guilty about her preoccupation with the new baby while her

287

friend was suffering.

But Sam was also worried that the sight of Anna's new baby and happy family might again highlight Eve's loss.

As it turned out, she needn't have worried. When she got off the phone to Anna and broached the subject of a visit with Eve, her sister seemed very open to it and especially to spending time with Baby Ciara.

"Yes, that would be nice. I can hardly remember what she looks like," she said with a rare smile, agreeing that they should call over later that same evening.

"Well, Anna says Ronan is convinced she's the milkman's!" Sam joked, pleased that the prospect of the visit seemed to have brought Eve out of herself. "Apparently she doesn't look a bit like him."

"That would suit your theory then, wouldn't it?" Eve said wryly, and duly chastened Sam hung her head in shame.

"Well – I – I think I may have been a bit unfair on her really," she stammered. "Obviously they're very happy together now, and I was just being silly."

In the great scheme of things, her stupid obsession with Ronan seemed now incredibly foolish and immature, and she had resolved to just forget all about it and let him, and everyone else, get on with their own lives. And she was too wrapped up in taking care of Eve at the moment to even think about her own feelings.

No, tonight would be a good excuse for everyone to get together and hopefully try and bring Eve out of herself and set her on the road back to some kind of normality.

*　　*　　*

"She's absolutely beautiful, Anna," Sam said with feeling, as she, Anna and Eve gazed admiringly at five-week-old baby Ciara, who was sleeping peacefully in her cradle in Anna and Ronan's living room. She was indeed a pretty little thing, with her shock of jet-black hair, long dark eyelashes and peaches-and-cream skin, and again Sam felt intensely guilty for even contemplating that she might not be Ronan's child.

Granted, she didn't look remotely like him, but again it was impossible to tell at this early age, wasn't it?

"She's lovely," Eve agreed.

Sam watched her sister closely for any signs of distress or emotion, but to her relief Eve seemed at ease with and largely unaffected by the sight of her friend's newborn.

"And she's the image of you, Anna," Eve continued.

Ronan, who was sitting on the sofa, laughed and rolled his eyes. "Typical! Everyone only sees Anna in her. Anyone would think I had nothing to do with her at all!"

"Don't be silly – of course she looks like you," Anna replied briskly. "She has your eyes, hasn't she?"

Ronan shrugged his shoulders. "I suppose so, but aren't all newborn babies' eyes blue?"

Just then, little Ciara stirred and began to wake up, and when her eyelids eventually opened and a beautiful pair of striking blue eyes stared up at them, Sam thought that Anna was right; the baby seemed to have inherited Ronan's eyes.

"Can I hold her?" Eve asked then, and when Anna gave a relieved smile, Sam realised that she also had been worried about Eve's reaction to her daughter.

"Of course," Anna said, gently lifting Ciara from her cradle and placing her into Eve's arms. As she did, the baby seemed to give Eve a joyful smile, although again at that age, Sam wondered if such a thing was possible. Ciara could just as easily have been breaking wind.

"She's so beautiful," Eve whispered almost to herself, gently carrying the baby in her arms as she went to sit beside Ronan on the sofa.

"She's not so beautiful when she's screaming her head off at all hours of the morning," Ronan remarked wryly, sharing a knowing glance with Anna.

"True, she started off well but she's been a bit narky lately, what with the chest infection and all," his fiancée agreed. "We were hoping to bring her over to France for a few days when things were a little bit more settled, but I don't think that's going to happen anytime soon."

"Your sister hasn't seen her yet, then?" Sam recalled Eve telling her before that one of Ronan's sisters, Martha, was married to a Frenchman.

"No, and of course she's dying to!" Ronan groaned, rolling his eyes. "She and Thierry were going to come over, but it isn't all that long since they were here for Mam's anniversary, so we said we'd go to them instead."

"But not until Ciara's fully fit and able to travel," Anna added firmly.

"Well, great that she's over the worst of it now," Sam said, relieved that Eve seemed totally preoccupied by, and almost in thrall to, the baby in her arms. The joy surrounding the new baby's arrival had today at least taken her sister's mind off her own awful situation and given her something else to concentrate on.

And despite the horror of the last few weeks, Sam decided, as she watched her baby sister smile tenderly at the little bundle in her arms, it seemed that Eve was finally on her way back.

CHAPTER

31. The Last to Know

"It was really good of Eve to offer to mind Ciara for us today, wasn't it?" Ronan said, straightening his tie in front of the mirror over the dressing table in their bedroom. "And great to see her keeping so well."

Anna grimaced. "It is, but I'm still not sure about being away from Ciara for so long," she said mournfully.

It was now the middle of September, and she and Ronan were today heading off to attend Denis and Lauren's eagerly awaited wedding. As they needed a baby-sitter, Eve, who seemed to be coping remarkably well these days, had offered to come over to the house and look after Ciara for the day.

Although Anna was happy for Lauren, and eager to share in her friend's big day, this would be her first time being parted from Ciara since she was born eight weeks before.

No doubt she would be fine with Eve, but still . . .

"Don't be worrying, she'll be grand here," Ronan reassured her. "Anyway, she'll probably sleep all day and won't even notice we're away." He grimaced. "Hopefully she'll do the same on the plane to France in a few weeks' time!"

"You're right – I'm fretting over nothing." Anna smoothed down the front of her three-quarter-length ruffle-hemmed floral dress – the only item in her wardrobe that went some way towards concealing her still-rounded tummy, although luckily the majority of the baby weight had begun to disappear soon after Ciara's birth.

"You look stunning," Ronan said, as if reading her thoughts. He reached across and kissed her gently on the lips. "Look, just try and relax and enjoy yourself today. It's been tough the last while, and you deserve it – we both do."

Anna knew he was referring not only to Ciara's premature arrival, but also to the death of Liam and the kids. Although for Ronan the pain and shock of losing his best friend had been tempered somewhat by the birth of his first child, the last few weeks had been hugely draining for both of them, particularly in the early days after the crash. Now, by concentrating on the new baby, he and Anna were at least managing to return to some sort of normality.

As, it seemed, was Eve. Anna, like everyone else, had been greatly concerned about her withdrawn behaviour in the immediate aftermath of the accident. And although she still didn't speak freely about the crash, or outwardly acknowledge her grief, at least she now seemed to have a hold on the fact that Liam and the kids weren't coming back – and according to Sam, despite the fact that she would likely never fully recover from the tragedy, seemed to be coping reasonably well and taking each day at a time.

"But she still doesn't mention it, and neither do I," Sam told Anna when she'd recently enquired after Eve's welfare. "Still, as long as she's coping, that's the main thing."

Because Ciara's arrival had coincided with Liam's death, Anna hadn't been able to spend any great length of time with Eve or provide comfort in the aftermath of her friend's loss. She'd been so caught up in looking after and getting used to the new baby that spending quality time with Eve had been difficult.

At least, that was what Anna tried to convince herself, but deep down she knew that the real reason she hadn't been around Eve in the immediate aftermath of the accident was because she found it just too difficult to face her.

And like Sam, Anna too worried that Eve could be negatively affected by the sight of her new baby girl, that Ciara would highlight all that she had lost even more.

But no, when Eve and Sam called round recently, Eve had seemed just as enamoured with the baby as everyone else – perhaps even more so – and hadn't outwardly displayed any signs of discomfort or distress. Eve had always adored babies, Anna thought sadly, recalling how she used to talk almost incessantly about how she'd love to have another baby with Liam.

Anna hung her head. Sometimes, life could be impossibly cruel.

Just before they were due to leave, Eve arrived at Anna and Ronan's house, and when she answered the door to her friend, Anna was struck by how much better she looked these days.

Granted, she'd lost quite a lot of weight in the weeks following the accident, and her face was still gaunt and tired looking, but despite this the colour in her cheeks and the brightness in her eyes today almost belied her recent trauma and made her appear much more like the old Eve.

Ronan was still getting ready upstairs, and as Eve followed her through to the kitchen, Anna realised that this was the first time that they'd spent any time alone together since the accident.

Sam, who had pretty much shadowed her younger sister after the accident, had only recently returned to her own apartment in the city centre, evidently satisfied that Eve now needed time on her own.

"So, how are you?" Anna asked, feeling decidedly uncomfortable and more than a little ashamed that she'd kept her distance.

But Eve seemed unperturbed. "I'm fine. How are you?"

Her voice sounded unnaturally bright, Anna thought. Evidently, she still didn't want to talk about or dwell upon the tragedy, and if a complete avoidance of the subject helped her get through it, then Anna certainly wasn't going to push it.

"Great. Listen, thanks again for offering to look after Ciara. We really appreciate it."

"It's no problem. I'm glad to do it."

"Well, er – thanks again," Anna babbled. "I've made up some bottles and as she mostly sleeps between feeds she shouldn't be too much of a problem. Of course, she has her moments but –"

"I'm sure she'll be fine."

"I'm sure she will."

Their conversation felt stilted and unnatural, and for reasons she couldn't comprehend, Anna felt as though she was talking to a stranger instead of her friend of many years.

Of course, her guilt following the accident probably had a lot to do with it, but Eve didn't know anything about that, did she? And, given what she'd been through, it was also a bit stupid of Anna to expect Eve to be laughing and joking like her old self, wasn't it? No, it was only natural that things would be a bit awkward for a while, particularly when Eve was unwilling to share her bereavement and everyone needed to tiptoe around the subject.

Well, mostly everyone.

"Hello!" Just then, Ronan entered the room fully dressed in his wedding attire. "How are you these days, pet?" he said, reaching for Eve and engulfing her in a heartfelt hug. "Great to see you."

"I'm fine." Evidently discomfited by this obvious show of emotion, Eve returned the hug briefly before just as quickly stepping back and away from him.

"We'd better get going soon, Ronan," Anna said, hoping to alleviate the awkwardness. "Lauren's due at the church at two." Too late she realised that the mention of Lauren's wedding would of course highlight the fact that the wedding Eve had wanted for so long would now never take place.

"Yes, you'd better get going," Eve agreed, raising a brave smile, and Anna's heart went out to her.

"Right, well, I'll just check on Ciara one more time, and then we're off."

"I've just been in there and she's fast asleep, love," Ronan said. "Might be better to just leave her be. If you wake her up now, Eve might have terrible trouble getting her back down."

"I suppose you're right." Still, it was bad enough having to leave her daughter for the first time ever, let alone not being able to say goodbye before she left.

"Seriously, Anna, she's fine. Now come on, we'd better head away – we're already running late as it is." Ronan was insistent.

"All right then. Eve, you have the number – phone us if you need anything. Anything at all, OK?"

Eve nodded. "I will."

"And we'll be back straight after the meal. It's supposed to be served at seven but you know how these things can go. Hopefully we'll be back around ten at the very latest."

"Fine. See you then."

"OK . . ." Anna floundered, at a loss for anything more to say. "Well, I'll see you later. I just hope you get on OK and don't have any problems. But I'll try and phone a few times throughout the day just to see how you're getting on, all right?"

"Better not, Anna – that could very well cause problems if she's asleep when the phone rings," Ronan chided gently. He turned to Eve. "Probably best just to leave her be, and you can phone us if you've any problems," he said and Eve nodded.

"I suppose that probably makes more sense . . ." Anna agreed reluctantly, although she would have preferred to talk to Eve whenever she felt like it rather than waiting for Eve to ring her.

But Ronan was right; this arrangement probably did make a lot more sense in the end. God, this was mad! Never in a million years did she think she'd be this obsessive about anything! But motherhood turned you into a different person – that was for sure. And just then, Anna got a brief idea of what Eve must have felt when she found out her children were lost to her forever. No wonder she wanted to shut out her pain for so long afterwards – if anything like that ever happened to Ciara, Anna would go out of her mind.

"Right, I'll just check on her so and . . ." Then she grinned and shook her head. "No, I said I'd just let her be, didn't I?"

"Yes, you did." Ronan grinned, amused by his fiancée's uncharacteristically flustered behaviour.

"Check on her if you like," Eve said in an odd-sounding voice. "If she wakes up, so be it. You'll feel better having said goodbye to her properly."

Anna reddened, now regretting her neurotic behaviour as she realised that Eve was most likely thinking about how she'd love to have had the chance to say goodbye to her own children. It was written all over Eve's pained expression and plain to see in the haunted look in her eyes. She'd been wrong in assuming that her friend was moving on, Anna thought. Eve had obviously just been trying to put a brave face on things and was making a great effort to hide the pain and anguish she continued to experience. And here Anna was bringing it all back to the forefront by making a huge fuss over nothing.

"No, really, it's fine," she said, chuckling awkwardly at her own silliness. "I'll leave her alone. I know she'll be fine."

And Ciara would be fine, Anna decided as she and Ronan left the house, having again said their goodbyes to Eve. Having had plenty of experience as a mother herself, no doubt Eve would look after her daughter better than anyone.

*　*　*

The wedding was a lavish, pompous affair and Anna couldn't wait to leave. While Lauren looked amazing and was absolutely glowing with pride as she walked down the aisle with Denis, Anna couldn't help but think that the whole arrangement had served more as a showcase for the couple's obvious wealth than an expression of their love for one another.

As if she could talk, she thought wryly, glancing sideways at Ronan who was deep in conversation with one of the other guests at their table. Although in fairness, Ciara's arrival had definitely changed her outlook when it came to making things official with Ronan.

Now that they were a proper family, it was the right thing to do, wasn't it?

So when Ciara got a bit older, they were going to sit down and talk about setting a date once and for all.

Still, whatever they decided upon, Anna knew that their wedding would be nothing at all like this. No, they'd do something small and intimate, with just a few friends and family in attendance. Then, yet again recalling poor Eve and her hastily ended plans for her own wedding, Anna began to have second thoughts.

No, much better to wait until her friend had a chance to get past all this. No point in making things harder for Eve by forcing her to sit through someone else's big day.

Anna shook her head and smiled softly, deciding that she'd come a very long way indeed when she was seriously thinking about arranging her wedding. But again, Ciara's arrival had changed everything – in more ways than one. She recalled how elated and empowered she'd felt when she held her daughter in her arms for the very first time and how she'd realised then that this was the best thing she'd ever done in her life, her greatest achievement. And right then, she'd wanted to tell Liam that he'd been wrong, that the accusations he'd levelled at her had been completely off the mark.

Liam.

Anna's heart sank yet again as she thought about what had happened between them.

A couple of weeks after Eve and Liam's engagement party, not long after her pregnancy first became public knowledge, Liam had one evening appeared at Anna's front door.

"Ronan's not here," she'd said, her heart – as usual – giving a little flip when she saw him. It had always been that way. "He's at work."

"I know," Liam replied, studying her. "I know he's not here."

"So . . . what is it you want?" she said, looking away quickly, unable to hold his gaze.

"What are you playing at, Anna?"

"What do you mean?"

"You don't love him. You've never loved him."

Anna's heart sank. Somehow she'd expected this, although she'd never in a million years expected him to be so upfront in this way. "Of course I love him," she replied, trying to give her words enough conviction. "I've always loved him."

"That's not true and you know it."

Anna closed her eyes. "Liam, don't do this."

"Do what? Speak the truth? Something I should have done a long time ago as it happens."

"Liam –"

"But I didn't and I was stupid and now the two of us are stuck in relationships we both know are all wrong."

"How can you say that?" Anna retorted, outraged and at the same time guilty on her friend's behalf. "You and Eve have two children together, you've been together forever and now you're getting married!"

"You and I both know that things weren't meant to turn out like this. Yes, I love Eve but it's not the same, not the same as –"

"The same way as I love Ronan," Anna interjected quickly, unwilling to let him say anything more.

"And now you're pregnant," Liam said.

"Yes, I am."

"But waited a while before telling him, apparently?"

"That's nobody's business but mine and Ronan's."

"Are you sure about that, Anna?"

"Of course I'm sure! Liam, who the hell do you think you are coming here and talking to me like this? How dare you!"

"I know exactly who I am, Anna. I'm the one who could have really made you happy. I'm the one you should be spending the rest of your life with, instead of spending it trying to convince yourself that you made the right decision."

Her heart plummeted into her stomach. "Go away, Liam, please!" she cried, unable to listen to any more of this.

"But instead you decided to do the cowardly thing and stay with Ronan – poor innocent Ronan who never had a clue what was happening right in front of him, who never had a clue that his precious Anna might have had eyes for someone other than him."

"You've got it all wrong, Liam. Now, please, just *leave!*"

"What was it that stopped you back then, Anna?" Liam kept talking. "Was it guilt? Or fear – fear of hurting and disappointing your childhood sweetheart or fear of leaving the one person who had always been a constant in your life? Fear of breaking free from what you knew best?"

"You're wrong, Liam. I loved Ronan – I still love him!" she said, catching herself quickly. "Nothing is ever going to change that."

"You can kid yourself all you like, Anna. But you and I both know that that's not true and up to now most of your life has been founded on lies."

"Stop it." She went to close the door in his face.

"Think about that," Liam went on. "Think about what kind of a life that child will be born into. A mother who is too cowardly to admit how she really feels, and a father who doesn't know any different and thinks all is fine in his happy little world. Bloody ironic, isn't it, considering that Ronan advised me to think twice about marrying someone for the wrong reasons. If only he knew that his own girlfriend was planning on doing the very same thing."

"You have absolutely no idea what you're talking about!" Anna cried, finally shutting the door in Liam's face and wishing it were just as easy to shut him out of her life.

Afterwards, she wondered whether Liam might take things farther – tell Ronan or, more likely, tell Eve as a way of escaping from their engagement. There was an air of desperation about him that frightened her.

And then a only few weeks later, Anna discovered with equal measures of relief and horror that Liam was indeed out of her, and everyone else's, life, for good.

CHAPTER

32. The Last to Know

Eve was really enjoying looking after baby Ciara. She was such an adorable little thing with her big blue eyes and soft downy black hair and that lovely flawless and sweet-smelling baby skin. And she reminded Eve so much of Lily as a baby that it hurt.

But she couldn't think about that now. She tried to hold back the tears. She wouldn't allow herself to think about it. It was better that way – much better to try and concentrate on something else.

She hoped Anna and Ronan were enjoying the wedding. They really needed a day out the two of them, and she wondered if there would soon be another wedding on the cards – this time for them. Again, her heart tightened as she tried to push thoughts of her own longed-for wedding out of her mind. Don't think about it, she warned herself once more. But it was very difficult not to.

Since Sam had moved back to her own place a while back and the house was completely empty all the time, it was impossible to *not* think about . . . things, so in order to stop herself going crazy, most of the time she tried to busy herself with something else. The relentless obsession with housework that Lily always used to tease her about had lately become her friend, a companion of sorts, but she had quickly found that a house without a family was a lot easier to keep clean, and so time and time again she found herself thinking about . . . *That.*

Just then, Ciara moaned softly from her cradle, which was situated in the living room beside the sofa.

Eve looked at the clock. Two thirty. Time for the baby's next feed.

She got up from the sofa and went into the kitchen to warm one of the bottles Anna had prepared earlier, all the time thinking that this should have been her, that *she* should have been the one preparing bottles and feeds for her baby, the third baby she'd so desperately wanted with Liam.

And she'd really felt that she could get him to come round to the idea, in the same way he'd started to come round to the idea of going on a family holiday soon, in the same way he'd come round to the idea of getting married.

Why, when life was finally coming together for them, did something like this have to happen? How was it fair? She believed herself to be a good person and had tried her best to be a good mother and partner to Liam. So why had God decided to take her family – the people she loved most in the world – away from her?

Having sworn to herself she wouldn't think about it, Eve busied herself with Ciara's bottle before going back into the living room, picking her up and sitting back down on the sofa, the baby now wide awake and ready for her feed.

She really was a gorgeous little thing, Eve thought again, as in her arms Ciara sucked away on her bottle, her dark eyelashes so tiny and delicate looking.

In truth, she really didn't look a whole lot like Anna or indeed Ronan – despite Anna's insistence that she had his eyes. Maybe

Sam had a point about something being up there, she thought, chuckling faintly at the stupidity of the idea.

She was glad that all that seemed to be over and done with too, that Sam seemed to have now given up on her infatuation with Ronan and concluded that it had all been just a silly phase she was going through. She smiled softly as she thought about her sister. Sam had been wonderful – an absolute rock these last few weeks – and Eve didn't know how she'd have coped without her.

But was she coping – really? Eve wasn't sure. She wasn't sure what coping really was and how it was supposed to feel and –

All of a sudden, Ciara stopped sucking from the bottle and shifted her mouth away from it, dribbling milk all over her mouth and onto her bib.

"Oh, honey, have you had enough for now?" Eve smiled down at the baby and spoke aloud in a sing-song voice. Reacting to the sound of her voice, just then Ciara seemed to grin back, her tiny mouth widening in the semblance of a smile and her huge blue eyes focusing intently on Eve's face.

God, she loved that, Eve thought as she wiped the baby's face with the bib before removing it altogether. Those tiny features, the so-called smile, the almost addictive new-baby smell of her – she was just gorgeous. Anna was so lucky to have her, so lucky to have . . . to have everything Eve didn't.

She hugged the baby closer to her chest and then, almost without realising it, tears began streaming down her cheeks.

Eve sat that way for a few minutes, holding the baby close as she became lost in her own thoughts, grieving for everything she'd lost and the future she no longer had.

It was only when Ciara began to whine a little and then launched into a full-blown cry that Eve managed to recollect herself. Then, remembering that she was here to take care of the baby and not drown her in tears, she saw to her dismay that while crying she'd accidentally spilled the bottle onto Ciara's babygro and the soft towelling material was now wet with milk. She'd better change it for a dry one, particularly when the poor thing wasn't long over her chest infection.

Getting up from the sofa with a still-whimpering Ciara in her arms, Eve made her way upstairs to Anna and Ronan's bedroom, planning to put her down in her cot for a few minutes while she went to find a change of clothes in the other bedroom. This was where – according to Anna – most of the baby's clothes and toys were located, and which would undoubtedly be Ciara's own room once she was old enough to be moved out of her mum and dad's.

Laying the baby down in her cot alongside Anna and Ronan's large double bed, Eve went into the next room and headed straight to a chest of drawers where Anna apparently kept most of Ciara's clothes.

There was nothing suitable in the first drawer, only lots of bills and letters, insurance documents, passports . . . She picked up Anna's passport and her breath caught when she looked inside to see the baby registered on it, in the same way that she herself had recently registered Lily and Max on her own. Anna had obviously done this for their upcoming trip to France, and again Eve felt stricken by the unfairness of it all. Lucky Anna that she was able to go on a nice family holiday, the same happy event that Eve had sorely wished for with hers. Fighting back tears, she put the passport back in the drawer and slammed it shut.

Once she'd searched further and found a clean babygro, Eve stood up and looked around the prettily decorated room. She marvelled at the collection of baby gifts Ciara had already accumulated – baby mobiles, loads of teddy bears and other stuffed toys.

She smiled sadly, remembering. There had been nothing like

that when Lily was born. Back then, because she and Liam were so young and so tight for money, her first-born had to make do with hand-me-down clothes from relatives and a borrowed carrycot from a neighbour. Her mum and dad, despite the fact that they adored their new granddaughter (whom Eve had named Lillian after her own mother) were at the same time unwilling to make a huge fuss over Lily's birth, considering the circumstances and the fact that their daughter remained unmarried, despite Liam's promise to stand by her. But in fairness, at the time, Sam had given Lily a gorgeous new teddy bear – the only gift the baby had that wasn't second hand.

And while there had been some improvement in the quality of baby paraphernalia she and Liam had managed to secure second time round for Max, and indeed in his presents, it was still nothing compared to all this.

So many teddy bears and dolls and so much . . . stuff! Still smiling, Eve's gaze travelled along the row of cuddly toys and stuffed animals, lined up neatly side by side on a nearby shelf.

But when she caught sight of one of the toys – a pink-coloured teddy bear with a big red heart on its chest – the smile quickly froze on her face.

Care Bear – Pink 6.99

Immediately, Eve's thoughts flashed back to the empty gift-store bag that had been delivered with her family's personal belongings and how its appearance had puzzled her at the time. She remembered taking out the receipt and naively concluding that Liam had bought her something for her birthday. She remembered holding the receipt to her lips and crying, wondering where her gift had ended up and if it had – like the rest of her family, and indeed her life – been destroyed in the accident.

But now Eve realised she'd been wrong – so, so wrong it was agonising.

Liam *hadn't* bought her a pink teddy bear as a gift. He'd bought it certainly – as Eve knew she definitely hadn't and Lily didn't have that kind of money or indeed the wherewithal to get to the shops without Eve knowing. No, the purchase had definitely been Liam's, and he'd bought it for Ciara and had evidently given it to Anna shortly before the accident.

But why? Eve puzzled. Why would Liam go out and buy something for Anna's new baby and not tell . . .

Then, with a burst of comprehension that literally took her breath away, Eve thought she understood *exactly* why.

CHAPTER

33. The Last to Know

After a delayed meal, and the interminably long wedding speeches that followed, Anna and Ronan eventually made their excuses to Lauren and Denis and headed for home.

"Thank God for that!" Anna muttered as they walked out of the hotel and towards the taxi Ronan had called. "I thought we'd never get out of there!"

"Jesus, will you relax, woman!" he teased, walking alongside her. He grinned. "You really can't wait to get back to her, can you?"

"No," Anna smiled guiltily, getting into the waiting cab, "I really can't. It's strange, Ronan. Even though she's only been around a few weeks, I can hardly remember what life was like without her. She's in my thoughts every second of every day and, to be honest, most of today was like torture for me."

"Oh, you're a real mammy all right," Ronan chuckled as the cab drove away. "But to be honest, I'm looking forward to getting back to her too. It's hard to believe, isn't it?" he said proudly. "You and me being parents. It doesn't seem that long ago since we were kids ourselves, and now we've got one of our own."

"I know."

Things had changed a lot for them over the last while. For a start, Anna was feeling much more positive about their future together; it was as if the arrival of Ciara had finally clarified things for her after all this time. But hadn't Liam's death helped in this regard too? The thought crept unbidden into her mind and Anna gulped guiltily, feeling awful for thinking such a thing, especially when by contrast Eve's life was in ruins.

"I meant what I said at the hospital, too," Ronan continued, his tone becoming more serious as he took Anna's hand and gave it a light squeeze. "No matter what happens, I'm going to make sure I do my best for her – for both of you."

"We'll both do our best for her," she said, smiling back at him.

Some fifteen minutes later, Anna and Ronan let themselves into the house. Assuming that Ciara would be asleep, they quietly removed their coats and jackets in the hallway before announcing their return to Eve.

"I'm desperate for a pee," Ronan whispered, handing Anna his jacket. "Will you hang this up for me while I make a dash for it?"

"Go on," she said, rolling her eyes. "But don't make too much noise on your way up in case you wake her."

While Ronan went upstairs to answer the call of nature, Anna hung up the jackets and then went into the kitchen in search of Eve to see how the day had gone.

Evidently, everything was fine, as Eve hadn't phoned once throughout the day and, while Anna was relieved, she thought her friend might have at least contacted her to reassure her that all was well.

But what would be the point of that? she decided, realising that she was being neurotic yet again. Eve was well used to looking after babies – newborn or otherwise – so if there was nothing to report, then there was nothing to report.

Still, she was eager to find out if Ciara had been feeding properly, or if indeed her daughter had even missed her. Although she wouldn't have wished a crying baby on anyone, and hoped that Ciara hadn't been distressed, at the same time she kind of hoped the baby did at least realise that her mother wasn't around – or at eight weeks was she way too young to know the difference?

The kitchen was empty, so Anna went back out into the hallway and then into the living room, where Eve was no doubt watching TV or listening to the radio.

"Hi, how did you . . . ?" But the remainder of her question was cut short when she realised that the room was empty and she actually was addressing thin air. The TV was on, but where was Eve?

Upstairs – either in their bedroom with the baby's cot, which meant Ciara might be awake, or in the household's only bathroom. Poor Ronan might have to wait a little longer to answer the call of nature!

"Eve?" Anna called out softly as she began to ascend the stairs. "Eve, we're home! Eve?"

She heard a toilet flush, and then Ronan appeared on the landing.

"They're downstairs," he said. "I checked the bedroom on the way into the bathroom."

"What?" A wave of unreasoning panic crashed over Anna. "You mean they're not in there and Ciara's not in her cot?"

"No, did you look downstairs?" he replied, frowning at the vibes he was getting from her.

"Yes, they're not there!" Anna cried, her voice rising considerably as she rushed towards the bedroom. "Eve!" she called out once more, her heart racing. "Eve, are you here?"

As Anna continued to search for Eve in the other bedrooms, Ronan stared wildly around him on the landing. "What the hell is going on?" he asked, following Anna as she rushed downstairs. "Why aren't they here?"

"I don't know, I don't know. Maybe she went out somewhere. I think some of Ciara's things are missing – the bag with her nappies and stuff – her blanket –" Anna was trying to think rationally, but deep down something told her that this was all wrong.

"Out somewhere with Ciara? In what? Her pram's still in the hallway. Anyway, wouldn't she have told us if she was planning on taking her out? Shouldn't she have phoned first?" Ronan went on, his tone rising with every utterance. "Or even left a note? Could she have left a note somewhere? Check downstairs while I look upstairs." He was already halfway up the stairs as he spoke.

But there was no note.

"What was she thinking of?" said Ronan. "She knew we were due home around now."

Sensing the fear in his tone, Anna realised that her own panic wasn't as neurotic or unfounded as she'd thought; he was just as concerned as she was.

"I know that, Ronan. I can't understand why she's not here! Eve!" she cried again, overwhelming panic now seizing her.

"She should know better than to be bringing her out in the dark like that! She's not long over her chest infection! Oh God, maybe she had to take Ciara to the hospital? But surely she would have phoned us? Yes, without a doubt she would have phoned us – or the hospital would." He paused, thinking desperately. "Wait – let me take a look outside in case she just stepped outside the door or took a walk down the street."

Anna waited, gazing hopefully out into the dark after him. But he returned a few minutes later, shaking his head.

"Look," he said, "maybe she brought Ciara to Sam's – for a visit or something."

"To *Sam's*? You said it yourself – her pram is still here!" Anna blustered, knowing full well that this was clutching at straws. "And why on earth would she take her all the way into town to Sam's without telling us?"

Ronan was already dialling Sam's number. "Well, one way or the other, we'll soon find out."

For Anna, time seemed to stop while they waited for Sam to answer the phone. Yes, there was a good chance that Eve had gone there, although if she had, why hadn't she or Sam –

"Sam? Hi, Ronan here. Yes . . . yes." Ronan's eyes met Anna's, and in that instant she understood from his reaction that Eve wasn't at Sam's place. Oh God . . .

"Sam, listen a second," Ronan spoke quickly. "I need to ask you something very important. Is Eve there with you? With the baby?"

But both Ronan and Anna already knew the reply. Eve wasn't at Sam's.

"No . . . there was no one here when we got home just now . . . no, we looked everywhere . . . no, no note, nothing. If she contacts you, let me know, will you? I know that . . . yes, of course. " Judging from Ronan's side of the conversation, Sam was now as worried as they were. "I know that. OK, bye."

"Oh my God, Ronan, what the hell is happening?" Anna said, her body shaking. "What has she done with the baby? Where has she taken her?" What the hell had they been *thinking* allowing Eve to look after Ciara? The woman had been through hell and back these last few weeks, and she had just lost her own children – her entire family! Chances were she was still unbalanced . . . possibly dangerous!

"Slow down, slow down – maybe we're jumping to conclusions here," Ronan said as if reading his fiancée's thoughts. But what else *could* Anna think given the circumstances? "Let's not panic." He picked up the phone again and dialled. "I'm ringing Eve's house . . . there might have been some emergency and she had to rush off there . . ."

Anna watched his face as he listened to the ring tone.

"No answer," he said eventually, putting down the phone.

He brushed past a now distraught Anna and headed for the door.

"Stay here in case she comes back," he called back over his shoulder.

"Where are you going?" Anna shouted after him, tears streaming down her face.

"Over to Eve's house – and if she's not there, I'll check the hospital. If I don't find them, I'm going straight to the guards."

Anna nodded dumbly, but deep down she knew that Ronan wouldn't find Eve and the baby at her house.

Chances were he wouldn't find them at all.

* * *

The older member of the two garda síochána who arrived at Anna and Ronan's house had a kind face and seemed genuinely sympathetic to their plight, as opposed to his younger colleague, who gave them a bit of a hard time.

"You're saying you left a newly bereaved and clearly unbalanced woman in charge of an eight-week-old baby?" he repeated when Anna, through her tears, tried to explain the situation as best she could.

"We didn't realise she was unbalanced!" Sam, who had rushed immediately to Anna's side following Ronan's call, shot back. "Yes, she was bereaved, but lately she seemed to be coping!"

"And you are?" the policeman asked her, flicking a page in his notebook.

"I'm Eve's sister, and before you ask, I have no idea where she might have gone with the baby. I wish I did."

She and Anna had subsequently followed Ronan to Eve's house, where, to their absolute horror they discovered hastily discarded clothes in Eve's bedroom and emptied-out drawers and open wardrobes – clear signs of someone in a hurry, or worse: someone in the throes of an escape.

"She's taken her!" Anna cried, distraught, as she tore through Eve's house, the significance of the messed-up room overwhelming her. "She's taken my baby!"

"Oh God!" Taking in the state of her sister's bedroom, Sam ran both hands through her hair, unable to think clearly, unable to comprehend what was happening.

What had Eve done?

"Look, she's probably just had a bit of an episode or something," she said, trying to calm Anna. "She'll be back, I know she will."

Ronan wasn't having any of it. "You know we can't take that chance, Sam. I'm sorry but we have to call the guards. For all we know she could be miles away by now. We were gone all day, remember?"

"I knew I shouldn't have left her!" Anna was quickly becoming hysterical. "I never should have left her! What was I *thinking*?"

Sam looked helplessly at the other woman. Damn it, she should have known that Eve's behaviour wasn't right, that it wasn't normal for someone who had experienced such a tragedy to bounce back so quickly.

But she really did think that Eve's closed and distant behaviour had been her way of coping, that it had been her own method of working her way through the bereavement process. But it just wasn't normal – it was probably the farthest thing from normal – and while of course Sam had her concerns at the time, Eve's subsequent improvement had convinced her otherwise.

God, she was an idiot! And was as much to blame for this as anyone for not keeping a closer on eye on her. Granted, Sam could never have *conceived* of Eve doing something like this but –

"Eve wouldn't do anything to hurt Ciara," she insisted now to the gardaí in Anna's front room, trying to convince herself more than anyone else. "Yes, she might be a little mixed up at the moment, but she wouldn't do anything to that child."

"We don't know that!" Anna cried once again. "We don't know that at all!"

"Anna, Eve wouldn't hurt a fly," Sam said softly. "I think she's probably just had some kind of a breakdown. Maybe being on her own with Ciara triggered off something inside her and reminded her of what she's lost."

"And that gives her the right to steal my baby?" Anna shot back incredulously, her eyes wild.

Ronan put a comforting arm around his fiancée's shoulder. "Look, love, Sam's not trying to make excuses – she's just trying to figure out what happened, same as the rest of us."

But Anna couldn't be placated. "I *knew* we shouldn't have left her, Ronan! I should have realised something wasn't right! And now she's gone, and I never even got to say goodbye!" She looked pleadingly at the two gardaí. "She's only eight weeks old."

The younger man exhaled loudly. "You can't think of anywhere she might have gone – relatives, friends . . .?"

"I've tried absolutely everyone," Sam replied, shaking her head.

She and Ronan had been in contact with Eve's friends and had questioned her neighbours, none of whom had seen her return to the house at all that day – baby in tow or not. Nor had Anna and Ronan's neighbours seen any trace of her.

"No, I haven't seen her since . . . well, you know," said her neighbour Sara. "I was planning to call in and see how she was, but I just didn't get the time what with looking after Jack and all . . ."

In her desperation, Sam had even managed to contact Liam's still-distraught mother, but Noreen also hadn't seen Eve since the funeral.

"Well, I wouldn't panic just yet," said the older garda reassuringly. "There's probably a simple explanation – there usually is. And if – as you say – she's had a bit of turn, I'd imagine she'll soon realise what she's done and your little baby will be back before you know it."

"You don't know that for sure," Ronan said. "She could be halfway across the country by now for all we know. She may have had this planned for a while and could have taken the baby anywhere by now. Who knows, she may have done something . . . something stupid."

Anna looked as though she were about to faint at the suggestion that Eve might have planned to do harm to herself along with the baby.

Sam didn't even want to consider something like that, but she knew that it was impossible at this stage to guess at what Eve would or wouldn't do.

"We have to consider a worst-case scenario," Ronan continued to the other men. "You can't just assume she'll turn tail and come back home. The woman isn't well, and although we didn't know it at the time, we certainly know that now!"

Sam looked away, ashamed. She just couldn't comprehend that her sister could have done something like this – that she had gone on the run with someone else's baby. And not just any person's baby, but the child of two of her closest friends!

It was the kind of stuff you read about in the newspapers or saw on TV, not the kind of thing a normal person would do in real life. But Eve wasn't in a normal state of mind, was she? Which was where the ultimate problem lay. What exactly was Eve's state of mind at the moment? And where on earth would she have taken little Ciara?

Anna could no longer understand what they were saying; by this stage, it was all just a continuous babble in the background. She didn't know why the gardaí were still standing there, while Ronan kept gesturing madly at them and Sam just kept shaking her head.

Oh God, this was really happening, this was all too real! Her baby was gone, stolen away somewhere and by someone Anna considered a friend. Why would Eve do that? Why would she want to hurt them like that? And what was she planning to do, or what . . . what might she have already done? The possibilities were so horrific and so overwhelming that Anna's brain felt like it could explode any minute. She closed her eyes, willing herself to stop thinking about it, stop imagining the terrible things Eve might do. No, no, Eve wasn't like that, Anna reassured herself just as quickly: she adored babies, adored children, she'd bring Ciara back, surely she'd bring her back? But if she didn't . . . Anna squeezed her eyes shut, her brain simply unable to cope with the enormity of not knowing.

Why had she left her? Why had she gone to that stupid wedding? And why, oh why hadn't she kissed her daughter goodbye? Tears gushed out of her eyes and raced down her cheeks, tears Anna didn't think she had. How could she have left her daughter without kissing her goodbye? How could she have left her at all? What kind of a mother was she?

And why the hell wasn't Ronan doing something? A wave of intense anger suddenly unseated her intense grief. Why wasn't he out there trying to get Ciara back instead of just standing around chatting away to the police as if it was all no big deal? Why wasn't he breaking down doors, turning over every stone he could think of to find the baby and bring her back? Why the hell wasn't he doing that?

Because, Anna realised suddenly, the realisation hitting her so hard she thought she might die, because Ronan, like herself, hadn't the faintest idea where to start.

CHAPTER

34. The Last to Know

None of them would have considered starting their search in a small nondescript travel agency in Liverpool, where a tired-looking Irishwoman carrying a suitcase and a carrycot had disembarked from the previous evening's ferry and was now in the process of arranging the next leg of her journey.

The travel agent, a helpful and cheery Liverpudlian, smiled as she handed over the tickets, while Frankie Goes to Hollywood's "Relax" blasted out of the stereo in the background.

"You're all booked, love," the woman said. "The next train out of Lime Street leaves in a hour and arrives in London Victoria this afternoon. From there, you take the next service out to Heathrow, where your flight leaves at nine a.m. tomorrow morning."

"And that's all included in the price?" her customer enquired. "All the flights and everything?" Eve had never been on an airplane before, and although the long journey sounded a little frightening, she knew she could manage it. She *had* to manage it.

Thank goodness the woman hadn't asked too many questions or thought it odd that she was arranging such a mammoth journey at such short notice. But then again, as a gateway to and from the UK, this place was probably used to Irish people coming and going, and lots of people who got the ferry to Liverpool were on their way to somewhere else.

In truth, Eve hadn't had the faintest idea where to go next once she'd arrived in the city the previous night – she just knew she had to keep moving no matter what.

Because as long as she kept moving, she wouldn't have time to think about what she was doing. All she could think about was that she had to get out of Dublin in order to keep the baby – *Liam's* baby and the only piece of him she had left, the only piece of her family she had left – safe.

That was the most important thing.

And there was no doubt in her mind whatsoever that Ciara was Liam's. She had known something wasn't right from the very first second she'd spotted the pink and white teddy bear sitting on the shelf in the baby's room the afternoon before, but initially her mind had refused to consider the implications, and she wondered if she might well be jumping to conclusions like Sam had.

But when she'd picked up the toy bear and held it in her hand and then read the little tag attached . . . well, then there really was no doubt.

It read simply, in Liam's handwriting: *To baby Ciara, with love xxxx.*

Four x's – one for every letter of Liam's name.

Clearly he had something to hide – why else wouldn't he sign his name? Or the names of his family, or at least his own along with the name of the woman who was soon supposed to become his wife?

But at the same time, as she stood rooted to the spot in Ciara's bedroom, Eve knew that the questions she was asking herself then were meaningless because somewhere in the recesses of her mind she began to understand exactly why Liam had bought the baby the gift in the first place. Her head spun as a myriad different thoughts tumbled around in her brain, and feeling faint she grabbed onto the chest of drawers to try and keep her balance.

While the discovery of the bear might have seemed innocent enough in isolation, the events leading up to the accident served to validate her suspicions even more and her heart raced as her brain frantically tried to put the pieces together.

Anna had kept her condition hidden for months and had only told Ronan about the baby when it had become impossible to deny its existence any longer. In fact, Eve knew that Ronan had suspected she might be pregnant long before Anna brought herself to admit it, and had even confided his suspicions to Liam. And like Sam had suggested, there could really only have been one good reason for keeping her pregnancy hidden from him.

She remembered too how the news of Anna's pregnancy seemed to have provoked a rather odd reaction in Liam and how he'd seemed quite put out by it all. Why would something that should by rights have had nothing at all to do with Liam concern him so much? At the time, Eve had simply assumed he was afraid she would start putting more pressure on him to have another child and that his rather scathing reaction to Anna and Ronan's news stemmed from his own reluctance to become a father again. But little did she know that her instincts had been spot on, although certainly not in the way she'd anticipated.

Her heart twisted. Liam must certainly have suspected Ciara was his if he went to the trouble of buying her a gift and gave it to her so secretly, mustn't he?

There were so many thoughts, so many questions racing around in her brain that Eve could barely focus.

Anna and Liam . . .

When had all this happened, and why hadn't she seen it? She shook her head wildly from side to side. No, no, maybe she *was* over-analysing things, seeing things that weren't even there. With all that had happened recently, it was only natural, wasn't it?

Anyway, Liam and Anna had never been that close, had they? Even Lily had commented on the fact that her father had always seemed quite unfriendly towards Ronan's fiancée. But Eve had always explained away the frostiness between them as Liam's way of letting Anna know he didn't approve of how she treated his best friend by continually refusing to set a date for their wedding and being so casual about the whole thing. And, despite the threesome's close teenage friendship, Anna and Liam always seemed decidedly uncomfortable and ill-at-ease around one another – chances were for that very same reason.

But what if their behaviour had suggested something else entirely? What if – as Sam had been at pains to point out – Anna and Ronan's relationship wasn't as perfect as it seemed and Liam's refusal to get married stemmed from a very different reason than just 'never getting round to it' or a natural aversion because of his parents' marriage?

The pain in her heart was almost unbearable as Eve eventually began to come to an inevitable and devastating conclusion, the only conclusion she could possibly come to that might rationally explain the reasons behind Liam's baby gift – a gift that had been bought and given in secret.

Sam had been right all along in her assessment that things between Anna and Ronan weren't right. Anna, instead of jumping for joy like any normal woman in a loving relationship would do, had kept her pregnancy secret for almost six months! Why would she do that unless she had something to hide? And not just from Ronan but from everyone else too? The pain in Eve's chest was crucifying as all the pieces finally began to fall into place.

Anna and Liam were clearly not the old friends and now more distant acquaintances she had always assumed they were. Evidently, they were much, much closer than Eve – or indeed Ronan – had thought. And even worse, they had been making fools of Eve and Ronan for years . . .

Eve leaned back against the chest of drawers and tried to stop her thoughts, her mind, her *world* from spinning out of control. As she did, a sharp cry from the room next door brought her back to the present.

Ciara.

Liam's baby – the baby Eve should have had, and the child whose existence Anna had denied and tried to hide for months on end.

Anna, who didn't care about the baby or Ronan or indeed about anyone other than herself. Anna, who was supposed to be Eve's friend but didn't care a jot about their friendship or Eve's feelings; all she'd been interested in was stealing Liam away from her. Anna who had everything – a new baby, a loving and devoted fiancé, a big white wedding and the rest of her life to look forward to – in short, everything that Eve didn't.

And through Ciara, she'd even managed to hold onto a piece of Liam.

For the second time in as many months, Eve's world again began to spin on a three-hundred-and-sixty-degree axis, and she felt a familiar and almost welcome dull ache in the pit of her stomach. And when the baby cried out once more in the hope of getting her attention, Eve realised right then with blistering clarity exactly what she needed to do.

*   *   *

The previous evening, having taken the ferry from Dun Laoghaire long before Anna and Ronan were due to return from their friend's wedding, Eve had exited the terminal and almost in a daze had walked the short distance to the centre of Liverpool in the hope of finding a place to eat and somewhere to feed and change the baby.

She was doing the right thing, she reassured herself. Anna didn't care about the baby she didn't care about anyone. No, it was up to her to keep Liam's baby safe – the baby that she, and not Anna, should have had – and if she had to go to the ends of the earth to do so, she would. On her way up the street, a brightly coloured advertisement in the window of a nearby travel agency caught her eye, and as she drew closer and read the words, she realised that this had to be a sign – a sign that she was doing the right thing and that someone from up above – Liam maybe? – was trying to give her a helping hand.

Special Offer – This Week Only!
Fly to Sydney, Australia – The End of the Earth!

The accompanying pictures in the advertisement looked beautiful: snow-white beaches, aquamarine seas, weird-shaped mountains and exotic-looking animals. She remembered how Liam had loved travelling to Australia, how much he'd talked about how beautiful the country was, how everything about this faraway land was awe-inspiring – the scenery, the wildlife, the people.

The End of the Earth . . .

Eve looked down at the baby, now fast asleep in Max's old carrycot, and knew exactly what to do next.

So, first thing the following morning, having found a bed for the night in a nearby hostel, she found herself inside that same travel agency and in front of the counter, the baby's carrycot at her side.

"All the tickets are definitely included?" she queried again, raising her voice slightly in order to be heard over the radio, on which Frankie were still urging people to "Relax". Then just as quickly, the song ended and the opening bars of Queen's Radio Ga-Ga began. Liam had been a huge Queen fan and had most of their albums apart from the latest one, Eve thought sadly.

"Yes, love, all the flights, your train tickets – everything is included in the price," the woman confirmed in her lilting Liverpool accent. "All you need is your passport and you're ready to go!"

Eve nodded. It had been *another* sign that she'd just happened upon that passport only seconds before her awful discovery and mere minutes before she'd made the decision to take Ciara and leave. In truth, at the time she wasn't exactly sure what she was going to do when she left the house or where she was going to go, but despite this, everything seemed to be falling into place of its own accord. Yes, she was *supposed* to do this, Eve reassured herself, it was meant to be, and thanks to the passport with the baby's name on it, she also had the means to do it. Liam *must* be guiding her on her way.

The agent was still chatting. "This is such a fantastic offer too – you're really lucky. Of course, there are tons of people emigrating down there these days, and who could blame them?" She gestured helplessly out at the dark and dreary morning. "You certainly won't miss any of this!"

"No, I won't," Eve replied quietly.

The woman smiled at the baby who was wide awake in her carrycot. "Aren't you a cute little thing!" she said, beaming. "How old is she?"

"Eight weeks."

"Ah, they're lovely at that age, aren't they? So innocent and sweet. Well, I really hope you and your daughter have a lovely trip to Sydney. I'm sure your husband is really looking forward to the two of you joining him out there. It must have been hard on him having to start his new job without you all the same."

Eve smiled tightly. "Yes, it was."

"But I think you were right to wait until she was old enough to travel. Although sometimes the younger they are, the easier they are to handle, aren't they?"

"I certainly think so." Eve picked up her suitcase in preparation to leave. "Thanks for everything," she said then, reaching for the carrycot. "So the train station's not far from here?"

"No, love – only a short walk. Just go back out the door, turn left and then head for that large stone building with all those steps in front of it. That's Lime Street station."

"OK, thanks again." With that, and the tickets safely stowed in her bag, Eve turned and walked towards the door.

"You have a lovely trip now – you and . . . by the way, what's her name?"

"What?" Eve stopped in her tracks.

The travel agent smiled again. "Your daughter – what's her name? I didn't think to ask when writing out your tickets – I just put her down as an infant."

"Her name is . . ." Eve looked down at the carrycot and for a moment, she seemed to falter, but almost just as quickly recollected herself. "Her name is . . . her name is Brooke."

The other woman beamed. "Brooke – what a beautiful name!"

Eve smiled softly. "Yes, I've always liked it." It had always been on her list of favourite baby names and she'd long ago decided that if she and Liam ever had another girl, then they would call her Brooke. So it was only right then, that –

"After Brooke Shields, I suppose," said the other woman, interrupting her train of thought. "Did you see the *Blue Lagoon*? It was great! Me and me boyfriend went to see it in the cinema when it came out a couple of years back. Anyway, I'm sure Brooke will just *love* living in Australia, with all those kangaroos and koalas and stuff. You know, if I had the money, I'd do the very same as you and emigrate there myself."

Eve nodded but said nothing.

"You and your husband are doing the right thing getting away from this part of the world, you know," the travel agent went on, clearly on a roll now. "Nothing here but misery and unemployment and bloody miners' strikes! And I hear Ireland is the very same – not a job to be found over there either by the amount of people we get looking to find work here. Honestly, I thought the seventies were bad but these miserable bloody eighties . . ." She rolled her eyes at Eve. "And love, we're not even *half* way through them yet!"

CHAPTER 40

In her office in Sydney, Brooke stared unseeingly at the last page of the manuscript in front of her, unable to comprehend, unwilling to believe . . .

Realising that her throat had gone dry, she swallowed hard, trying to get a grip on herself. No, no, no, this couldn't be right. This *couldn't* be right.

It couldn't be . . . be what she thought it was, could it?

That the story she'd spent the last couple of weeks reading wasn't a story at all, but was some kind of . . . some kind of *personal* message to her! That this wasn't just a hopeful submission but a carefully constructed ploy to make her aware of a true story, a story about *her* . . . the story behind her birth! Which meant that the people she'd been reading about were not only *real* people but people she knew, people close to her and her mother . . . Brooke shook her head. Could it be possible? Or was she going mad?

Her mother . . .

No, of course not, she was completely overreacting and now that she thought about it overreaching, she decided, sitting up straight.

So what if this Eve woman had kidnapped a child, named her Brooke and brought her to Sydney? OK, so the fact that the story wasn't – as she'd thought – based in contemporary Dublin but in the eighties, around the same time she herself was born . . . yes, that was certainly a bit weird. And of course the baby having the same name as her own and being brought to Sydney was more than a little coincidental but . . .

No, Brooke reassured herself, what she was thinking now was complete and utter nonsense. OK, so her mother might have been Irish, but for one thing, her mother's name was *Lynn*, not Eve and . . .

All of a sudden, something struck her. Everyone had indeed called her mum Lynn but her mother's name had actually been *Evelyn*, which again seemed a bit weird in the scheme of things.

And then something else about Brooke's parentage struck her – this time about her father.

William. Her father's name had been William. But wasn't Liam a shortened version of that? And he had died in a car crash – in the same way Liam had died in the story . . .

Brooke's mind spun in a thousand different directions, trying to figure out exactly what was going on here. She thought again about the reason she'd picked up the manuscript in the first place, the note that had been left on the front page. *Think this one should certainly interest you!* And despite assuming that the note was from someone in-house, she still hadn't managed to find out exactly who had recommended it to her or how it had got onto her reading pile. But why would somebody go to such lengths to ensure she read the script unless . . .?

So, Brooke tried to rationalise, her thoughts going a mile a minute, if it were indeed possible that this was no ordinary manuscript and was in fact some kind of personal message to her . . . then was it also possible that her mother wasn't her real mother at all? That she was just some crazy bereaved woman who had kidnapped her and brought her all the way to Australia? No, no, that wasn't right! Her mother wasn't a crazy woman, far from it – and for all of her life Lynn had been the most important person in her life . . .

Yet there was no denying that there had always been a slight undertone of something, a slight sadness about her mother that Brooke had subconsciously always been aware of but had never been able to understand. Nor had she ever questioned Lynn about it, assuming that her sadness had everything to do with losing her husband William at such an early age. Oh God, that was something else! she realised now. Apparently her father had died at twenty-eight, exactly the same age that Liam was in that story – him supposedly being twenty-one when Eve had Lily. *The story.*

It was just a story, wasn't it? she tried to reassure herself again, studying the sheaf of pages she was still holding in her hand. A story about the lives and loves of three women who lived in Dublin and, OK, so there were more than a few parallels with her own life . . . but those things didn't have to mean anything, did they?

She shook her head, trying to work it out. No, of course they didn't. This was a story – a piece of fiction, no different to the thousands of other manuscripts seeking publication that passed across her desk from year to year.

Yet, despite all that, Brooke realised with growing trepidation, it was a story that had somehow found its way directly onto her desk and had been left there by someone who had so far appeared unusually reticent. In fact, nobody in the company seemed to have any idea where this particular script had come from. When Brooke had finally managed to ask Mary about it, her reader didn't have the faintest notion what she was talking about. While yes, she had recommended a script recently, it had been a multi-generational saga – a completely different type of story to the one Brooke was asking about. At the time, she wasn't too worried about this, figuring that she'd find out eventually, but thinking about it all now . . .

OK, *really* think about this for a second, Brooke told herself, taking a deep breath and trying to be rational. She had to try and get the entire scenario into perspective. Still, her heart continued to race ahead at high-speed, as she began to realise that *everything* surrounding this manuscript did indeed seem out of kilter.

As well as having absolutely no idea how it had ended up on her desk, there was no author name, no address and no contact details whatsoever. So even if Brooke did want to publish *The Last to Know*, she had no idea how to get in contact with the author in any case. Then she bit her lip as she realised something. Clearly the author's intention when sending this story hadn't been publication at all. But if that was the case, then what on the earth *did* she want?

Assuming for a second that all these coincidences and parallels in the story did mean something, and this *did* have something to do with her, then what was the author trying to prove by sending this? Why try and turn her life upside-down and upend everything she thought she knew to be true, everything she loved – her mother, and her father to some degree – and render her entire life in Australia a lie?

Why would anyone do something like that – *who* would do something like that?

Then all at once it hit her. Suddenly Brooke realised exactly why someone would want her to know the painful and earth-shattering truth about her life. And she thought, the air freezing in her lungs as realisation dawned, she also knew exactly who that person was.

CHAPTER 41

"What do you mean you're going to Ireland?" That evening at her house, Will was flabbergasted. "When did this all come about?"

Brooke wasn't yet ready to tell him about the manuscript and explain its significance.

For one thing, he probably wouldn't believe her; for another, even if he did believe her, he'd probably try to talk her out of what she was about to do.

"It's business," she told him calmly as she continued packing a small case. "There's an author from there that Julie really wants, so we're trying to snap her up before somebody else does."

"But you never get involved with acquisitions to that degree!" he replied, his tone suspicious as he sat on the bed watching her.

He was right, Brooke rarely met with prospective authors to discuss terms; and especially not when they lived on the other side of the world! That was usually Julie's job and even then the publishing director rarely travelled outside the country.

"This is different – I already have a relationship with the author, and Julie wants me to do it." With a jolt, she realised the significance of her words. *I have a relationship with the author.* Now, she just hoped that an already doubtful Will wouldn't try and corroborate her explanation by contacting Julie. Nah, that wasn't her boyfriend's style. But he was certainly taken aback in any case. As had Julie been when, the following day, Brooke informed her boss she needed to take time off for a family emergency.

"Compassionate leave?" she'd said, eyebrows raised. "I didn't know you had family in Ireland."

Neither did I, Brooke replied silently. "My mother was Irish," she told her, without further explanation.

"I see. Well, take as much time as you need." Julie was cool about it all. "Although I certainly don't envy you *that* journey. I get nosebleeds if I have to move anywhere further than striking distance of Sydney, let alone the country. Try and book Club Class if you can – that should make the trek easier."

"I will," Brooke replied flatly. Six years as Horizon's publishing director had evidently erased all memories of Julie's former editorial position there and its accompanying meagre wages. "But thanks for being so understanding. I know it's short notice but –"

"No worries" Julie waved her apologies away. "You do what you have to do."

*   *   *

A couple of hours later, she was on the flight. There would be a short layover at Singapore airport – a couple of hours to refuel before going on to London – and Brooke realised that if the story of *The Last to Know* was true – which she had to assume it was – she was taking the exact reverse of the route she and Lynn – Eve – had twenty-five years before.

Brooke had never travelled this far outside her homeland before, and certainly never on her own. A few years back she and a friend had gone on a short trip to New Zealand for a week's holiday, but that was only a few hours away – nothing like the mammoth trip she was embarking on now.

What was it like, she wondered, as she stared at the computer-generated flight path on the screen in front of her seat – the tiny plane inching slowly out over the Pacific. What must it have been like for Lynn, flying for the first time to a strange, faraway country, leaving behind everything she had and everything she knew, with absolutely no clue as to what was ahead? But then again, her mum had already lost everything, hadn't she? She'd lost her children – her own siblings, she realised with a start – the love of her life and evidently – she admitted sadly – had also lost quite bit of her sanity.

But regardless of everything Brooke had learned, she couldn't reconcile the portrayal of Eve in the story with that of Lynn, the only mother she'd ever known and the woman whom she'd always adored and for whom she'd grieved so profoundly.

It had always been just the two of them, and despite Brooke's best efforts her mother had never had any interest in finding someone to take the place of William. Although, given what she'd recently learned of the man, and her mother's profound adoration of him, perhaps this was understandable.

And despite what she'd done, despite the fact that she'd stolen her away from her real mother, Brooke couldn't hate Lynn, she couldn't resent her, and strangely it made her love her all the more – the fact that her mother must have carried an incredible amount of guilt and remorse for what she'd done to Anna. Yet, Anna had done something even worse, hadn't she? She'd stolen William's heart and had conceived a child with him, all the time knowing that Lynn – Eve – the mother of his older children was madly in love with him. And that wasn't right.

Ironic really, how she'd never actually taken to Anna in the story and had always thought her to be somewhat cold and unsympathetic. And even now, despite knowing what Lynn had done, and the pain her actions had undoubtedly caused Anna – her real mother – she still couldn't summon up any great measure of feeling for her. Yes, it must have been horrific to have a child stolen away like that but . . . Brooke shook her head, still unable to reconcile herself with being the 'child' in question, let alone try to put herself in Anna's shoes.

Why had she really done this? OK, so naturally enough she wanted to try and find her daughter after all these years, but didn't she stop to consider what kind of effect all of this might have on her? And if so, what kind of mother was she if she felt it necessary to disrupt her child's life like this, to turn on its head everything she'd ever known, everything she'd thought was real? What kind of mother would do something like that? And in such a way?

Brooke sighed. There was so much she wanted to know, so much more she needed explained. Why had Anna gone to the trouble of writing the manuscript? OK, so the reason she'd sent it was pretty clear – obviously she wanted Brooke to know the truth – but why that method, and why now? And how had she managed to ensure it landed directly on her desk like that? Was it deliberate, the way the note sounded so casual and personal, so that Brooke had assumed it was from someone in-house? But that would have been a long shot at best and required such a level of planning it seemed unlikely. Not to mention that there would have been no need to go to so much trouble. Surely instead she could have attempted to contact her by some other, more straightforward means, like a letter or an email . . .

Yet, Brooke realised now, if some strange woman had contacted her with such, such an improbable tale of deceit, tragedy and eventual kidnap, she wouldn't have believed it – and in all honesty would probably have attempted to have the woman arrested, if not committed. Evidently, this was Anna's way of making Brooke understand the circumstances surrounding her birth and the mindset behind Lynn's behaviour. But why take such a huge chance?

Brooke didn't know but she was going to find out very soon.

* * *

But when a day later she finally arrived in Dublin airport, having taken a connecting flight from Heathrow, Brooke began to have second thoughts.

What did she think she was doing travelling halfway across the world with the intention of confronting a perfect stranger, a stranger whose fictional story might very well turn out to be just that?

Perhaps she'd only imagined that the author of the manuscript had been trying to tell her something, and the supposed coincidences apparent in the story had been just that: coincidences. Talk about making a fool of herself!

Yet, deep down Brooke knew that the manuscript of *The Last to Know* had ended up on her desk for a very good reason. She was supposed to read it and by the end was supposed to figure out exactly how it had all happened. What she didn't yet know was the meaning of the whole exercise.

What did the author (presumably her mother – real mother) expect? Evidently, Anna assumed she'd be shocked, emotional and presumably curious to find her. At least, Brooke hoped the woman's name was Anna, because if for the sake of the story, her name had been changed or modified – as Lynn's had – then she was on a bit of a wild-goose chase, wasn't she?

As it was, she wasn't really sure where to start. All she knew was that Anna lived in Dublin, was likely married to someone called Ronan . . . what was it again? Brooke searched frantically for the surname . . . yes, Fraser, that was it. Some poor sod called Ronan Fraser who had come across in the story as a nice guy and way too good for Anna.

In fact, Brooke recalled when reading the story how she'd been routing for the other girl, Sam, to end up with . . .

Sam.

Brooke stopped dead in her tracks, causing the traveller pushing a trolley behind her to swerve suddenly. "Hey, watch where you're going, you silly cow!" the man muttered, causing Brooke to decide that the idea she'd had of her parents' and Will's homeland as a friendly, easygoing place had been rather rose-tinted. Then again, *she* had stopped suddenly, so the man could hardly be blamed . . .

Yes, Brooke thought, recalling exactly why she had stopped in her tracks like that; she'd stopped because the thought of Sam – the other major character in the book – had caused her to have a major brainwave.

In the book, Sam had been Eve's – Lynn's – sister and presumably this was also the case in real life. But not only that, in the book Sam was supposed to have been a successful author of women's fiction, and assuming that the personalities and their accompanying professions were true, then chances were *Sam* was the one who had written the story in the first place. Brooke couldn't *believe* she hadn't thought of this before! To think that she'd had so much time on the plane to think it over and that hadn't dawned on her! And not only that, she realised, her thoughts racing ahead of themselves as the realisation came to her, she already *knew* of a successful and well-known Irish author called Sam – one who would have been quite close to her mother's age now that she thought of it – Samantha . . . Samantha Reynolds.

Brooke began to perspire. There it was. The final, most convincing and possibly most devastating of all coincidences.

Sam Reynolds' first novel was indeed called *Lucky* and while it had been changed to just *Lucky You* in the story, Brooke really should have realised, should have twigged that something about the author's name combined with that title felt familiar. But then again, why *would* she have noticed something like that when as far as she was concerned this was a fictional story written by a brand new author?

But at least this last piece of the puzzle had, if nothing else, given her the proof she needed to reassure herself she wasn't going crazy or making wild coincidental leaps. Now there was no longer any doubt. The Sam in the story was almost definitely her mother's sister. And although this too had been changed – evidently not to unduly alert Brooke of anything untoward early in the story – they even shared the same surname.

Samantha Reynolds, author of umpteen bestsellers and someone who clearly knew how to tell a story. So, if Brooke wanted answers – and quickly – she now knew exactly where to start.

CHAPTER

Sam Reynolds was having a very bad start to the day but had no idea that it was about to get a whole lot worse.

Her husband had been like a bear with a sore head over breakfast that morning, and when he was like that Sam knew she was better off just staying out of his way until he headed off to his golf game. Additionally, some time mid-morning, she'd got a telephone call from her agent in London, who'd informed her that her latest book had been reviewed – and savaged – by one of the Saturday newspapers. Great. Make that another bad review, Sam thought, deeply stung by the negative reaction, but in truth, she knew the book deserved it – *she* deserved it.

With an effort like this, perennial women's fiction favourite Samantha Reynolds is in grave danger of losing her crown as one of Ireland's top-selling female writers. An almost permanent fixture in the UK and Irish bestseller lists for decades, since her debut Lucky was published in 1982, Reynolds seriously disappoints with this stilted, unimaginative effort, causing some industry experts to wonder if she might be following in the footsteps of other long-time 'brand name' authors.

"You know what that means, don't you?" Ellen, her agent, asked, having read the review word for word over the telephone to Sam. "Reading between the lines, they're trying to imply you've used a ghost."

Sam was horrified. "Never in a million years would I ... Ellen, you know that's not the case!" Despite the fact that she was now in her mid-fifties and writing less and less, there was no way she would ever put her name to a story someone else had written in order to capitalise on her brand status. The very idea was despicable to Sam, as indeed it should be to Ellen.

But of course the critics didn't know the real reason Sam's latest novel had been stilted and unimaginative, whereas she did. That book had been written in record time – less than a year (as opposed to two which was now Sam's typical writing schedule) – and it had been a plodding, half-hearted effort. But she couldn't help it. All throughout the time of writing it, she'd been too engrossed in another project of hers, one that in the end had turned out to be a royal waste of time.

"Ellen, you know well that I'm not interested in that kind of thing. Maybe I can't write as quickly or as well as I used to, but there's no way I'd resort to using a ghost-writer."

"I know that, Sam, but there's no denying that this one was under par. How's the next one coming along?" Ellen asked hopefully and Sam realised she might as well tell her the truth.

"I haven't started it yet," she admitted. "It's been tough, what with everything that's been going on."

"I understand that," Ellen replied, her tone sympathetic, "but try and at least make a start. With the reviews this one's been getting, people will start to feel a bit edgy."

By 'people' Sam knew Ellen meant her publishers.

"Tell them not to worry," she assured her. "This one will be bigger and better than the last, I promise you."

"I know it will. You're a pro, Samantha Reynolds, and really, the reviewers would be appalled if they realised what was really going on in your life, and they certainly wouldn't dream of criticising you like this. I still don't know why you won't speak out about it. Maybe it would help and –"

"Because it is my life, Ellen," Sam interjected crisply. "That's why."

And despite what her agent and her PR team thought, Sam wasn't about to share her private business with the world. She'd done enough of that throughout her career, although in fairness, the media didn't know the half of it, and would indeed be appalled if they did.

She spent the rest of the day in her study, trying to do as Ellen asked and get a start on what would be her twentieth book. Sam exhaled deeply. Her twentieth book, who'd have thought it? Of course, if she were being really honest with herself, this next one would be her twenty-first book. But, no one knew about the other book, did they? In fact, only a handful of people knew about the one that had been written with as much effort and heartfelt dedication as any of the others – even more so. But better to put that one out of her head now, Sam thought. Much better to concentrate on the *real* book number twenty.

Despite her state of mind, she'd made a quite decent start on her new novel and had written a couple of hundred words when later that afternoon she heard the doorbell ring.

Sam looked up and smiled. She would be willing to bet she knew exactly who that was and what they wanted. Ellen had a very kind but completely unnecessary habit of sending Sam a bouquet of flowers whenever one of her books got a bad review, and given that her agent had been the one to break the bad news earlier that morning, this was undoubtedly a dual attempt at an apology and a cheering up.

Sam got up from her desk and went downstairs to answer the door.

"Hello," she said to the attractive young woman standing on the porch outside who, devoid of flowers, was clearly not from the local florist's. "Can I help you?"

Melissa Hill

The woman's expression, which at first glance looked rather fierce and determined, suddenly seemed to melt into something else – something that Sam couldn't quite put her finger on.

"Can I help you?" she repeated when the woman didn't reply. Instead, she just continued to stare at Sam as if she couldn't quite believe what she was seeing. Oh dear, thought Sam, suddenly recognising the expression all too well. One of her readers must have sought her out, probably looking for an autograph or something, although she looked a little bit too young to be a fan of Sam's books, and it was rather unusual for readers to appear at her home in any case.

Generally, they were much too respectful to interrupt her at home and, despite her fame, even people on the street were usually happy to leave her be and respect her privacy. But there was always one or two that wanted to –

"Are you Sam Reynolds?" the woman asked, and Sam frowned. Nobody except family, close friends and her agent called her that; to everyone else she was known by her full professional name, Samantha. And it was uncommonly cheeky for a reader – a complete stranger – to be so casual and familiar towards her.

"I am Samantha Reynolds, yes," she replied, haughtily emphasising her full name. No point in letting her think she could get away with being familiar. Next thing she knew the girl would be inside the house and making herself at home! "And you are?"

"Well," the girl said, in an accent that right then Sam couldn't quite place but would later wonder why she hadn't recognised immediately, "if the story you sent me is to be believed, then apparently in a way I'm your niece."

*   *   *

"Come . . . come in," Sam said, when she had finally regained her composure. She couldn't believe this.

Despite what they'd thought at first – it had worked, the manuscript had worked! All the months of effort and pain trying to get the story to read just right, trying to ensure she'd understand, and at the same time hoping against hope that their efforts would bring her back to them, had worked!

And now here was Ciara – or Brooke, as Eve had called her – standing right in front of her, here in Sam's front room. Nobody could have anticipated her appearing in person; the very most they'd expected (and hoped for) was a brief email or a note – some tentative and remote form of contact. And of course they'd also ensured to have someone on standby, ready and waiting for her to finish the manuscript, to fill in the blanks and give her the necessary support when she did. But obviously, things hadn't worked out that way.

Yet, after all this time, all the heartache and years spent wondering about her niece, Sam thought she'd feel more elated and thrilled to finally meet her, that she'd feel relieved that they had finally managed to bring her home.

But it was difficult to feel that way when the girl had such a thunderous expression on her face.

"What did you think you were doing?" Brooke said, her cheeks flushed and her eyes flashing as she stood in front of Sam in the living room. "What the hell did you think you were doing, playing mind games with me like that?"

"Mind games!" Even though of course she'd expected an initial negative reaction, Sam was still taken aback by the vehemence in the girl's tone. "Love, it wasn't like that – we were simply trying to find a way of letting you know so that –"

"So that what? So that you could wreck my life, turn everything I know and love upside down, and try and turn me against my mother?"

"No!" Sam cried, horrified. "It was never our intention to turn you against Eve! We just wanted to explain –"

"Oh, don't worry, you didn't succeed on that count," Brooke interjected. "I adored my mother and still do. She was a wonderful person and there's nothing you or anyone else could do to change that. The way I see it, it was Anna who was the villain in your story!"

"Brooke –"

"So where is she?" Brooke asked then. "Where is the famous Anna, the one they were all supposedly in love with, the one who's behind all this! Tell me where to find her, so I can tell her to her face that I don't want anything to do with her!"

Sam stared at the angry woman in front of her and realised that they'd badly misjudged the depth of her reaction to the truth, or at least the negative reactions. Brooke hadn't come here in order to seek out Anna for a tearful reunion; she'd come here to tell her to get lost.

The girl had already admitted that her life had been turned upside down, that she didn't know what to think or who to believe. And while they had of course tried to imagine all possible consequences and foresee every eventuality, facing the reality was now very different.

Then again, did they honestly think that having read the story, and realised its earth-shattering significance, Brooke would simply put the pages aside and think, 'Amazing – I must try and contact them all at home and see if we can meet up sometime.'

Of course not. Granted, they hadn't expected her to be blasé about the whole thing, but they certainly hadn't expected her to be so angry either. But, Sam realised now, they'd obviously gone about it the wrong way.

She swallowed hard. "Brooke," she began, speaking slowly and carefully, in a weak attempt to try and calm the girl down, "it was never our intention to upset you like this. Of course, we realised that it would be a huge shock to the system and that you might very well react like this, but your mother was certain that –"

"Who gave this Anna person the right to decide what was right for me? How dare she! How dare the selfish cow presume to know what is best for me! My mother, the one who raised me, the one who spent the last twenty-four years of my life loving me – she's the one who got to decide what was right for me and, do you know something, I'm proud of her for doing what she did back then! Who knows, having faced such a tragedy and then discovering what her *hag* of a friend had done – I might have done the same thing! Any woman might have! So to think that just because this Anna gave birth to me that it gives her the right to decide what I should and shouldn't know, well, how dare she? I had a mother and a bloody good one at that! And I don't need anyone else trying to step into her shoes."

"Brooke," Sam said, unable to believe the ferocity of the girl's emotions, "you're right, nobody has a right to decide something like this for you. Nobody except Eve – or Lynn as I understand she called herself over there. But, love, try and understand that she did exactly that."

"What?" Brooke frowned. "I don't follow. What do you mean?"

"Love, Anna didn't decide that you should be told the truth about your past and about your real mother," Sam told her quietly. "Eve did."

CHAPTER

B rooke looked shell-shocked and again Sam's heart went out to her. "What do you mean? How could Mum possibly . . .?"

"Brooke, love, will you please sit down and let me make you a cup of coffee . . . or tea or something," Sam said, leading her gently by the arm towards a chair. "Then, I promise I'll tell you everything."

"I'm fine," she insisted sharply but at the same time allowed herself to be led.

The poor girl looked like she was about to collapse on her feet; she'd been through so much in the last few days. And then after that long flight . . .

"Look, I just want to know what's going on and what you people want from me."

Sam swallowed hard. It was only natural that Brooke would now view them as "you people" rather than the close relatives they actually were.

Despite all she'd learnt from the manuscript, Eve was the only family the girl had ever known and possibly, Sam thought worriedly, the only one she'd ever want to know. She'd been a little taken aback at Brooke's staunch loyalty towards Eve given what her sister had done – but then again, why wouldn't Brooke defend her? Why wouldn't she want to preserve the loving memories she had of life with the woman she had always considered her mother?

She looked at the clock on the mantelpiece and, with a jolt, realised that her husband would shortly be returning from his golf session. With any luck, he wouldn't appear until after she'd managed to calm Brooke down and explain things properly to her. The last thing the poor girl needed now was someone else barging in on them unexpectedly.

"You're lying," Brooke was saying now. "Who else but Anna would want me to know that I was stolen away as a baby and brought up by someone else? Obviously she's thrilled that my mum is gone now so that we can all be friends and play happy families. Well, she can forget it –"

"You're so wrong," Sam replied sadly. "In the beginning, Anna was hugely opposed to contacting you in the first place, let alone telling you the truth. She felt it would be cruel to drop a bombshell like that on you. You wouldn't believe how upset she was when she realised that she had no choice in the matter, and we had to do it."

"Oh, I see," Brooke said petulantly. "Mum was right then; she didn't give a shit about me and was obviously thrilled to be rid of me in the first place!"

"Now you listen here, young lady!" Sam wasn't having any of it, even though she knew Brooke's anger was simply a manifestation of the huge shock she'd had – a sort of self-preservation. Yes, she could understand the myriad confusing emotions the girl might be going through at the moment, but she wasn't going to let her think that Anna didn't care. "Anna did nothing wrong in any of this. She adored you and was absolutely distraught when you went missing. But the reason she didn't want you to know the truth is because she was terrified of what it would do to you, and she didn't want you hurt. So stop trying to put the blame on Anna. She was the victim back then – her and Ronan."

"Give me a break. According to the story, your own story, Anna had been screwing around and possibly didn't even know who my father was!"

Sam took a deep breath. "OK, if you're determined to aim the brunt of your anger at Anna, then fine, you do that. But perhaps you should reserve judgement at least until you hear what I've got to say."

"Fine." Brooke bit her lip and looked away, refusing to meet Sam's eyes.

Sam sat in the chair across from Brooke and took another deep breath. "Right, as I said, the decision to tell you the truth about your parenthood didn't come from us," she began, her thoughts drifting back to the way all of this had come about. "In fact, it came from Eve."

*   *   *

It had been a nightmare of a time in all of their lives – hers, Ronan's, Anna's, Sam reflected. They felt that the gardaí weren't taking their abduction concerns seriously enough at first; as far as they were concerned there were a number of possible explanations for Eve's absence.

Back then, Sam reflected, such an incident would naturally have been viewed with less suspicion by the authorities who – in those more innocent days – tended to be more rational and optimistic about the reasons for a child's disappearance, rather than immediately assuming the worst like everyone did now.

"For God's sake, can't you do something?" Ronan pleaded with them on the evening of his and Anna's horrifying discovery. "Send out someone to check the train stations, the ferry-ports – get the English police involved – something!"

"Sir, look at it from our point of view. You left the baby in the care of this person of your own free will – she's a family friend – she isn't just some stranger who sneaked into your house and abducted your child. If she had, then that would be a different story altogether, but as of yet there's no evidence of abduction. In the majority of such cases we find –"

"No evidence?" Anna bawled. "She's stolen my baby! Why can't you see that? We told you she's taken some clothes! *And* her passport!"

Back at Eve's house, they had searched high and low for her passport but there had been no trace of it.

"I'm sorry," the guard insisted, his tone firm. "We can't just jump right in and assume she's abducted the child. You may be mistaken about the clothes and she may well keep her passport in her handbag – many women do. So if you just let us have a detailed description of the woman and the child, we'll circulate the information and check all the Dublin hospitals – I know you checked the baby's usual one, sir, but in the case of an accident they could have been taken to any of them. Then, if she doesn't show up by morning," he glanced at his watch, "which is only a matter of hours now . . . we'll reassess the situation and put the proper procedures into place."

"Proper procedures? What the fuck does that mean?" Ronan was red-faced. "All we're doing by wasting time like this is giving her even more of a head-start! She could be anywhere by now!"

But the gardaí were insistent that they could not launch a full-scale search until it was clear that Eve had indeed abducted the baby.

Sam felt so frustrated she wanted to scream. But this was nothing compared to what Anna and Ronan were feeling.

"Fucking idiots!" Ronan yelled when the gardaí had left, slamming his fist into a nearby wall. "How can they do that, just walk away and tell us not to worry, that everything will be grand?" There were tears in his eyes as he said it. "How the hell can they say that?"

"I don't know," Sam whispered, shell-shocked. Maybe Eve *had* gone out for a walk and there had been some kind of an accident or something. Or was she just clutching at straws, unable to believe that her sister had really done such a terrible thing? And there was no denying that the missing belongings from Eve's house did little to support such a harmless theory. The fact that her passport was nowhere to be found did even more to indicate that her intentions weren't entirely innocent.

"Well, I'm not going to just sit around waiting to see if Eve comes back," Ronan said, grabbing Ciara's baby picture from the mantelpiece and putting on a coat. "I'm going down to Dun Laoghaire to see if anyone saw them there. If not, I'll go to Heuston and after that . . ." His voice trailed off, as if realising the hopelessness of his task. At this late hour and without police involvement, it was unlikely he'd get much help from anyone.

Anna had said nothing at all since the gardaí left, instead she was just sitting on the sofa with her arms wrapped around herself, shaking furiously.

And as Sam looked from grieving mother back to helpless and frustrated father, she had to remind herself yet again that her sister – her own flesh and blood – had been the cause of all this anguish.

Where could Eve have gone? The car was still parked outside the house, so wherever she'd gone it had been on foot or by bus or taxi, which Sam supposed was a positive as it indicated a short trip. Of course, there was always the chance – as Ronan had suggested and assuming she *had* abducted Ciara – that she'd headed straight for the ferry-port and gone across to the UK. Then again she could have just taken a bus into town and gone from there, but where would she be heading?

But when night turned into day and still there was no sign of Eve and Ciara, the gardaí agreed that their disappearance could no longer be explained away. But by the time they launched a full-scale search and sent out alerts to the relevant authorities, serious time had already been lost.

First, they arranged to check passenger lists of all scheduled flights out of Irish airports but to no avail. As for the ferry-ports, records proved useless, as there was so much migratory movement between Ireland and the UK at the time that passengers simply bought a ticket in the same way they would when taking a bus. The stringent security measures that nowadays characterise every means of travel were, back then, still a long way off.

The UK police were then informed, and the authorities there ensured that all ports and airports were on alert and all flight passenger lists for that same week were checked. But there was still no sign and each passing day brought the three closer to the realisation that it was like searching for a needle in a haystack, and they might not find Eve and Ciara at all.

They had little choice. After days and weeks of investigation, by both the gardaí and the authorities in Britain, nothing was found, nothing at all that could help point to where Eve and the baby might have gone.

Sam didn't know how Anna could stand it. She wasn't a mother and couldn't comprehend how it must feel losing a child like that – especially one so young and in such horrendous circumstances. While she'd tried everything she possibly could to help with the search in the early days, after a while Sam could see that Anna was finding it increasingly difficult having her around all the time. It was understandable, given that her sister had been the cause of all this anguish in the first place, so Sam eventually decided to step back a little and give the couple some space. As Ciara's parents, they needed time on their own too, time to get through it as a couple.

She recalled one particular night when the three of them were yet again going over Eve's behaviour in the run-up to the abduction, trying to figure out if she'd given off some clue, some idea of what was about to happen. Sam had left the room to use the loo and upon her return had overheard a conversation they were having in the living room.

"You know, I don't think she planned it in advance, Anna." Ronan was saying. "That day, to all intents and purposes, she seemed perfectly normal."

"Obviously she wasn't," Anna hissed in the embittered tone that so characterised her back then. And who would blame her? "Why else did she make a point of telling me to say goodbye to her? She must have been planning something then. And of course you were too busy tiptoeing around and being all nicey-nice to her that you couldn't let me do that one thing."

Outside the door, Sam paused. Oh no. While Ronan and Anna had up to now been trying their best to be strong for one another, clearly some resentment was beginning to show.

"For fuck's sake, Anna!" Ronan said, and there was a crash that sounded to Sam as if he'd pounded his fist on the table. "As if *I* could possibly know what she was going to do!" Then his voice softened. "Oh God, I'm sorry, I'm so sorry, I just feel so fucking helpless!"

"I know, I feel the same way. Except it's worse for me because I should have known better!" Anna cried, her voice plaintive. "Because I'm her mother and I should never have left her. Why did I do that, Ro?" she gasped. "She was only a baby, only eight weeks old! Who knows where she's gone with her or what . . . she might have done to her! Oh God, Ronan, what if she's done something . . . something awful?"

Sam's heart twisted. No, no, Eve wouldn't do something like that; she didn't have it in her to hurt anyone, let alone a helpless baby.

"You can't think like that," Ronan insisted. "Remember it's Eve we're talking about here – she wouldn't hurt Ciara, she wouldn't hurt a fly."

"But she has!" Anna cried forcibly. "Look at what she's already done to me – to us! Oh, it's all my fault for leaving her – why did I do it? Why?" There was a loud, heartbreaking sob. "I don't know . . . I just don't know."

After that visit, Sam stepped back considerably in order to let Anna and Ronan try and deal with their loss in their own time and in their own way.

Poor Anna soon became consumed by her own guilt, believing it to be all her fault for not recognising that Eve wasn't well and for putting her baby in danger in the first place by leaving her. Sam too carried her own considerable guilt for not understanding how much her sister had suffered and how much pain she was in. Eve's family had been her life, how could Sam *not* have known that losing them all could send her over the edge?

The only thing they could all realistically agree upon was that baby Ciara had likely been the catalyst for Eve's breakdown; that the baby had represented everything she had lost and the life she would never have. Losing Liam, Lily and Max in one fell swoop and while planning her long-awaited wedding – it had all been way too much for Eve to take.

But as to where she'd gone and what she'd done, the questions continued to pile up. And eventually Sam, Ronan and Anna had little choice but to try and come to terms with the fact that the baby was likely lost to them for good and that she and Eve might never be seen again. The question as to whether or not Eve had done 'something terrible' was always in the background, and as the search eventually began to grind to a halt, this seemed to the authorities the most likely scenario, although naturally neither Ronan, Anna nor Sam would ever admit it out loud.

And as the years passed they all tried to move on with their lives, and while of course they couldn't just forget what had happened, they felt they had to at least try and put it aside somehow, otherwise there was no doubt they would have ended up losing their minds.

* * *

"Look, this is all very well, but I still can't understand how sending me this manuscript was all Mum's idea," Brooke said, interrupting the story. Tears sprang to her eyes. "She died last year, do you know that?"

Sam nodded sadly. "I know. I found out when –"

Just then the front door banged, and at the sound of the noise, she and Brooke looked up.

"Sam?" a male voice called out from the hallway.

"Don't worry, it's just my husband – back from his golf," Sam explained to Brooke quickly, when the other woman began furiously wiping her eyes.

"Sam, where are you . . . oh!" He came into the living room and smiled apologetically at his wife. "Sorry, I didn't realise you had company."

"This is . . . an old friend," Sam said quickly, giving him a look that she hoped conveyed that his interruption was ill timed. "We haven't seen each other for a few years and she was in the area so she dropped by for a quick visit. Now, leave us alone so we can have a good girlie chat," she dismissed lightly, winking at Brooke out of the corner of her eye.

"Oh right . . . I'll leave you guys to catch up then," he said, nodding briefly at Brooke, who said nothing. "Can I get you anything? A coffee or some tea or –"

"We're fine, dear," Sam interjected with a tight smile. "See you later."

But rather than upsetting Brooke, instead the brief interruption seemed to have had the effect of calming her somewhat. It also had the effect of helping Sam find the courage to keep going. Even now, after all these years . . . it was still hard.

"So how did you find me?" Brooke prompted, when they were once again alone. "How did you know where to send the story?"

Sam smiled softly at the memory. In the years following the abduction, she'd thrown herself into her writing: it had been her saving grace, had kept her from dwelling upon what her sister had done and whether or not she and the baby were alive or dead. And somehow, her career had gone from strength to strength, and soon she was almost a permanent fixture on the bestseller lists in Ireland and the UK. She stayed on in Ireland, as London certainly held no attraction for her now, and she supposed there was always some form of hope – futile and all as it might have been – that Eve might return.

Then one day, almost twenty-two years later, the postman delivered a handwritten envelope addressed to her. She remembered thinking at the time that there was something oddly familiar about the handwriting, but in truth she could never have anticipated who it was from. And then, when she opened up the letter and began to read . . .

"I was flabbergasted," she said to Brooke, her eyes glistening with tears. "I just couldn't believe it. Well over twenty years and nothing and then . . . just like that a letter arrives here in the post. At first I couldn't understand how she knew where I was, but of course I suppose I was easier than most to find. She found me in the same way that I'd imagine you did – through my publisher." She looked at Brooke for confirmation.

"Not exactly" Brooke shrugged. "When I realised who you were, I knew your publishers wouldn't give out your address so instead I picked up one of your books, read your biog and found out that you lived in Killiney. Then I just asked someone in the village where your house was. It wasn't too hard. And even though I didn't ask, the guy told me where Bono lives too."

"I'm sure he did," Sam smiled wryly. "Well, apparently Eve had been keeping tabs on me through the Internet."

Brooke smiled. "She loved the Internet. I could never figure how she could spend hours and hours on the bloody thing." Then her face clouded slightly. "I guess I know now."

Sam nodded. "I suppose it was only natural that she'd try and maintain some links with home. Especially after what she'd done. Of course, there had been a piece in one of the nationals about the . . . incident," Sam had been about to say kidnapping but realising how upsetting this could be for Brooke she caught herself just in time, "but of course, most newspaper records from the eighties are kept on microfiche and not online so she wouldn't have found any coverage. But luckily, I was easy enough to find and very easy to keep track of. Through the net, Eve managed to keep an eye on my career, discovered that I'd got married and that I moved to this house . . ." She smiled softly. "Then one day, as I said, about two years ago, I got this letter. And while of course I was appalled about what she'd done, at the same time I was overjoyed to hear from her. She was my sister after all, and it was overwhelming to discover that she was indeed still alive and that the two of you were OK."

It had been the happiest and at the same time one of the most difficult experiences of her life. And of course, while it was wonderful to know that Eve hadn't lost her mind completely, and maybe done the baby or herself some harm, the letter had left her equally confused as to what had actually happened. Eve didn't tell her too much in that first letter other than that they were both OK and now living in a different country, and that she knew she'd hurt some people but she still truly believed she'd done the right thing.

Sam shook her head. "This admission shocked me, Brooke. While I believed she had certainly taken leave of her senses when she took you away, I'd also believed that after a while she would realise what she'd done and how wrong it had been, but by then it was too late to bring you back, as she would get in so much trouble. Knowing Eve as I did, I had to assume that she'd found it easier not to think too much about what she'd done – buried her head in the sand, if you like, rather than think about the consequences. So to discover that she was still convinced that doing such a terrible thing had been right . . . obviously I wasn't quite sure how to feel about that."

But perhaps more importantly, Sam also had something else to consider when she heard from Eve – her conscience. Should she tell Ronan and Anna that she'd heard from her, and that Ciara was OK? She *had* to, hadn't she? Put them out of the misery they'd been suffering all these years and give them something to hold onto? But at the same time, she had no idea where Eve was, had she? Eve didn't give anything away about where she was in her letter, although Sam did spot that the postmark on the envelope was Australian. But Australia was a very big country and Eve hadn't mentioned anywhere specific . . . and there was always the chance she had changed her name . . .

Now, Sam sighed and her gaze focused on a piece of lint on the floor. "So I battled with that same conscience for a very long time," she explained to Brooke. "On the one hand, Eve was my flesh and blood and the only sister I had, so how could I turn her in? On the other, what she'd done had ruined many people's lives – Ronan's, Anna's and perhaps yours to a certain extent, as back then I didn't know what your life was like in Australia. The two of you could well have been living hand to mouth for all I knew."

"Our life was wonderful," Brooke cut in defensively. "Mum worked very hard to keep us going. We have a nice house and loads of friends and we were very happy. I couldn't have wished for better."

"Well, I'm pleased about that," Sam replied, realising that she needed to choose her words more carefully when talking about Eve, who evidently Brooke had adored. "But if I told Ronan and Anna where you were, I knew that they would want to go straight down there and try to find you – certainly Ronan would have *swum* there if he knew," she added, smiling softly. "You have no idea how desperate he was to find you."

Brooke sniffed. "He might have felt differently had he known that I wasn't even his," she said. "Then he wouldn't have to worry about finding me."

For a long moment, Sam didn't know how to reply to that, and eventually she decided not to yet.

"So obviously you didn't tell them you knew where I was," Brooke concluded, "seeing as nobody ever did try to find me."

Sam shook her head. She didn't tell them then. It was hard to explain but at the time she didn't want to break the connection with Eve so abruptly. It had been over twenty years, and she suspected it had taken a lot of courage for Eve to contact her in the first place . . . and, at such an early stage, Sam didn't want to scare her off. And it seemed to work. In Eve's first letter she'd been very cautious and very deliberate in her words, obviously not sure how Sam was going to react. She didn't give an address so Sam had no way of writing back to let her know one way or the other if she was going to turn her in. She wanted to let Eve know she could trust her, but at the same time it was very frustrating not being able to communicate with her.

So, a few more months passed, and then Sam got another letter. Evidently Eve had deduced in view of the fact that the police hadn't appeared at her door that Sam hadn't given her up, which was why she felt brave enough to write another letter. Sam supposed it must have been cathartic for her in a way, having some form of contact with the life she'd left behind, and of course with the only remaining member of her family.

The second letter was warmer and a little more relaxed. Eve explained that she and Brooke were happy with their new life and had settled in wonderfully in Australia. The weather was nice, the people friendly and helpful, she got a job very easily and in Brooke she felt she still had a piece of Liam. As far as Eve was concerned, all the bad stuff had been left behind.

Sam looked at Brooke. "I had to read through the letter again and again before I could truly take it in, and when I did, I finally began to understand why she seemed so untroubled by what she'd done, why she was still, even then, convinced that what she'd done was right."

"What do you mean?" Brooke asked frowning. "What did you have to take in?"

Sam looked at Brooke. "Those words – 'a piece of Liam'."

"Well, of course," Brooke said as if it was all totally obvious. "You all knew that was why she'd done it in the first place, and perhaps who could blame her? Such a horrible thing –"

Sam shook her head. "Brooke, we had no idea."

"What?" Brooke frowned again. "But in the manuscript –"

"Yes, we know *now* what her motivations were, but at the time we hadn't a clue why she'd done what she did that day. We were sure she'd just had some kind of breakdown or a relapse or something. It was the only way we could explain it."

"But it was obvious why she did it!" Brooke cried. "Anna being so secretive about her pregnancy, Liam not wanting to marry Eve and the teddy bear in Ciara's room –" She stopped short, realising what she'd just said. "I mean . . ."

"I know. But you must understand that this story was written only after Eve had put together all the missing pieces. At that stage, she wanted me to know everything so that *you* would know everything, and she hoped that you wouldn't judge her as a result."

"But if she'd been so convinced she'd done the right thing, then why would she worry about my judging her? I do understand why she did it and, to be honest, I'm not sure whether or not I wouldn't have done the same myself, had I been in her shoes. To think that her so-called best friend . . ."

Sam decided it was best to try and explain this now, although it was still hugely complicated, even to her. "Look, the whole Anna and Liam situation was always a bit of a puzzle. As you know, Anna and Ronan had been together forever, and that was the way it was supposed to stay. I suppose you've probably also figured out from the story that when they were younger, Anna and Liam both knew they had feelings for one another but were afraid to act on them. After all, it had always been just Ronan and Anna, and Liam only appeared on the scene when they were in their teens. So while they both felt something for one another, they never acted on it, mostly because they didn't want to hurt Ronan, and also because they were never really sure if their feelings for one another were real. So it was easier to just carry on with the status quo. Anna was Ronan's girlfriend and that was that. Then Liam met Eve and you know what happened."

"But why did Liam stay with her if he didn't really love her?"

"It was the seventies, Brooke, and back then, that was the way things were in Ireland. Single mothers were mostly unheard of – either they got married or else they gave their babies up for adoption. In any case, respectability needed to be maintained."

Brooke nodded blankly, and Sam remembered that the girl had no experience of Catholic Ireland and, she thought wryly, was probably all the better for it.

"Anyway, as I said the entire situation between Liam and Anna was complicated. He and Eve got on with their lives, and Ronan and Anna – as always – got on with theirs. They got engaged in their mid-twenties, bought a house and as far as Ronan was concerned everything was going according to plan. Please understand that this is very difficult for me to explain properly, and you have to realise that most of what I know is second-hand."

Brooke nodded. "OK."

"But for Anna the feelings she had for Liam had never really gone away, which I suppose was the real reason she could never bring herself to set a date. She loved Ronan, of course she did – but as long as the doubts were there she couldn't move forward. Yet she was caught. She couldn't act on her feelings for Liam, as by then he and Eve had settled down and had two children, and at the same time she was afraid to leave Ronan. They were childhood sweethearts, remember, and he was her best friend; she was afraid to step out of the comfort zone and it was easier to just continue on as things were and hope that eventually things would work themselves out. Again, that was the way things were back then. Liam did the very same, but his feelings for Anna also still remained and, although Anna didn't know this, for as long as she dilly-dallied and delayed marrying Ronan, he wondered if there might be hope. I know what you're thinking," she said, when Brooke looked sceptical, "but suppressing your feelings was par for the course back then. As I said, people were just expected to carry out their responsibilities and get on with their lives. In fact, I think that if Anna and Liam had given into their feelings back when they were teenagers and just got the entire thing out of their systems, it all would have come to nothing. But that's me."

"So the longer they denied how they felt, the stronger those feelings became?" Brooke mused.

"Apparently yes. So, when Anna discovered she was pregnant, all of sudden, everything seemed to come to a head. She knew that the pregnancy meant that there was no going back and she would be with Ronan for good. And when Liam accepted Eve's proposal and then discovered that Anna was pregnant, it seemed that that was it; there was no going back. But for some reason, all of this prompted Liam to give it one last shot and, as you read in the book, he went to see Anna to try and have it out with her once and for all. By then, it was a now or never situation for both of them. Either they continued along the path they'd created for themselves with other people or they gave into what they had always known existed between them. As far as he was concerned they had to admit their feelings and act on them. But of course, by then, Anna had already decided. Despite her feelings for Liam, out of loyalty to Ronan and especially for the sake of the new baby, she decided to forget all about him and really make a proper go of it with Ronan."

"What? But the baby was Liam's – that was obvious!"

Sam knew Brooke had now forgotten that they were talking about reality and that *she* was the baby involved. Instead, she was right back in the story.

"No, Brooke," Sam said, shaking her head sadly. "Ronan was – *is* your father, there was never any doubt about that. There had been something between them, yes, but Anna and Liam never did anything like . . . Anna did not cheat on Ronan."

Brooke sat up in her chair, wide-eyed. "But why be so secretive about the pregnancy then? And what about Liam giving Anna the teddy bear and calling to her house like that? In the story, it was obvious that they'd been together! Why else did she feel so guilty? And who was that guy she met outside the theatre that time – it had to have been someone who saw Liam and her together!"

Sam shook her head. "No – that person was Anna's doctor, Dr Ryan. That night, she worried that he'd mention something to Ronan about her pregnancy, when she hadn't yet said anything about it."

"Oh."

"She felt guilty about Liam because she knew that what she was feeling wasn't fair to Ronan or to Eve or to anyone. And then when he was killed, she knew that it was finally all over, now she no longer had to battle with her feelings; and she could get on with her life. And she hated herself for that. Eve had lost everything and all Anna could think about was that she was finally free. It's so difficult for me, Brooke – Anna is really the only one who can explain all this. I tried my best to put it all across in the story, but mostly so that you could understand why Eve might have made the mistake in assuming that Liam was your father. Only Anna knows how she truly felt, and much of what you read or what I'm telling you now is merely my own interpretation of what little she shared with me." She paused for a moment. "Do you remember that scene in the story – the one just after the guards left the house, where Anna was trying to make sense of what had happened?"

Brooke nodded but seemed confused.

"In all my years as a writer, I think that was the most difficult piece

I ever had to write," Sam said sadly. "How could I put myself in her shoes or even begin to imagine the horror of what she was feeling? I tried my best, certainly, but doing so drained the life out of me, and I hadn't suffered a fraction of what Anna did. I'm merely pointing out why it's so difficult for me to illustrate her feelings to you in any case, let alone the ones surrounding Liam."

"But I don't understand! What about the teddy bear? If he wasn't her father, why did Liam buy the baby . . ." Brooke faltered again, realising that she was talking about herself. "Why did he do that behind Eve's back?"

Sam shook her head. "We're really not sure. Anna can hardly remember getting it. She thinks it might have been Liam's way of apologising for calling to the house and upsetting her. At the time, we had no idea that this was what had sparked Eve's breakdown that day. As I said, I only realised from her second letter that she'd suspected as much." Then Sam sat forward. "But you might also remember from the story that I too had my suspicions back then about Anna's reasons for keeping her pregnancy a secret from Ronan. And I wasted no time in feeding those suspicions to Eve either. So for all I knew, Eve could very well have been right; it certainly made a lot more sense than any scenario I'd concocted back then.

"So some time after I got Eve's second letter, I contacted Anna upon some pretext or another, and we arranged to meet up. Again, I didn't tell her I'd heard from Eve, although naturally it was very difficult not to but, as I said, I felt some sense of loyalty towards Eve and in truth I must admit that I was curious to find out if the idea of the baby being Liam's was true. Over the years, we'd all raised various possible reasons for Eve's behaviour, so it wasn't that out of the ordinary to ask about it. But when I said this, Anna almost fainted, and by her face I knew that there was no question of Liam having fathered . . . you. Eve had it all wrong – you're Ronan's, no doubt about it." She smiled softly. "And believe me, sitting here looking at you now, there really *is* no doubt about it."

When there was no visible reaction from Brooke, Sam went on.

"So, having learnt that Eve was mistaken about this, I began thinking about all the times I'd questioned Anna and Ronan's relationship and the times I'd suggested to Eve – not long before Liam's accident – that Anna's reasons for keeping her pregnancy secret might be for a suspicious reason. Of course, I know now that the combination of all these things were what set Eve off on that train of thought, although none of us could ever have known about the teddy bear. That triggered everything."

"So what did you do? Did you tell Mum that she'd got it all wrong? That William wasn't my dad after all?"

Sam looked up quickly. "She called him William?"

"Yes."

"Interesting. I suppose she felt it was safer using different versions of both their names, William for him and Lynn for her. But his name was indeed Liam."

"She told me that he'd died in an accident shortly after I was born," Brooke said now, and Sam could see that the truth – and more importantly, what it meant – was now really beginning to sink in. But they could deal with that later.

"Well, if she honestly believed that Liam was your father, then she was telling the truth," she replied. "And I know now that she truly did believe this, so when she discovered that this wasn't the case, all the reasons she'd used over the years to rationalise what she'd done went right out the window."

"But how did she find this out?" Brooke asked again. "How were you able to tell her that she'd got it all wrong?"

Sam exhaled deeply.

"At first I didn't know what to do. I wanted to let her know firstly that Liam hadn't betrayed her like she'd thought, and secondly help her realise the actual damage she'd caused. I don't know – maybe I thought that knowing the truth would change things and perhaps she might bring you back, but of course this was impossible. So I read through both letters trying to find some clue, trying to find some way of contacting her. I tried resealing one of the envelopes she'd sent me with a letter of my own inside and marking it 'return to sender' but it came right back to me. For a while, I thought about trying all sorts of things and at one stage I was so out of ideas that I even considered sending a message in a bottle." She laughed. "But then I hit on something."

"How?" Brooke was transfixed.

"She mentioned in her letter that she'd looked me up on the Internet and found my website. Now and again I send out newsletters to all my readers and post a copy of it on the site. I was hoping that Eve might be reading this as a way of keeping up to date with what was happening in my life. So in my next newsletter, I included a sentence that I hoped she'd realise was aimed at her. I wrote something like. 'Could the reader from Australia who has recently sent me the nicest letters send me her email address? I would really love to contact her and promise I won't hound her' or something to that effect – it was years ago now, I can hardly remember. But it worked, because a few days later an email arrived from Eve. Finally, I had some way of contacting her."

"So you told her she'd been wrong about Anna and Liam?"

Sam shook her head. "Naturally I didn't want to drop such a bombshell on her at such an early stage. Instead, I began telling her about my life and gradually here and there dropping in questions about you, until she got to the stage where she was comfortable discussing you. This might seem underhand to you, but you have to realise how delicate the situation was. I couldn't risk alienating her completely. And as you'll soon discover, I had a very good reason for taking my time in breaking the news."

Brooke frowned.

"Anyway, after a while she began discussing you more frequently. She told me that you were both fine and that you'd had a happy life. But Brooke, you could have knocked me down with a feather when she explained how she'd taken Anna's passport and used it to get you away. No wonder we could never find out where she went, as we'd naturally assumed she travelled under her own passport and her own name." Sam shook her head. "And it seemed nobody was any the wiser. Of course with all the trauma that followed, Anna never even noticed it was missing. Why would she when she had so much else on her mind? But having admitted this much and solved the mystery as to how we'd never found her, Eve still didn't want to tell me where you were because she didn't want to be found. She was still convinced she'd done the right thing. 'She's Liam's,' she wrote in one of her letters. 'What else could I have done?'

"So I knew then that the time was right to tell her and, when I did, I know I pulled the rug from under her. All those years in Australia with you, I don't honestly think she ever felt guilty for taking you; she was so certain she'd done the right thing. She'd rationalised it to herself so often that after a while she managed to convince herself that everyone was better off. But then, when she realised that she'd been wrong about Anna, and that she'd stolen you not only from your real mother – but also from your real father – she began to see things differently. And that was when the guilt crept in – particularly when I was able to tell her at first hand how devastated he'd been and how –"

"How long and hard I tried to find you."

They both looked up quickly at the sound of the male voice coming from the doorway, quivering as he spoke.

Sam looked at her husband, willing him to understand. She'd worried that he might have recognised the visitor when he arrived home earlier, but because he'd left her and Brooke alone again so quickly and without protest, she knew he hadn't had a clue. Now tears sprang to her eyes when she saw the way her husband was staring at Brooke – the daughter he'd lost twenty-five years before and up until now was certain he'd never, ever find again.

CHAPTER 44

Amazed, Brooke stared at the man standing in the living-room doorway, a man who looked to be in his mid-fifties and who had a kind, weather-beaten face and was greying slightly at the temples.

"I'm sorry, love," he said, looking helplessly at Sam. "I was passing by and overheard some of what you were saying . . . I couldn't believe it and I couldn't help myself . . . I couldn't stay out there any longer. I just had to . . . you know."

Brooke turned to Sam in disbelief, remembering what she'd said before about her mother getting in contact when she discovered on the Internet that she'd got married. "Ronan?" she gasped. "You married Ronan?"

Sam stood up and went to stand beside her husband. She looked nervously at him, concerned about the effect seeing his long-lost daughter now was having on him.

She turned again to Brooke, who heard a trace of guilt in her tone. "Yes, we got together a few years after . . . well, after Eve had taken you away. As I said earlier, he and Anna never really –"

"We never really got over losing you," Ronan finished, a catch in

369

his voice. He continued standing there – hesitant, unsure and, Brooke thought, seemingly unable to believe that she was really there.

As for her, well, she didn't know how to behave either. This man, this *stranger* was her father. And contrary to what she'd always believed, he was alive and well and had been for all of her life.

Every muscle in her body tensed. What was she supposed to say? How was she supposed to feel? And how crazy was this, sitting in the same room with Ronan and Sam – two people she'd been reading about for the last few months, people she'd presumed were fictional but instead were actual, live people, people of real significance in her life. It was totally and absolutely surreal and Brooke didn't know how to behave or what to say . . .

Ronan seemed to be having the very same problems. "Your mother and I – Anna, I mean . . ." he added blushing, "it was so hard . . . we were devastated after . . ."

"We were all in bits over what happened to you," Sam finished on his behalf. "But of course, it was particularly difficult for Ronan and Anna. Love, why don't you sit down here beside me." She gave Brooke an apologetic look, which seemed to convey that she hadn't intended on him interrupting them.

"We were under fierce pressure, and none of us knew how to handle it," Ronan said, sitting down across from Brooke. He sounded cautious and hesitant, as if afraid that his mere presence might now make her run away.

Brooke couldn't blame him. At that stage she was so confused by the whole thing that she couldn't be sure that she *wouldn't* run away.

"At the beginning we both blamed Eve, but after a while we started blaming each other. Anna blamed me for the fact that she'd never got the chance to kiss you goodbye that day we went to the wedding. I blamed her for not realising that Eve wasn't . . . wasn't herself," he added quickly, unable to look Brooke in the eye. "We couldn't talk about it, couldn't work through it . . ."

And although there was a degree of regret in his tone, Brooke sensed that it was a rather distant, faraway regret.

"The relationship had been fragile for a long time before you were born, and I think we both knew it," he went on. "Then, when we had you, everything seemed to be going great again, we'd begun planning our future and then . . . then we lost you . . ." He looked away, the sadness in his eyes immense. "We just felt so helpless. I was supposed to be your father, the one who swore to take care of you, and yet I couldn't find you – couldn't bring you back. I felt so bloody powerless . . ." He looked away. "I know Anna began to feel that way about me too. I'd disappointed the two of you, let you both down . . . I couldn't do anything to make it better."

"It wasn't for the want of trying, and you know there was nothing you could have done. Anna did too," Sam soothed and Brooke suspected they'd gone over the same ground time and time again over the years.

"Anyway, it was hard for me and Anna after that," Ronan went on, recovering slightly. "We started snapping and sniping at each other over every little thing. Eventually it was difficult for us to be in the same room together, we were so caught up in our own feelings."

Brooke could only imagine how difficult it must have been for them as a couple, and it brought to mind what Sam had told her about how, in the immediate aftermath, he and Anna had very quickly started blaming each other.

"After a while, there was very little to keep us together. We tried to muddle through of course, but by then there was nothing left between us but shared guilt and loss. So eventually, we decided to part ways."

Brooke looked at Sam, recalling what she'd written in the story about how she'd felt that she – and not Anna – was the one who'd end up spending the rest of her life with Ronan. Evidently she'd been right.

Sam seemed to read her thoughts. "Ronan and I didn't get together until a long time after he and Anna finished," she said almost apologetically. "Soon after they parted ways, Anna moved away from Dublin, and she didn't keep up much contact with me or her old life here. I suppose it was easier for her not having to face me, knowing that I was related to the woman who had caused her such pain. But for Ronan and me, well . . ." She looked fondly at her husband. "Strangely, this seemed to have the opposite effect. We stayed in touch a lot and began confiding in one another, which eventually had the effect of bringing us closer together."

"It was easier – each of us knew how the other was feeling," Ronan said, taking one of Sam's hands in his, and as he did Brooke realised that whatever love he might have had for Anna was undeniably now long gone.

How strange that Sam's premonition had been right after all! Ronan was indeed the man she'd ended up spending her life with, although obviously nobody could have anticipated exactly how that would come about.

"Anna and I were much better off without one another in the end," Ronan reiterated. "It was easier – easier for us to move on. Had we stayed together, we would have ended up hating one another and, to be honest, I think it was a huge relief for Anna when we finally did call it a day. So it was much better for everyone." Then he gazed at Brooke. "I still can't believe you're really here," he said, shaking his head. "It's been so long . . . I never ever thought we'd find you."

Brooke tensed. She couldn't deal with this – not now. She couldn't even think about dealing with it until all her questions about how all of this had come about were answered.

"I'm here because I need to know why you did this," she replied quickly, trying her best not to offend him. "Sam, why did you send me that manuscript? Obviously you wanted me to know the truth but –"

"*Eve* wanted you to know the truth," Sam replied. "I was just getting to that before Ronan came in." She smiled again at her husband before lapsing back into the story.

"When she found out that she'd been wrong about who your father really was, she was overcome with guilt. She knew she'd made a big mistake and had got things badly wrong. The excuses she'd used to justify her actions for all those years suddenly disintegrated into nothing, and for the first time ever she was wracked with guilt. And of course at this stage, she also knew she was ill, although I had no idea of that at the time." She swallowed hard. "Then, a couple of weeks after I told her the truth, she wrote back telling us lots of things – almost everything about you, what you did for a living, how wonderful you were. I knew she was doing this because of Ronan – in a way, it was a means of trying to apologise for what she'd done. She knew that I'd married him and that I would have known how much he'd suffered. You see, I don't think it ever crossed her mind that you might not have been Liam's, and the fact that you weren't changed everything."

"She sent us photographs of you at different times when you were growing up," said Ronan. "Pictures of the two of you having picnics on the beach, laughing with friends in your back garden, all tanned and healthy and . . . happy. She thought this would help, although when I first heard from Sam where you were I literally wanted to tear the woman limb from limb and was planning to hop on the first plane to Australia to do just that and then take you back here with me. But after a while I realised I couldn't do that. To all intents and purposes Eve *was* your mother, the only family you'd ever had. I couldn't just swan in and pull the rug from under you. How could anyone?"

"But as time went by Eve became convinced that you should be told," Sam went on. "She knew the cancer had spread and was getting worse and that it might not be long until . . ." she looked away, unshed tears in her eyes, "until it was too late. She worried that when she was gone, you'd have nobody – no family, no relations, nothing. And she felt more guilty about that than anything else, especially when your parents – your real family – were alive and well and still missing you like crazy."

Brooke couldn't help but wonder why Lynn didn't explain all this before she died, let her know that she'd made a huge mistake but now wanted to bring the family together again. She and her mother had been so close; why couldn't she tell her the truth and give her the chance to have the father she'd always wondered about?

But Sam soon answered this unspoken question. "One day, she wrote to us again, asking us to explain everything to you but to do it only after she'd died. And although it might seem cowardly to some people – and perhaps to you too – I think I can understand why she wanted to wait until then. Had she told you the truth before she died, I don't think she would have been able to bear it if, after all this time, you cut her out of your life and perhaps went running back to your real parents. You were all she had and the two of you had been through so much together. Her telling you the truth would be a huge risk, and I know she just couldn't face the prospect of something like that happening, especially when she was ill."

Brooke did understand this somewhat. Even though she adored her mother, there was no way of knowing how she *would* have reacted to a bombshell like that. Evidently, it was a risk her mum hadn't wanted to take.

"Either way, Eve wanted you to know that you had a family back here in Ireland and that you wouldn't be alone after she was gone. She thought I should send you a letter explaining things a few months after she died, but I couldn't imagine how anyone could possibly get across everything that had happened in a few pages of a letter. And we had to consider strongly how you'd feel, learning this after all this time and learning such terrible things about your mother. We had no way of knowing how you – or anyone else – would react to something like that."

"Then we flirted with the idea of going over there and telling you in person," Ronan said. "That's what *I* wanted to do, what I'd wanted to do from the very beginning, but again, we knew it might be too much for you to take in. How could we even begin to explain something like that to you? Chances were you wouldn't believe us."

Brooke nodded almost to herself. She'd thought the very same thing on her way here on the plane. She *definitely* wouldn't have believed it.

Sam smiled and went on. "'Sam, I know you'll come up with something,' Eve told me in the email. 'You're the one who was always good with words.' So then one day, I sat down and started writing all about what had happened. At that stage I didn't know how long Eve had left and of course I wanted her to see the letter before I sent it to you. Once I knew that there was no chance I would ever see my sister again, I suppose I wanted to make sure I did it right. And although Eve would never have admitted it, I too had played my part in helping her make the mistake of thinking Liam was your father. I'd spent too much time trying to pick holes in Anna and Ronan's relationship, and there was no doubt that this had contributed."

"We don't really know that," Ronan soothed, patting his wife's hand.

"Yes, we do," his wife replied firmly, before continuing. "I thought the best thing to do was to firstly give you some idea of the background surrounding the whole thing, so I went into detail about Anna and Ronan's relationship, and also about Eve and Liam's. Then, before I knew it, I had written hundreds upon hundreds of words and yet I was nowhere near explaining anything. But having read what I'd written at that stage, your dad . . . I mean Ronan," she said quickly, "hit on the idea of writing it all down in story form and sending it to you as a novel."

"Seeing as you worked in publishing and everything," Ronan supplied, slightly pink-cheeked.

"But Eve thought this idea was perfect. After all, I knew all the main players in the story very well; all I had to do was find a way of outlining their motivations in order to explain their behaviour. Eve and I were corresponding regularly at this stage, and she'd told me everything she'd felt and experienced in the run-up to . . . that day, and it was very easy to write about myself and Ronan. But of course, if we were going to explain all of this to you properly, there was one major player we needed to include."

"Anna," Brooke supplied breathlessly. She'd been so caught up in the fact that her real father was not only alive but sitting two feet across from her that she'd almost forgotten about her.

"Yes. In fact, by then Eve had insisted on getting her involved. She'd written to Anna in the meantime, shortly after discovering her mistake in assuming you were Liam's. By all accounts that must have been a *very* long letter. I don't know what she said in it or how she managed to explain away her actions . . . how could anyone? And in the meantime, Ronan and I spoke to Anna and tried to explain to her that you were fine and that Eve had made a very big mistake." She sighed. "As you can imagine, that was a very difficult conversation."

Brooke *couldn't* imagine it, couldn't comprehend how hard that must have been. "What happened when my mother wrote to her?" she prompted, afraid to dwell too much on Anna's reaction to finding out what had happened to her daughter.

"Well, I know Eve did her best to try and apologise and explain everything as best she could, but as you can imagine Anna didn't want to know. How do you even *begin* to explain something like that? She was inconsolable and, naturally enough, felt even guiltier about giving up the search and moving on with her life. We *all* did. But, as I explained before, we really didn't know if you and Eve were alive or dead, and in order to try and gain some closure, we had no choice but to assume the worst. But Anna . . . well, she was your mother and as far as she was concerned she had let you down even more by giving up. So to find out after all this time that you were still alive . . ." Sam paused, her eyes shining with tears. "Then, when Anna discovered from us the reason Eve had taken you and the mistake she'd made, she tried her utmost to understand Eve's motivations a little better, but there was no denying that Eve had done a terrible, terrible thing. She'd ruined lives, and there's no apology in the world that can make up for that. I'm sure Eve knew that too, but it didn't stop her trying to atone for it."

How sad for her mother to have to deal with all of this alongside her illness, Brooke thought, and how awful that she couldn't trust her enough to share it with her! She must have been terrified that Brooke would abandon her and run off back to Ireland. How on earth had she managed to keep all this pain and worry to herself?

Now Sam looked Brooke in the eye. "But irrespective of how she felt about what had happened, or how angry she was with Eve, Anna was initially dead set against telling you –"

"Whereas I wanted to get on the first plane down there," Ronan interjected, and Sam gave him a stern look

"Yes, well, Anna was more concerned about the consequences than perhaps the rest of us were. She felt it was much better to just let you be, let you carry on being happy where you were and with what you were doing, happy believing that Eve was your mother. There was nothing to be gained by upsetting you and sullying your and Eve's relationship and the memories you had together, she argued. She knew by then that the two of you were extremely close and that Eve had reared you well. But Eve kept at her, kept at *us* to ensure that you'd know the truth, and eventually we wore Anna down."

Brooke didn't know how to feel about this. On the one hand, she was appreciative of Anna for considering the effect all of this would have on her, yet on the other she wondered how the woman – supposedly her real mother – wouldn't have wanted to move heaven and earth to get her back?

"I know what you're thinking," Sam said, seeing Brooke's

expression. "Maybe 'worn her down' isn't the best way of putting it. Believe me, Anna was torn in two. On the one hand, she desperately wanted to find you and bring you back, but on the other, and perhaps like any mother, she tried to put your welfare before her own. Which is why she was so insistent that we didn't upset you."

"OK, maybe I can understand that," Brooke said reluctantly, although she was still unsure how to feel. Lynn had been behind all of this. Lynn, who'd made a huge mistake in stealing her away from her parents all those years ago and who now wanted to make up for her actions by bringing them back into her life. She wanted to make sure that Brooke would never be lonely.

"So, with Anna's help, we were able to write the story and able to include everyone's point of view and all our motivations. Don't get me wrong – it wasn't easy for me to write about my feelings for Ronan knowing that Anna would read about them, and it certainly wasn't easy for Anna trying to explain how she felt about Liam. And even though they'd parted ways a good twenty years before, obviously, this bit was difficult for Ronan too."

Ronan smiled tightly. "I'd love to be able to say that I suspected there was something between them all along, but I didn't. I never had a clue that Anna and Liam were attracted to one another like that and that they'd battled with their feelings for all those years. It was hard to take, certainly, particularly as I was sure back then that Anna loved me as much as I'd always loved her. So considering what we'd gone through, to hear that all this had been the background while she was carrying you . . ." He shook his head. "It was a huge shock to the system – despite the fact that I was now with Sam and we were very happy, but to find out after all that time that everything you thought you knew was totally wrong, well . . ." Then he looked directly at Brooke. "Although, I suppose you have some idea of how that feels, all the same," he added wryly, and despite herself, Brooke smiled.

"But, we knew that the reasons for doing all this were more

important than our own feelings, so we had to get past all that," Sam went on. "Still, as you can imagine, it was quite a heavy-going process, laying out all our innermost thoughts and actions like that – and then having to put them all down on paper," she added, locking eyes with Ronan who nodded gently in agreement. "Still, we really believed we were doing the right thing."

For the first time since her arrival, Brooke began to get some inkling of what all of this must have been like for them and how they too had been affected by writing the story. Up until now, she'd been so caught up in her own feelings and in her own anger that she hadn't really considered how difficult writing the story must have been for each and every one of them. They must have laboured over every sentence, trying to make things clear, hoping that she would understand Eve's reasoning all those years ago. And despite that it had been Eve who had done something terrible and caused all this trouble and heartache, and whose mistaken assumptions had started it all in the first place, they were still prepared to help her mother make things right. All for her – Brooke's – sake.

And right then, she realised that she could no longer stay angry with them for wanting to tell her the truth, and perhaps instead she should think about being grateful.

Sam was still talking. "But while coming up with the idea of sending you a manuscript was one thing, ensuring you'd actually read it was a different story altogether. I myself know how things work in publishing and that even if we addressed the script directly to you it would no doubt be opened by someone else in-house, and because it was unsolicited it would likely end up in the slush pile." She laughed. "Even with twenty books behind me, I still wasn't confident it was good enough to catch anyone's attention!"

Brooke smiled at this self-deprecation, but as Sam continued talking something in her mind began to click.

"So I knew we had to bypass the slush pile somehow and –"

"The note!" Brooke interjected, as things finally began to make sense. "There was a yellow sticky on the manuscript urging me to read it! I assumed it was from someone in the office but never did figure out who. How on earth did you manage that?"

Sam smiled softly. "Your mother did actually. After listening to me argue in great detail about how sending you the script unsolicited would be a huge long-shot and might never come to anything, she went off and had a little think about it. And a few days later, she came back and told me that someone else was willing to help. Someone who could ensure the manuscript went directly to you and who would also try and make sure you read it. A fail-safe if you like. And then – and this is the bit we all liked – when you *had* read it, this person would also act as a shoulder to cry on afterwards, someone to help you make sense of all of this."

Brooke frowned. "You mean someone back home – in Sydney? But who the hell could *possibly* . . . oh my God!" she gasped, her hand flying to her mouth as everything slotted into place. "It was *Bev*, wasn't it? She kept asking me how work was going, and if I was reading anything interesting . . ." Brooke remembered too how in the run-up to Christmas – not long before she started reading the manuscript – she'd been seeing a lot of her mother's best friend. There had been more than a few supposedly casual lunches, which Brooke had interpreted as Bev trying to be there for her at what would be a lonely time without her mother, but, she now realised, were instead good opportunities to come to the office. And thinking back on it now, hadn't she and Bev met for lunch a day or so before she'd come across this mysterious manuscript? Her mind raced as she thought about it. Yes, actually, that very same morning she'd come out of a cover meeting and had found Bev sitting in her office, her assistant having allowed her wait there until the meeting was over . . .

"Sorry I'm early," Bev had said, "but I needed a break from those all those Christmas shoppers."

At the time, Brooke hadn't thought twice about it. Why would she?

"It took the poor woman three attempts before she managed it," Sam said with a smile, confirming Brooke's suspicions. "Apparently she used all kinds of excuses to visit you at the office so she could sneak it in and –"

"So Bev *knew* all along what Mum had done?" Brooke cried as a horrifying thought suddenly struck her. "My mother's best friend knew all throughout my life that I had a family and a father somewhere else but *I* didn't?"

"No, no, no," Sam was quick to disabuse her of this rather disturbing notion. "She didn't know a thing until recently – as I said, even Eve didn't fully understand the full extent of what she'd done up until a year or two ago. But when we came up against that hurdle in bypassing the slush pile, Eve knew she had no choice but to enlist someone else's help. And in order to do this she had to run the risk of letting that other person in on her secret. Think about how risky that must have been for her, Brooke. This Bev must be a pretty special friend."

Brooke couldn't believe the extent of this conspiracy. She'd strangle Bev when she saw her again! But then again, would she really? As Sam had pointed out, she'd been a great friend of her mother's and had been such a support to her too since Lynn's death. And by all accounts Bev was preparing to be there for Brooke even more when she discovered the truth. So how could she fault her for that? Or indeed for standing by Lynn in spite of what she'd done?

"So the manuscript didn't come from someone in-house at all," Brooke said, shaking her head in amazement. "Bev put it there."

"On our behalf, yes. But to tell you the truth, when Eve died and Bev was on board and it was all systems go for sending the script to you, it was only then that we really started to consider what would happen once you'd read it. We were all on tenterhooks wondering if she'd manage to get it to you personally or if someone else in your office might pick it up, in which case all of our work would have come to nothing. So then when we got an email from Bev confirming that you'd got it and she was almost certain you were actually *reading* it . . ." she looked at Ronan, "we knew then that it would all come to a head soon. But of course, it took you much longer than we expected to read it."

"I know – but work was crazy, and I had new books in from my published authors: it was almost impossible for me to get any time at all for reading new stuff."

"I understood that all those things would be a possibility," Sam smiled. "but Ronan here was going out of his mind, wondering why Bev hadn't emailed with more news, why you hadn't tried to get in contact. I think he expected you to have it read in a week or so! Despite being married to an author, he clearly hasn't learned anything about the publishing industry," she teased and Ronan looked sheepish. "But then, as time went by, I too started to worry that I hadn't made things clear enough, that perhaps you had finished it but maybe hadn't spotted the coincidences or realised the implications . . . or indeed that you had become bored with it and thrown it away halfway through!"

"Well, I might have realised sooner if you'd made it clearer that the story was set way back in the eighties!" Brooke chided, feeling somewhat more relaxed in their company now. "As far as I was concerned this was a modern story about modern Ireland – although thinking of it now, I did wonder why nobody ever seemed to use mobile phones!"

Sam blushed. "Well, I was trying to keep the time and setting authentic. Force of habit, I suppose."

"See, I told you – ever the bloody novelist!" Ronan teased, winking at Brooke, who couldn't help but smile at how easy and happy husband and wife were in each other's company. It was sweet in a way, and given everything they'd been through she was glad that they'd gained comfort from one another.

"But whenever you did finish it, we certainly didn't expect you to jump straight on a plane and come here like this," Sam went on. "I don't know, I think we all – Bev included – expected that you'd confide in her about what you'd discovered and that she'd try and help you come to terms with the news before you even considered contacting us."

"It was why Anna – more than anyone I think – liked the idea of having someone in Australia to hand, not just to drop off the manuscript, but to help you deal with the aftermath," Ronan said. "But you're obviously an act-first, think-later kind of person and I think I know where you got that from."

Again, Brooke felt a slight jolt at the mention of Anna and the traits she might have inherited from either of them, but at the same time it made her think of something else. "Sam, in the story I felt you made Anna the least sympathetic character. Why was that? Surely if anything Eve should have been the one I identified least with – considering the circumstances, and especially once I found out the truth."

There was a strange expression on Sam's face. "That was the way Anna wanted it," she replied softly.

CHAPTER

Despite the myriad thoughts and emotions she was experiencing – or perhaps because of them – that night, in Sam's spare room, Brooke slept like a baby. The three stayed up late into the night talking, and the more she learned about how the decision to tell her the truth came about, the less distressed she felt. Certainly, the intense anger she'd felt in the immediate aftermath of completing the manuscript and subsequently arriving at Sam's door, had all but dissipated – especially when discovering that their intentions hadn't been to upset her to the point that she needed to do that. She supposed she should have thought about confiding in Bev or even Will, but she'd been so overwhelmed that she hadn't even given herself time to think. Ronan was right – she *was* an act-first, think-later kind of person, Lynn had always teased her about that.

Lynn . . .

It was still difficult to take in the extent of what her mother had done. While her love for Lynn hadn't changed, there was no doubt that the truth now cast a huge shadow over Brooke's memories of her and the life they shared together. To think that her mother had made her way to Australia with a young baby and then forged a brand new life for them all on her own and thousands of miles away from friends and family! Thinking of it now, Brooke recalled that Lynn had never again travelled outside of Australia, despite her own repeated attempts to get her to do so.

"Why would I want to when I've got everything I need here?" Lynn had insisted, and eventually Brooke gave up trying, not suspecting for a second that there might have been a more suspicious reason behind her mother's reluctance. Ironic to think that she'd had two passports all along too . . . though of course they would have eventually been out of date, she supposed . . .

Brooke still couldn't truthfully say how she felt about it all and knew she probably wouldn't be able to for some time. But there was no denying that in the end her mother had done a very good thing by ensuring she wouldn't be alone after her death, so perhaps she had to give her credit for that, at least.

The following morning, she woke bright and early, feeling refreshed and considerably more alert than she'd been for the last couple of days. Getting out of bed, she wrapped herself in the dressing gown Sam had given her the night before and stepped out onto the terrace outside her room.

The house was built in such a way that every room at the rear of the property had double doors leading out onto a wooden-decked terrace which ran the full length of the house and had magnificent views out over Killiney Bay. On that bright and clear morning, the views were simply stunning and watching the sunlight dance and sparkle on the water below, Brooke almost had to remind herself that she was no longer in Australia but instead in the country of her birth.

"Sleep well?" Hearing a voice, she looked to her left and saw that Ronan was also out on the terrace, enjoying the view and what smelled like a breakfast of freshly made coffee and toast.

She nodded and slowly approached the table. "Yes – surprisingly," she said, realising that, unlike last night when he'd first entered the room, she didn't feel at all nervous around him now. He was like that, though, very restful and easygoing, and the night before he hadn't once tried to embrace or embarrass her by making a huge fuss over her – even though he surely must have wanted to.

And even though they'd met for the first time not twelve hours before, Brooke almost felt as if she'd known him for a very long time. Which in a way she did, she thought wryly.

"I'm glad to hear it," he said, pouring Brooke a fresh cup of coffee. "What will you have to eat? I'm just having toast, but I can get you a bagel, or some croissants, if you like." He wrinkled his nose. "I don't like all that fancy stuff that Sam eats myself, but it's there if you want it."

"No, toast would be perfect," Brooke said, picking up a fresh slice and putting it on a plate. "I'm not much into the fancy stuff either."

Ronan grinned and passed her the milk. "Well, we have one thing in common so!" Then, evidently realising he might have spoken out of turn, he blushed. "Ah, sorry about that – I didn't mean to make you uncomfortable –"

"It's OK," she said smiling back at him. "And you're right, we do have something in common." She took a sip of coffee, trying to get over the weirdness of sitting here and having breakfast with her father, something she'd never, ever thought would happen. And despite herself, Brooke discovered she liked it.

They chatted companionably for a few minutes, Ronan enquiring some more after Brooke's wellbeing and whether or not the bed had been comfortable enough for her.

"It was fine, honestly. Anyway, I was so shattered last night, I would have slept on stone, I reckon."

He looked sideways at her. "Your accent is gas. Even though I didn't expect you to be yapping away at us like a Dub, it still took me by surprise when I heard it."

"I didn't think I had *that* much of an accent!" Brooke was smiling at the idea.

"Well, you do – *mate*," Ronan replied, feigning an Australian accent. "So do you all *really* go around saying 'Crikey!' over there?"

"In the same way that you all go around saying 'Top o' the morning to ya' over here?" she shot back quickly.

"Fair point," Ronan said winking at her, and as they laughed together like they'd been doing this all their lives, a lovely warm glow began to envelop her and yet again she had to remind herself: *This is my father.*

For a while, the two of them continued eating breakfast in comfortable silence until, eventually, Ronan spoke again. "All of this must be hard for you to take in, I'm sure."

Brooke exhaled deeply. "It is, and to be honest, I still don't how to feel about it, you know? To think my mother could do something like that . . . it all seems totally surreal. And, you know, I thought of something else when I woke this morning . . ."

"Yes?"

"My birth certificate . . . my Irish birth certificate . . . with Evelyn and William on it as my parents . . . it can't be genuine. It has to be some kind of a . . ."

"Forgery?"

"Yes. How in God's name did she pull that off?"

"She would have moved mountains to protect you and keep you for herself," said Ronan. "She thought she was doing the right thing."

"How can you defend her?" Brooke's eyes widened. "After everything you went through back then, you and . . . Anna." For some reason, Brooke still found it difficult to say the woman's name. Probably because she was still almost a figment of her imagination (or more like *Sam's* imagination), a character in a book she'd read recently. It was hard to comprehend that Anna was not only a real person, but also her real mother.

But yet, hadn't she felt that way about Ronan too in the beginning, and now here she was having breakfast with him and chatting to him like she'd known him forever?

"I'm not defending her as such," Ronan said. "Believe me, many times over the last couple of years I wanted to wring the bloody woman's neck!" He laughed, but despite his apparent offhandedness, Brooke knew there was a lot of truth in his words. "But there's no doubt that she wasn't herself when it happened, and maybe we were as much to blame for not seeing that." He shrugged. "Anyway, what's the point holding a grudge at this stage? The poor woman is gone now, and in the end she did the right thing, didn't she? She told us where you were and she helped us bring you back."

Brooke didn't know what to say. She couldn't believe that after everything that had happened, he could find it in his heart to forgive Eve. It was unimaginable. Sam had been right; there really *was* something special about him, and just then Brooke felt enormous pride that Ronan – and not Liam – had turned out to be her father.

"So *you've* forgiven her, but what about . . . about . . .?"

"About Anna?" Ronan seemed to sense her hesitancy. "To be honest, it was she who convinced me to forgive Eve – eventually. As I said, I wanted to hunt her down so many times . . ." He shook his head. "But by then, Anna's feeling was that we'd all had a part to play in what had happened. Maybe if she'd been happier and more upfront about the pregnancy, then Eve wouldn't have made that great leap when she spotted the teddy bear. As parents, maybe we should have realised what a chance we were taking in leaving you alone with a newly bereaved mother. Maybe if Sam hadn't been so convinced that there was something up with me and Anna . . ." He shrugged. "The way Anna saw it, in the end, none of us was completely blameless. And then when we eventually found out that Eve had used Anna's passport, well, then the poor thing felt doubly guilty for not even considering something like that. It nearly broke her heart to think that if she'd just realised that sooner . . ." He shook his head. "Anyway, when we finally found out where you were . . . well, I thought wild horses couldn't hold me back from going straight down there and getting you back. But Anna was the one who convinced us not to – like Sam said, she was the only one who had really considered how upsetting it all would be for you, and for Eve. At this stage, we knew Eve was ill, so obviously the notion of me going to Australia and kicking your front door down wouldn't have been the best idea and would be massively upsetting for both of you. Anna was the only one who realised that. I think even Sam was the same as me, so eager to find you and Eve that we didn't think beyond that – to what would happen once we did. So I think she did us all a favour in the end, and for that alone maybe she deserves something."

Brooke met his eyes, realising what he was getting at. "You want me to meet her, don't you?" she asked, more troubled by the idea than she had expected. She'd gone through so much in the past few days; she didn't think she was ready for this yet – if at all.

Ronan looked right back at her. "Love, it would mean the world to her," he said simply.

* * *

That same morning, Sam made the call that Anna had been waiting twenty-five years for.

Brooke didn't know what the other woman's reply had been, but judging by Sam's tearful reaction on the other end, she could almost guess. So when, much later that afternoon, Sam and Ronan's doorbell rang to announce her arrival, Brooke prepared herself for what would undoubtedly be an emotional meeting on Anna's side, but a downright uncomfortable one on hers.

She wasn't sure why, but while it had been much easier to accept Ronan as her father – possibly because he was so easy to be around and had nothing to live up to – she wasn't at all looking forward to meeting Anna. As far as she was concerned, Lynn was still her mother, her best friend and (despite the circumstances) she knew she couldn't have hoped for better. This woman on the other hand was a complete and utter stranger.

She knew absolutely nothing about Brooke, her bad habits, likes and dislikes. She hadn't been around when Brooke had learned to walk, ride a bike, surf or drive a car. She hadn't been around when Brooke had her leg broken at fifteen and her heart not long after. She hadn't been around for any of it.

So when a slim, middle-aged woman with an attractive face and apprehensive smile followed Sam into the living room, Brooke didn't expect to feel anything other than indifference, as well as considerable embarrassment that they needed to do this at all.

But one look at the woman's overjoyed but, at the same time, utterly terrified expression changed everything.

"I'm so sorry," Anna whispered. "I never should have left you."

In the background, Brooke barely noticed Sam and Ronan quietly leave the room.

And when her eyes eventually met Anna's frightened and tear-filled ones, she finally realised just how wrong her mother had been and how much damage Lynn – *Eve* – had done by stealing her away all those years ago.

This was the face of a woman who had experienced a world of hurt, who had her life upended in such an immense way it was almost unimaginable. And yet here she was, evidently terrified of what Brooke would think of *her*, obviously worried about how *she'd* feel. Anna wasn't here to claim what was rightfully hers or to try and take up where she'd left off: she was here to beg for forgiveness.

Brooke loved Lynn and perhaps back then her mother had thought she had her reasons, but there was no denying that she had done a terrible thing, a selfish, cruel thing. This woman didn't deserve that; no one deserved that. Anna hadn't been around for all those things Brooke listed through no fault of her own, and looking at her now, she understood that this had almost killed her.

And as she and Anna just stood there in Sam's living room, staring wordlessly at one another for what seemed like the longest time, she decided there and then that she was going to do her utmost to try and make up for it.

"It wasn't your fault," were the first words Brooke uttered to her real mother, and the ones she knew Anna had waited most of her life to hear.

EPILOGUE

'No doubt about it, this is the story that will make or break your career. Publish this and you will be forever known as the editor who had the balls to support this genre-busting, edge-of-your-seat, spellbinding story; one that will grip the reading public like nothing that has ever gone before!'

Brooke's eyes widened. "Well, mate, I don't actually have any balls, but you've certainly grabbed my attention," she muttered aloud as she read through the rest of the hugely enthusiastic submission letter. "Now let's see if you can follow it through."

She flicked over the page to find the accompanying synopsis for this self-styled genre-busting submission called *The Apocalypse Conundrum*.

Right.

Brooke bit back a smile, sat back in her office chair and began to read.

Manhattan: New York City 1.45 a.m.

An old man lies dead on the floor of Grand Central Terminal; his eyes wide-open, his body twisted at an awkward angle, his arms and legs arranged in a seemingly random position. But upon closer inspection, the NYPD realise that what at first appears to be a random dead body is, in fact, a carefully constructed signpost. The dead man is pointing upwards to the astronomical symbols on Grand Central's world-famous ceiling. But what do these symbols mean, and more importantly what is the dead man trying to say? Only one man, cosmologist Richard Langford, can understand the symbolology and their meanings, and in doing so, uncovers a conspiracy that –

Brooke rolled her eyes in exasperation. Symbols, codes and bloody conspiracies – again! Was she ever again going to come across something fresh and new, an idea that someone had actually taken some thought in dreaming up, instead of just recycling the same old raw material from previous bestsellers?

She smiled then, thinking about how just a few short months ago, she had thought she'd found just that, although in the case of *The Last to Know*, there had been a real conspiracy at play.

Following her recent last-minute dash to Ireland, she'd spent a full week at Sam's house getting to know her, Ronan and Anna, and now, barely two months since her return home, she was already thinking about planning another visit.

Although it had been very weird and totally surreal getting her head around the fact that she had, not just a family, but two real live parents on the other side of the world, Brooke was now beginning to come to terms with what her mother had done.

And through spending time with Anna and Ronan, she'd begun to imagine the gravity of Lynn's actions.

But despite those actions back when she was eight weeks old, Brooke found that, although she couldn't quite understand it, she still bore no ill will towards her mother for what she'd done.

How could she when they'd had such a wonderful life together? And at the same time – although blinded by grief – Lynn had truly believed that she was doing the right thing in taking her away from Anna and trying to hold onto a piece of her family.

It was even stranger to think that she and Lynn hadn't been related at all, despite the many comments over the years about them supposedly looking alike.

Brooke now knew she looked very much like Ronan, which considering the circumstances was pretty ironic. And although she'd missed growing up with a father, she had to admit (as she had to Anna and Ronan) that she really hadn't wanted for anything. Her mother had done her best for her and had been a father and mother wrapped up in one. So how could Brooke hate her for that?

After that initial meeting at Sam's house, Anna and Brooke had spent hours talking together and slowly getting to know one another, or in Anna's case – catching up on Brooke's life.

And while she knew that Anna had no intention of trying to fill Lynn's shoes, she understood that it was important to her real mother that they become, if not mother and daughter, then at least friends. She'd spent so long blaming herself for Brooke's disappearance that it was almost heartbreaking to behold and was the main reason she'd insisted that, as Brooke's real mother, Sam didn't give her any preferential or subjective treatment in the story.

"I didn't want to sway you in any way or make you feel sorry for me," Anna explained. "It was mostly my fault that Eve jumped to such a conclusion in thinking you might have been Liam's. If I hadn't been acting so strangely about the pregnancy – or had been more upfront about how I really felt about it – then it might never have happened."

"There was nothing you could have done. She wasn't herself – we know that now," Brooke replied, hoping to comfort her.

She had to admire the calm, serene and upstanding way Anna had borne her loss, because although she herself didn't yet have any children and couldn't comprehend what it must have been like losing a child, Brooke could imagine how much Anna must have yearned for her return. And again, it was testament to the other woman's character that she expected nothing at all from her.

"I don't want you to feel as though you have to keep in contact or that you owe me any more of your time. After all these years, all I wanted was to see you again and make sure that you were safe and happy. That's all."

But despite this, Brooke found that she did want to keep up contact with her and in a way satisfy Anna that Lynn had indeed done a good job in raising her. And she definitely wanted to keep up contact with Ronan, who had already made a huge impression on her, his easy-going persona and loveable traits already endearing him to her no end. And seeing as she'd spent most of her life yearning for a father, it was easy for such a kind and loveable man to fit that slot.

And of course, there was Sam, who was the only person who knew what her mother was really like and who had known her all her life. Strangely, she still considered Sam her aunt, despite the fact that there was no blood relation between them, and thankfully, Sam seemed to view her in the same way.

"Thank you," Brooke told her before she left for the airport, having spent the week being fussed over by Sam at her house. Anna, evidently afraid of crowding Brooke, had opted to stay in a guesthouse nearby. "Thank you for writing it all down. I know it must have been hard for you, trying to make it right, trying to ensure that I understood." Then she grimaced apologetically. "And I'm so sorry that your other book suffered as a result."

Sam smiled. "You're so welcome," she said, hugging her effusively. "And don't worry about me – bad reviews are par for the course in this business, as you well know."

"Come back and visit us soon, won't you?" Ronan said in a suspiciously tearful-sounding voice, while Brooke hugged him warmly and promised him that she definitely would return.

"And try and keep in touch, let us know how you are – if you can," Anna said, her apparently relaxed tone – Brooke knew – belying her desire to play some part in her life, however small.

And again, Brooke respected her wholeheartedly for that and resolved to keep Anna, and indeed them all, up to date with what was going on her life. And depending on how things went, maybe sometime in the future they could come and visit her and see exactly what her life in Australia was like.

Shortly after returning home, she'd gone straight to Bev's house.

"I can't believe you just took off to Ireland like that!" her mother's friend cried when Brooke confronted her. "I was so sure when you learned what had happened that you'd come straight to me and –"

"I might have done if I'd known you were in on it!" Brooke shot back quickly, but at the same time she couldn't be annoyed with Bev for doing what she'd done. It had been Lynn's last request, hadn't it?

"So how did it go then?" Bev asked, putting a mug of coffee in front of her. "That Sam seems nice, I reckon. I didn't get to speak to her much, though – it was easier to keep in touch by email and it was really Lynn I was doing it for . . ."

"She's great – they all are," Brooke replied truthfully. "It was a hell of a shock, to be honest, and it took me a while to get over it."

"I can imagine, love." Bev looked pained. "I didn't know how to react when Lynn told me about how the two of you came to be here. The whole thing just seemed so . . . crazy, almost too outrageous to believe. But at the same time, there was no doubting your mother's guilt or her determination to put things right."

"I just can't figure out why she couldn't tell me herself – wouldn't it have been so much easier than having to do all of this? Get so many people involved?"

"Believe me, I tried to get her to do just that. But, love, she was terrified of losing you and, even worse, terrified of what you might think of her. I don't think I'll ever forget the shame on her face when she was telling me – having to confess something like that was tearing her to pieces. After that, I knew I'd do anything I could to help her make amends."

"I still can't believe it was you who put the manuscript on my desk!"

"Strewth, that was hard – believe me! I was racking my brains trying to come up with different excuses for me to be in the city."

"It did seem strange, particularly for someone who supposedly prefers the peace and quiet over here."

"Ah, you know me – I'm getting too bloody old for city life, I reckon." Bev smiled. "Your mother always said . . ." Then she coloured suddenly and the rest of the sentence trailed off.

"It's OK," Brooke said. "As far as I'm concerned she's still my mother and always will be."

A few days later, Brooke found the courage to confess all to Will who, when hearing about the manuscript and the story behind it, had been unexpectedly livid at the idea – much to Brooke's dismay. They'd been having a picnic in a quiet spot on the beach near her house when she'd told him the real reason behind her rushed trip to Ireland.

"What kind of a person would do such a thing?" he'd thundered, causing Brooke to worry whether he meant Lynn for kidnapping her or Sam for telling her the truth.

If he had meant Lynn then she was sorry she'd told him, and knew that if he couldn't appreciate how much she'd loved her mother, Will wasn't the person she'd thought he was. "I mean, putting you through all that heartache and worry . . . it's a terrible thing to do."

Relieved that he hadn't been casting judgement on her mother, Brooke went on to explain that it was Lynn's decision that she should be told the truth and that her real parents had up until then been afraid to make contact. "She wanted to make sure that I wasn't alone."

"But you're not alone," Will said, drawing her close as they sat together on the sand. "Haven't you got me? And yes, I know I've hardly been around this last while, but I've been trying so hard to get this bloody promotion. If I didn't get it they might not have renewed my visa, and then . . . well, you know what would happen then."

Brooke did. He would have to return to Ireland. "Don't you miss seeing your family, though?" she asked him. "Two years is a very long time to be away from them."

"Of course I do, but to be honest I'd miss you a hell of a lot more. Anyway," he added, "once my visa's sorted properly, then I can go back for a visit." He looked sideways at her. "And maybe you could come along with me. See what you think of my lot."

"You mean to meet your parents?" she said, amazed at this apparent breakthrough in their relationship. Will had never suggested something like this before; in fact, up until then, she had been hard pressed to get him to acknowledge – outwardly or otherwise – that they were serious.

"Why not?" He shrugged, as if it was no big deal. "And if you wanted to," he added casually, "we could always go and see yours again too – your other parents – if you wanted to, I mean," he repeated quickly.

She smiled, thinking that sounded like a very nice idea.

"Is it any good?" Brooke looked up quickly, the voice bringing her right back to the present. Julie was standing in the doorway of her office.

"What?"

"That manuscript you're reading – is it any good?" her boss asked again. "I certainly hope it's better than some of the rubbish I've been getting recently. The ways things are going, we'll be lucky to have a catalogue next year, I reckon."

Brooke shook her head. "Sorry, it's another *Da Vinci Code* rip-off – and a bad one by the looks of things," she added, putting it aside.

Julie rolled her eyes. "Is there any other? Jeez, I really thought we'd have seen the last of those by now," she said, coming inside and eyeing the rest of Brooke's slush pile. "Anything interesting in there, I wonder? Oh, and now that I think of it, I'm going to pass on that other one, you know that Irish one you were talking about before?"

Brooke sat rigidly in her seat. "*The Last to Know?*" she queried, her voice trembling. How the hell had Julie got hold of that? Brooke was certain she'd taken it home with her. In fact, following her discovery she remembered deciding to take it home with her that same day, in case anyone from the office read it and realised exactly what it was all about . . .

But either she hadn't taken it home or else her boss had found a copy of it somewhere or perhaps Karen had given *her* copy to her . . . shit, she'd forgotten all about that!

"I wasn't blown away by it, to be honest," Julie said, wrinkling her nose. "It started well enough, and the characters were pretty good but that ending . . ." she rolled her eyes, "talk about melodramatic!"

Brooke nodded wordlessly.

"I felt it needed too much editing. The writing was amateurish and the dialogue a bit stiff, I reckon," Julie went on, totally oblivious to the fact that the book had, in fact, been written by one of the UK's long-time top-selling authors. Sam would certainly get a kick out of that! "So I think we should pass all the same."

Well, that was publishing for you, Brooke thought wryly. One man's meat was *definitely* another man's poison. "You're probably right," she told her boss. "It's just . . . well, for a while there, I really thought it had something."

"Yeah, well, it just didn't do it for me in the end," Julie continued with a shake of her head. "But yes, I can see why it caught your eye all the same."

Brooke was trying desperately to keep from smiling.

THE END

Direct to your home!

If you enjoyed this book why not
visit our website:

www.poolbeg.com

and get another book delivered straight to your
home or to a friend's home!

www.poolbeg.com

All orders are despatched within 24 hours.

all because
of you

Melissa
Hill

'Some things really do happen for a reason . . .'

Tara Harrington's life seems perfect – a successful career as a life coach, the flashy sports car to match and a happy home with Glenn.

But when Tara's difficult younger sister Emma announces she's pregnant, and refuses to divulge who the father is, suspicions are aroused all round. Best-friend Liz's fairytale husband, Eric, suddenly doesn't seem so Prince Charming any more, and their move from the city to the country isn't working out as planned. Can Tara help her friend through it?

Glamorous London PR girl Natalie has everything she ever wanted – except a husband. And when Tara agrees to coach her in landing the latest 'man of her dreams', the two women soon find they have more in common than either had imagined.

ISBN 978-1-84223-274-3

Also published by Poolbeg.com

never say never
Melissa Hill

Sometimes hopes and dreams don't go according to plan
– sometimes, real life gets in the way.

It's the late nineties and seven friends finishing college make a
pact to meet up in five years and find out whether their
predicted futures came true.

Who will be an environmentalist, and who dreams of being a
famous sports star? Will Leah be a chef, Robin an accountant
and Olivia the one who holds it all together?

But when we meet the gang years later it's clear that life has not
gone according to plan. Why is Robin in New York and
determined never to return to Dublin?

Why is Olivia grieving over a lost love? What happened to
Andrew's rugby career? And why does Leah feel so left out as she
heads towards the big three-o?

When Robin is eventually forced to return home, the friends find
themselves face to face with the past and nothing will ever be the
same again.

Sometimes it's best to never say never.

ISBN 978-1-84223-221-7

not what you think

Melissa Hill

Good friends are there through thick and thin – or are they?

Laura Fanning has the wonderful Neil, talent to burn and her brand-new jewellery design company.

Her best friend Nicola Peters has independence, a job she loves, her own home, great friends and the lovely Ken.

Glamorous and successful Helen Jackson has legs to die for, a killer wardrobe, a thriving career and her cute daughter Kerry.

Social climber Chloe Fallon is marrying the gorgeous Dan Hunt and planning the wedding of the year.

But all is not what it seems. Under the surface Laura struggles to live up to her parents' impossible expectations, Nicola is coping with a life-changing event, Helen resents Kerry for putting an end to her love life and Chloe wants to know why Dan is being so mysterious about his divorce.

When times get tough you find out who your friends really are.

ISBN 978-1-84223-170-8

Also published by Poolbeg.com

Something you should know

Melissa Hill

Just when everything was going so well for Jenny and Mike,
Roan Williams had to come back into their lives.

Four years earlier, while her friends Tessa, Gerry, Karen and
Shane were falling in love and heading for happy ever after,
love-rat Roan had broken Jenny's heart and completely
shattered her life.

Harbouring a terrible lie, Jenny had struggled
to pick up the pieces of her life, but if Roan was going to be
around, the truth would have to come out.

It would ruin everything but Mike had a
right to know . . .

ISBN 978-1-84223-161-6